ABUNDANCE

AN ENDEARING ROMANCE NOVEL

SHANNA SWENSON

Enjoy your
trip to
abundance :)

Shanna
Swens

Abundance
Shanna Swenson

Abundance is an original work of fiction. Names, characters, places, organizations and incidents either are the product of the author's imagination or are used fictitiously. Any resemblance to actual persons, living or dead, events, or locales is entirely coincidental.

www.shannaswenson.com

❀ Created with Vellum

ALSO BY SHANNA SWENSON

Return to Abundance (The Abundance Series: Book 2)

Starlight Valley (The Prequel to Abundance)
Coming March 2019

Escape from Abundance (The Abundance Series: Book 3)
Coming Summer 2019

This book is dedicated to my wonderful family whose never wavering support made this book possible. To my sweet niece, Camryn, for her budding attitude, my mother, Anne, for her pride and determination in me, my darling husband, Jeff for his strength in pushing me to finally publish this book and last, but certainly not least, my angel of a sister, Katie for her words of encouragement and critique. Each of you has inspired some portion of this novel and I want to thank you from the bottom of my heart. I love you!

FOREWORD

To My Readers:
I actually started the ideas for this book some twenty years ago and went through several spells of writer's block before I was finally able to complete it. Oh, how many times I went through each detail of each scene in my head and then typed it out, working to portray each character as I would have them seen. Many nights I stayed up well beyond exhaustion pouring my soul into this novel. I've edited, written and rewritten to tell this story. So, without further ado, I hope you enjoy reading this book as much as I enjoyed writing it... And don't miss the next book, Return to Abundance, in this saga.

PROLOGUE

$\mathcal{N}$atalie Cameron sat in the driver's seat of her Honda Accord with her head on the steering wheel and tears in her eyes. Her car had broken down on the side of an old dusty Texas road that stretched as far as the eye could see. Save for randomly scattered clusters of trees, nothing but open fields of pasture land covered both sides of the road; an endless row of fence line and posts marched ahead. Her childhood home, settled on the west end of her hometown of Abundance, Texas, was still a good 15 minutes away and the sun was slowly sinking low in the sky, falling below the tree lines.

Natalie had just brought her four-year-old daughter over 950 miles across the Midwest. She was completely exhausted and didn't know how much longer she could run on an empty stomach. Her head was pounding, her back ached, and her rear-end was numb. She just wanted to be home with her parents then she would finally feel safe. However, now she was stuck in the middle of nowhere and the only question she could ask herself was: *How could this be happening to me?*

She raised her trembling, tear-stricken face off the steering wheel and looked in the rear-view mirror. She saw her daughter staring back at her and turned around in the seat.

"What's wrong, Mommy?" her daughter asked, her expression full of concern, as she rubbed at her eye with her small hand.

"Nothing, angel! I'm just tired, that's all," Natalie said, wiping at the tears on her cheeks and giving a weak smile, so as not to alarm her little girl.

"I'm hungry, Mommy," the little blonde cherub replied, rubbing at her eyes again with her tiny fists, trying to wake herself.

Natalie had naively assumed they would be to her parent's house by now so they had both eaten only snacks since being on the road.

"I know, baby. We should be at Grandma and Paw-Paw's house soon. I promise."

And it was high time for her to decide how on earth they were going to get there because the sun, now a beautiful array of purple, pink and orange hues, was slowly disappearing behind the trees and it didn't look as if her car, with all the gray smoke billowing from the engine, would be getting them there. She grabbed her cell phone from her purse. Knowing there was no way that it was going to work on this desolate country road that stretched for miles on end with no visible sign of a cell phone tower anywhere in sight, she tried dialing her parents' number anyway. Her phone had no service and her ears were bombarded by a series of loud beeping noises.

"Dallas, will you be okay if I step out of the car for a minute?"

"Yes," she replied quickly, "but I'm hungry." She confirmed once again.

"I know Dallie. I'll hurry."

She opened the door and stepped out of the car. The wind softly blew her hair from her face, and she took a deep breath as she shut the door back, trying her best to keep what was left of her composure. She knew that if she gave in and lost it that she would do them both more harm than good, and right now she needed to keep it together because they were stranded here in the middle of nowhere with no way out. She walked around to the front of the car honestly not knowing what she could possibly do, just subconsciously willing the engine to heal itself. She was no mechanic; she knew absolutely nothing about cars. Stubbornly, she opened the hood anyway and yelped as the heat from the engine burned her fingers as she raised the hood.

"Ow, dammit!" The wreckage that was her engine hissed and sputtered, rivulets of smoke coiled out at her. "Oh, this is bad, really bad," she mumbled aloud as she stood transfixed at her current situation. *Ok, so what am I going to do? I can stand here all night and stare at this mess with no clue what to do or come up with a plan...* She couldn't walk to her parents' house; it was at least 10 miles or more so that would take her about 15 minutes by car. She couldn't even fathom how far it would take her to walk it, especially in the dark and carrying Dallie most the way. She was ready to scream when Dallas called for her. She stepped back toward the driver's side of the car and opened the back door, looking down at her daughter. Her big blue eyes were curious and worried, and her curly blonde head was tilted.

"Is the car broken, Mommy?" she asked softly, her little bottom lip pouting out.

Natalie couldn't help but smile at her daughter's innocence. It was very much broken and completely useless to them at this moment.

"Yes, Dallie. Our car is dead."

"What are we gonna do now?" Dallie asked, so unaware.

That was her line of questioning, not her daughter's worry; she smiled again at her little blonde angel.

"Everything will be fine, baby. Mommy will think of something, okay?"

The truth was that Natalie hadn't a *clue* what to do. She decided against walking. It wasn't a good idea, she thought, not with Dallie; if she were alone, she would, but not with her daughter. She felt hopeless, and she felt like she was out of options. She should be better prepared for something like this, but her mind had stopped functioning at full capacity months ago. All she wanted to do was cry, but she prayed instead. Praying had been the one thing she had held onto throughout all this... *God, please, help me out!* Her parents had no idea that she was coming, she wasn't expected to arrive until the following week. She hoped for a miracle.

CHAPTER 1

*J*ack Kinsen raced forward in his brand new rust colored Dodge Ram Laramie pickup. The sun was setting, turning the sky crimson, pink, and gold. Subtle darkness began to cover the pastures of east Texas. It was the first day of fall, but the temperature stated otherwise. It was at best 70 degrees on this windy evening.

He had gone into town an hour earlier to have drinks with his best friend, Luther Boyd, and was on his way back home. He rolled his window down, so he could smell the sweet fragrance of the autumn that had begun. The leaves were already starting to change on the oaks, elms and sweetgum trees. He also picked up a smell that he was all too familiar with, cow manure.

As he continued down the long straight road that went on for miles, he spotted a silver car that hadn't been there when he left for town earlier. The incident was unusual simply for the fact that the car was where it was, in the middle of nowhere, the hood was raised and smoke was coming off the engine. The car was compact, probably a Toyota or Honda. As he closed in on it, he saw a woman with long, wavy, dark hair leaning into the open door of the back seat.

Although he was tired from the long day, he decided to stop and see if she could use some help. As it was, he was accustomed to giving his southern hospitality to a "damsel in distress" or his fellow man in distress... if that be the case. That was just the cowboy way...

He parked his truck a few feet behind her car, grabbed his work gloves from the dash and hopped out. It appeared that she hadn't noticed him pulling up, which seemed odd since his diesel engine could easily be heard; perhaps she was otherwise preoccupied or was simply ignoring him.

But boy, he found it hard to ignore her... Her hair was a shiny, dark brown that glimmered with red and copper hues where the setting sun touched it. She wore khaki slacks that outlined a very shapely backside, if he did say so himself. As he came closer to the car, he noticed her radio was blaring loudly and she was singing and laughing. He was within a few steps of her now and to get her attention, he cleared his throat.

She immediately tensed and spun quickly around to confront the intruder. Her face was full of terror from his sudden manifestation, but the color soon returned, and she regained her composure. It occurred to him that she *really* hadn't heard him approaching. *Odd*, he thought.

He took in her soft, feminine features. She had an oval, slender face with a small straight nose, high cheekbones, and the most beautiful mouth he had ever seen on a woman. Her baby blue eyes matched the tank top that she was wearing, her skin was creamy, like that of a peach, and her breasts were full and high as they heaved from her unexpected fright.

"I didn't mean to startle you, ma'am," Jack stated truthfully as he tipped his cowboy hat at the lady whose face suddenly looked familiar to him. He knew that he'd definitely seen her before...but where?

"Well, you did," she remarked angrily as her chest continued to rise. "What do you want?"

"I was just driving down the road and saw your car." He tilted his head, pointing out his truck to her. She looked at it as if it had suddenly appeared out of thin air. "I thought that you could use some help," he continued.

She stiffened and backed up slightly as if trying to distance herself from him.

"You thought wrong." She looked him straight in the eyes, daring him to say otherwise. She crossed her arms over her chest giving off the demeanor of a drill sergeant.

He didn't give up that easily. "Would you mind if I take a look? You do seem to be in quite a predicament, especially with all that smoke coming out from under the hood. I would assume the car's not drivable." He adjusted his hat.

She turned her head to look at the smoke, sighed, and then turned her face back to him, not directly acknowledging his response. Jack got it as clear as if she'd said no.

"Mind if I take a look?" he requested again as he put on his gloves and started walking toward the front of her car.

She had other plans. She came up behind him and grabbed his thick arm, the gesture stopping him in his tracks.

He turned toward her, appalled by her attitude. Here he was trying his damnedest to be a Good Samaritan, and she was acting as if she were angered by his friendly gesture. She was probably some damn rich yankee who'd taken a wrong turn, he thought. He crossed his arms and set his jaw. He towered over her by almost a foot and outweighed her by at least eighty pounds, but instead of being frightened by him, a man much bigger than she was, she confidently stood her ground.

"We're fine," she stated firmly, "and I would appreciate it if you would leave us alone." She planted her hands on her hips as her sexy lips tightened into a frown.

Jack was getting angrier by the minute. *Who the Hell did she think she was?* "Look, in all sincerity ma'am, we both know that's not true."

"Look sir, in all sincerity, we both know that it is *none* of your business."

He couldn't believe the audacity of this woman! Did she think that she was too good for his help? Was she in some kind of trouble? What in Hell was her problem?

Just as he was about to tell her where she could shove it, a tiny little voice intervened, and Jack noticed for the first time who the lady had been talking to when he'd approached the car.

It was a little girl, no older than five, sitting in a car seat with a cup in her hand. She had blonde hair with curly tendrils that flowed to her shoulders and the same blue eyes and full lips as the woman. There no mistaking that this child belonged to the woman. The little girl, like the woman, was very beautiful. However, unlike the woman, the little girl looked sweet. She smiled at him and his heart melted.

She spoke, looking directly at him, "Are you a cowboy?" Her lovable little blue eyes lit up in eagerness.

He belted out a rich laugh. "I sure am, little lady."

"Wow...a real cowboy..." She looked at him mesmerized before she suddenly spoke again, "Hi, I'm Dallas. What's your name?"

"Hi, Dallas. I'm Jack." He reached out to shake her tiny hand, but the lady suddenly came between them and gave him a look that dared him to touch the child.

His patience was wearing thin. "Listen lady, do you wanna stand out here and bicker with me or do you want to let me see if I can help you? It doesn't much matter to me. I can be on my merry way if you want me to leave you to it... But town is a good ways away from here, and it doesn't much look like you have a lot of options right now. There are some strange creatures out here after dark. In the child's best interests, I don't think you wanna be out here then," he said, once again crossing his arms over his chest.

She looked down, and her features softened then as he watched her process his words carefully. She finally spoke after a long silence, "Of course! You're right. Will you please see if you can help us Mr. ..." She trailed off, looking up at him.

"Kinsen, but call me Jack. And you are?" he asked, extending his hand.

"Natalie...Natalie Cameron."

Her name was familiar too, first her face, now her name... But he couldn't place it to save his life. She extended her much smaller hand, and he shook it gently, but firmly.

"Now, what seems to be the problem?" he asked, getting down to business. She led him to the front of the car. Smoke continued to spew from the engine as he stepped in front of the small, now confirmed, Honda.

"It made this big horrible noise and then just started sputtering. It won't crank. I tried to pull off the road as it died and saw that smoke was coming out from under the hood," she explained as she moved beside him in front of the car.

"Well," he remarked, bending over the car and examining the engine closely, "I'm no mechanic, but I think your engine has over-heated, and I can see that you've got a busted water hose, looks like the radiator's boiled dry." He pointed out the radiator and busted hose to her, then propped his forearms on the grill as he continued to survey the damage. "Depending on how hot it got, it could have done some damage to the engine, but it's hard to say," he said, looking over at her. She didn't look happy about that, he noticed. She looked extremely tired. She grimaced and rubbed her cheek in thought.

"Did you notice your temperature gauge while you were driving?" he asked, turning his body toward her. "How far have you driven?"

"I drove here from Chicago. I guess I didn't notice the temperature..."

"Chicago?" *Damn!* She'd driven a long way...halfway across the country.

"Yeah... So, can you fix it?" she asked hopefully.

"*I* can't, but I know someone who can," he said, closing the hood of the car and turning toward her as he swiped the gloves off his hands and shoved them into his Wranglers. "I tell you what, ma'am… Just a suggestion… I work just about 10 minutes from here. How about I take you there and you can use the phone? Cause as you probably could tell… cell phones won't work out here," he smirked.

"Where do you work?" she asked curiously, her eyes narrowing.

"Starlight Valley Stables."

"No way!" she stated, her tone softening in surprise. "That's my parent's ranch! That's where I'm going." She smiled suddenly and burst into a quick laugh, making her even more beautiful than he'd originally thought.

"Wow! *You* are David and Corrine Butler's daughter?" He shook his head in disbelief.

"One and the same!" She smiled again.

"No kidding!" He couldn't help but smile at her as he watched her whole face come to life. "That just works out good for the both of us, then doesn't it?" he asked.

Her parents, huh? That's why she seemed familiar, she was. There were pictures of her throughout the house and the little girl too. How on earth had he not connected the two?

"Yeah, I guess it does," she said, smiling back.

~

So, she'd prayed for a miracle and ended up with a guy somewhere between the Marlboro man and Wyatt Earp…

"Thank you so much for the ride," Natalie said to the handsome stranger sitting next to her as they rode toward her parents' house. She appeared confident to this kind gentleman who had rescued her on the side of the road, but inside, she was trembling. However, she would never let him see that. Although it calmed her to know that he worked for her parents, everything she had been through in the last year made her feel uneasy being alone with this stranger in his truck.

He had helped her unload the two big suitcases and several medium-sized bags that held all that she and Dallie had left in the world into his truck. He also helped them into the passenger side, while he made sure her car was locked. The man appeared to be such a Good Samaritan that Natalie felt bad about being so rude to him just minutes before.

"It's my pleasure, ma'am." He smiled over at her.

Dallie held tight to the stuffed, pink horse she had appropriately named Pinky Pie. Instead of choosing to sit in one of the back seats, she had chosen to sit in Natalie's lap. She laid her head on Natalie's breast, playing the shy card towards Jack and closed her eyes.

"She looks tired," Jack said as he looked over at Dallie.

"Yeah, she's pretty exhausted. She has been through a lot lately." *A lot more than you could ever know*, she thought. She wanted to get her mind off her past, so she decided to find out more about this good-looking man. "So, how long have you been working for my parents?"

"About a year and a half now," he stated and smiled. "They're great people to work for."

"I bet!" She returned the smiled. "What do you do there?" She wanted to know as much about him as possible. She wanted to know exactly who she had chosen to hop a ride with.

"I'm the foreman, although mostly I do the training and handling of the horses alongside your father," he said casually while he adjusted the black Stetson that rode on his head.

Everyone in the small town of Abundance knew the Butlers and their 500-acre horse ranch. Her father had bred, raised and trained thoroughbreds and quarter horses there since before Natalie was born. The ranch had been in operation for over 30 years. Jack, Natalie thought, must be great with horses if he helped him with training. Her father had never allowed anyone to help him train and break the horses... except for her and her brother. He'd said it was too important of a job. Of course, it had been years since either of them had been active at the ranch.

The man sitting next to her in the spacious truck was gorgeous; she would give him that much. He looked like he was approaching thirty years of age. His kind eyes were the color of soft green moss, the most amazing shade of green she'd ever seen. His light brown hair peeked out where his cowboy hat didn't cover. His face was ruggedly handsome with a square jaw, long, straight nose and full lips. He had a broad chest and a large build, she had noticed that when he was standing in front of her earlier. His arms were muscular, his skin lightly tanned, the hair on his arms blonde, bleached by the sun. The green polo shirt that he wore looked new and clashed with his jeans, which seemed to be well worn in. The truck was new, leather interior; it even had that fresh new car smell.

He looked at her and smiled, interrupting her reverie. "Would it be impolite of me to ask you why you drove all the way here from Chicago? That sure is a long ride!"

"I decided to come back home. I left Chicago forever." Her answer was short and to the point.

"Call me absent-minded, but I apologize for not recognizing you back there. I knew that your parents had a daughter and a granddaughter and I knew that you lived in a big city. Heck, they talk about you all the time, and there are tons of pictures of you both all over the house, yet I didn't even notice the resemblance...Talk about embarrassing."

"It's okay, really! We've never met each other. You can be told about someone, but you probably wouldn't recognize them even from a photo unless you've met them."

"Yeah, I guess you're right! Things have been really hectic around here lately, your father and mother have been gone a lot throughout the year..."

"They've been with me." She interrupted.

"Oh, I see, I had only been working at the ranch less than six months when your father put me in charge while they were gone. He didn't say where they were going or how long they'd be gone. Your parents are very private people. I mean, of course they talked about you, but I just wasn't expecting to meet you now, so suddenly. They haven't mentioned your arrival..."

That's because they aren't expecting me yet. Natalie knew all too well the reason for her parent's privacy was because of her situation in Chicago. She could only imagine how helpless they felt with her being so far from them and knowing it was hard, if not almost impossible, to just leave the ranch to come be with her. She was ever grateful to them for all they'd done for her in the past year; yet it upset her to know that they were so withdrawn, with friends, with co-workers. It wasn't something they could easily talk to anyone about. It was a blow that hit the entire family and not just her and Dallie.

"Now... aren't you married?" he asked, trying to sound nonchalant.

Instead of tensing, which is what she initially expected to feel, she almost laughed. She found it humorous that this man was interested in her marital status.

"Divorced!" she stated proudly for the first time. It seemed to lift a huge burden from her shoulders, and she found herself smiling knowing that she could say it with liberation.

"No wonder I haven't seen a photo of a son-in-law..." He looked almost relieved as he smiled over at her. This man, this rugged cowboy was flirting with her, and she couldn't help but feel flattered by it. She smiled back over at him, she couldn't help herself.

"How old is your daughter?" he asked, turning his head to Dallie.

"She's four, soon to be five." She smiled down at Dallie who was trying to drift off to sleep. She looked up at him. "So, now you've met me and Dallie, did you ever get to meet my brother?"

"Yes, I've met Nathan. I met him in the rodeo circuit. He's as wild and free as the bulls he rides." He laughed.

Natalie would love to forget that her older brother had left the ranch to go and ride Brahma bulls. She wanted to laugh at Jack's comment, but what Nate had said to her the day she'd left was something she could never forget; something that haunted her to this day, ten years after the fact.

"Yeah, Nate *is* quite a character. He and I loved the ranch..." She trailed off, and then decided to change the subject; it was just too painful to talk about with this stranger. "Do you have any brothers or sisters?"

"I have two brothers, one older, one younger. My older brother lives in Cheyenne and my younger brother lives in Corpus Christi."

"That's good, how about your parents, where do they live?"

"Oh, uh…they…they're deceased." He stiffened a little when he answered her.

"Oh… I'm sorry, I didn't mean to—" She flushed as she stuttered her apology.

"No, no, it's okay! Really! They died about eight years ago in a car wreck while I was in college. But they lived in Louisville, Kentucky. That's where I'm originally from."

"I'm so sorry to hear that." She was quiet for a moment to show her respect, and then asked, "Where did you go to college?"

"I went to Texas A & M."

"Wow, that's great, what was your major?"

"Animal Science. I specialized in Equine Science." She was impressed to say the least and was surprised when he continued. "I've worked with horses all of my life. Go figure, being from Kentucky and all. My father had a small horse ranch while I was growing up, and I became obsessed with the lifestyle. I plan to start a horse ranch of my own within the year."

"Wow, well, good luck with that," she stated, smiling.

"Thanks. I appreciate it." He smiled back at her. His eyes seemed so deep that Natalie found it easy to get lost in them. He was so easy to talk to and seemed truly genuine. She tore her eyes from his before she became lost in their emerald depths and stared ahead for a few minutes.

It seemed as though the road stretched on endlessly. Blackness from the approaching night began to consume the land, the sky, the truck.

"It's amazing how it gets dark so much faster in the fall time… maybe it's just me," he muttered, absent-mindedly.

"No, you're right. I was just thinking how quickly it came myself."

She looked over at him and suddenly felt very ashamed of how rude she'd been to him. "I…uh…I want to apologize for my behavior back there."

"Please, don't apologize. I understand. You were just concerned for your daughter. I'm just glad I could help out." The look in his eyes was sincere as he spoke.

Dallie chose that moment to move around, and when she couldn't get comfortable, she cried out.

"Mommy, I'm *so* hungry," she cried, sitting up and wrapping her arms around her mother's neck.

"We'll be at Grandma and Paw-Paw's soon, honey. I promise." Natalie soothed her, patting her on the back and cradling her head. "Even though they aren't expecting us yet, I'm sure they'll be grateful to feed us." She laughed to ease the tension she felt from Dallie, but Dallie continued to cry despite Natalie's words. "She's just tired," Natalie explained to Jack.

"Hey, Dallas?" Jack asked her with a smile on his face.

Dallie quieted down for a second and looked up at him and said, "Yeah?"

"Do you like horses?" he asked. She gave him a slight smile and nodded. Jack laughed. "How about you and I ride one when we get to your grandparents house? That is, after you get something to eat."

"I never rode on a horse before!" she exclaimed, smiling brightly.

"Oh, Dallie. Yes you have!" Natalie replied. "Well, you were probably too little to remember it… You don't remember riding with me on Cheshire?" Dallie shook her head indicating that she didn't.

"Can Mommy come too?" Dallie's eye lit up as she looked over at Jack.

Jack looked up at Natalie as he said, "Sure! That's fine with me, whatever she wants to do."

Natalie met his eyes, but didn't smile. Instead, she spoke to her daughter. "We'll see Dallie. Mommy's really tired. We'll just have to see."

Instead of going into a fit which Natalie expected her to do,

Dallie just laid her head back onto Natalie's breast. She didn't utter a word of protest. Natalie was surprised, but she realized that Dallie was just as tired as she was. Although she hated disappointing her child, maybe one day Dallie would understand how exhausted and weak Natalie felt.

"It's because of Daddy isn't it?" Dallie asked, looking up at her mother after several moments of silence. Tears clouded her little eyes.

Natalie was taken aback. "No Dallie, this has nothing to do with your father." Even though it had everything to do with him and possibly always would.

"It's because I was a bad girl… isn't it?"

"What?" Natalie asked angrier than she felt.

Dallie repeated her statement only she whispered it this time, "It's because I was bad."

"Dallie," Natalie spoke firmly but soothingly. "Look at me." Dallie turned toward her mother. Natalie took Dallie's soft, plump little face in her hands and spoke gently to her. "Baby, you never did anything wrong. *Nothing.* Do you understand me? You were *never* bad. You have no reason to ever feel like you did anything bad. Never say that again."

Dallie just nodded her head and again rested it on Natalie's breast.

Natalie couldn't have been happier when flood lights began to shine onto the road. They had finally reached her parents' driveway. *Finally*, she thought. Dallie sat up and looked too. Jack didn't say anything, but Natalie could tell he was curious about the conversation that had taken place. Who wouldn't be?

"Well, here we are," Jack stated as they pulled into the gravel driveway. It was almost truly dark now, but Natalie could still read the arch over the driveway: *Starlight Valley Stables.*

The driveway separated two pastures that were enclosed by newly painted white picket fences, several horses contained in each fence. A couple of paints, quarter horses and thoroughbreds, she noted. Each pasture was only about half the size of a football field. The fences ended parallel to each other. Her parent's driveway ended with the fences into a fork. If you went straight ahead you'd go into the driveway toward the house, if you went either left or right you'd end up at the barn, that road made a circle. The large blue three-story house sat about 60 yards past the fences centered in the middle of a grove of oak and pecan trees. To the left was a carport big enough for two cars. The barn couldn't be seen for the house, but it was big and bright red, she knew, with fenced pasture-land that spread out as far as the eye could see.

The house was a beautiful sight to behold. The trim and shutters were covered in a creamy beige. It had clapboard siding, adorned gables and a wrap-around porch with elaborate spindlework giving the house a Victorian charm. There were four rocking chairs lined in a row to the left of the front door and a swing to the right. The third floor with its three dormers housed their attic which was full of old chests of clothes and books. It had always intrigued Natalie when she was a child.

God, she had missed this house. It brought back so many memories. She remembered the many mornings she eagerly ate her breakfast anticipating the moment when she would be able to go riding, the soul- rendering talks Natalie and her mother used to have in her bedroom upstairs as her mother brushed her long hair, her first kiss had been experienced there on the porch swing. Maybe here she would find the peace she so desired to feel.

Her reverie was interrupted as a waiting Jack tapped her on the shoulder.

"We're here, Natalie." His brows were raised in question as her head spun around to him. "We're here."

"Oh! Sorry!" She recovered. Dallie was already sitting up, ready to go.

Jack took that as his cue to get out and began hauling the luggage out of the bed of his truck. Natalie helped her daughter out of the seat and sat her gently on the ground while she gathered her purse and stepped down out of the truck. Natalie looked up to see her mother curiously looking out at the truck from the kitchen window. She watched as her mother realized it was her and came rushing out of the screen door of the house. Corrine ran to her and embraced her just as Natalie fell into her arms, her body wrenched by uncontrollable sobs.

"Hush now, baby. You're home. Everything's gonna be alright," Corrine said soothingly into Natalie's ear, holding her and stroking her back. She pulled Natalie's face up so she could look at her. "Nat, it's over, darling. It's over." She kept repeating those words like a chant until they finally sank into Natalie's brain. She sniffled and wiped her eyes. Her mother was right. It *was* over. She was home!

CHAPTER 2

"Jack, dear, would you be so kind as to take Natalie's things upstairs while I get everything ready for dinner?" Corrine asked as they all stood in the foyer. She handed Natalie a tissue as she picked up her granddaughter. Natalie wiped her eyes and nose on it and checked her appearance in the mirror adjacent to the staircase.

"Yes ma'am. I sure will," Jack stated and retreated upstairs with Natalie's luggage.

"How's Grandma's little angel doing?" Corrine asked Dallie as she kissed her cheek.

"I'm really hungry," Dallie remarked matter-of-factly smiling into her grandmother's kind face.

Corrine laughed and kissed her again. "Well, darlin', its ready when you are." She sat Dallie down and turned to Natalie as they all walked toward the kitchen. She looped her arm through her daughter's. "So, where's your car? How on earth did you end up with Jack?"

"Oh, it started sputtering and smoking. I had to pull over on the side of the road. Then it went dead! Luckily, Jack saw my car, and offered to bring me back here."

"Well, bless his sweet heart! I'm sure glad he found you. Especially since you didn't *tell* anyone you were coming early," her mother accused.

"I know. I'm sorry. I finished everything up and just wanted to get out of there."

"I know darlin', it's alright! The house is a mess, but now I have someone to help me with it..."

Natalie smiled at her mother as she led them into the kitchen. It was decorated in creams and reds with cherry wood cabinets. She had helped her mother redecorate it about two years ago when she'd come to visit. There was now a large island in the middle of the kitchen with a pot rack hanging over it and Natalie had replaced their old appliances with stainless steel ones. She had also tiled the floors and added rooster prints into the décor. When they'd finished, her mother had said it was too fancy, but Natalie could tell she loved it.

Corrine walked over to the stove and opened the lid of a huge pot sitting on one of the stove eyes. A delicious aroma filled the kitchen as her mother stirred the contents of the pot and added spices to it. Natalie's belly rumbled with hunger pains, she couldn't remember the last time she'd eaten a decent meal.

Natalie continued her explanation, "I had tried to call, but my cell didn't work, so I was kinda out of options. I just hoped for a miracle." *And I ended up with a good-looking cowboy.*

"Well don't worry about the car! We'll tow it in the morning; it should be fine where it is. No one should mess with it." Her mother had taken a spoon and was testing the consistency of whatever it was that was cooking. She sipped at the wooden spoon, wrinkled her nose in thought and said, "Just a bit more cream and butter," then wiped her hand on her bright red apron as she walked over to the fridge.

"Well, everything of value is out of it. Thank goodness. Can I help you with anything?"

"No, no, sit yourself down and take a load off!"

20

Natalie sighed and sat down in one of the chairs at the small breakfast table located in front of the kitchen's bay window as she watched her mother maneuver her way around the kitchen adding this and that to the large, steaming pot as her belly grumbled once again. Her eyes burned from lack of sleep and her muscles felt like liquid. She trembled with exhaustion. It felt so good to sit down and relax for the moment. Dallie had found one of her grandmother's kittens on the floor so she'd busied herself playing with it.

"Mommy, look. Grandma has kitties." Dallie giggled. "Oh, they're so cute." Natalie just smiled down at her and then laid her head on her arms.

"Natalie," her mother said, looking over at her with her hands planted on her hips, a look of pity in her eyes, "Why on earth didn't you let me and your father stay with you longer than we did out there? If I had known it was still wearing you down, I wouldn't have left you."

"Oh Mom, I'm fine, just overwhelmed. Dallie and I both are, but we'll be okay. I'm just glad to be home now. I'm glad it is finally over."

Corrine's voice dropped to a whisper, "And it *is* over, Nat. The sooner you realize that, the sooner you can move on with your life. I'm just glad to see you home now. You can start over here. I know you won't ever forget what happened, but you're still young and so is Dallie. He's in prison and he can't hurt either of you ever again."

"I know," Natalie said and relaxed a bit at her mother's calming words. She looked down at Dallie playing with the kitten and smiled. She was home; no one could hurt her or Dallie here.

Corrine turned on her then and scolded her, one hand on her hip, the other shaking the wooden spoon at her daughter. "You look awful, Natalie. You're too skinny, and you look like you haven't slept in days. If nothing else good comes out of this at least you'll get plenty to eat and some well deserved rest. For God's sake, you must keep your strength, honey."

Natalie just closed her eyes and smiled. It felt good to be fussed over that way; it made her feel young again and she realized how much she had missed being home with her family. She opened her eyes then and took in her mother's appearance. Her mother was small and petite as she'd always been. Her long hair had been put up in a bun, but the hairstyle didn't hide the few lines of gray that were starting to streak it. Despite that, her mother didn't look her age of fifty-three years.

Jack chose that time to come into the kitchen. "Boy Mrs. Butler, whatever you're cooking sure smells good!"

Corrine laughed and patted Jack on the back as he kissed her on the cheek. "Nat, this man is the biggest pig next to your father that you'll ever have the pleasure to meet. I have never met anyone as eager to eat as he is. And Jack I want to thank you for rescuing my daughter."

Jack smiled and pulled his dusty hat off, hanging it on the hat rack that hung on the far right wall in the hallway off the foyer. "Well, it was nothing ma'am. I was just glad I could help her out."

"David and the guys should be here any minute now. So, why don't you three go wash up for supper?" Corrine suggested.

He looked over at Natalie, who got up and called Dallie to come as well. She and Dallie followed Jack to the small bathroom just beyond the kitchen. He scooted over enough to make room for the two girls as Natalie sat Dallie on the sink. He turned the water on, grabbed the soap and passed it to Dallie who took it.

"Thank you very much," Dallie said as she began lathering her hands.

"You're very welcome, little lady." Jack smiled at her. "Aren't you polite?" Dallie just beamed up at him, her cheeks looking like little red apples.

"Thank you," Natalie said. "I tried to teach her proper manners. Sometimes she uses them." Natalie smirked, lifting her eyebrow at Dallie who suddenly gave Natalie a mischievous look.

"Well, it looks like you did a very good job of it. It's rare to hear a child be polite nowadays." Boy was that statement all too true…

Natalie's father bolted through the back door at that time, followed by his hands. Nat couldn't see them, but she could hear the sounds of scuffling boots and loud boisterous laughter and she smiled to herself.

"Cavalry's here!" Jack boomed loudly. Natalie laughed and Dallie gave a squeal, followed by a surprised, "Paw-paw!" Dallie rinsed her hands quickly and jumped off the counter to go greet her grandfather, squealing in delight as she raced to meet him.

Natalie grabbed the soap and lathered her hands then handed the bar to Jack who did the same. She noticed the calluses on the palms of his hands and the deep tan that came from working outside all day. His hands looked so strong and capable. The sun had bleached the hair on his arms blonde giving it that shiny look that was typical of cowboys.

She grabbed the towel from its rack and began vigorously drying his hands as Jack rinsed his. She waited on him to dry his then they headed towards the ruckus coming from the living room.

As they entered the living room, David was holding Dallie over his shoulder like she was a sack of potatoes.

"Where'd my lil' darlin' go?"

"Paw-paw, I am right here." Dallie laughed. She pounded her little fists on his back. He swung her around to the side of him and began tickling her belly. Natalie stopped behind them and smiled. Dallie was the most precious thing in the world, even if she was her own. Corrine came in then and scolded David for tickling Dallie, then as he sat her down Corrine kissed him on the cheek. David rubbed her back as he returned the kiss. Dallie hugged at her grandfather's legs then Corrine called her to the kitchen to help her bring the food into the dining room, and she obliged happily. Natalie was glad to see Dallie's spirit and enthusiasm return. It had been too long since she'd seen her truly smile. All the hands had gone to wash up and were returning to the table as Natalie approached her father.

"Hey Daddy!" Natalie said, hugging her father for the first time in four months. She held tight to him taking comfort from his strong embrace.

"Hey darlin', you doin' alright?" he asked in her ear as he held her close.

"Yeah, I'm good. Doing much better now that I'm home." She smiled into eyes that were almost identical to hers and took in her father's features. He was the tall, dark, and handsome type of man that was read about in novels. Although he was approaching fifty-five, his dark hair had few silver strands. He smiled back at her and held her cheek in his large palm.

"Everything's gonna be fine. I promise you, baby," he said. Tears filled her eyes as she thought of how grateful she was for the rock that he'd been for the last twenty eight years of her life. "I better go and wash up before supper starts without me, huh?" With that, he kissed her cheek and hurried to the bathroom.

She laughed and wiped at her eyes. Jack had disappeared into the kitchen, so she decided to see if she could help as well. Natalie knew all too well that feeding a crew of hungry ranch hands was a big job.

He was filling up glasses with tea, and Dallie was watching her grandmother scoop up the contents of the huge pot that sat on the stove, asking her what it was. Natalie now recognized it and smiled. Her mother had made one of Natalie's favorite dishes, chicken and dumplings. It had been ages since she had eaten that wonderful southern meal and her stomach began to rumble.

"Jack, honey, you don't have to do that. Let Natalie do it and you go and sit down." Corrine tilted her head at Jack.

"No ma'am. I can get this just fine," he replied, pouring sweet tea into several glass tumblers.

"I can help," Natalie said.

She grabbed the glasses that he had filled and began taking them into the dining room. She sat them in front of the hands. Three of the men were new, and two she recognized as familiar faces. One was the face of a man who had worked for her father as long as she could remember, Billy Bob Anderson. His once dark hair was now silver, and his mustache showed the same signs of aging. He looked a lot like her father except for the fact that Billy Bob was a bit older and darker. His face was still handsome if only slightly more rugged with crows feet surrounding his eyes. His soft smile was just as sincere as always, she noted as she sat his glass down in front of him.

"Miss Natalie, you have grown into quite the young woman. Come give your Uncle Billy Bob a hug for old time's sake." She came around the side of the table to hug the old man who really was more like her uncle than her father's co-worker. His big arms wrapped around her.

"Well thank you, Billy Bob," she said, returning his smile and giving him a kiss on the cheek as he released her.

Her eyes fell on the other ranch hand that she recognized. He was much younger than the other and had only been there for about two and half years. He looked at her with the young pride of a man who knew how to get the ladies. His beguiling smile and come-hither eyes always annoyed Natalie beyond sanity. His name was Dan Wilson. He was like a peacock with the bite of a snake; arrogant, charming… and a complete male chauvinist. He thought he could get any woman he wanted, and Natalie hated that in a man. He'd had his big brown eyes set on her since she met him two years ago in the barn on her parent's property. That first impression had showed her just what type of man Dan really was.

She had just come back from riding her favorite horse, Cheshire, a privilege that had been taken away from her when she'd moved to Chicago. She was brushing the thoroughbred gelding down when Dan came up behind her and pressed himself intimately into her buttocks while grabbing her hips. His rough voice reverberated in her ear as he placed his hand over the one of hers that was brushing the horse down its back.

"Let me show you how this is done, darlin'," he'd voiced in a thick southern drawl.

Natalie had immediately tensed when she'd felt his unfamiliar frame against her. After she had gotten over the initial shock of him, she had pushed him off her, informed him never to lay a hand on her again and, for good measure, that Hell would freeze over before he could ever teach her something about horses that she didn't already know. Ever since then, she had appeared to be a challenge to him because she was not only the daughter of the man he worked for, but also a married woman. And judging by the look he was giving her now, she was fair game once again now that was divorced... *Great!*

He looked at her, a crooked smile on his face, as she sat his glass down in front of him. His eyes licked at her body; she could feel them burning through her clothes. It made her incredibly nervous, but she didn't show that to him.

"It's a pleasure to see you again, Natalie! You're looking as beautiful as ever." He smiled his charming, devilish smile.

"Nice to see you again too, Dan," she lied and gave him the same shit-eating grin.

He laughed then and crossed his arms over his chest, pleased that he knew he could still get to her. She cursed herself silently, but it was useless. He knew that she hated him; it was written all over her face.

She practically stalked away to the kitchen not just to get more glasses, but to take a breath. She hated his egotistical attitude. He was such a jerk. Her mother looked at her as she quickly came through the swinging kitchen door and knew the reason for her daughter's obvious disgust.

"Ew! He's horrid!" she said in an expulsion of breath.

Her mother laughed. "I take it you and Dan got to catch up."

Dallie looked up from the salad she was doing her best to toss and Natalie couldn't help but smile at her capability. Nat then looked back at her mother with indignation.

"I can't believe Daddy hasn't fired him," she said, placing her hands on her hips. Jack was now looking at her with immense curiosity as well but said nothing.

"He's a good worker," Corrine replied, slicing tomatoes for the salads. "Just because he annoys you doesn't mean he doesn't do his job. Ignore him, Natalie. He has to be someone you must get used to because I doubt he's going anywhere anytime soon. You won't have to see him too much anyway. Besides, you know that there aren't a lot of people willing to put up with the stuff that hands have to put up with."

Why did her mother always have to be right? She sighed and picked up some more glasses to take to the table.

She returned to the dining room with three glasses and moved along the table sitting the glasses down, taking in the appearance of the three hands she didn't recognize. One was a man who looked to be in his mid-thirties with dark black hair. He seemed quiet but kind and thanked her when she set his glass down. The one sitting next to Dan was just a kid, about eighteen/nineteen years of age. He was laughing at something Dan said. Natalie bet that he was quite the jokester; he had that look that said he was trouble with a capital T. The other hand next to Dan was Hispanic and sat very quietly with his hands in his lap. Her father took that moment to walk in and take his seat at the head of the large oval table.

"Nat, honey, let me introduce you to the guys," he said, calling her to come to him. He placed his hand in the small of her back as he introduced her to his ranch hands. "Of course you know Billy Bob, and I am sure you remember Dan." When Natalie nodded her head mechanically, he continued, "The one beside Dan is Kyle. That's Miguel and the quiet one is Cass."

The men all shook their heads obligingly. Kyle stood and gave her his hand. "Pleasure to meet you ma'am. You look nothing like your brother ...Thank God."

The table broke into laughter then and even Natalie smiled about his statement.

She didn't think her brother was even close to remotely bad-looking, but she took it as a compliment and thanked him.

When all of them finally got to the table and the food was served, Natalie started feeling the effects of the long trip. She found herself yawning as she began cutting Dallie's salad. She found her mother's cooking exceptional, and it felt good to sit down and have a home-cooked meal again. It had been a long time since she had eaten that way, and she thoroughly enjoyed it. Her mother added her into the conversations she had with the hands. It was nice to know a little more about each one of them. Jack especially made it a point to talk to Natalie and Dallie as well. That he was kind to her child gave Natalie a newfound respect for him. Dan, however, did not have that same respect. He appeared to dislike Jack for some reason, and it appeared that the dislike was mutual. Jack never spoke directly to him or vice versa. If they were brought into conversation with one another, there was tension between the two men. It was quite interesting, and it made her curious as to the hostility between them.

For dessert, her mother had made banana pudding. By the time it was passed around the table it was completely gone. Dallie loved it and Natalie even tried a little. She helped her mother take up the dishes and put them in the dish washer. By then she was completely exhausted and yawned as she sat down at the small table in the kitchen. Dallie was in the living room with David, so Natalie rested her eyes knowing that she was safe with him. She could finally relax here not having to worry about where Dallie was and if she was safe with whomever she was with. She propped her elbow on the table and laid her head in her hands. She watched her mother wipe the counter off and put the tea away.

"Mom, how long has it been since you talked to Nathan?"

"Oh honey, at least a month. You know he calls when he wants to, never leaves a number. We never know where he is or what he's doing."

Natalie looked down. Sadly, she knew it had been her and Nathan that had put the few grays hairs in her mother's once dark mahogany hair. She hated the fact that Nathan was the one doing it now. Even though Natalie, like Nathan, had left, at least she had been in complete contact with her parents. Unfortunately, the day she'd left for Chicago was the day she had lost touch with her brother forever. He had nothing to do with her now. He felt betrayed by her, and he had every right to feel that way. She had forgotten who she was, and he had made her never forget it.

"Honey, why don't you go on up to bed?" Corrine requested, looking at her with sympathy.

"Yeah, I know, I look like death warmed over," Nat said, trying to laugh.

"No, you just look exhausted. Go on up to bed and I will bring Dallie up in a little while, okay?"

Natalie gave into reason. The thought of curling up in her warm soft bed just got the best of her, so she kissed her mother and headed up the stairs to her old bedroom.

～

The whole house heard the words despite the loud laughter of three of the hands coming from the living room and the Cowboys vs. Giants game showing on the television.

"*What* in the *Hell?*"

Jack knew immediately who had said it and why. He rushed to catch up to Corrine who was climbing the stairs two at a time. They stopped just short of Natalie whose face showed absolute confusion and anger. Jack held his breath.

"What *happened* to my room?" Natalie yelled.

"Natalie, your father and I gave it to Jack." Corrine approached the subject with a soft soothing tone of voice as if she were talking to a small child.

"*What?*" The colors on her face deepened from a light pink to a crimson color. "Why? You gave my room to a *complete* stranger?"

"Well, Natalie, just calm down." Corrine stepped forward. Natalie took a step backward.

"Calm down! Calm down? You let some outsider have your daughter's bedroom. How am I supposed to calm down?" She exhaled in shock.

David came up behind Jack at that time with a disapproving look

29

on his face. Jack continued to hold his breath, despite the discomfort in his lungs.

"Natalie Anne, what is the meaning of this?" David demanded.

"Daddy, how could you?" Natalie turned to her father, pain in her eyes.

"Natalie, we've always been very hospitable to our guests in this house, young lady, and you know better than to act any such a way as this. I'm appalled at your behavior," her father's voice was laced with anger and authority.

"But you gave him my *room*! That is what the guest bedroom is for."

"Honey," her mother intervened, "the guest bedroom was much too small for Jack. We thought he would be more comfortable if he had a bigger bed, more closet space, a room closer to the bathroom... Besides, at the time, you had your own house and family. We never thought you would come back home to stay, just to visit, so we saved the guest room for that. We didn't think you would have a problem with our giving a permanent guest your room," she explained, emphasized the word permanent.

"Well I do! What's wrong with the bunk house? Why couldn't he stay there? Or Nathan's room?"

"We didn't have enough room at the bunk house. There are only three bedrooms. It's overcrowded as it is. Besides, Jack helps out more around the house than the other hands do and Nathan's room is full of boxes and junk, there isn't even a bed in there anymore."

"He's still a complete stranger!" She was grasping at straws now.

"He is to *you* Natalie, but not to me and your mother. You forget that he has been with us for over a year and half now," her father replied.

Natalie was totally defeated, and Jack felt bad for her. She looked so exhausted and now humiliated. Her face was pale; all the color had drained from it.

"I'm sorry, Natalie," Jack spoke for the first time. "I never knew you would take this so hard. If you want me to move my things into the guest bedroom I will, no problem." He softened his tone a little, "It is *your* room after all."

Her head came up slowly but her eyes looked at him in what appeared to be contempt. "Oh, forget it, Jack! I wouldn't have the room back." It wasn't the words that struck him. It was the conviction in her tone of voice. It was like a blow straight to his heart. She hated him now, and all he'd wanted since he'd found out that she was the beloved daughter of his employers was her approval, he couldn't figure out for the life of him why, but he wanted her approval all the same. Her parents looked like they had been slapped, and he felt embarrassed for them too.

Dallie chose that moment to come to the bottom of the stairs. Her little footsteps sounded softly on the wood floor, she held the big pink stuffed horse in the crook of her arm.

"Mommy? Are you okay?" she asked, her voice almost cracking. Big fat tears had formed in her little eyes. They all turned back to look at Natalie and saw that she was upset at herself for the way she'd acted in earshot of her child. She raced down the stairs and scooped up her child, holding her to her shoulder.

"Come on, baby. Let's go get some fresh air, okay?" she said as she walked toward the back door.

The house fell completely silent. David and Corrine both looked humiliated and hurt. Jack felt like a total ass. If it weren't for him, they would never have had to feel this way.

Corrine was the first to speak. "I've never seen her act that way before Jack. I'm so very sorry." She shook her head then looked away in embarrassment.

"No, Mrs. Butler, it's ok, really. She has every right to be upset. I understand." Even though he didn't...at all.

David looked severely pissed off. "That bastard she married did this to her, Corrine. She wasn't like this before she married him. I swear to God if I could get my hands on him..." His fists balled up at his sides.

"David," Corrine scolded, "this is not the time or the place." She then moved closer to her husband, putting a hand to his chest and one on his right hand, looking up at him.

Something bad had happened between Natalie and her ex husband. Jack had assumed that much when Dallie had made the comment she'd made in the truck on the way to the ranch. It made him curious, but not curious enough to ask. After all, it was none of his business. He felt bad though; he had upset Natalie. Not intentionally, not directly, but he had upset her just the same. He felt responsible, so maybe he should try to work it out.

"I'm gonna go talk to her," he said cautiously. He was afraid that they would warn him not to.

"Maybe that would help," Corrine offered. She didn't know what to do either. *Whatever that man had done to Natalie had been pretty bad,* Jack thought.

David nodded in approval so Jack walked slowly down the stairs. The hands had congregated to the back porch after probably hearing everything that had gone on, he was sure. He opened the screen door and walked out to the porch. Two of them were smoking, the other three were cracking jokes about God only knew what.

As Jack passed by them, Dan bumped his arm. "It would probably be best if you didn't go running after her, you know?"

"And why is that, Dan?" Jack demanded, confronting the man he despised, his arms crossed over his chest. He wanted to tell Dan that it was nothing to him whether he went after her or not.

"Trust me, I *know* Natalie." He cocked an eyebrow, the mischief in his smile deliberate.

Jack frowned. Surely she hadn't been with Dan. Surely not… She couldn't have, she didn't…he hoped she hadn't. Jack gave Dan the mother of all "go to Hell" looks and rushed down the porch steps.

Leave it up to a man like Dan to brag about sleeping with a woman like Natalie. Jack was surprised that Dan hadn't said something more vulgar than he had. Dan's take on women was cut and dry, he used them for one thing and one thing only.

Jack felt incredibly disappointed, but he couldn't really say why.

If Natalie wanted to sleep with Dan, then it was nothing to him, but just the thought of the two of them together upset Jack more than he wanted to admit.

As he headed down through a big pasture where a number of horses grazed, he thought about what he was going to say to her. He opened the gate and followed the dirt trail that led down to the barn. What would he say? Would he apologize again? *Oh this was a bad idea,* He thought. She'd looked at him as though she hated him. Maybe he should just turn around and forget it.

The moonlight was scarce, but the flood lights around the house plus the lights around the barn lit the area up like it was daylight. He entered the barn cautiously, afraid he might scare them. He saw Natalie with Dallie on her hip. They were petting Cheshire, David's thoroughbred. He smiled at little Dallie who was letting the horse feed out of the palm of her hand. She was a little angel, the cutest little girl that Jack had ever seen.

"Keep your hand flat, Dallie, and he'll eat out of your hand," Natalie said, giving Dallie some hay to feed the horse.

"Ew! Mommy his whiskers tickle me." She giggled and moved her hand back. Jack laughed softly, but they didn't hear him.

Natalie laughed too, a deep throaty laugh. A sexy laugh and Jack smiled. God, she was such a beautiful woman.

"Do I get to ride this one?" Dallie asked, looking up at her mother. Her blonde locks bouncing with the turn of her head.

"Well I don't know babe, I might have to ride this one with you. He's pretty big."

"Do you still hate horses, Mommy?"

"NO! I *never* hated horses. Your father hated them, so he expected me to do the same."

"How could he hate them? They are so beautiful!" she asked unbelieving, mesmerized by the horse. She reached up to pet the horse again but was too short, finding his mouth instead and was almost bitten by his large flat teeth. She screamed. By that time, Jack was right by their sides. Natalie had grabbed

Dallie's hands and was searching her fingers for any signs of damage.

Dallie was mad and her face had formed a snarl, her eyebrows were drawn down. She directed her finger at the horse and scolded him, "Bad horse! Don't do that... no... more!"

Jack and Natalie broke out then into hysterical laughter. Dallie was fine and her temperament seemed to be as well.

"You have to be careful sweetie. His teeth could snap one of your fingers off," Jack said, warning her.

"That's okay. I think I got him under control now, Jack." This brought forth even more laughter. After they caught their breath, Dallie asked to go see the "pony", so Natalie sat her down then and brushed the dirt off her hands as Dallie ran to find Blaze, the six month old colt.

After a long uncomfortable silence, Natalie looked up at Jack. So many things showed in her eyes, but she said nothing. Jack spoke first when Dallie had walked out of ear shot.

"I'm really sorry. I never meant to intrude on your family... or you for that matter. If you want the room back, it's yours. I'll have my stuff moved out of it in no time and you—"

She was shaking her head and interrupted him. "I don't want the room, Jack."

"Well, surely there is *something* I can do to make up for the inconvenience I've caused you?" Jack asked eagerly. He wanted badly to make amends with her.

The contempt showed in her eyes again as she answered him. Contempt that had no grounds, contempt that he didn't understand.

"Jack, just leave me alone that's what you can do. Just stay out of my way." With that she stalked off, grabbing Dallie and headed back towards the house. Dallie waved at him as Natalie pulled the side door behind her.

Her statement stung as bad as the bite of a rattlesnake, the poison sinking deep into his body. *Damn!* She really did hate him. He had known it was a bad idea to try to talk to her. Obviously she was really upset that he'd "stolen" her room.

He swallowed the pain that her words had caused him. Go figure that a woman as beautiful as Natalie would hate him and sleep with Dan. Women had never made any sense to him, what made this one an exception to the rule? It must have been wishful thinking.

Natalie had been the captain of the cheerleading squad, had graduated with honors, married the star quarterback of the football team, majored in Journalism, gone on to write for a big magazine in Chicago… He knew her life story because her parents had always sang her praises, he'd seen the pictures in her room; her cheerleading pictures, her awards, her graduation pictures, but he didn't know anything about her. She didn't even appear to be the same woman her parent's had described. The woman they had described was sweet, loving, funny, giving; the list went on and on. Looking back now, he could remember the things Corrine had said about Natalie, she was a daughter that would make any mother proud. She was all the things that made up an incredible person, but the person he had seen thus far must be her evil twin.

They had gotten off on the wrong foot from the very beginning. He'd blown his first impression to Hell and back then to add insult to injury, he, the "outsider", had come in and taken over her bedroom even though it was her parents that had given him the room…. But even so, she hated him! How could he blame her? He was nothing compared to her, nothing! He was raised on a small horse farm in Kentucky and was bred with the value that a person had to work hard to go far in life. His family never had very much of anything. He had gone to college, but he had worked his ass off to get there, and his degree wasn't quite as grand as hers had been. He was a simple country boy who took pleasure in his work. He didn't live the life of a famous person like Natalie had. He had nothing to offer a woman like her, so why shouldn't she hate him and want nothing to do with him? He was a nobody.

Well, by God, he might be a nobody, but he was still a nice guy!

He could sulk or he could try again. He wasn't raised to be a quitter, and he would be damned if he started doing it now. He wouldn't give up! He was determined to get her at least to like him, she just needed time to cool off and get used to this adjusted living arrangement. It was only a matter of time. She would get to know him and she would like him. That was all there was to it!

He gave her enough time to get back to the house before he started that way too. When he got to the porch, Kyle looked at him and laughed.

"Damn, son what did you say to her? She was as mad as a bull with a rubber band around his nuts."

"I didn't say anything to her. Besides, it's none of your business." His mood was sour, but that's how he felt.

"Yeah? Well, I guess we can't all have charm oozin' from us like Dan does, huh?" Kyle laughed.

"Yeah," Jack said, raising his eyebrows as he looked Dan straight in the eyes. "We can't all be cold-blooded, conniving, woman-users now can we?"

Dan cut his eyes at Jack, but recovered quickly. "She'll never touch you, Jack. You can count on that!"

Jack ignored him before he shoved his fist down Dan's egotistical throat and walked into the house. His ears were greeted with laughter from Dallie, and he couldn't help but smile. The sound of her laughter took all his anger and pain away. It was like magic. He stepped into the den where she sat with her grandmother and several tabby kittens. They were chasing a string that she held; they were all paws and tails. It was a humorous sight, and he sat down with her to play because it just seemed so inviting. She smiled at him, and his heart melted for the second time that day.

"You like kitties, Jack?"

"Yeah, I sure do."

"My daddy didn't like kitties…or horses…or *any* animals."

"Why not?" Jack was suddenly curious to know more about Dallie's father.

"Because he said they were gross," she frowned then looked up at him with those deep blue eyes of hers. "Do you think animals are gross, Jack?"

He could tell his answer was very important to her, so he chose his words carefully.

"No Dallie, animals aren't gross. I like them very much."

"I do too," she said with a huge grin. Corrine added that she liked animals too, and Dallie just beamed bright as the sun. Jack picked one of the kittens up and began stroking its little head as it purred back at him.

"She likes you."

"Does she? How can you tell?" Jack was amused by Dallie's eagerness to talk to him.

"She's purring. That means she likes you, Grandma said so," Dallie said, her head bobbing up and down in a nod, curls bouncing.

Dallie continued to tease the kittens with the string then suddenly she looked up at Corrine.

"Grandma, where's the momma cat?"

Corrine looked up from the book she was reading. "Well, honey… She died." Corrine failed to mention how she died, but Jack was glad she didn't go into details about it. A motorcycle had hit her just last week and Jack buried her while Corrine sobbed. Tabitha had been Corrine's baby for the last eight years.

Dallie bowed her head looking rather upset by what Corrine had said, and then she looked back up at her grandmother a serious look on her face.

"They can't live without their mother!" Dallie said in shock.

Corrine smiled, "Oh honey, sure they can. They are old enough now that they can take care of themselves. They really don't have a choice about living without their mother."

"Kinda like I don't have a choice living without my Daddy?"

Her statement took Corrine by surprise. She was silent for a moment.

"Well…yes Dallie. But you have your mother to care for you."

Dallie sat quietly for a moment, looking down. Then she got up, put her hands on her grandmother's knees and looked into her eyes. She spoke quickly, her lip trembling, "What will happen to my Daddy? Will I ever see him again? Will I get a new Daddy?"

The blood had drained from Corrine's face, and Jack could tell that she didn't know how to answer Dallie's questions. Jack was suddenly dying to know what had happened to her father, but he dared not ask. Dallie was obviously very distressed about losing her father. If he wasn't dead then where was he?

"Dallie," Natalie said, coming from out of nowhere. She spoke softly, but her eyes were intense as she spoke. "Don't talk about your father. He's gone and that's all you need to know. You'll never see him again."

"Natalie!" Corrine intervened, appalled at Natalie's answer to Dallie's questions. "Dallas look at me." Corrine brought her to her lap smoothing her hair down as a tear formed in Dallie's eye. "Your daddy isn't someone you need to be around or someone you would want to be around. He isn't a nice man, baby. Maybe one day you will see him again..."

"She will *never* see him again!" Natalie said louder than she'd been seconds before, a grim determination in her tone.

"Despite what he has done, he's still her father, and she still loves him," Corrine stated, trying to calm her daughter down, reasoning with her.

"I don't care. There will be no visitations. You *know* what he's done to her, to me... He's crazy, mother. He has no rights to her now, so there is no way I will ever allow him to see her."

They had obviously forgotten that Jack was in the room. He tried to busy himself playing with the kittens and pretend that he was indifferent to what they were saying, but he was hanging onto every word.

"Yes, I understand that, Natalie. But you can't say that to her right now. She has been traumatized. She's lost her father, her home, her friends, her whole life and in such a short period of time. One day she'll understand, but right now she's four years old. She didn't just stop loving him because you did."

Natalie sighed knowing that she was out of line speaking to her daughter like she had. She looked down, then at Jack and took her anger out on him. "What are *you* doing in here?" She crossed her arms over her chest.

Oh, Jeez! What did he do now? He should have left the room, but no he just had to stay, didn't he? He just had to stay. He shrugged his shoulders in surrender. "Um... I was playing with Dallie and—"

"Well don't you believe in a little privacy?" Her voice was so calm it was creepy.

"Natalie!" Corrine shouted at her. Her voice was the loudest Jack had ever heard it before, "Just go to bed!"

Natalie looked at her and didn't even argue with her, just turned and walked upstairs. Jack's heart went out to her, she echoed misery. It oozed out of every pore. He felt complete sorrow for her. Whatever her ex-husband had done to her had been really bad... bad enough to where he was out of the picture forever. The way they had talked it sounded as if he were in prison. Had he been a member of the mafia? Did he kill someone? Had he beaten them, threatened their lives? Is that why Natalie had run from him?

Corrine looked over at him then, her bright blue eyes trying to help him understand her daughter's rudeness toward him, but it wasn't necessary because Jack understood pain all to well and Natalie was suffering from a huge dose of it.

Dallie spoke first, "Mommy's sad. Is it my fault Grandma, is she mad at me?"

"No darling! She loves you more than anything in this world. You know how much she loves you. She's just upset and tired. She'll be fine though, I promise you. Give her a few days to relax, and she'll be okay. She just needs to rest."

Dallie yawned, and Corrine scooped her little body up and cradled her in her arms. She started to rock her and softly sang an old gospel hymn. Slowly, Dallie's eyes fell and her breathing slowed.

She surrendered to sleep in her grandmother's comforting arms. It was such a contented scene that Jack yearned for bed as well. He yawned big and stretched and felt the muscles of his arms and back ache from working that day.

"Well, I think I'm going to head on to bed too. Good night Corrine." He stood and stretched as he covered a yawn.

"Goodnight honey. Sleep well…oh, and Jack?"

"Yeah?" he asked, turning slowly around.

"I apologize again for my daughter's behavior and I thank you for all your help today."

"Don't apologize, ma'am. It's fine, really. And don't thank me either. That's what I'm here for." With that Corrine gave him a big appreciative smile and squeezed his hand as he passed by her. He returned it, leaned down to kiss her cheek and headed up the stairs to hit the hay.

He felt bad about going to Natalie's room. After all, he was "the stranger" as she had put it. As he stepped inside the door, he pulled his boots off and curled his toes, enjoying the feeling of have his feet free from the confinement of shoes. He pulled his shirt over his head and unsnapped his jeans. His gaze flew over to the wall of photos of Natalie that he hadn't really bothered to pay much mind to until now. He walked closer and one picture caught his eye. Her slender yet curvy figure clad in a red and white cheerleading outfit, her long hair curled in ribbons with braces adorning her pearly white teeth as she smiled at him in youthful bliss. This was the smile of a sweet, innocent young woman who hadn't yet known what pain was. He sighed and felt guilt tear at him. He walked out the door then and walked into the bathroom to brush his teeth and wash the dirt off his face. When he finished that, he turned the light off and headed out the door.

A noise caught his attention and he looked toward the guest bedroom, the door at the far end of the hall that was directly opposite his bedroom door. The light had been cut off, and the door was closed. The noise was soft and constant, and Jack finally recognized it as sobs. The sound twisted his stomach. Natalie was sobbing! He walked forward toward the door listening to her heart wrenching cries. He hesitated. For a moment he thought about going to her, but decided against it, knowing that she would only yell at him to leave her alone again. He turned then and walked to the room that had once been hers as guilt knocked at his heart once again. He didn't shut the door when he fell into bed... just in case she needed him. Just in case.

CHAPTER 3

The sound of birds and the heat of the sun coming through the window woke Natalie that morning. She stretched and felt groggy still, her eyes itchy from crying all night. The red digits of the bedside clock confirmed that it was 10:30 in the morning. Wow! How long had it been since she had slept that late? It had been a long time. She looked down at the cover beside her. Dallie wasn't there.

Where is she? Panic flooded her veins. Natalie was supposed to be protecting her, some one could hurt her. Where could she possibly be? She threw the covers off herself and searched frantically for some shoes. She found her flip flops and almost broke her toes trying to shove them on. She opened the door and raced down the stairs. She could smell the scent of food cooking and knew her mother must be in the kitchen.

She bolted through the swinging doors, startling her mother.

"Where's Dallie?" She screamed, her chest heaving.

Her mother's mouth had dropped in surprise. "Nat, she's outside... What on earth is the matter?"

She didn't give an answer as she ran to the back door and onto the porch. She had to see for herself if Dallie was okay. She flew down the stairs as her mother yelled for her. She ignored her and ran through the pasture, out the gate, and made her way down to the barn. She was running so fast that her flip-flops almost gave way, but she ignored them. She had to find her daughter, had to know she was safe… and she did.

Jack was sitting on her horse, Cheshire, with Dallie in front of him. Cowboy hats sat on both their heads and the horse panted like it was out of breath. Natalie's father was beside the horse looking up at them, he was talking to Jack.

"Dallie!" she cried in relief. All three of them looked at her. She ran straight for Jack, she was gonna tear him apart. "Give me my daughter!" she demanded as she extended her arms, her waist brushing against the saddle. Her father stepped back from the horse.

They all looked at her like she was a maniac and she knew that she must look a mess. Her hair had curled in wavy ringlets down her back like it did each night that she slept, her face hadn't been washed last night, so there had to be some traces of her makeup left, probably raccoon eyes from her mascara, and she was sure she was quite a sight, bra-less with her skin tight pink Victoria's Secret tank top and matching shorts, but she couldn't care less; she wanted her daughter and demanded that Jack give Dallie to her again. Jack pulled Dallie from the horse and handed her to Natalie. She grabbed her and hugged her tightly to her chest. Jack followed and came off the horse to stand before Natalie. She looked at the two men with flames in her eyes; she was completely outraged. She sat Dallie down, stepping in front of her as if she were protecting her from them. Jack stepped forward to explain himself, but Natalie didn't want an explanation. She slapped him across the face as hard as she could, and his head snapped to one side. He turned his face back to her with confusion in his eyes as she lashed out at him.

"You *bastard*, who in the Hell do you think you are? How *dare* you take my daughter *anywhere*, especially without asking me first?"

Tears had formed in her eyes and her accusing tone of voice deepened with hurt.

"Natalie," David interrupted, astonished by his daughter's actions, "I took her. Jack had nothing to do with it. Dallie wanted to go riding and I volunteered Jack to take her. I'm sorry." Her father had a soothing tone in his voice, and she saw the shame in his face as he looked at her.

"Natalie, I…" Jack began only to be interrupted.

"Don't say *another* word to me. I have nothing more to say to you. Just leave me alone and leave my daughter alone." With that she turned and grabbed Dallie up as tears streamed down her face. Her mother ran into her then, and saw the tears on Natalie's face. She looked at David and shook her head. She put her arm around Natalie as they walked back to the house. Dallie was sat on the ground to follow behind her mother and grandmother. When they reached the house, Corrine sat Natalie down in a chair in the kitchen and went to go get some tissues for her. Dallie walked up to Natalie and placed her hands on her mother's thighs looking guilt-ridden.

"I'm sorry, Mommy. I didn't mean to make you cry. I had fun riding the horsy with Jack. I'm sorry, Mommy. Please don't cry no more!"

Natalie's heart broke, knowing that she had hurt her child. How could she be so heartless? Why did she have such anger in her, such a thirst for blood, especially Jack's?

"Oh baby, you didn't make me cry. I'm very glad you had fun. I just…" How could she explain to her daughter the fear she felt for her. How could she explain that if she couldn't even trust her own husband with her daughter, how could she trust any other man? If her child's own father could hurt her, then why wouldn't another man do the same? How could she explain the humiliation, the anger and resentment of herself for not knowing what had been happening behind her back? How could she voice that to Dallie? She was so innocent and pure of heart, so trusting of Jack…of everyone.

Corrine came in then with a hot wet washcloth and some tissues.

"Dallie, baby, Mommy isn't feeling too well. Why don't you go into the living room and watch TV?" Corrine suggested as she handed Natalie the rag.

Dallie looked at her mother and grandmother then trotted off silently. Corrine watched her go then she turned and crouched in front of Natalie. She sighed looking at her daughter with understanding and Natalie broke into another bout of tears.

"Oh, Momma!" she cried as she fell into her mother's arms. Corrine crooned to her and held her as she sobbed uncontrollably into her shoulder.

"That's it baby, let it out," Corrine said, stroking her daughter's hair. "Cry it all out, honey."

~

"*T*hat bitch!" Troy Cameron mumbled to himself as he approached the cafeteria. This place was the very pits of Hell, he'd decided. He'd had the life of a celebrity. He had his own sports show on ESPN, a mansion, a Cadillac, a yacht, a Porsche, the list went on and on… Now he was forced to sleep on a hard lumpy piece of shit they called a bed, share a dirty toilet with another man, and had no privacy whatsoever. The meals sucked, he was bullied constantly, and the shrink treated him like he was some kind of freak. He hated prison, he hated *her*. That bitch had put him here. Why had he listened to his lawyer?

"If you take an insanity plea then they might not seek the death penalty."

His lawyer hadn't told him that there was no way out. Hell, the death penalty would probably have been better than this place, he might as well be dead.

He was in a state penitentiary locked up like some barbarian and had to see a psychologist who every day analyzed every minute detail of his brain, making him recite every wrong thing he'd ever done in his life, talk about his spoiled childhood and ask him about the remorse he felt for what he'd done. An insanity plea…what kind of idea had that been? And how had they found out about that girl in college… and the little girl a few years later? He had been so careful. Forensics, they said, DNA testing. That had given him away. Once he'd been arrested, they were able to trace his fingerprints to his victims. He had no defense at all. Then there were witnesses and evidence that he hadn't known existed…There were others too, they just didn't know it… no one did, but him.

He would crack that lawyer's head wide open if he ever got out of this Hell hole. Oh and he would, he was sure of that… And Natalie… He should have watched his step, been more cautious, more careful… She was his wife, goddammit, and her loyalty was supposed to be to him….he'd come to hate her for betraying him. His hatred had slowly grown each day he'd had to spend in this place of torture that rotted his very soul. He wanted to taste her blood. She had it coming. Boy, did she ever have it coming to her!

He walked forward toward the metal galley to the line where the inmates were standing for food. He kept his eyes down; he had learned better the first day, especially with the bigger inmates. *Never make eye contact.* That was what his roommate Bob had said. Bob was a good guy, and Troy was grateful to him for his advice. He had killed someone too and they shared a bond that only people who have seen into the faces of primal fear can share. It was nice to know that he had a person to help him out. Bob and he were planning an escape.

The biggest of Troy's three bullies approached him, a huge smirk on his ugly face. Troy's blood clotted; he was scared shitless. He looked down, hiding his thoughts from the thug as if he could read his mind.

"Hey pretty boy!" His thick hand rested on Troy's shoulder as he licked his lips. Bile rose in his throat, his stomach churned. *Do whatever they want you to do.* Bob had said to him. *Never argue; never fight back…if you want to live that is.*

Bull, the biggest one, was white, huge, tattooed and had the most horrific breath in the world. The quiet one was black, not quite as big as Bull but just as menacing. Bull called him Shorty. The last one resembled a weasel, he rarely ever spoke but when he did his words had a hint of a Spanish accent. He wasn't as big as a rail, but had crazy eyes and crooked teeth. He was definitely a serial killer, Troy decided. They called him Dagger because of the lightning shaped scar that ran the length of his face. The name fit him all too well.

Bull smiled as he looked down at Troy. "You in line?" When Troy didn't answer he continued, "Good, because I'm starving." He and his buddies shoved their way in front of him, carrying him with them. Their big sweaty bodies pressing against him, his heart filled with hate and anger. Bull shoved his hand down to Troy's crotch and grabbed at him suggestively. "I'll be waiting for you in the shower, pretty boy." He laughed as he shoved Troy out of his way and proceeded toward the front of the line. Troy hesitated, wanting to tell the son of a bitch to bust Hell wide open, but then thought of Bob's advice. *Never argue or fight back*. He nodded.

One of the only perks about this place was that Troy had endless time to work out, tone his body to be as fit as possible…not that it hadn't been once, not too long ago as a professional athlete, that was until his knee got all busted up. He still had a tall, lean, muscular build, he just wasn't as ripped as the days of his prime, but all that would change when he built his physique back to its former strength. He would need it to keep these bullies off of him and for the escape…

When he finally got his tray and sat down his hands were shaking with anger at his predicament. He felt cold and uneasy. He ate two bites of his meal, he was too sick to his stomach to eat any more than that. As he stared out the bars of the windows, he made a vow to himself… Natalie would pay for this if it was the last thing he did… she would pay heavily.

*T*hat last outburst was the first of several to come. A week later, Jack was ready to throw all the things he'd said about not giving up down the drain. He was about fed up with Natalie's blaming him for everything. It was as if he were the cause of all that was bad in her life and he was sick and tired of it. She directed all her anger and hatred at him. Every little thing, no matter how miniscule it was, was Jack's fault. She rolled her eyes at him, cut her eyes at him, and spoke down to him like he was the very cause of every screw up, whether he had been around or not. She would find something to direct at him, then at night he would hear her crying in her bedroom. It was crazy! Corrine had suggested that Dallie sleep on the trundle bed in her and David's room, and Jack really couldn't blame her for it. David and Corrine were appalled at Natalie's behavior and tried to talk to her about it, but eventually they gave up as well. Her attitude got worse and worse...

It was driving him crazy. He couldn't get within 5 feet of her without her having some sarcastic remark about it. He was ready to pull his hair out strand by strand. He'd been patient, sympathetic, and nothing but kind to her, but all that was about to run out. He almost lost it after he walked in the bathroom while Natalie was giving Dallie a bath.

It was after dinner one night, and he hadn't even known that they were in the upstairs bathroom. She hadn't bothered to close the door, which wasn't *his* fault. It wasn't like he meant to walk in, he didn't even see anything. Besides if he had of, what would have been the problem? Dallie was a four-year old child. He wasn't some kind of pervert who enjoyed looking at naked little girls. It was an honest mistake...but not in Natalie's eyes.

"GET OUT!" She had screamed at him while frantically covering Dallie with a towel. She even stood up, shielding Dallie's nakedness with her own body. It was outrageous; she was a child for God's sake.

He had apologized and apologized, but still there was that same look in her eyes as if he were the epitome of disgust to her. It made him feel like a bad person and he knew beyond the shadow of a doubt that he wasn't. He hadn't ever done anything wrong in his life...well okay, except for getting drunk that time and crashing into a neighbor's fence when he was just 16, and that time he got in a bar room brawl with a bouncer and spent the night in handcuffs. The bouncer had it coming though, treating that poor girl like she was a ten-dollar hooker... And then there had been his bull-riding days, but he wasn't a bad person. He would never hurt anyone. He'd grown up since his younger, wilder days, and he was no longer a boy, but a respectful man just working his ass off trying to make a living. Not only was he *not* a bad person, he was also *not* a pedophile, but damned if Natalie didn't make him feel like he was when the whole incident happened. She hated him so much and he really couldn't figure out why.

She had gotten him so mad that night that he almost told her to go straight to Hell, but not in front of Dallie. His head pounded in anger while she went on with her tyrant about privacy, and knocking on doors and his being a pervert. He could feel his face heat up as his blood pressure rose... She was gonna give him an aneurysm before it was all over. He had never been violent or short-tempered which was something he had prided himself on, but with her around, his fuse got shorter and shorter. Something had to be done. She simply had to be put in her place.

He'd worked his hands to the bone that last week too and coming in from a long day at work to an ill woman who fussed about pretty much everything he did was not his idea of relaxing. He couldn't be around Dallie very much because of her either. So, he resorted to working on anything and everything to keep from being around her. He had even begun dreading dinner with the people he worked for, and that had been his favorite part of the day. She had even ruined that for him too. She not only drove him crazy, but everyone one else around. All of them were irritated by her hostility. Her parents gave up trying to reprimand her for her rudeness and finally gave in to walking on egg shells around her, which really pissed Jack off since they, of all people, didn't deserve her hostility. Jack would be damned if he continued to ignore her outbursts. That Thursday night he'd had all of Ms. Natalie Cameron's piss poor attitude that he could stand.

They were eating dinner at the table, him and Natalie and the Butlers and all the hands and Dallie too. Then Natalie started in about how the beans were overcooked, how the roast was too tough, the potatoes were too mushy... Jack went off on her before he even knew it.

"*Jeeeesus* Christ, can you find one more thing to bitch about? Dammit, Natalie!" he said, slamming his fist down on the table. Corrine flinched and David looked his way, but he ignored them, all of them, and riveted his eyes on her. "I think this food is pretty damn good considering the fact that your mother took the time to stand over a hot stove and it almost 90 degrees outside. So, if I were you I would be grateful enough to eat it and stop complaining about it."

That statement had everyone's eyebrows raised. The hands had gotten used to sitting quietly at dinner, even Dan, so they just looked on at the scene like bystanders. Dallie's eyes never left Jack's face, and Natalie looked at him as if he had taken on the form of a space creature. Corrine tried to hide behind a grateful grin, but said nothing. No one did. There was complete silence except for the soothing sounds of crickets and frogs outside. The statement had taken Natalie completely off guard, and for once she was speechless...so he continued.

"You know what Corrine? I love your cooking," he said looking at her, then back to Natalie, "but here lately, I haven't enjoyed it so much because ever since Miss Big Shot Chicago came along I've been having trouble eating or working or doing anything for that matter... So, I hate to be rude, but I think I'm going to pass on my dinner tonight. Thank you, Corrine. It was delicious." He took Corrine's hand and kissed it gently. "If y'all will excuse me..." He gave one final glimpse at Natalie, her mouth still wide open, as he picked his napkin up off his lap, set it down, stood and scooted his chair under the table. He grabbed his hat off the rack and headed out the back door knowing that all eyes were on him as he let it shut behind him.

~

*H*er mouth was still hanging open as she watched the door slam behind him, never in her life had anyone spoken to her so rudely. She was both shocked and impressed that someone, Jack, had finally stood up to her. She'd had it coming; she'd known that beyond the shadow of a doubt. But she still had her pride; he couldn't take that from her. So she closed her mouth, she knew her face had to be flushed as she looked at the people surrounding the table. They were all looking at her. Every single eye was on her. Silence filled the dining room, even Dan had nothing to say. She tried to recompose herself and lifted her napkin off her lap as well.

She laughed sarcastically, "Just who the Hell does he think he is?" She stood up and scooted her chair in like he had done just moments before. "No one talks to me like that!"

"Natalie…" her mother sighed as she grabbed for her arm, but Natalie was already heading toward the back screen door, she nearly tore it off its hinges as she violently pushed it open, it squealed in protest as it swung to the wall and gave a loud thump, then retracted to close behind her.

She was just plain mad now… slightly impressed, but still angry all the same. She hurried down the porch steps and headed down the trail through the pasture, opened the gate and shut it, picking up a run in the process. What he did was just rude, embarrassing her in front of everyone like he had. Her pace was kicking up dust she knew. She let her anger speed her on. The sun had yet to set and the dry heat of the night made her sweat beneath her cotton dress, but she was on a mission so she ignored that fact. She was gonna let him have it tooth and nail, she decided as she approached the barn.

She opened the side door and was ready to confront him and give him a piece of her mind, when she realized that he wasn't in sight. She looked around cautiously and started down the length of the barn. She looked in each stall, left and right, until she found him in one of them brushing down a black stallion. The sign above his door deemed him Jackson's Star of Midnight. Jack was focused on the horse as he lifted the saddle onto the stud's back.

She watched his large arm muscles flex and his broad shoulders tighten as he worked. She sighed internally. She felt a longing so deep within her that it took her breath away, the longing to be wrapped in those strong arms, Jack's arms. She had begun to feel this way each time he walked into a room and knew that her attitude toward him lately had been caused by these feelings; that and the fact that her parents treated him like he was God's gift to the world. She felt as if she'd been replaced with Jack over the past year. They didn't *need* her or Nathan anymore; they had Jack. It was easy to envy him, his life was practically uncomplicated. He was unmarried, childless; he just had his work, his passion. He was about to own his own ranch and have the job of his dreams… He was a simple target for her anger and aggression simply because his attitude and life was so care-free and hers was filled with disorder and heartache. She was jealous of him, and the sheer truth of it was that he made her want to rip her clothes off and beg him to take her breath away. This unwelcome knowledge made the anger surge through her veins again, and she planted her hands on her hips, preparing herself for a battle with him.

He had left the stall door open, so she ducked underneath the Dutch window and turned toward him.

"What the Hell is your *problem?*" she demanded, crossing her arms over her chest, her skin tingled with the eagerness to spar. She was anticipating this fight; this was the only way she could express herself because no one else would tangle with her. He looked back at her then focused his attention back to the horse, obviously seeing no threat.

"If you can't figure that one out on your own, then why should I tell you?" He spoke calmly, like he was speaking to a child. It infuriated her.

"How *dare* you embarrass me like that!"

"Hey, I was being nice. You're lucky I wasn't really mad." He busied himself with the horse, placing the bridle on his face and putting the bit in his mouth.

"Nice? You were being an absolute jerk. That was the rudest thing anyone's ever said to me." Her voice was getting louder; it was starting to echo off the stall walls so loud that even the horse jerked in response.

He laughed, pointing his massive chest her way. "Me? Look at how rude you've been to me since I met you, Natalie. You don't even know me, yet you've treated me like I'm your worst enemy. Now I would call *that* being rude." By this time, he had turned around to face her, his huge arms crossed at his chest. "You are the most difficult person to get along with that I've ever met in my life. You've been a lot more hateful to me in the last week than I've been to you in the last 30 seconds, so how was *my* statement to you rude?"

She had no defense against that; she knew it and he did to. She *had* been horrible to him. She started with, "Well…" only to be interrupted by Jack as he silenced her with one look. Her mouth was going dry just looking at him; his sweaty pectoral muscles clung to his thin white tank top tracing each breath he took.

God, he was sexy…

He took a step forward and was within reach of her; she could feel the heat coming off of his body and she gulped.

"Let me let you in on a little secret, sweetheart. I would give my left arm… no, I take that back, *both* of my arms, if I could have my mother cook just *one* more meal for me. I don't have that luxury like you do. My mother is dead and has been for several years now. So, you should cherish each and every meal you get to eat with your mother, especially if she cooks it. There was no call for the way you acted about dinner."

She was speechless again. She'd never thought of it like that. How thoughtless she had been. She could see the glimmer of sadness in his eyes and it made her yearn to apologize, but again she put her guard up. She didn't handle problems by lying down. The past year of her life, she'd lived as if she were at war with the world; she'd fought for herself and for her daughter. There was no backing down, no weaknesses, no giving up without a fight...

"Well, you just had no right..."

Once again he interrupted her, only this time by putting his finger to her lips. When he removed his finger, her lips burned as if they were on fire and her heart hammered in her chest. Her core started to tingle with a sensation she hadn't felt in a long time, but recognized immediately. He glanced thoughtfully up at the ceiling as if he were in deep reflection.

"You know what, Mrs. Cameron? You are nothing like your parents said you would be!" He stated, looking back down at her.

The statement took her off guard.

"What?" Her forehead wrinkled. "Why do you say that?" she asked numbly, still stunned by the touch of his finger to her lips.

"Because they said their daughter was sweet, caring, fun-loving... And so far, all I've seen is a spoiled rotten brat who finds nothing that she's satisfied with."

"*What?*" She couldn't believe what she was hearing. "I am *not!*" She planted her hands on her hips and glared at him.

"Yes you are!" He took a step closer to drive his point home. "You've had your life handed to you on a silver platter. You've never had to work hard a day in your life. You have two incredible parents, a home, and a daughter who loves you." Natalie was taken off guard, he was jealous of her, just as she was jealous of him; Irony in its truest form. "You have nothing in this world to be so angry about, especially at *me*, yet you treat me no better than you would the dirt on your shoe. All I have ever wanted since the day I saw you was your approval. However, the only time you've been nice to me in the past week since you've known me was in my truck when you knew I was your *only* way home. I have done nothing but *kiss your ass* since you got here, and I'm not doing it any more.... I don't care *how* gorgeous you are..." He trailed off then and Natalie had the feeling that she wasn't supposed to hear that last sentence. It took her aback. He sighed and cleared his throat, looking down suddenly. *He thought she was gorgeous?*

"You think I'm gorgeous?" She looked up at him, amazed and flattered at the same time.

"Oh come on, Natalie. You say it like no one's ever told you that before," he scoffed and rolled his eyes.

She shrugged; she couldn't remember the last time someone had earnestly called her gorgeous.

"Oh please, like I'm supposed to believe that!" he smirked.

Wow! He was good for the ego.

"Well, believe it because it's the gospel," she said matter-of-factly.

"Ok, fine, whatever... And you know, when people give you a compliment it's considered polite for you to say thank you."

"Oh... thank you!" she said, smiling earnestly.

"And you know something else, it doesn't hurt to be nice to people either, but you wouldn't know anything about that, now would you?"

The sarcasm in that statement caused her smile to fade and her brows to draw downward.

"I can be nice..."

"Yeah, to everyone but me. You hate me, and I can't figure out why."

"I don't *hate* you!" she said as if she were surprised to hear him say that, even though she knew she had been worse than a bitch to him. For some reason his compliment had put her on cloud nine, and she couldn't seem to get back down on the ground.

"Ok! Then how come you act like you do?" He asked a question she didn't have an answer to. Well, actually she did have an answer, just not a certifiable one… She was jealous, she was horny, she had a past that wouldn't let her live…It was clear to her, but she couldn't explain it to him. "Am I that easy to hate?" he asked impatiently, waiting for an answer.

"No!" she said, looking down. She had no excuse for her behavior, not even the bitter past. "I'm sorry, Jack. Honestly! That's all I can say…"

Instead of responding, he turned back to the horse.

"I said, I'm sorry, Jack." She stepped closer to him, making sure he could hear her, knowing clearly that he could.

"Yeah, I know. I heard you." He busied himself fooling with the saddlebags.

"Well, when people say I'm sorry it's considered polite to respond to it, you know, like I forgive you, perhaps….I mean, the least you could give me is proper forgiveness!" she replied sarcastically. Two could play at his little Etiquette by Jack game.

"You want me to properly forgive you?" He turned then, and he was dangerously close. Too close for comfort. When he looked at her, his sea green eyes smoldered like fire, she recognized the want in his eyes and with her answer accepted it.

"Yes."

It was whispered so softly that both of them barely heard it, and before she knew what was happening, she was being pulled into arms that felt stronger than any she'd had wrapped around her before. They were like steel coils as he wrapped one of them around her waist, the other worked its way up her back as he planted his hand in her hair. His head fell then and she could feel his sweet, hot breath on her face as he came ever closer. Her eyelids fluttered closed as she felt his soft full lips press gently against hers. Her hands immediately went to his hard chest and she could feel the muscles move beneath her palms. Her lips softened as she absorbed his kiss then her hands slid to his sides and then to his back, holding him as if she were afraid she would fall if she didn't. He pulled her even closer, crushing her into his chest as his mouth moved over hers. She opened her mouth to him and let him trace her lips with his tongue. She moaned longingly and he complied with a very masculine sound of his own. His tongue touched her teeth then it dipped deeply into her mouth, tasting her. Her knees turned to mush and she melted against him. She'd never experienced passion quite like this and she let it envelope her and carry her into a world where her past didn't exist. Nothing existed, but this sexy cowboy and his taste and smell and feel.

His exploration was gentle yet forceful all at the same time. His kiss was expert, yet he kissed her as if it were his first time ever kissing a woman. He took his time, tasting, exploring, teasing…it felt so wonderful. His hands were everywhere, in her hair, stroking her back, touching her face. His lips were soft and experienced. She felt as if she'd been carried away. He kissed her breathlessly, and when he finally pulled away, he sighed and looked into her eyes.

"There you've been properly forgiven!" He said as his chest heaved against hers and Natalie was slowly brought back to reality. And boy did it come crashing down hard.

She pushed him away from her; huge tears suddenly filled her eyes. What the Hell was she doing? How could she have let him kiss her like that? How thoughtless she had been! How stupid! Had she learned nothing? She felt the pains of nausea tear at her stomach, and her lungs suddenly stopped taking in air. Her head reeled, and she felt faint.

"I'm sorry, Jack. I can't do this. I'm so sorry. I have to go now," she said, her hands trembling as she pulled herself out of his embrace.

"Natalie." He grabbed her hand as she started to exit the stall.

He pulled her back into his chest, his arms locking around her waist, as he looked into her eyes. "It's okay to let someone in, you know?" He brushed a strand of hair off her face, allowing her to see into his deep green eyes. They were so sincere it was painful.

She closed her eyes so he couldn't see the tears in them.

"No, it's not Jack," she protested as he leaned his face down again to kiss her, but her hands pushed against his hard chest. "Please stop,

Jack. I can't. I can't *do* this." He stared at her for a moment longer before he sighed and eased up, dropping his arms to his sides in defeat.

She fled, tears streaming down her face all the way to the house.

When she reached the stairs of the back porch, she expelled her breath and wiped her face free of tears. She had her hand on the rail, when she looked over to see her mother on the swing beneath the porch staring at her.

"Natalie!" The tone in her mother's voice conveyed a threatening note. It had been a long time since her mother had spoken to her in that tone of voice.

"Yes, mother?" she asked. Corrine motioned for her to sit next to her. She felt like a child again being scolded for unruly behavior.

"Come. I want to have a word with you."

Natalie walked to where her mother sat and slumped down to sit next to her. Corrine was quiet for several moments then looked at Natalie with a stern face.

"Nat, you know I'm usually a go-with-the-flow type of person. I'm very tolerable, and I don't usually say much bad about anyone." Natalie nodded her head. Suddenly, she was very interested in what her mother had to say to her. "But, here lately, your attitude has been worse than offensive. It's as if my daughter has become someone that I do not know any longer. I can't tolerate who you are becoming, Natalie. I'm personally tired of it, and I know that Jack is too. I understand your pain, not firsthand, mind you, but I can empathize with you, and Natalie it is long past time to leave your past exactly where it belongs. You have hurt long enough over what happened in Chicago. You have a new life now, and it's time to move on. It's over! Maybe you need to speak with someone who can help you through this, because obviously I can't… Your behavior with Jack is puzzling to me. Why must you take all your anger out on him, Natalie? He hasn't done anything to you … or Dallie. If I can remember correctly, he has been anything but unkind to you. I understand that this behavior of yours started when you found out that we gave him your room, but honey, it has to stop…" She looked up into Natalie's eyes and took her hands. She sighed and continued.

"Jack is part of this family now. You have to remember that you and Nathan chose to go your own ways, but Jack has been here like a son to us. Your father gave him a chance for a better life, but he's given us so much more. He came along when we needed someone most. He has helped us out more than you'll ever know. Your father and I are getting older, Natalie, and we can't do as much as we once could. Jack knows the business, he knows how to run the ranch, and he knows everything there is to know about it. We trust him… What I'm saying is; I want my daughter back. Jack is a wonderful person and I know that the Natalie that I gave birth to would love him as much as your father and I do if she would only open her eyes… and her heart." Corrine smiled at Natalie, whose face was once again streaked with tears. Corrine wiped at Natalie's cheek and opened her arms to her daughter. Natalie leaned into her and sighed.

Her mother was right. She hadn't been herself. Who *had* she become? But how long had it been since she had been herself? A long time, she concluded. Jack had been so kind to her and giving and she had been such a pain in his ass. Maybe she should give him a chance; this whole jealousy thing had to stop. She couldn't make up for lost time with her parents, but she could give them the best she had from now on. And her best meant to accept Jack as her parent's had, unconditionally; to let go of the past and move forward.

No sooner had the thought crossed her mind than the person she was thinking of approached. He glanced over at them, then turned red, embarrassed at his intrusion. He apologized and headed for the stairs.

"No wait, Jack," Corrine said and held her hand out to him. He gave Natalie an unsure glance before walking up and obediently taking Corrine's hand. "Natalie, I want you to apologize for your rudeness toward Jack this past week."

He shook his head vigorously. "No, Mrs. Butler, that isn't necessary at all."

Natalie intervened then and brought her head off her mother's shoulder.

"No, Jack, she's right. I owe you an apology...and I *am* sorry. I apologize for my behavior to you this past week, and I promise to be nice to you from now on."

Jack just smiled into her eyes and Corrine sighed in relief. Corrine said nothing, but Natalie knew that she thought, *It's about time.*

～

*T*hat night before she lay down to go to sleep, Natalie took a long, hot, relaxing bath. Everyone else was either down stairs or heading off to bed, and she decided she needed the luxury. A soaking would do her mind and body good, besides she needed to relax and think, and what better way to do it than stretched out in a tub of hot water. She closed her eyes and let her body rest in the mass of suds, wondering when she had actually gotten the chance to relax since coming home. Her skin pebbled with goose bumps until she grew accustomed to the heat of the water. It covered her like a blanket and she let herself slip into thought as she relaxed her muscles. She really shouldn't have but let her mind drift to think about Jack Kinsen. She thought about everything he'd said that night to her then she imagined the man behind those words. His muscular arms, his hard chest as she'd crashed into it, his hands in her hair, his lips kissing hers, the noise that came from his throat as he had... Everything about him had made her body come alive and the realization scared her to death. Was she crazy? She had just gotten out of a horrible marriage, she had a daughter who'd been traumatized by her father, and now she was letting herself get all hot and bothered by a handsome cowboy she really didn't know. It alarmed her; her attraction to this man. What was she thinking? How had she let him just kiss her without stopping him? He had no idea all the chaos that had ensued her life up to this point. He had no idea what had happened in Chicago. How on earth could she dare trust another man after what Troy had done to her and Dallie?

But Jack had kissed her so passionately, so tenderly, and sincerely. It had felt wonderful. Troy had never kissed her the way Jack had; even from day one, she had never had that kind of passion with Troy, what she'd had with him was only superficial, puppy love, teenage lust at best. He'd never made her tingle all the way to her toes like Jack had tonight. But Troy wasn't exactly a good person to compare anyone to. Everything Troy had been in the time she'd known him was a lie. He was a false person, the devil even. It terrified her to know that she had been with Troy for almost ten years and never knew the real person behind the mask. Her husband had been hiding behind his own sick shadows, and she had never suspected a thing. Then one day, her world came crashing down on her, her husband came out from behind his facade, and she realized that almost the last nine years of her life had been built on false pretenses.

Her divorce happened almost over night. Troy had been arrested and was held in a cell until they met for the divorce finalization. Due to the allegations against him, Troy had no choice but to forfeit everything while awaiting trial. He'd been denied bail by the judge. Natalie had been given it all, sole rights to their daughter, the house, the furniture, the vehicles, and their money; everything that was hers and Troy's. But she sold all their belongings, house, furniture, cars, everything, not wanting any of it because it all reminded her of him. She kept only their clothes, a few pictures, hardly any jewelry, and some of Dallie's toys. She investing some of the money, put some in bank accounts and opened a savings account and trust fund for Dallie, then bought a car for her road trip. She figured that all she needed to start over was her and her daughter.

Then there was the other trial, the one that no one would have ever suspected would happen, the one where Dallie was called to take the stand against her own father. The trial that would reveal a whole other side of Troy Cameron. Natalie would never forget the day her lawyer, Jerry Sheffield, had showed up at her door really early one morning. It had been about three months after Troy'd been arrested. He'd been anxious and amped up and yet also saddened. He'd made her sit down as soon as he'd walked in the door.

"Natalie, I have something that I have to tell you right away. Where's Dallie?" His voice had been uneven as he took her hands.

"She's sleeping, Jerry. What is it?" She had started to tremble.

"Natalie, the police have more evidence on Troy. When they ran his fingerprints and DNA through the system, there were multiple matches. Nat, this is going to come as a huge shock..."

"Evidence, what kind of evidence?" Her eyes widened. She knew that he was about to tell her something terrible. The hairs on her arms began to stand on end.

"Jeez, I really don't know how to tell you this..."

"Just say it, dammit!" Panic rose in her throat.

"Natalie, Troy, well, he...he's going to be tried for murder." The look she'd given him had been of shock, disbelief and horror. She'd come close to fainting then, she remembered. Although she hadn't really wanted more detail than that, Jerry had given it to her. The woman was killed while they were attending college, the little six year old girl, only four years ago, after Dallie had been born. The woman had been raped and murdered, strangled to death with a zip tie and left in the woods. The little girl suffered a much worse fate although according to Troy, her death had not been planned...it just happened.

He'd apparently used his fame and legend as a pro football star and sports broadcaster to hide behind what he'd done. He thought he was invincible and used his stardom to make himself look innocent to the public, playing upon their sympathies, but his DNA couldn't lie for him. Natalie closed her eyes, remembering the utter shock and disgust that had come over her when she'd sat that day in court as they questioned him on the stand, the details he'd given about the murders, the reasoning behind the deaths. She'd looked straight at Troy and found no remorse, no regret, just a hard, cold stare right back at her. It chilled her blood to hear his admissions and know that she'd married and bore the child of a cold-blooded killer. She'd gotten physically sick and had to leave. She'd puked her guts out…Who had she married? Who was this man, this monster?

It had all happened so fast, even though it took over a year to get Troy where he belonged, and it left Natalie feeling overwhelmed. She had lost her husband, or the man she thought her husband was, her life in Chicago, and her trust in human beings all at once. She was horrified and stunned. She felt betrayed, stupid, and naïve. She remembered when it was all said and done that she couldn't wait to leave Chicago. Her own fame had begun and ended in that city and it seemed from the moment of her arrival it had all been a mistake. She'd loved Chicago at one time and then a dark cloud had descended upon her life. She figured that her love for it had ended when her love for Troy had ended; the night she found him molesting their three year old daughter.

The betrayal was enough to bear, but then there was the burden of what Dallie had suffered. It had been over a year ago and yet Natalie still had no faith in other people and she worried immensely about her daughter. How long had he been tormenting their daughter at night when she was away? Had this event traumatized her for life? Would Dallie interact with people, especially men, differently? Would she have nightmares forever? Could she live the life of a normal child or an adult woman for that matter? Would Dallie be able to have a relationship in her future without fear? Those questions haunted her each night. She also blamed herself for not seeing the truth, maybe there was something more she could have done. She should never have left him alone with her daughter.

However, despite all that had happened, Dallie seemed to be faring rather well…only the nightmares bothered her now. She hadn't had one in about a week, but that didn't mean she wouldn't. The child psychologist Natalie had taken Dallie to after the ordeal had said the nightmares were normal and they would probably eventually stop. She warned her of Dallie pitching temper tantrums out of the blue, being extremely clingy, getting angry or upset over nothing, avoiding men in all circumstances. She had also said that Dallie could become entirely introverted and ask questions about her body or bodies of the opposite sex. She'd also said that it could be just the opposite, since Dallie was so young that maybe she would forget all about it. She explained that sometimes people simply block out traumatic events in their lives to avoid the pain of remembering. The doctor had told her that it was too early to see how her molestation affected Dallie's psyche, but to expect anything since it would depend on Dallie and how she mentally handled the situation; whether she regressed or repressed or simply moved on as if nothing had happened.

Natalie didn't know what to expect, but so far Dallie seemed like any normal four year old, especially now that she was surrounded by her loving grandparents. In the beginning, Dallie had started pitching fits immediately for the first three months over nothing. Natalie assumed this behavior had been amplified by the fact that everything had changed so quickly for her and Dallie. In addition to the trauma of what had been done to her, Dallie had lost her father and her home... She'd been thrown into a new daycare, a new apartment, nothing had been familiar to her. But the tantrums had passed as quickly as they'd started much to Natalie's relief. She'd also asked about her body and a few questions about men's bodies, and Natalie had answered her as best as she could, but she didn't really know how to answer her without being too straightforward. She'd left those questions to the professionals. She simply just tried to encourage Dallie to be a normal fun loving child.

Dallie didn't seem to be avoiding men. In fact, she opened right up to them... well, Jack anyway, and that fact scared Natalie as well. Of course, he was the only man she'd frequently been around other than Natalie's father, her lawyer and the ranch hands since the night Natalie had left Troy. Plus, Dallie had always been an outgoing and outspoken little girl.

Just then, the bathroom door creaked open. Natalie covered her breasts with one hand while opening the shower curtain with the other hand to see who was intruding on her privacy. It was Dallie. She smiled at her daughter. "Hey, baby girl."

Dallie gave her a weak smile and bowed her head down as if she were in trouble then looked up inquisitively at her mother. "Mommy, is it okay to tell Jack that I love him before I go to bed?"

Natalie's first thought was *why?* But she didn't ask that. "Well, Dallie, I guess it would be okay," she said reassuringly.

"Well, its bedtime Mommy, and Grandma and Paw-Paw say 'I love you' to me and to you, but nobody says it to Jack." Natalie had never thought about it that way...Dallie had a point. "Maybe he likes to feel loved too Mommy."

That caused Natalie to grin. Everyone needed to feel loved once in a while. "Sure Dallie, honey, you go right ahead. I'm sure it would make his night," Nat said patting her little hand.

Dallie broke out into a huge grin. "Grandma said that too." With that said she hurried out the door as Natalie reminded her to close it behind her.

Natalie relaxed back into the tub and smiled to herself. Her daughter had such a kind heart. She sat and soaked until she felt like a prune, then she got out and dressed herself for bed. She set her mind as she brushed her teeth that tomorrow she would take Dallie riding and spend some desperately needed one on one time with her.

CHAPTER 4

*J*ack was standing on the porch looking up at the stars trying to ignore the smell of the vanilla cigar Dan was smoking. He had given them up years ago, but he couldn't help but yearn for a taste when someone else was smoking one. He was certain Dan was doing it just out of spite.

He was thinking about Natalie, that's why he needed a cigar. The kiss they had shared in the barn was more than incredible. He'd wanted her more in those few minutes of simply kissing her than he'd ever wanted any other woman in his life. He couldn't explain it! She had been nothing but rude to him in the past week and now he was having all kinds of thoughts about her. Sure he'd been attracted to her from the very beginning, but his feelings had obviously been dampened this past week as her moods had been as unpredictable as the weather.

She'd done a 360 degree turn around just since he'd given her a piece of his mind. He'd known she was feisty and headstrong, but she didn't know how to take it when someone was standing up to her. That seemed funny to him. *She could dish it out, but boy, she sure couldn't take it!* He smiled remembering how clueless she had been when he'd told her she was gorgeous. The innocent face she'd given him was so genuine and unaware. Her trying to call his bluff implying his lack of proper manners as she'd said "...the least you could give me is proper forgiveness," the look in those eyes, full of anger, passion, yearning, those pouty lips pursed out at him, he couldn't resist that challenge in her eyes. So, he'd tested the waters, if she wanted him she would let him know and she had with that sexy little invitation...so he'd took the bait and gave her all he'd had bottled up inside, the passion, the fury, the desire. If someone hadn't told her how beautiful she was, it'd only been because of her attitude because she sure as Hell had an incredible body with her wavy, sexy hair and full...

"You know what Natalie needs to straighten her up?" Dan asked completely out of the blue, interrupting Jack's thoughts. He turned to see Dan facing him, puffing on his cigar. With Dan, there was no telling the answer to that one.

"What is that, Dan?" Jack sighed and rolled his eyes as he responded, but didn't turn around.

"Someone needs to fuck her brains out." Dan laughed and continued, "I'd let her go every which way, but loose. I guarantee you she'd lose that attitude *real* fast..."

Jack saw red. He could feel the blood boil in his face. In two strides, he had Dan jerked up by his shirt collar. Jack's face was little more than an inch from Dan's, his jaw muscle ticking as he gritted his teeth.

"So help me God, if you so much as think about touching her Dan, I swear I'll..."

"Oh, come off it Jack, would you?" He tried easing out of the grip Jack had on his shirt, but Jack held him still. "You know you want to do the exact same thing and don't say you don't, cause then I'll know you're a goddamn liar. Admit it...you'd like to take her any way you could get er.'"

"No, Dan. I'm not you and I don't see women the same way you do. Natalie's a lady, and I'll be damned if I talk about her like she's some white trash whore. She deserves better than that."

"You ain't got a hair on your ass, Jack. I *know* you want her! I've seen the way you look at her, even though she's been nothing but a bitch to you, you'd like nothing more than to fuck her til she can't stand up straight. I'm no fool, Jack. It's that curvy little body of hers isn't it, the way she walks, like she's begging for it..."

Jack would never admit to Dan's foul accusations if it would save him from damnation, despite Jack's feelings for Natalie...and her body. "Violence is not in my vocabulary, Dan. But you're wearing my patience thin. If you don't shut your damn mouth, I'm gonna shut it for you." His tone was getting deeper as his anger increased.

"Oh, c'mon just admit it, Jack. You want to know what her sweet body feels like!" Dan was egging him on, pushing Jack to see how far he would go and Dan was about to find out just how far Jack could be pushed.

"I mean it, Dan, I'm not kidding. I said to shut the *Hell* up!" Jack's grip on Dan's collar was getting tighter and tighter.

"I can tell you... I've felt it before." He laughed that sinister laugh of his and before Jack knew what he was doing, his fist was buried in Dan's face and Dan was rolling on the porch.

"You son of a bitch, you broke my nose!" Dan yelled, holding his nose with both hands, the sweet smelling cigar had fallen to the ground.

David came running out onto the porch at that time, hearing the commotion. Jack just stood there, arms crossed, eyebrows drawn. He would never apologize. David looked at Dan, then Jack inquisitively. Jack shrugged, rage still smeared across his face. There had always been bad blood between Dan and Jack, and Jack had remedied it...for now anyway. Corrine came out at that time and helped Dan to his feet.

Obligingly, she walked him into the house to doctor his nose, but Jack saw her wink at him. She knew that if Jack hit Dan it was for good reason, just as David knew the same. Back when David was younger that's how arguments were handled in the west, with fists drawn… guns before that.

David came to stand beside Jack. He knew what the fuss was about before he ever even asked.

"My daughter has caused more trouble on this ranch in the past week than we've had all year," David said, shaking his head. Jack smiled to himself. "What happened, Jack?"

"Well, David, no one's going to talk crudely about a lady while I'm around. I won't stand for it." He looked down as he flexed out his hand, it felt as if he'd slammed it into a brick wall.

"Well thanks, Jack. I appreciate you defending my daughter's honor, even though she has done nothin' but treat you like shit since the day she got here. Why break someone's nose for her?" Jack was silent for a moment then shrugged and David laughed. "Ah, Hell, women do some crazy things to us men, I tell ya." He laughed again and patted Jack on the back.

Dallie burst out the door then, in a hurry to get to Jack. She rushed up to him, her pink Barbie nightgown swishing and those little blonde locks bouncing as she came to stand in front of him. She extended her arms upward towards him in a gesture signaling for him to pick her up. He did and she crossed her arms over her chest, looking into his face.

"Jack, did you punch Dan?" Dallie asked. Jack turned red, that was the last thing he wanted Dallie to know, that he had hurt someone intentionally, but he admitted it to her.

"Yeah, I did, Dallie."

"Why?" she asked, looking shocked with her little eyebrows drawn downward.

"Well, Dallie, he said some things that he shouldn't have said, and I didn't like it. But I shouldn't have punched him. I'm sorry you had to see that."

"Well, I guess I can let it slip this one time," she said thoughtfully. Jack smiled at her. "But, next time, we'll sic Mommy on him." This brought hysterical laughter from David and Jack. When they finished, their eyes had tears in them.

"I could see that one happening, couldn't you, Jack? She'd tear the poor fool to shreds..." David laughed and slapped Jack on his back.

"Could see what happening?" All of the ruckus had brought Natalie downstairs. Her hair was damp and hung in curls down her shoulders, her body wrapped in a soft pink robe. Jack's heart did a flip flop as she approached them. "Why's Dan's nose bleeding?" she asked.

Dallie looked at her mother and spoke matter-of-factly, "Mommy, Jack punched him."

"What?" she asked and looked at Jack like he was insane. "Why?"

"He said things he shouldn't have said, Mommy," Dallie answered for Jack, which relieved him of having to tell her.

Natalie looked taken aback, but grateful as she looked into Jack's eyes, knowing without a doubt that it was her that Dan had been talking about. She spoke a thank you without the words and when she gave him a soft smile, he saw that she respected the fact that he had taken up for her. To see the respect in that smile, he would do it again a thousand times, despite the throbbing in his knuckles.

"Jack," Dallie said grabbing his face so his attention was riveted on her and not Natalie.

"Yes?" He laughed at her attempt to get his attention.

"I love you."

Jack smiled. It had been a long time since anyone had said that to him, a really long time. It melted his heart to hear her say it.

"I love you too, Dallie." With that he gave her a big hug, and she kissed him on his cheek.

Natalie just stood there, a tear fell down her cheek, a tear that she thought no one had seen her wipe away, but Jack had seen it. She smiled at them, then turned and walked back into the house.

*T*he next morning there was much for Natalie to think about. Witnessing last night's saga had made her unsure about her and Dallie's growing fondness for Jack. He was wonderful, she had come to that conclusion, but Dallie was already telling him she loved him and getting so attached to him. He'd talked in the truck about how he wanted a ranch of his own. What if tomorrow he came up with all the money he needed, then what? He'd be gone! It would break Dallie's heart into pieces. Nat couldn't allow that to happen. Dallie had never been so open and loving to a man other than her father and grandfather before now, and that scared Natalie. She shouldn't be getting this close to someone whom she'd known such a short time. Of course Natalie was one to be talking; her feelings for Jack were becoming deeper the more she saw him. Maybe it was those sincere eyes of his that held the epitome of kindness. Maybe it was that smile of his that promised honesty and dependability. She didn't know, but her heart turned in circles each time she laid eyes on him.

Like this morning, she had been roused from a deep sleep by a loud banging that came from outside her window. She'd crawled out of bed to see Jack, shirtless, hammering away at a fence that had taken some damage, his tanned muscles shiny and sweaty from the heat of the sun. He was facing away from her, his back and arm muscles rippled with each swing of the hammer to the wood. Her mouth had gone dry and her pulse had quickened, her veins humming the way the wood did with each strike of the hammer. She sighed at the masculinity that radiated from him. Suddenly, he'd grabbed his tan Stetson off his head and wiped at the sweat beading on his forehead. In the process, he'd turned around so that she had gotten a clear view of his broad, muscled chest. He reminded her of the Marlboro man in that moment, and she might have laughed if she hadn't been so stunned by the pure sexuality of seeing him half-naked. She'd been suddenly overpowered by lust, the stirrings deep in her belly so raw with hunger that it took her breath away, the desire to have him take her and make her his. She wondered if maybe her attraction to him was due to the fact that she hadn't been touched by a man in almost two years, which was something she hadn't realized until now how desperately she'd missed.

But to lust over a stranger was not the solution to her problems, and she also realized that. However, this man was so incredibly sexy that she had a hard time allowing herself to forget the way he looked, and felt, and tasted... She had to keep her distance before she lost her sanity. Allowing herself to draw comfort from him, allowing him to ease her pain was a dangerous thought. Oh, how easy it would be to get lost in his touch, his eyes, it would only leave her bereft and alone when it was all over. She *knew* that. She couldn't get too close, it was pointless.

She'd thought about all this while helping her mother cook biscuits and gravy for that morning's breakfast. Well, she made the dough and took the biscuits out of the oven if that was helping; her mind was too involved in her thoughts of Jack to do much else. It was all too funny to her mother who seemed amused at having to remind her to put the biscuits in the oven and to take them out again.

She'd showered with Dallie that morning so they could eat and head off after breakfast. She looked forward to spending time with Dallie; it had been too long since they had done anything fun together. The last year they'd been tied up in visits to her psychiatrist, visits to the lawyer, court dates...

Natalie smiled as Dallie laid forks in each plate surrounding the table while she set the food at random around the table for the hands to eat before they started that morning. Her mother had already yelled for them to come eat, so she knew that they would be filing in before too long. She had teased her mother about them working up an appetite because there were virtually no leftovers...ever. She also said that if Corrine had any dogs that they would probably starve. Her mother rolled in the floor at that one. Before Natalie could set the last of the deer tenderloin on the table, the men started piling in.

They sounded like a herd of cattle, and Natalie was almost expecting to hear a couple moos and a snort or two come from them. She smiled to herself.

She stilled as she watched Jack come to the table. The shirt that he'd previously removed was now tied around his waist and his face and hands were washed and ready for breakfast. Unfortunately, that couldn't be said for his chest and stomach. His entire chest and midsection were covered in sweat and dirt. It clung to every crevice of his torso, defining the lines of chiseled muscles there. He looked like he'd stepped straight off the set of a Stetson commercial.

She stared at the fan of light brown hair that dusted his chest and the happy trail that ran down his abdomen and disappeared into his jeans. He greeted Dallie and they engaged in a conversation like always. Natalie, however, could not remove her eyes from his bare midriff. It was magnificent, seeing his nakedness up close and personal. The muscles of his chest and abdomen were considerable and well-defined; the width of his chest was impressive to say the least... She longed to rub the gritty dirt scattered across it just to be able to feel the strength of his muscles on her palms. She'd always loved a man with muscles, the bigger the better.

The other hands piled in as well, one by one until everyone was seated except for her and her mother. Her mother bumped into her on her way out of the kitchen. Only then did she realize that she had been staring at Jack's torso...the whole time. She blushed, embarrassed at calling attention to herself, but no one seemed to notice. She sat next to Dallie and greeted Jack with a red face when he spoke to her. Her father said the blessing and all the food was passed around. Natalie began preparing Dallie's plate for her and Jack teased her about not liking deer tenderloin.

"It's good for you, Dallie," he said. "It'll give you big strong muscles."

"Like yours?" she asked, smiling.

"Me? I ain't got no muscles. See?" Jack replied, giving them a shot of his massive bicep as he flexed it up. Natalie gulped.

"Yes, you do, Jack. You got BIG muscles, a lot bigger than Paw-Paws. Don't he Mommy?"

*Oh, **yes** he does,* was what she wanted to say but mumbled an "uh huh", busying herself with Dallie's plate, forcing herself to look away from his arms, although she really wanted to ogle him.

Jack laughed and teased Dallie some more then spoke to Natalie, "You look lovely today." The compliment made her stall in pouring gravy over Dallie's biscuits.

She looked over at him and smiled gratefully. "Thank you, Jack." She didn't think that the old denim jeans and simple tank top did wonders for her, but she wouldn't argue with him. It was nice to know that someone took pleasure in her appearance. She sat Dallie's plate down in front of her and Dallie looked up at her and smiled.

"You *do* look nice today, Mommy. And you smell good too, like flowers."

"Thank you, sweetie! You look pretty good yourself." Natalie gave her a grateful grin.

"Mommy's taking me horseback riding today," Dallie announced to the table loudly. Everyone smiled and nodded their heads. Everyone except Dan, who looked like he'd tangled with a tiger, a black and blue bruise streaking his nose and eyes. He had been observing the exchanges between Jack and Natalie silently, but kept looking at Jack with evil eyes and the smirk that always adorned his face when he did. Jack ignored him.

"I'll be glad to help you saddle up the horses, if you need me to, Natalie," Dan said, looking straight at Jack.

Natalie hesitated only a moment before she said, "No, thank you though, Dan. I can handle it on my own. It's been a while, but I'm sure I can manage it." He looked defeated, and Natalie didn't look at Jack, but she could almost feel his smile at her response.

Jack continued to watch her as they all ate. When Natalie would catch his eyes on her she'd blush, he'd smile and the process would repeat itself. She felt like a schoolgirl again. It felt wonderful.

After breakfast, she and Dallie left to go to the barn. Her mother said she could do the dishes on her own and had dismissed her. They walked hand in hand, Dallie smiling up at her. When they reached the barn, Natalie saddled Cheshire up and picked Dallie up to put her on his back then hauled herself up as well using his mane and stirrup. She shuffled around until she got comfortable and gently tapped the horse's flank with her heel as she placed her feet into the stirrups and grabbed the reigns. He trotted forward and out the back barn door into the pasture through the gate. He led them out through the open land that went on for miles. The scent of the changing leaves filled their nostrils as they rode. The sun shown brightly and birds flew above their heads into the trees on the outskirts of the back pasture. She set the horse at a faster pace until he was in a soft canter. Dallie squealed, delighted at the thrill of it. Natalie laughed as well. She ran Cheshire around for a good hour or so, until he was quite winded, then she led him to the creek for some water. He gulped it down in a hurry, and she and Dallie rested there for a moment under a big shady oak tree before trotting back toward the barn. It was growing hot outside, and they both were beginning to sweat. Natalie also realized that neither of them had sunscreen on. She headed back home. Dallie didn't argue, she was resting the back of her head on Natalie's breast, and Natalie knew she would be out like a light in no time. She brought the horse to a stop in the middle of the barn and got off of him then she grabbed for Dallie and set her down on the ground in front of the horse. Dallie wiped at her eyes sleepily and Natalie smiled.

"Let's go brush him down, okay?"

Dallie's eyes came alert at the sound of that and the sleepiness melted from her face. She nodded her head vigorously.

They took him to his stall and removed the saddle and blanket from his back. She then unhooked his bit and his reigns, pulling his foaming mouth down to a big bucket of water. He drank greedily. Dallie grabbed the currycomb and Natalie picked her up and showed Dallie how to brush the horse. She was intrigued and after a few strokes, Natalie handed the brush to her. She'd never seen Dallie so delighted, and it brought newfound joy to her to know that her daughter loved the animals that she'd, at one time, won blue ribbons with.

Jack approached the stall then, smiling. "How'd your ride go, little lady?" Natalie was slightly disappointed to see that he'd replaced his shirt, but glad to see him all the same.

"Great!" Dallie grinned as she looked at Jack.

"You brushin' him down now?"

"Yup! Almost done," she spoke with such an accent that Natalie laughed as did Jack.

"Well, how about you brush some more down for me while you're at it?"

She looked at him with stars in her eyes. "Really?"

He looked over at Natalie, "If it's alright with your mom." Natalie nodded and Dallie squealed in excitement. Natalie and Jack smiled at each other, and Natalie's heart rate quickened when her eyes met his. Jack told Dallie to go get the step stool out of the closet next to her grandfather's office, and she ran hurriedly to do as he'd said. He smiled at Natalie as he stepped into the stall with her, pulling the top of the Dutch door closed as he did so to give them a little more privacy.

"You've just made her incredibly happy," Natalie said, admiring his everlasting kindness to her daughter.

"Well, I take pleasure in seeing her smile, but not as much pleasure as I get from seeing *you* smile." He took a step forward, planting his hand in her soft dark hair. He stroked her cheek with his thumb, and she sighed enjoying the gentle peace she felt from his touch. His fingers tilted her jaw bone up, her face lifted up to his for the taking. She anticipated the moment she could feel him take a breath in, the feel of his lips on hers, the touch of his tongue to hers. She yearned for it, but she knew it was danger, and she tried to tell him so.

"Jack...We can't."

"Yes, I know, but I can't help it. I *have* to touch you...I can't stop myself. I've wanted to kiss you all morning."

She looked up at him, her eyes pleading with him. He looked so gorgeous standing there, so manly, so kissable. He smelled like leather and sweat and a scent that was wholly Jack and she said the unthinkable before she ever knew it had come from her lips, "What are you waiting for then?"

And he kissed her. Softly. Gently. Her hands embraced his neck, bringing him closer to her. His chest pressed against her breasts as she opened her mouth to him, giving him more of her and he took it. He teased her tongue and nibbled at her lips until they were both aching for one another, then he stopped suddenly. He removed his lips from hers, looking into her face in confusion. He turned his head from her, listening hard for...something.

"Jack, what is it?"

"You don't hear that?" he asked, eyebrows drawn in concentration.

He stepped out of her embrace and left her side, leaving her feeling bereft. He walked to the door of the stall and listened. She came up behind him. He looked out into the hall of the barn. Dallie came prancing out of David's office then with the step stool at the far end of the barn and that's when Natalie saw what Jack was so transfixed with. It was a horse galloping at a dead speed toward the barn...heading right for Dallie. It looked like a horse that would have drawn the chariot of Hades. It was shiny and black and was running like the very gates of Hell were behind it.

Natalie screamed out at Dallie, but knew there was nothing she or Jack could do. The horse was right on her as she turned to face him, and Natalie could hear its evil whinny as he reared up. Natalie buried her head in Jack's shoulder and closed her eyes, waiting for the moment when she heard the sound of the horse's hooves hit the ground. Her stomach pitched and she knew she would puke her guts out at any second. Jack's muscles had become rigid, like a tree trunk. He didn't move, but Natalie knew he had turned his head away from the scene as she had because she felt him look up when not another sound was heard.

"Dallie, don't move," he instructed.

~

*I*t was the most magnificent thing that Jack had ever witnessed. He too had hid his eyes from what he thought would be the inevitable death of the child that had become so precious to him. He had froze knowing he couldn't save her, knowing she would be crushed before their very eyes. But, she was there right in front of them; standing on the stool he had asked her to go get, petting the horse that had almost murdered her. He couldn't believe it. The horse that had reared up on her as if it were crazed now stood there like the most domesticated animal alive. *Incredible*, Jack thought. She was whispering to him and stroking his muzzle lovingly. Jack approached wearily. Natalie stayed put, her body trembling as he let her go.

As he came up to Dallie, he put a hand at her back ready to grab her from harm's way if need be.

"Dallie, How on earth?" Jack started.

"I just reached up and touched him, Jack. He was just scared that's all. You just have to whisper softly, he likes that."

Jack was speechless. Never in his life had he seen someone with the ability to control a horse as spooked as that one had been…just by touching it.

At that moment, Miguel came barreling in the barn heaving along with the other three hands, Dan, Cass, and Kyle. They were all out of breath and it took them a minute to regain themselves. Finally, Miguel spoke.

"Sorry, señor. He ran through the fence. Rattlesnake. He was too fast for us to run after him…. Madre de Dios!"

"Sonovabitch was huge, Jack…" Kyle began then his mouth dropped.

They all paused as they saw the scene before them; Dallie calmly stroking the horse, the horse standing there allowing her to do so. They looked at Jack in confusion and he shrugged.

Dan was the first to speak, "How the Hell? What did she—?"

Jack didn't know what to say, he turned to look at Natalie, whose eyes had filled with tears. His heart went out to her; she must have been terrified. She walked over to him and he hugged her to him as she regained herself. He stroked her hair and reassured her.

"Shh... it's okay now. She's fine. It's over."

"I know Jack, but what would have happened? I shouldn't have left her by herself."

Jack's heart broke; she was blaming herself for something that was his fault. He should never have let her go alone to get that stool even if it was just to David's office. The barn wasn't the place for a four-year-old child. It wasn't safe with all the horses around; she was too small to be let loose in there.

Guilt ate at him as he looked into her eyes. Natalie turned then to Dallie and grabbed her, hugging her tightly. The horse nudged them. Natalie ignored him and stroked her daughter's hair.

"Oh, my baby, are you okay?" She pushed Dallie away from her and searched for any type of damage she could find, and then sat her down.

"Its okay, Mommy. See? He's okay now," Dallie said, pointing to the horse and stroking his neck as far as she could reach.

"Uh...Jack." It was Cass that spoke this time.

"Yeah?" He turned to look at him.

"That horse is wild," Cass said, still looking as if he couldn't believe his eyes.

"Yeah, I figured as much when he came tearing in here like a bat out of Hell. He the same one that wrecked the fence this morning?"

"No, I mean he was just brought in the other day from Wyoming, a wild Mustang."

"What?"

Surely they were mistaken. This horse...Well, it just had to be domesticated. There was no way it would allow Dallie to pet it like this if it weren't.

Jack reached his hand out to touch the horse on the head. It snorted and stepped away from Jack's touch. Jack was at a loss for words. Horses became tame through hard work and discipline, respect. He had been a horse trainer all his life and never witnessed anything like this. It was simply...amazing.

Later that night at dinner, Jack related what had happened to David.

"We had to get her to help us take the horse back to a stall, David. He wouldn't leave her side. I swear I've never seen anything like it. He wouldn't allow anyone else to touch him or try to lead him in. It's like Dallie has a way with him that none of us have... You know, I've been thinking, what if we can get Dallie to help us tame this horse?" he remarked, cramming a bite of mashed potatoes into his mouth.

They all stared at him as if he'd just sprouted antlers, especially the six men. Dallie nodded her head, delighted.

"You *can't* be serious!" Natalie spoke first.

"But I am, Nat. I think she can help us. Hell, the horse has already warmed up to her. I think it would work."

Natalie was already immediately shaking her head. "I don't think so Jack. It's not a good idea."

"Actually, I don't think its half bad, Natalie," Dan said, intervening.

"What?" She stared at him.

"Well, Jack's right. The horse likes Dallie; none of us four could get him to cooperate at all. He nearly killed us jumping that fence like he did. I think Jack is on to somethin'."

Jack nodded his gratification at Dan then looked back at Natalie for her approval.

Her face was red with confusion and anger. "I said no, it's not safe. She's only four years old. You saw what could've happened today. Being around those horses is no place for a small child like Dallie. That horse could kill her without even trying."

"But, Nat, I'll be right beside Dallie the whole time. I won't let anything happen to her, I swear. You can trust me."

Natalie looked down for a moment and sat in silence. No one said anything just waited for her decision. Finally, she looked up at Jack.

"No Jack, No." She shook her head in determination.

"Natalie." David took her hand across the table. "It's worth a try."

Natalie stood up then, hurt showing on her face, her eyes fixed on Jack. "Dallie is *my* child and I said no, end of story." With that, she threw her napkin in her chair and headed out the back door.

Jack looked at David. "I'll go talk to her."

"Yeah, that gets you *real* far…" Dan trailed off as Jack gave him one of his looks. Dan looked away as Jack passed him on his way out the back door, and then mumbled something incoherent.

Jack was gonna talk her into it if it took him all night. He walked onto the porch and spotted her. She had her hands through the fence petting one of the horses in the back pasture. He walked down the steps and came up beside her, placing his boot on the middle rail of the fence and propping his arm on his knee. He looked at her for a long time before she spoke.

Nat sighed, looking into his eyes as she brought her hands back through the fence.

"Jack, she's all I have in this world. You can't ask me to allow this to happen. You don't have a child, how could you possibly understand?"

She was the most beautiful woman he had ever seen, he decided. Her eyes held such warmth, how had he ever thought she was cold hearted?

"I understand more than you think I do…" He bowed his head. "Do you trust me, Natalie?"

She sighed again. "Oh Jack, it has nothing to do with that… I want to trust you but…you just don't understand, okay?"

"Well, how will I ever understand if you don't talk to me, huh?"

She laughed cynically. "Let's put it this way, Jack! Dallie and I have been through Hell and back, and I don't think this is the best idea. Dallie doesn't need the stress of all this. I don't need the stress of worrying over her."

"Nat, I would take perfect care of her. I would never let anything happen to your daughter. You know that! Just think? If a four year old can tame a wild stallion then she could be famous."

Natalie laughed again. "That is the last thing she needs. Look, I said no Jack, and that's what I meant. We don't need another stressor right now."

Jack felt defeated, but he refused to give up. Dallie had a gift, he knew it, and he wouldn't let it be wasted.

"Nat, she loves horses. Isn't there anything in this world you wanted when you were her age? This would thrill her to death."

"Yes, and death is the key word here. Stop trying to get me to say yes because I won't do it," she said, looking hard at him, willing him to be satisfied with her answer.

"Not for anything?" Jack asked, glancing at her with sultry eyes.

"No!" She tried backing away from him, but he grabbed her wrists and pulled her against his chest.

"Not even for a kiss?" he asked, looking down into her face. She tried pulling away from the hand that held her, but gave up after a minute when she couldn't budge him. He brought her hand around her back and secured her other hand so she couldn't move, she was trapped.

"Jack, you can't bribe me." She stifled a laugh, trying to hold her composure.

"Oh really... wanna bet?" He smiled as well and tilted her face up with his other hand.

"This isn't fair, not at all." She pouted, gazing at the mouth that was about to kiss her.

"Well, I don't think it's fair that I can't kiss you more often."

"Who's stopping you?" She raised her eyebrow at him in challenge.

With that he planted his lips on hers, feeling the warmth of them.

It felt so incredible that he moaned aloud. She was ready for his tongue when he eased it into her mouth gently. He stroked the interior of her mouth with it, loving the noises she made each time it brushed over her tongue. He let her hand go and she threw her arms over his shoulders as he backed her into the fence. She used her tongue on him as well and he could feel his growing desire for her manifest itself snugly between them. It throbbed with his need for her softness, her femininity. He ached for her, craved to be nestled inside her silky warmth.

He continued his feast of her mouth, until the fire between them raged and they were both breathing heavily. His hands played in the thick mass of her dark hair, gently playing with it and tugging on it. His mouth left hers to explore her cheek, her neck, the base of her throat to her pulse point. His tongue lapped at her skin as if he were licking the sweetness from it. She gasped when his tongue traced circles at her collarbone. He sucked there gently, placing his mark on her.

His arms fell to encircle her waist, his mouth returning to taste the sweetness that was hers alone. His hands moved over her lean back then went low down to her bottom and pulled her against his rock hard erection.

She gasped and moaned; the most erotic sound he'd ever heard, as she felt his manhood, long and solid against her. It was the first time he'd pressed himself so close to her and she rubbed him with her own sex, rocking her hips against him. He immediately pulled away, knowing that he'd pushed himself to his limit. His body ached for her, her touch, her softness. He forced himself not to give in to his desire and then took a step forward again, taking her hands in his. He felt apologetic suddenly.

Their attraction to one another was both thrilling and irresistible, but Jack felt that they were rushing things a bit. Natalie had voiced the fact that she wasn't ready. She wasn't like the women of his past and he didn't want to treat her as such. He wanted to take his time with her; he wanted more than just casual sex with her. He gave them both a moment to breathe before he spoke.

"I want you to trust me, Natalie. I'm not a bad guy and I would never hurt you. I want you to know that I would never do anything that you wouldn't want me to do."

"I know you wouldn't." Her sapphire eyes burned into his.

"Then trust me...trust me with Dallie...with yourself. That's all I want."

He could tell she had trouble with that. She looked into his eyes so unsure, and he thought she would deny the request, but then she sighed.

"So help me, if my daughter gets hurt by that damn horse, I will castrate you."

Jack laughed out loud. "You have my word as a gentleman, that horse won't hurt your daughter." She cocked her eyebrow at him then smiled.

"Ok, Jack. I trust you." She sighed, as if a heavy burden had been lifted from her body, as if admitting to trusting him was the hardest thing she'd ever had to do.

He smiled at her and then pulled her back into his arms to kiss her softly on the lips. She returned the kiss then pulled back enough to look up at him.

"Jack, can I ask you something?"

"Sure," he said, playing in her hair again.

"Have you ever been married?" Wow, such a bold question at such an awkward moment.

"Nope." He nuzzled her neck and she pulled back.

"So, why is a good-looking guy like you not taken?"

"You think I'm good-looking? Wow, thanks." He smiled and brought his face down to kiss her again but again she pulled away.

"Seriously, Jack..." she said, looking up into his eyes, wanting to know about him, about his life.

Well, he might as well tell her now. No sense in putting it off.

"Seriously? You wanna know the truth?"

"Yes."

"It's quite a long story…"

"I've got nothing but time." She shrugged, smiled and planted her hands on her hips.

He smiled too. "Alright, I'll tell you, but let's go to your dad's office, so I can get something to drink. Kissing you has made me thirsty." He watched her cheeks turn crimson and laughed. He took her hand and led her to the office. Her hand was so soft and small in his, unlike his hard calloused palms.

He showed her in first then he took a paper cup and filled it up at the water cooler that sat on one of the walls of David's office. He turned the cup up and gulped the water down quickly then filled the cup up again before he headed to the couch. Natalie sat down on the old couch, it creaked under her weight. Jack sat down beside her and crossed his ankle over his leg in front of him, stretching out. He then turned to her. Noticing that he was comfortable; comfortable telling her about his past, trusting her with it. He was unsure how to start and wanted her to know that he didn't open up to a lot of people. He cleared his throat and began.

"Natalie, this isn't something I talk about. I think the only one who knows the whole story is your father…" He sighed before beginning. "After my parents died, I went back to college, because honestly I didn't really know what else to do. Besides, I was almost done anyway and what do you do when something like that happens? The same thing you've always done, right?" He'd answered his own rhetorical question. "I became withdrawn socially and became somewhat of a loner. I had myself and my schoolwork and the horses. I thought that was all I needed to make me happy. I graduated with honors and got a job at a ranch as a trainer. I worked hard to prove myself to my boss. I was good at what I did and moved up to foreman within two years. I'd made friends and even met a girl, her name was Karen. I thought I was head over heels in love. At the time, I thought she was the one and didn't realize that she wasn't quite as nice as she made out to be. Needless to say, after a few months of dating, I found her in bed with one of my co-workers; I'll let you take one stab at who that was..."

"Dan?" she asked, her eyes widening in shock.

"You guessed it!"

"Dan Wilson, you knew him that long ago?"

"Yup, we both worked in Amarillo at Long Winds Ranch."

"Oh my God, Jack, I had no idea!"

"Yeah, that makes two of us. He apparently hated the fact that I was made foreman over him because he'd been there longer than I had. He seduced her to get back at me."

"No wonder you hate him..." she said. Jack just shrugged.

"It was as much her fault as it was his," he stated, no longer hurt over the infidelity of his former girlfriend.

"So what did you do?" Natalie asked.

"I, of course, was heartbroken. I didn't even stay for an excuse. I left and never saw her again. I didn't stay in one place for very long after that; I went from job to job. I even went into the rodeo circuit for a few years, thinking I was tough and could do it. That's where I met your brother and then your father... I met him the night they disqualified me because I was staggering drunk. He found me lying on the ground with a bottle of Wild Turkey in my hands, next to my horse." Jack laughed at the memory then sighed.

"I'd gone wild, spending most of my time in the bottle and... with women. I had no job, no place to live, no where to go, no one to turn to. I had no friends. I'd run them all off with my horrible temper and drinking. I had nothing, I *was* nothing... I'd wasted the last five years of my life pining over that damn whore, sorry." Natalie smiled and shook her head indicating that she took no offense from his statement.

"Your father looked at me in the pathetic state I was in and told me that he would give me an opportunity to turn my life around. He said he'd seen me with the horses and thought I was good enough to be a trainer on his ranch. I told him I surprisingly had a degree in Equine Science and he laughed. He said he needed a foreman. So I took his offer, I had nothing to lose and nothing to gain or so I thought... Ever since I met your dad I've become a different person, Natalie. He's been like a father to me; he scooped my ass up off the ground and knocked some sense into me. He gave me an opportunity, a great job, a place to live. He saw the potential in me when no one else did and that meant a lot to me. He took me for what I am, and for that, I am ever grateful to him. No one else has ever done for me what he did." Jack paused then looked Natalie deeply in the eyes.

"So why have I never married? After Karen, I didn't want another relationship of any kind. Love, commitment, trust...it was all a joke to me. I, of course, still acted like a man back in my rodeo days, I won't lie. But after your father took me in, I just wanted to prove myself to him. So I worked hard every day and up until recently haven't even thought about dating again. Dating is something I've been dreading to be honest, simply because I haven't done it in so long, but I do want to find someone to settle down with."

He'd just spilled his past to her, and it'd flowed so easily, like a river, out of him. He hadn't meant to say so much, but maybe that would let her know what she wanted to know. She grabbed his hand and stroked it and when he looked over at her, he saw warmth in her eyes. She smiled almost apologetically and kissed him on the cheek. He turned his head to capture her lips then and savored the touch of them on his. God, she was all woman! He thought about how long it had been since he'd really kissed a woman, a woman like Natalie, a woman who deserved to be kissed, a woman who didn't want to be just another mark on his belt. It'd been a while, a long while, he thought. Then curiosity got the best of him and he wanted to know more about her life, her secrets, and her past.

"Now it's your turn, Nat." He put out the bait, even though he knew she wouldn't be talking about her past as easily as he had.

He thought he glimpsed a look of panic, then she started to speak but was reluctant, then she sighed.

"Mommy?" Dallie's voice called from the interior of the barn.

Natalie jumped up from the couch and raced toward the door. Jack was right behind her.

"Dallie, what are you doing down here by yourself?" Nat asked as she ran to Dallie and picked her up, dusting her feet off. Dallie was dressed in a pink nightgown with butterflies on it. David came racing in after Dallie.

"That little booger is hard to keep up with," he said slightly out of breath.

"Mommy, I wanted Jack to tuck me in," Dallie said, looking over at Jack. She gave him one of her sweet smiles, and he melted. She had the tendency to do that a lot. Jack knew that he couldn't love that child more if she were his own. It was funny, he could almost see her being his child, even though he hadn't been a part of her conception. He would have liked to have been though... Natalie was one of those women that a man could make love to forever and never stop wanting to.

"Ok, well, let's head back to the house, baby," Natalie said, breaking him out of his reverie. *Good thing*, he thought. He didn't want David to see him getting all worked up over his daughter.

"I want Jack to carry me," Dallie said, reaching for him.

"What makes you think I want to lug you back to the house? What do you weigh now?" Jack asked, teasing with her even as he easily took her from Natalie's arms.

Dallie laughed innocently. "You're Superman, Jack. You can carry anything."

"Superman? I don't think I'm quite *that* strong, sweetheart."

"You are to me," she said and smiled down into his face as he put her on his shoulders, and he felt his heart melt once again.

Once they reached the house, David headed off for the living room, and Natalie followed Jack to her parent's room to lay Dallie down. He lifted her gently onto the bed and brought the covers up around her. Natalie was behind him as he sat beside the little trundle bed to bid her a goodnight.

"Now you lay right down here, little cowgirl, and you rest that pretty head of yours."

"Okay, Jack. I will," She said, giggling.

"Goodnight, Dallie. Sweet dreams." He took her hand and kissed the back of it.

He switched places with Natalie as she leaned down to kiss her child on the forehead.

"I love you, Mommy! Goodnight."

"I love you too, my little angel. Sweet dreams."

Jack followed Natalie out the door, and Dallie blew him a kiss. He made every effort to pretend that he caught it in his shirt pocket, and she giggled once again.

Natalie shut the door and turned to Jack. "You know she thinks the world of you?" The eyes that looked up at him sparkled with admiration.

"Yeah, well, I think she's pretty incredible myself," he confirmed.

Natalie laughed at that. "She's quite a handful."

"Well, you are too," he said, looking down at her chest and giving her a Cheshire cat grin.

Her mouth fell open in a big O. "Jack Kinsen, of all the pigheaded, chauvinistic-" She never finished because he pulled her tightly against his body, loving the feel of her in his arms. He only pulled away because he heard footsteps in the hallway.

It was David. Jack tensed suddenly and stepped away from Natalie.

"Hey, kids, y'all wanna play some cards?"

They nodded because they were too baffled to do anything else.

CHAPTER 5

"Y̶ou give me that card, Jack. I know you have it!" Natalie shot snake eyes at him.

"I said GO FISH. I don't have it." He shrugged and gave her that charming smile of his.

"Well, I don't believe you. That's what you said last time and you pulled a sly one on me."

"Well I ain't got it, now go fish." He stuck his tongue out at her.

"Ew! I swear I'm gonna…" Natalie said as she pulled the top card of the stack. It wasn't the one she wanted, so she made a big deal about it and told Jack it was his turn.

She could swear there was a conspiracy going on. Her father and Jack had won all the games so far of the three they had played. Her mother just giggled, she was just enjoying the fun of it. Natalie smiled to herself and watched the love bubble in her mother's eyes. She was happy, Nat noted. It had been a long time since she had seen her mother smile so much.

"David, you got any fours?" Jack asked with a lot more confidence than was called for, in Natalie's opinion.

"Well, I want you to look at that. I do Jack; I got two of 'em."

Natalie was horrified, "No way?" But sure enough he showed her that he had two of the cards Jack had specified.

"Well, if that ain't something," Jack replied, looking at the cards like they were something magical.

"This is bull shit...total bull shit," Natalie rebuked, throwing her cards down on the table.

Her mother laughed hysterically and both men broke out into laughter as well.

"I can't believe you boys are cheating. Look at how upset you've made my Natalie," her mother piped in, wiping the tears from her eyes.

Natalie was mad as a wet hen.

"Aww, poor Natalie," Jack offered, mocking her by pushing his lips out in a pout and chucking her chin as if she were a child.

"Jack, I'm warning you," Natalie said smiling, grabbing at his hand.

He continued with his mockery until she reached for his chest to pinch him, but he blocked her hand. She used the other one, but she wasn't quick enough and he blocked that hand too. Her parents were hysterical, and she tried her best to push against his grasp but was unsuccessful. So, she pulled away from it, tilting his chair sideways and brought the two of them crashing to the floor. Jack laughed even as he tried bringing both him and Natalie upright. By this time Natalie was laughing as well. They managed to get the chair upright and deposit themselves back in their seats, all the while, their bellies throbbing from laughter. Corrine got up to go get some tea and Jack asked if Nat was okay.

She was punching him in the arm when a horrified scream pierced the air.

"MOMMY!"

"Oh my God, Dallie," she cried hardly above a whisper.

She flung herself from her chair and ran as fast as she could toward her parent's bedroom, Jack close on her heels and her father behind him. She pushed the door open and raced to her daughter's side. She was just sitting there on the bed holding her big floppy pony, big tears rolling down her cheeks, a frightened look on her pale face. She stretched her arms out for her mother as Natalie scooped her up and into her arms. She buried her head in Natalie's breasts, sobbing gently. Natalie crooned to her and rocked her gently.

"Baby, what is it? Are you okay?" Natalie forced Dallie's head up so she could look at her. Her little blue eyes were filled with tears, her cheeks streaked with red.

"Mommy, he was come—coming after us. He was right out—outside the window. I saw him; he gr—grinned at me. Please, Mommy, don't let him get m—me," Dallie sobbed uncontrollably.

"Who, baby girl? Who?" Natalie asked, stroking her daughter's curly ringlets. Her heart was filled with fear for worry of her daughter.

"Daddy!" With that word, Dallie's body was once again racked with sobs.

Natalie sighed in relief, knowing that she had just had a nightmare and nothing or no one had tried to hurt her daughter. "Baby, listen, your daddy isn't here. He's gone forever."

"But I saw him…I did Mommy, I did."

"Shh, its okay, Dallie. Honey, it was just a bad dream."

Dallie sobbed harder then. She cried so violently that she shook Natalie. Natalie looked pleadingly up at Jack and her father, pleading for what, she didn't know.

Jack sat down beside Natalie, his eyes full of understanding, silently reassuring her. He spoke to the terrified little angel in her arms.

"Come here, Dallie," Jack said, lifting Dallie's tiny frame from Natalie's arms to his shoulder. "Look at me, sweetie." She hugged his big shoulder like a vise grip then looked up into his handsome face, tears streaming her round little cheeks.

"You won't let him get me will you, Jack?" she asked. Her nose was running and she wiped at it as he answered her.

"No, Dallie, I won't. I will *never* let anything happen to you. Ever. You have to believe that. Okay?" Dallie nodded her little head, curls flying. "He'll never get in here, not past me." He wiped at a tear on her cheek as he smiled into her red eyes.

She smiled at that and hugged Jack's neck. "I love you, Jack."

"I love you too, Dallie." He embraced her, his arms wrapping around her almost twice. He patted her back as she squeezed tighter around his neck.

Natalie felt her heart burst with happiness; he continued to amaze her where her daughter was concerned. She was astounded at the way Jack had reassured Dallie and made her feel safe, probably safer than anyone could ever make her feel. A tear came to Natalie's eye as she thought of how important what Jack had said was to Dallie. The way he'd handled her was the way that Natalie's own father had when she'd been scared as a child, like he was… well…a superhero. And to Dallie, Jack was her Superman.

Dallie drew back then and kissed Jack on the cheek then looked over at Natalie. "Jack? Will you protect Mommy, too?"

"As sure as the sun rises."

Dallie broke into a huge grin then and her eyes glittered as she looked at her mother. Natalie smiled at her in Jack's arms; his strong, comforting arms. She looked at the handsome man that set her heart and body on fire and realized that she knew deep down in her soul that he would do everything in his power to protect them both. The realization both terrified and relieved her. For her to be able to trust someone she hadn't known long after all that had happened made her feel naïve, but the knowledge that he was there to protect them gave her a strange sense of comfort. However, she had learned all to well that a person could trust no one. How could she even think about trusting anyone else? But she trusted that Jack would protect them both, for what reason she had no clue, but she trusted him.

"How 'bout you go on back to sleep now, darlin'?" Jack remarked, interrupting Natalie's wondering mind.

Dallie nodded her head, so he scooped her up as if she were

lighter than a feather and deposited her underneath the covers. He pulled the covers up to her arm pits and tucked them under her sides, wrapping her tightly as if she were in a papoose.

"Now you remember that I'm right here, and I won't let anything happen to you, okay?"

"Ok, Jack. Goodnight, Mommy."

"Do you want to come sleep with Mommy?" Nat asked. Dallie shook her head.

"I want Grandma." With that Corrine came in and reassured Natalie as she walked toward the door. Dallie blew her a kiss and Natalie blew one back, she let Jack and her father out the door before she closed it and sighed against the back of it when they were out of sight. Tears filled her eyes, and she knew she would break down if she didn't get away.

She yelled goodnight and headed toward the stairs, so she wouldn't have to face them with her newfound insight; she was disappointed with herself and needed time alone. Her mind was racing; her heart was so torn between her want for this man and her fear of falling for him. She headed up the steps and to the guest room to change her clothes. She undressed quickly, feeling vulnerable while she slipped her shirt over her head. The feeling made her blush; she didn't like feeling so helpless while she was naked. She quickly slipped off her pants and grabbed her shorts thrusting them on and grabbing her tank top, slinging it over her head. She was walking out of the door for the bathroom when Jack popped up the stairs.

"Jesus, Jack! You just scared the Hell out of me."

"Sorry… you just kinda jetted outta there didn't ya?" He grinned then his smile faded as he saw her face. "What's wrong, Nat?" He closed the distance between them, and she backed away, knowing that if he touched her she would fall apart.

She shook it off. "Nothing, I wanted to thank you for what you did back there." She bowed her head, not wanting him to see her face, fearing she might lose it.

"Hey, it was no problem." He smiled, bending his head to try to look at her.

"Yes, but you calmed her so easily. I've never been able to…And what you said—"

"I meant every word of it." He touched her then and she sighed knowing that with the turmoil between her head and her heart she couldn't resist him. He brought her chin up with his finger then ran it down the length of her throat. She felt the fire within her yearn to be quenched and felt herself blush against his touch, ashamed of how wanton he could make her feel. He wrapped his fingertips gently around the back of her neck, embracing her head with his hand as he pulled it up and forward. "I would *kill* any man who tried to hurt you," Jack said softly, looking sincerely into her eyes before he lowered his head to take her lips.

"Jack," she whispered almost inaudibly, trying not to give into him even as the implication of his words hit her. He kissed her gently, letting his hand slip to her waist to stroke her back. His other hand slipped into the mass of her hair, holding her to where he could have full access to her mouth. He twirled the curling ends of her hair with his fingers, and he pulled back just an inch and smiled.

"God, you're so soft and sexy," he muttered against her lips as he kissed her then dipped his head to her neck, nibbling the soft skin beneath her ear.

She closed her eyes against the tears that threatened to come. Had anyone ever said that to her? He felt so good, his strong muscled arms and chest taut against her. His lips gentle against her quivering flesh, his hot breath on her skin making her break out in goose bumps, his hands stroking the small of her back, his erection pressing hard against her aching belly. Breathy moans escaped her throat as he nibbled and licked at her neck and her ear, her head spinning as her desire for his masculine strength throbbed deep in her womb. At that moment, she wanted him more than she'd ever wanted anything in her life. She wanted this feeling of losing herself to him, to Jack, her daughter's Superman. She wanted his comfort, his strength, his gentleness. She ached for him to make love to her; take her away from all the pain she'd felt for far too long.

His hand was inching up her waist, higher on her torso. She longed for his hand to inch just a little closer, to touch her breasts, oh how she wanted him there. She feared her desire, even hated herself for it because it made her so vulnerable. His hand inched further, a slight movement, hesitation, then his palm and fingers enveloped her left breast. He moaned, a throaty growl, as his thumb grazed her hard nipple. It felt so good to have his strong hands on that soft, sensitive part of her. She closed her eyes and moaned in pleasure as unshed tears of bittersweet torment flooded her eyes.

"Jack, please…" she gasped, her voice quivered as she looked up at him, the uncontrolled tears rolling down her cheeks. He saw them, unsure at first if she was asking for more or wanting him to stop then suddenly he pulled back looking embarrassed. He'd decided himself that it must be the latter. He was quiet for a moment, his head bowed in deep regret, looking like a scolded child. Then he spoke softly looking up at her.

"I'm sorry, Natalie. I'm so sorry. It's just… you're just so beautiful, and it's just so damn hard to resist the way you taste, the way you feel against me." He bowed his head again, looking defeated. Maybe she wasn't the only one who was losing her self-control.

"It's okay, Jack. Don't apologize." She put her hands in his.

"No, Nat. It isn't okay. I don't want to push you into something you aren't ready for and it seems I just keep doing that…" His cheeks were crimson, his remorse so sincere. "I just want you *so* badly." His hand cupped her cheek, his thumb tracing her lip and he gulped as he looked back up into her eyes. "But I can wait and I will, darlin' for as long as you need for me to." His eyes glistened with unfulfilled desire as well as hope for that desire to be quenched.

She stared mesmerized by the deep emerald pools of his eyes until slowly all of her demons hit her at one time. Her past, first and foremost, and all the distrust and betrayal that had came along with it. Next came her fear and excitement of her desire for Jack, ever present. It hit her hard, swamping her with doubts. Finally, her fear of the future, the pain that Dallie had felt... all of it. It was as if she were fighting an internal battle within herself. It was all too much for her and she started to cry. To cry for time lost, time wasted, a past that wouldn't allow her to move forward, a past that wouldn't allow her to love this wonderful man who wanted her as desperately as she wanted him.

The walls she had built around herself were suffocating her. It was so hard to be strong for herself and Dallie when deep down all she wanted was for someone to take the burden away. It affected her everyday life, every decision she made, for herself, for Dallie, was based on her past, her ex-husband, her insecurities. Why did she have to be tormented daily, nightly? Why couldn't she just make love with this heartthrob and stop regretting every touch and every kiss like a born again virgin and move on with her life? Why couldn't she be the person she used to be without fear or pain or regrets?

She started to sob uncontrollably as these thoughts took hold of her mind and heart. Jack pulled her into him then, soothing her. Her head fell on his shoulder as he wrapped his big arms around her. Violent spasms racked her body as she gave into the tears that had waited so long for comfort.

"I'm so sorry, baby. Please don't cry. I just want you so much that I forget to think about what *you* want. I am *such* an asshole. I had no consideration for your feelings. God, what a jerk I am..." He was beating himself up, thinking that she was crying because of what he'd done.

She brought her head off his shoulder then and wiped at her eyes and nose. "But Jack, you don't understand, I *want* you to make love to me. I know that we've only known each other such a short time, but I still want to. Call me a slut, whatever, but I want you just as much as you want me!" There she'd admitted it.

He stared at her as if he were making sure the words really came from her mouth.

"Seriously?"

"Yes, so very badly, but— but I can't. I can't allow myself... I just can't! You don't understand... I wish I could just...it's because..." She trailed off and sighed looking up at him, silently begging for understanding. But how could he understand, how could he ever understand?

"Because of your ex husband?" Jack asked after several minutes. Natalie nodded.

He took her cheek in his hand again and rubbed it with his thumb, looking deeply into her eyes.

"God, Natalie, baby, what did he *do* to you?" His eyes were so full of compassion that she broke into tears again and turned her face away from him consumed by her tears.

"He did the most h—horrible th—thing a human b—eing can do, Jack. I ca—can't even talk about it. I'm so so—sorry."

He pulled her back into his strong, willing arms and picked her up, carrying her to her bedroom. He laid them down on the bed together and pulled her into him. She threw herself into his compassionate invitation, loving the feel of his arms around her and his giving her his comforting embrace.

He let her sob into his chest all the while stroking her back and hair, kissing her cheek and neck and soothing her with his calming words. She fell asleep in his comforting arms after some time and was so exhausted that she didn't notice when he got up several hours after that to go to his own room.

∼

Jack lay awake that night, tossing and turning. His mind would not allow him to let go of both Dallie's and Natalie's distress. It sickened him to think that a man could harm a woman in any way, but whatever the man had done had involved the child too and that infuriated Jack. Had he beat them? Beat Natalie in front of Dallie? Whatever it was, Natalie couldn't even talk about it without bursting into tears. Whatever he had done, he was in prison for it. But that didn't change the feeling in Jack's gut...His instinctive need to protect them was so strong it scared him because deep down he had the unsettling feeling that they needed his protection.

He also felt a deep-seated shame in the pit of his stomach. He'd caused Natalie to cry, and he felt like shit about it. She'd cried for half an hour before the sobs slowly fell to whimpers then to nothing but the sound of her breathing as she slept in his arms. He'd held her for hours after that watching her sleep, watching the moonlight bathe her creamy skin, shadowing it, making her look angelic in the blue light. He'd watched the rise and fall of her chest and watched her young slender face, deciding again that she was the most beautiful woman he'd ever seen. The hardest thing he'd ever had to do in his life was leave her side; he wanted to stay all night long and hold her in his arms and run his hands through her long dark hair, planting kisses on her lips as she slept. But he had to leave, if not for the dull throbbing ache in his groin simply for the fact that he would never get any sleep with her to distract him, and he desperately needed to rest. It was approaching three in the morning and he yawned, exhausted, cursing the time.

It was almost time to get up and he hadn't had a wink of sleep. He closed his eyes and tried to clear his mind, but it kept going back to Natalie. Her pain had deeply affected him, he hated seeing her that way and the fact that he couldn't do a damn thing about it frustrated him. He tried to close his eyes to rest them, but the images of both of their tear-streaked faces haunted him, the faces of the two females that were slowly becoming a major part of his life. He hated seeing their pain, and the source of it remained a mystery to him. He was dying to know what made them cry that way. But he would never push Natalie for information; she would have to give it willingly.

When he glanced at the clock again he cursed out loud, he had to get some sleep. He closed his eyes and cleared his mind and found himself awake again four hours later.

A nightmare had shaken him from his deep slumber, and he

couldn't go back to sleep. His nightmare had been so real and so terri-fying that it shook him to the core. He saw Natalie and Dallie in grave danger, but he didn't know what the danger was or how to find it and only he could save them, but he was helpless. The dream both terri-fied and angered him. He decided to go take a cold shower and shake it off. He wanted to forget the dream and never think of it again.

He took a long shower, letting it both wake and cool him. When he finally got out and shaved and dressed, he heard laughter coming from down stairs, so he decided to check next door and see if Natalie was awake. He slowly opened the door, not knocking.

Natalie stood there in front of the bed, naked from the waist up, breasts exposed, facing the door. She tried to cover them as she saw him, but it was too late.

"Jack!" she yelled. "Get out of here." Her cheeks had turned as red as apples.

"Well, Ms. Natalie, you've just made my morning!" He laughed and dodged the balled up sock that was tossed at his head. He shut the door behind him and grinned to himself as he walked downstairs to start his early morning chores.

~

Natalie called Jack every dirty thing she could think of before she came downstairs to eat breakfast with her family and the hands. What a pig he was! Not knocking and looking at her half naked. How rude! He grinned at her as she came into the kitchen and her cheeks turned crimson. She felt like a teenage girl, blushing like she did around him, although she was a grown woman who'd been married and had a child.

Her mother had laughed at something Jack had said. "Jack, you're in the best mood this morning," she replied.

"Yes I am, Mrs. Butler. I feel great this morning," he said, glancing at Natalie, looking at her with a cock-eyed grin. She felt her cheeks burn and knew that she was once again blushing. She cut her eyes at him.

"Mommy," Dallie yelled, coming up to Natalie, "do I really get to help Jack this morning, huh, huh?" She reached up to Natalie for her to pick her up, so she did.

"Yes, you really do!" she said, smiling as she carried her into the dining room to sit her down at the table.

"Oh, Boy!" Dallie responded as Natalie pulled her chair up to the table and began ladling grits into her plate and then left to go back to the kitchen to get the butter.

Dan grabbed her arm on the way to the kitchen, stopping her. "You're really gonna let him do this?" His brows were drawn in a frown.

"Don't touch me!" she said aloud, not liking him having his slimy hands on her, especially after knowing how manipulative he truly was. "And yes I am, so mind your own damn business."

Jack heard her cry and flew through the swinging kitchen door, coming up behind Dan. Dan immediately let go of her arm and spun around to face Jack.

"You just like her guard dog now, huh? Or better yet her mother hen!" Dan laughed heartily.

"Oh you think that's funny, huh?" Jack laughed along with him then his face turned as grim as death. "Touch her again and I'll break your arm, you get me?"

Dan just cut his eyes at him and walked away.

"Are you okay?" Jack asked, taking her arm and looking it over.

"Yes." She was too shocked to say anything else.

During breakfast, Jack continued to look at her as if she weren't wearing her top. She looked down several times to make sure that it was still there. Every time he looked at her, a tingling sensation spiraled through her tummy. It both thrilled and frightened her. Before Jack left to go to the barn with her child, she threatened him within an inch of his life if Dallie was harmed. He promised to take care of her and they headed off to the barn while she ran upstairs to take a shower.

She let the hot water seep into her weary muscles and as always, thought of Jack. As she ran the washcloth down her body, she imagined Jack's hand on her breast as it had been the night before, her nipples puckered under the soft cloth and she moaned. She shivered thinking about his mouth being there and then blushed, ashamed of herself. She hurriedly washed the rest of her body, and shampooed her hair. When she got out, she blew her hair dry, dressed in her jeans and a coral colored top and applied a little makeup to her red face. She walked down to the round pen where Jack was with her daughter in the center. She stepped up on the fence next to her father and propped her chin on her arm.

"So, what'd I miss?" Natalie asked as she looked over to see them with the stallion attached to a halter and lead rope.

"A good bit actually. They started out with leading and getting him used to the halter. He's gotten the hang of following and stopping and he took to desensitization pretty well. Spooked a little at first, but got comfortable pretty fast with Dallie around."

She gave him an exasperated look and turned to hear Jack.

"See, I stop and he stops..." The stallion stopped about a head behind Jack. "You want him to follow you, but not too close, make him keep his space a little." He showed Dallie the whip. "Now Dallie, I want you to understand that this isn't a torture device, it's simply a guide for the horse, ok? It's important for you to get the horse to trust you but you also want him to respect you. You need to get to where you can read his body language and be able to interpret his behavioral cues and he needs to be able to do the same with you."

"But, Jack, I don't want to hit him," Dallie said and frowned up at her instructor.

"No, no, you *don't* hit him. Just guide him, that's all."

"Jack's doing all the work, just explaining the techniques we use and why... the horse seems more responsive with her presence than without," David explained.

"Groundwork is the basis of getting him ready to ride," Jack told Dallie. "All we are doing is training him to get used to the movements that we will use once he's saddled up with a rider." Again Dallie just nodded. "Now we are going to work on longeing him. This will help develop the correct movements and gait." He gave the line some slack and made a move toward the stallion then and horse jerked his head up and snorted, but slowly moved in the direction of Jack's outstretched arm. "My right arm goes up and that's the direction I want him to go." Jack clucked his tongue and ushered the horse a bit faster and used a flicking motion of the whip with his wrist to guide the horse in a soft canter around the corral.

"See and once he gets going, he's got to keep going until we tell him otherwise. This is to get him used to continuing to walk while you ride and him not suddenly stopping. It's important for you to maintain communication with him."

"Ok, I think I can do that." She took the whip from Jack and used it as he had instructed, as Jack controlled the line. She moved along with him and needed a little help to keep the momentum going, but overall did a terrific job in keeping the horse in form.

David smiled over to Natalie and laid his hand on her back. "Remind you of two other people we know?"

Natalie laughed. "Yeah, that's us alright," she said, smiling lovingly at her father.

"You were just about that old when I started with you...Gosh it seems like it was just yesterday, Nat." He smiled even brighter, the thought, a sweet memory to him.

Natalie smiled as well, Jack and Dallie were her and her father made over. Dallie looked at Jack with the same trusting, admiring eyes that Natalie looked at her father with.

"Hey, Mommy, look!" Dallie called out. Natalie focused her attention to Dallie to see her and Jack guiding the horse in a circle around the corral.

Natalie grinned brightly at her beautiful little angel. "Yes baby, I see that. I'm so proud of you." Dallie's smile deepened and she giggled. Jack looked up at her as well and smiled his gorgeous smile taking her breath away.

They lead the horse in several circles, let him rest and got him going the opposite direction for a few revolutions, they then worked on backing up and again leading until the big black horse was out of breath and so were Jack and Dallie. Jack took the rope and tied it to one of the fence posts. He pulled the horse's face down to a bucket of water that he'd sat down in front of him. The big stallion drank greedily.

Jack then turned to Dallie, picking her up. "Well, little lady have we decided on a name for this big fella?" When Dallie shrugged, he went on. "What about Dallie's Close Call?" He laughed.

He said it as a joke, but Natalie thought it had a nice ring to it and she told him so.

"Hey Jack, that's not half bad," she replied as he walked up to the fence she was propped on.

"You really think so?" He looked at her like she was crazy.

"Absolutely! Dallie's Close Call. What do you think, hon?"

"I like it, Mommy." Dallie giggled.

"Yeah, me too," David chimed in. "Come on, Dallie. Let's reward him," he said making a move to come inside the gate and grabbed an apple from the top of a barrel that sat by the fence. Close Call was indulging himself on the grass that grew beyond the fence and wasn't paying them any mind. Jack sat Dallie down and approached Natalie; Dallie ran to help her grandfather.

Jack came close enough to where he could whisper to Natalie, propping his chin to rest on the top of the fence post where hers had been seconds before. His face was so close to hers that it made her heart flutter.

"After what I saw this morning I think I want to ask you to dinner. You know maybe some wining, some dining." His sexy green eyes sparkled.

"Why, what makes you think you could get any luckier in one day?" She cocked her brow at him as she smiled.

Jack gave her a big laugh showing off his pearly whites. "Go to dinner with me, Nat. Maybe we can catch a movie afterwards. What do you say?"

She smiled into his sexy green eyes. "Sure, Jack. I'd love to go out with you."

"Is tonight okay for you?"

"I don't think I have anything scheduled." She looked up thought-fully, baiting him.

"Great. Let's go… say… around… six?"

"Sounds good!"

"Okay, don't stiff me now," he warned with a wink.

She laughed. "I wouldn't dream of it."

He took her hand and kissed it before he turned his attention back to Dallie and David. Natalie stepped off the fence and headed back to the house to gather her thoughts.

Her heart swelled to bursting… she had a date with Jack Kinsen.

~

"*J*ack!" David called to him. He was feeding an apple to the horse as Dallie watched in glee.

"Yeah?" Jack's head was swimming, his heart was fluttering. Natalie had just accepted his request to go to dinner with him. He was blown away.

"Don't mind an old man being bold, but you and my daughter seem to be hitting it off pretty well I see." His words took Jack off guard and he was speechless for a few minutes then answered as best he could. He tried to answer cautiously. After all, he was talking about his boss's daughter here.

"Well, yes sir, I think that we are." He tucked his hands down into his jeans pockets and shuffled his foot in the dirt. *Oh, boy. Here it comes!*

"Well then, son. Why don't you ask her out to dinner one night?"

Once again Jack was blown away. David was giving his permission, no, his blessing for Jack to take Natalie out on a date. *Well, I'll be damned.* He thought. "Of course, sir, that is if you don't think that it's too soon."

"Nah, she needs to get out of the house for a while and spend some time with another adult. Take her somewhere nice, will ya?" David remarked, smiling as he handed Jack the lead rope. "I'm callin' it a day, gotta go into town to talk to a man about a load of horses he wants trained for some movie." He didn't give Jack time to respond as he headed out the gate.

Jack couldn't believe what he'd just heard. David was encouraging him to date Natalie. *Man, he must trust me.* That had to be it. David knew the life Jack had lived before coming to the ranch; he'd been wild, reckless, a complete womanizer. But David also knew that Jack had changed and was no longer the young, irresponsible man he'd once been.

He tried to focus back on the task at hand, but his mind kept drifting back to Natalie. He couldn't get the sight of her naked torso out of his head. Her slender belly and curvy hips… her breasts were more beautiful than he could have ever imagined. They were large and round and creamy with pink tips. He thought about how soft her skin had looked and had longed to touch it, to caress her and test her fullness. He cursed himself for getting worked up over her; getting all hot and bothered was not a comfortable way to spend the better part of his work day.

At lunch, he couldn't keep his eyes off Natalie. He would have an entire night just the two of them, and he couldn't control his excitement. He kept watching her eat and winking at her when no one was looking. When she left to go into the kitchen, he followed her. He just had to kiss her before he burst with anticipation.

She was getting something out of the fridge and didn't notice that he had come in right behind her. When she turned around, she jumped, startled.

"Jack!" she said, holding her chest. He just smiled. "Oh you think your funny huh, Mr. Kinsen? If you would have given me a heart attack, you'd have had to miss your date."

"I don't think I could handle that." He laughed and pulled her into him, running his fingers through her beautiful long locks loving the feel of her silky hair against his rough skin. "Natalie, I don't think I can make it through the rest of the day without kissing you," he confessed, bending his head down to hers.

"Well, I guess I should go ahead and tell you that I don't kiss on the first date," she replied, smiling even as she tilted her head up to meet his. He leaned forward anticipating the kiss before he ever met her lips. Just then the kitchen door swung open.

"Oh excuse me…" It was Corrine, and both Natalie and Jack shot away from each other as if a mortar had gone off.

Corrine grabbed something off the counter, and Jack stepped back, clearing his throat as Natalie shut the fridge door. Corrine looked back at the two of them, her cheeks flushed, and then went out the door. Natalie burst into laughter and Jack just stared at her in bewilderment.

"What about that was so funny?" he demanded to know.

She held her stomach and could not contain her laughter until he bent his head down again to take her lips. This time he hit his mark. Then she stopped laughing.

~

The hands had gone back outside to finish working, leaving Natalie and Corrine to the dishes and the clean up. Natalie was in the kitchen scrubbing away at the pots and pans when Corrine sat down at the small table located in the breakfast nook looking at Natalie in deep thought.

"I didn't realize that you and Jack…were…together," Corrine said, her cheeks tinted pink. Natalie smiled at her mother's embarrassment. She thought it was humorous that her mother thought that her and Jack were *together*.

"Well, we aren't actually together. We're having our first date tonight."

"Oh? Well…that's nice, but don't you think it's a little too early to be sleeping with him?" Natalie's hands stalled in the soapy water.

"Mother? I am *not* sleeping with him! We were just kissing for Pete's sake."

"Well that was quite an intimate embrace, don't you think?" Her mother's eyes were dark as if she didn't really believe her daughter's comment.

"Mother! I can not believe that you would honestly think I would sleep with a man I've only known for what… a week and a half now!" She looked over at her mother who was grinning like the Cheshire cat. "What is so funny, may I ask?"

"I knew I'd get it out of you one way or another," Corrine boasted. Natalie just stood with her wet hands on her hips and frowned at her mother. "I always wanted Jack for my son-in-law," she said, a smile lining her lips; a far away look gleamed in her eyes.

Natalie just rolled her eyes and continued to wash the dishes.

"I knew something was going on between the two of you! It's the way you look at each other." Natalie was too embarrassed to speak so Corrine continued, "So, where is he taking you?" She came over to the sink next to her then and began drying the dishes Natalie had rinsed.

"I don't know yet. He didn't say."

"Well, I don't know about you, but I am just tickled pink about all this. Jack is a wonderful man, Natalie, and I am so glad that you two are togeth…excuse me, dating." She corrected herself.

"Well, I'm glad you're happy, mother." Natalie smiled at her. Corrine smiled back.

Later that day, Natalie headed back down to the corral to see the progress her daughter and Jack were making. Jack was teaching her pressure and release.

When she got to the corral in front of the barn, she noticed that the two of the other hands along with her father were in one of the pastures lugging two horses behind them.

"What's going on down there?" Natalie asked Jack.

"Oh, they've been pairing the two the last couple of weeks to breed natural cover."

"A little late in the season, isn't it?" Natalie knew that breeding season for horses was usually in spring and summer months, occasionally early fall.

"Well, we've had several unsuccessful attempts. The vet's been in and out, the mare's had to take some medications, just bad timing really....I think you're father's ready to go to AI if they don't get them to copulate soon," Jack said, turning his attention back to the stallion he and Dallie were training.

"It's a better idea anyway, lessens the risk for injury...Well, uh, Jack, don't you think Dallie needs a break," Natalie rambled as she watched the stud taking increasing interest in the mare's backside. Jack looked up at her in confusion. "I just don't think she really should witness the...the uh, pairing. It's a little ...graphic."

"It's just natural, Nat," he said, looking over at her. "Besides, she's too young to know what's going on."

"I know what's going on, Jack. I know the differences between girls and boys and it's the same with animals too. Boys have a penis and girls have a vagina. And I know how babies are born too and that's what they are doing, the horses are going to make a baby," Dallie stated matter-of-factly.

Jack looked at Dallie, his eyes wide in shock. "Well, we... can't...get much by her...now can we?" He blushed and smiled at Dallie who was sitting on Close Call, reigns in her hands then looked over at Natalie who was propped on the fence. "I think we are almost ready to take him for a spin."

"Really?" Natalie asked, surprised. "Will he let anyone close to him besides her?"

"No, but it's a start," Jack said confidently, smiling up at Natalie who stood on the fence. She smiled back at him, and they both looked at each other for several minutes, lost in each other's eyes, pleased with the accomplishment.

Then the neighs from the coupling horses pierced the sky. Natalie turned to see the mare bombarded by the stallion. He had attempted to jump her back and was whinnying and rearing up as the hands assisted him to her. The female wanting no part of the mating ritual, fought to free herself from the stud, but was tied off and couldn't evade him. Natalie turned to Jack.

"Mommy, he's hurting her," Dallie cried, staring at the horses, her innocent eyes taking in the full view of it all.

"Jack!" Natalie pleaded with him to get her off of the horse and out of view of the mating pair; he took the hint.

"C'mon Dallie, let's take a break." He grabbed her from atop of Call's saddle and brought her to the ground, tearing her eyes from the scene before her.

"Mommy, he was hurting her. Make him stop!" Dallie said as she was passed from Jack to her mother, keeping her eyes on the stallion and mare in the other pasture the whole time.

Natalie didn't know what to say. She could say a lot of things, but they wouldn't make sense to her four-year old daughter.

"It's okay baby, Paw-Paw will handle it okay? Let's go into the office for a bit." Natalie had broken into a full run as she headed for the barn.

"But Mommy..." she trailed off as they entered the door of her father's office.

David Butler's plaques and awards hung on the walls of the small air-conditioned room. His cherry wood desk was littered with papers and his computer sat idle. An old metal filing cabinet sat on one wall and a bookshelf full of equestrian resources sat on the other. The walls themselves had been repainted since the last time Natalie had been home; they were a soft tan color. The navy sofa that had always been there remained and an entertainment center sat adjacent from it on the opposite wall with a large TV in the center of it. Natalie opened the Coke machine beside the door and pulled out a Dr. Pepper for Dallie who sipped at it obligingly. She pulled out a Diet Coke for herself and stopped in front of the window A/C. The air felt good against Natalie's sweat stained shirt and she sat Dallie's soda down on the coffee table when she passed it to her. Then her daughter sat on the sofa looking at the floor.

"Mommy?" she asked after a long silence.

"Yes, Dallie?" Nat answered, brushing her hand through Dallie's sweaty blonde curls as she sat down beside her.

"That horse was hurting that other one like Daddy hurt me."

Natalie sighed. They'd had conversations like this before. She should say nothing, but she did. "No, Dallie. Look at me. Your father had no right to do what he did to you. But one day you'll be married and...The horses are only doing what is natural, baby. They're animals. We aren't. All animals mate and so do humans. That is what they were doing. But in humans, it's not like that; it isn't supposed to be violent like that. It's..." She could say no more, she'd said too much already.

"So I will do that one day?" Dallie had understood Natalie all too well.

"Yes," Natalie said after a moment, "that is how *you* were made. Just like all babies are. But yes, you will do that some day when you are married in order to have children of your own."

"So, why did Daddy do those things to *me*?" She looked up at Natalie, tears in her eyes.

"Because he is sick baby, sick in his head. Other fathers, *normal* fathers, don't do things like that to their daughters. No one is supposed to touch you in your private places unless someone is bathing you. If anyone ever touches you like your father did, you tell me and don't keep it a secret like you did. It's okay to hug someone like we hug or to kiss someone like you kiss Jack on the cheek, but no one should ever touch you in your private places. Do you under-stand me?" Natalie asked, angling her daughter's face up and Dallie nodded that she did.

"So only mommies and daddies do what the horses were doing?" she asked.

Well, it was a little more complicated than that, but Dallie got the just of it, "That's right. Mommies and daddies who love each other very much do that. It's a special thing between a mommy and a daddy," Natalie replied encouragingly.

Jack came in about that time and sat down beside Natalie. He took the can of Diet Coke that she offered him, wrinkled his nose at it but then drank from it greedily. He chugged it dry then bent the can in his hand, giving a sigh of contentment. Dallie then looked up at Jack.

"Jack, are you and Mommy going to do what the horses did?"

"What?" He turned to look at Dallie, his eyes wide.

"Are you going to mate, like the horses did? You're a boy and she is a girl!" she stated matter-of-factly.

Jack looked at Natalie then back to Dallie. "Why on earth would you ask me a question like that?"

"Well, I saw you kissing Mommy last night by the fence. Does that mean that you are going to mate with her and have babies?"

Jack looked as if he'd been hit in the crotch. Natalie tried her best not to smile. Jack was on his own on this one, Natalie decided.

"Well, uh, Dallie, only if your mother and I ... only, uh, if we…get married." He tried to sound respectful, but Natalie knew better. She stifled a laugh.

"So are you gonna ask her to marry you?" Stars shown in Dallie's eyes as a smile crossed her lips.

With that, both Natalie and Dallie looked at Jack. Natalie's face contorted in a laugh that she couldn't let out. Jack was backed into a corner.

But he smiled and replied, "I'll tell you what little lady, let me take her out tonight first, and I'll tell you how it goes okay?"

"You are going to take her out? Like on a date?" Dallie grinned like it was Christmas morning.

Her curiosity amused Natalie and it seemed to do Jack the same way.

"How do you know what a date is?" he asked.

"'Cause me and Grandma watch *Days of Our Lives* at lunchtime when y'all are working."

"Well well, I guess I really can't get *anything* past you," he stated and tickled her.

"What will you wear, Mommy?" Dallie looked over at her mother, excitement in her eyes. If Natalie didn't know any better she would think that Dallie was more excited about this date of hers than she was… but she knew better.

"Well, I don't know yet. I was thinking maybe—"

"A skirt or a dress?" Dallie chimed in.

"Oh, yes, a skirt would be great," Jack added his two cents in, shining his green eyes at Natalie.

"We'll just have to see." She looked at Jack with snake eyes daring him to dispute her. He bowed his head like a scolded puppy, but looked at her with pleading eyes. She couldn't help but laugh.

⁓

*C*orrine sat in a rocking chair on the back porch and watched her granddaughter and Jack with Close Call. Natalie came up then and handed Jack a cold glass of water as he approached the fence. Dallie sat on her horse and stroked at his neck, completely oblivious to the couple in front of her ogling each other. Corrine had noticed the growing connection between her daughter and Jack and it made her smile. They were giggly and flirty like teenagers, like her and David had once been. Natalie looked happy for the first time in a long time and Corrine's heart burst with joy. Her daughter deserved this man and his love; she deserved to be able to fix her life and Dallie's. Jack had been like a son to her and David when all hope seemed gone and they were about to lose the ranch. He'd saved them

SHANNA SWENSON

from bankruptcy! He was their knight in shining armor and now it looked like he was becoming Natalie's as well.

"Boy, have I got some good news for you…" David boomed as he came to sit down next to her, pulling off his hat and wiping the sweat from his brow.

"What is it?" She yearned for good news.

"Well, we got the contract deal! We're getting three Tennessee Walkers to train for that movie in Houston. You know the one I told you about? Some movie about horses… Anyway, its big bucks and we got about 6 weeks. We're training with the crew too, so there will be a good bunch of them here off and on."

"Oh, honey! That's great." She reached over and patted his arm.

"I know. I'm relieved. I'll be going with them when they are shooting, so I thought maybe you might wanna go with me. I know how you love Houston." She nodded that she would. "They are also working with Thomason Farms too, so Bill will be helping me out."

"Well, that's wonderful!" she exclaimed, overjoyed; they really needed that deal for their nest egg.

He looked over at her and smiled. "You get more beautiful each day, you know that? I still can't believe I get to wake up to you each morning."

"Ha, I get *a new wrinkle* with each day…What are you wanting anyway?"

He had always been charming, but she wasn't sure he was being completely earnest. "What? I have to have a reason to give my wife a compliment? I mean it, woman, every word of it. I love you more than anything in this world." He leaned over to her and kissed her soundly on the lips.

"I think you've been around Natalie and Jack recently…" she trailed off, knowing that she wasn't the only one who'd noticed the way he and Natalie were looking at one another lately.

"Well, it *is* somewhat contagious, you know." He paused and smiled over at her, a twinkle gleaming in his eye. "I told him to take her out…"

114

"You did?" So *he* had been the spark to light Jack's fire.

"I sure did, I think he was hesitating because of you and me. 'Course Jack asked me if I thought it was too soon. But I don't think it is, do you?"

Corrine thought for a second then shook her head. "No, I don't."

"Yeah, that's what I thought. She really needs to get out of here for a while, get away and just have a little fun. It's been a while since she had any fun…"

"Well, how about we go have a little fun?" She might have wrinkles, but she wasn't too old to have a little fun herself.

"Baby, I like your thinking!"

CHAPTER 6

By four that afternoon, Jack was more than ready for his hot date with Natalie. He was also ready to get in out of the scorching heat. The air was so dry that it was stifling, the sun beat down hotter and hotter on the earth making the ground look like it would sizzle. Dallie was exhausted by three and went inside to lie down, so after he put the horse up and watered him, brushed him down and fed him, Jack called it a day as well. He had a few errands to run in town before his date. He wanted to clean his truck out and buy a new shirt; he wanted to impress Natalie so badly that he ached with it. When he went inside, the window air conditioner gave him goose bumps, but it felt so good that he removed his sweaty work shirt and stood in front of it for several minutes then he walked into the kitchen to get some water. Natalie stood at the sink sipping a glass of the coveted liquid and looked up at him as he came in.

"Want some water?" she asked, extending the glass to him.

"You read my mind." He grinned, taking the glass from her and downing it in one sup then sat it down on the countertop. "How'd you know?" he asked, wiping his mouth on his sweaty shirt.

"You're practically oozing it all out," she said, trailing a tear of sweat as it rolled down his abs. The sensation of her finger on his bare skin sent a different kind of heat radiating to his groin, and he yearned to have her pressed against him. The look he gave her was one of pure lust. She gulped, but stood his challenge and moved her hands up to his face. He reveled in the feel of her soft palms on his stubbly chin and cheeks. She moved her fingers down his neck and chest, tracing his muscles with her fingertips grazed his nipples and pectoral muscles. He could feel his sex pulsing with each movement of her hands. Oh, how he longed for them to be there, touching him. Her fingers continued their descent down his body to his navel, tickling his belly with her fingernails. As her fingertips traced the button of his jeans, he grabbed her wrists and pinned her with his hips to the sink where she stood. She gasped as his stubbly cheek tickled her neck.

"It's my turn now," he grumbled as he nibbled at the skin just below her ear. She let out a soft whimper, which sent a fiery chill all the way down to his erection. His tongue traced a path from her ear to her collarbone, and her skin broke out in goose bumps.

"Oh, Jack..." she gasped in his ear. He moved his hands from her waist to her belly, then up her torso and cupped both of her breasts in his hands. The shirt she wore was tight and he could feel the fabric of her bra underneath his fingers as he squeezed her gently, admiring her firmness. She moaned in pleasure. He pressed his arousal into her belly, letting her feel his need for her then as he kissed her lips longingly and teased her nipples with his thumbs, wishing they were exposed to him. She moved her hips against his hard arousal, and he felt as if he would die. He took her lips once again before finally pulling away from her, not quite ending his torture. She looked at him wantonly, gasping for air, her chest heaving from his loving of her skin. Her hair was tousled and sexy as all get out and he wanted to scoop her up, take her upstairs, and make her his.

"You're killing me, darlin'," he breathed out heavily.

"Well, then I'd better stop. I would like to at least have my date with you before I kill you..." She smiled up at him and cocked her eyebrow. There was a challenge in her eye that he hadn't noticed before, and he smiled, pulling her head to his again as he made love to her mouth with his tongue.

"I can't wait to have you all to myself tonight." The promise in his voice was unmistakable as he pulled back.

She just smiled at him and walked away. Maybe she *was* starting to trust him after all, he thought.

～

"*What* on earth is wrong with me?" Natalie asked herself while she shampooed her hair in the shower. She had practically thrown herself on Jack. Just last night she'd cried herself to sleep in his arms. Was she getting braver or was she just plain crazy? She knew better, yet some invisible force drove her to him. She couldn't explain it, when she was around him her body wasn't her own, but one of a seductress Hell bent on going to bed with a man she'd known for only a week and a half. It was as if a magnet pulled her to him, and she could not control herself in his presence. This game of hers was danger and she knew it, but for the life of her, she would not heed the warning. She wanted him, oh did she want him, but everything inside her head screamed at her to get a grip on herself. Had she learned nothing from her past? He couldn't be trusted, but she trusted him. He'd done nothing to her or Dallie for her to doubt him. He'd been nothing but kind to her. But she had to control herself or end up hurt when it was all over. Casual sex never promised anything but pain that she knew for a fact. Jack didn't love her, so where would that leave her when he'd lived out his fantasies?

She might fear having sex with him, but she was quite excited about her date with him, especially since she knew he would be a complete gentleman. It had been a long time since she'd gone out, with girlfriends even, and she felt giddy, like a child.

She'd decided to shower again before her date. The hot October day had left her sweaty and gritty, and she didn't want to go out with Jack feeling so disheveled. She finished soaping up and was just stepping out of the shower when Dallie popped in.

"Hi, Mommy!" her little angel said.

"Jeez, Dallie, you scared me…"

"Sorry, I just wanted to tell you a secret."

"Ok." She looked at her daughter with an amusing smile on her face.

"Jack's here and he has a surprise for you." She had the most mischievous look on her cherubic little face while she folded her arms behind her back.

"Oh, really?" Natalie dried herself off with the towel she'd laid out.

"Yup, and he told me not to tell you what it was."

"Then why did you even mention it, you stinker?" Natalie asked, cocking her eyebrow at Dallie.

Dallie just shrugged, "What are you wearing tonight, Mommy?"

"I'm not sure yet…did Jack put you up to asking me that question?"

"No… Can I help you?" Excitement sparkled in her little blue eyes.

Natalie smiled at her. "Sure you can."

When she was finished drying off, she applied lotion to her skin that Dallie said smelled like her Grandma's flower garden. She then wrapped the towel around herself, brushed her teeth, and ran into the guestroom to put on her panties and bra. Although she knew Jack wouldn't see them, she still picked her skimpiest black set. Dallie helped her pick out her makeup and curl her hair. They were right in the middle of dolling her up when Nat heard Jack come upstairs. Dallie ran out of the door to meet him.

"Don't come in," Dallie stated. "Mommy isn't decent."

Her reply made Natalie laugh. Jack laughed as well and said he would definitely knock before entering as he went into the bathroom. When Dallie came back in, Natalie smiled at her.

"Where did you hear that phrase, angel?" Nat asked, putting her blush on.

Dallie just stood there watching her. "From Grandma."

Natalie shook her head and applied some lipstick to her lips then Dallie helped her style her hair. When they were done, she looked at Dallie to judge the finished product.

"Well, what do you think, kiddo?"

"Wow, Mommy, you look like a princess," she giggled.

Natalie looked in the full-length mirror…and she did indeed look like a princess. She'd chosen honey brown and gold for her eyes to give herself an exotic look, and she'd curled her hair in ringlets, which framed her face rather well. Now, she just needed an outfit and some diamond studs for her ears.

She had the perfect outfit in mind, but hoped it wasn't too dressy for whatever place Jack was taking her. She pulled the silky, lacy two-piece black dress from the closet and held it out. It was a one shoulder Sophia Bradley dress. It was a little over knee length with a slit on one side that went up to mid-thigh, layers of silk gathered to the slit. The dress slimmed her and accentuated her curves. She decided it would be perfect for the evening as well as leave something to the imagination. Jack was going to love it. She slipped on both pieces of the dress, adjusted her bra strap to make it convertible and slid into her strappy heels.

Dallie's eyes lit up. "Wow, you're so pretty, Mommy. Jack is going to be so surprised when he sees you."

You can say that again, Natalie thought silently and smiled to herself as she sprayed on a soft floral perfume.

～

*J*ack was as nervous as a cat on a hot tin roof. He'd showered quickly and left his hair still damp as he slapped some gel on it. He was dressed in a new outfit and tented himself in the cologne he'd bought at the mall that day.

He'd opted for a tighter pair of black Wranglers than his usual looser fitting pair, brand new black Roper boots, and a silver silk button-down collar shirt. He also had a black Resistol cowboy hat in the truck for later. He looked the part of a modern day cowboy, but he felt like he was sixteen again on his first date. He smelled like a million bucks, and he hoped and prayed that Natalie would be impressed with his efforts. He took a deep breath as he knocked on the guest bedroom door. Dallie shyly opened the door up, and Jack felt his heart stop as his eyes fell on Natalie.

"My God, you... look...amazing!" he stuttered as he walked up to her and took her hand in his, kissing the top of it. He couldn't believe how gorgeous she looked tonight. Her hair dropped in curls like ribbons around her head, her silk and lace black dress was tight across her chest limiting him from seeing her cleavage, but it slit up her leg to expose her slender thigh. He secretly wondered what she had underneath it...that thought would drive him crazy before the night was over.

She gulped and he saw that he wasn't the only one that was nervous about tonight.

"Well, I wore this dress to a summer party my office had one evening. I just hope it isn't too flashy for the place we're going..."

"No, no, it's incredible. You look perfect."

"You don't look too bad yourself, cowboy. I love the shirt." She looked him up and down in that seductive little gaze of hers, touching his collar.

He shivered. "Thanks."

They stood speechless for another several moments, gazing into each other's eyes. Then Jack smiled as Dallie came up to them, welcoming the interruption since his heart felt like it would explode.

"Wanna show Mommy your surprise, Jack?" she asked, grabbing at Jack's hand.

"Oh, yes, of course." He told his date to stay put and walked out of the room. He returned with a bouquet of yellow roses wrapped in paper and handed them over to Natalie. "A yellow rose is a promise of a new beginning... and friendship," he stated softly.

A gentle smile crossed her lips as she looked upon the roses in admiration. When she looked up at him he could see tears glistening in her eyes. She lowered her head suddenly then looked back up at him. "Jack, this means a lot to me." She pulled him toward her and softly kissed his lips, then looked up into his eyes. "Thank you." He simply nodded. Her understanding of his reasoning touched him deeply.

She pulled away from Jack's embrace and took his hand so they could walk downstairs. Dallie followed and when they approached the door, Natalie turned to Dallie and wrapped her arms around her.

"Now you be a good girl for Grandma and Paw-Paw, okay. And do as you're told... and go to bed at 8:00 okay?"

"Yes, Mommy. Have fun." She looked slightly disappointed that her mother was getting to go out and she wasn't, but Jack promised her she could go the next time. That put a smile on her little face.

Just then, Corrine came in as if on cue and Natalie handed the roses over to her.

"I got this child, now y'all go and have fun and don't worry about a thing," she said and walked up to Dallie, putting her hands on her shoulders.

"Ok," Natalie said, "I won't. Be good Dallie." She repeated again looking over at Dallie, who was taking her Grandmothers hand, her other hand waving goodbye.

"She'll be fine with us, honey. You two go and have fun tonight. Me and Dallie are going to bake some cookies," Corrine said as Dallie's face lit up like a Christmas tree. "But not before we eat a good supper."

With that Dallie's smile faded and Jack and Natalie laughed as they walked out the door and shut it behind them.

Jack walked her slowly to his truck, which he'd washed up and cleaned out. He had to lift her into the cab when her heels got caught on his nerf bar. He laughed, but she didn't think it was too funny.

As they drove along down the road, he looked over at her. She looked so amazing tonight. That dress of hers was just plain sexy as Hell.

"Boy this seems familiar," he said, smiling.

"Oh, no it doesn't. My car isn't stuck on the side of the road forcing me to be riding with a complete stranger." Jack laughed heartily at that.

"Well, I'm not a *complete* stranger anymore, now am I?" He winked at her. She lifted a brow at him and he silenced.

"I haven't left Dallie alone in a really long time," Natalie said, turning and looking back out of the truck's back window after a few minutes.

"Oh, I know, but don't worry. I'm sure Dallie and your mom will have a great time," Jack said, patting her thigh reassuringly.

She took his hand and held it in hers. She smiled over at him and his heart did a flip flop. He really couldn't believe his luck; he was out on a date with Natalie Butler Cameron. How lucky did he feel? Like the luckiest guy in the world.

"Thank you for my roses. That was so thoughtful, Jack. It really touched me that you thought of something symbolic like that."

"Well, I just wanted you to know how I feel about you." It surprised him that his simple gesture had affected her so.

Once again she smiled, but there was something new to it, admiration, appreciation, he couldn't quit place his finger on it, but he loved the way she was looking at him and he smiled back at her.

He had refused to tell her where they were going, so when they finally pulled up to a fancy Italian restaurant outside of town she was thrilled.

"Ooh, I love Italian," she said delighted. "I can't even remember the last time I ate it."

"Really?" he sighed in relief. "I was hoping that you did." He turned the truck off and reached into his glove compartment. "Oh, I, uh, I forgot to give you this." He placed a big silver box in her hand and she looked at it shocked.

"Jack, what is this? You bought me something *else*?"

"Yeah, why don't you open it and see what's in it?" He smiled mischievously as she opened the box. Her mouth dropped and tears flooded her eyes as she looked up at him.

"Jack! This is gorgeous. Where did you—? Oh my God!" Her hands trembled as she pulled the diamond collar necklace out of the box. It was a white gold choker interweaved with endless rows of pave-set diamonds. She looked up at him. "I can't believe that you bought me this, Jack. This is—this is a *really* expensive piece of jewelry." He took the chain from her hands and placed it around her neck, latching it in the back.

"It's just a necklace."

"Just a necklace? This is a gift of incredible proportion." She touched it as if she couldn't believe it was actually there around her neck.

"An incredible gift for an incredible woman."

"An incredibly *expensive* gift! I can't accept this..." she said, shaking her head.

"Nonsense! You deserve this necklace." He touched it and traced the rows of diamonds with his finger admiring the look of it on her skin.

"Jack, I really can't—"

"Shh," he hushed her with a finger to her lips then replaced his finger with his lips. He kissed her softly at first then deepened the kiss. She threw her hands around his neck and kissed him back. Then he pulled back.

"Thank you, really, I—I've never been given anything as nice as this before," she said. Jack found that quite hard to believe.

"You're welcome, darlin'." He smiled, happy for her enjoyment of his gift.

"But don't think for one minute that you can buy your way into my pants..." Her smile was one of mischief.

"I wouldn't dream of taking advantage of you." He took her hand and kissed the back of it gently. "But if I wanted to get into that dress, there wouldn't be a *thing* you could do to stop me…" This time he was the one with a playful grin. He grabbed his keys and got out of the truck, came around to her side and opened the door.

"I could really get used to being treated like this", she said as he pulled her into him and out of the truck. Her body molded to his as he sat her on the ground.

"So could I," he said, rubbing her arm lightly and giving her a passionate glance.

~

*T*hey walked hand in hand to the entrance of the large brick and stone front restaurant. A neon sign laced with red and green labeled it Courtyard of Tuscany. It looked wholly formal and Natalie was glad she'd worn her expensive black dress. She smiled up at Jack as he opened the door for her. A host dressed in coat and tie greeted them, Jack rattled off that he had a reservation. The man smiled and told them to follow him. Natalie was impressed at his preparation for their date. He had really tried to make this an amazing evening for her and she was truly touched by his consideration.

The host led them through the restaurant on carpets of beautiful shades of maroon and hunter green. Large tapestries and oil paintings of Tuscan landscapes adorned the red brick walls, exquisite wine displays appeared on every corner. The dining room was a labyrinth of tables and booths; open in some parts and private in others. The smell of garlic and herbs lingered in the air and the voice of Frank Sinatra echoed through the dining room.

The host led them out large French doors to the cobblestone courtyard. Beautiful orchids and hydrangeas of all colors lined the walkways of the garden. He led them to a secluded table shaded by peach trees next to a large bubbling water fountain. It was beautiful and Natalie was pleased that Jack had reserved this specific place for them. Jack thanked the host and pulled Natalie's chair out for her.

She thanked him and sat down, noticing her chair was nice and comfortable. She also noticed that for the abundance of luxury, all of the guests were dressed casually and not in the formal attire she'd expected when she'd walked through the door. She was pondering this as Jack's wondering gaze met hers.

"Wow, Jack, this place is great," she said as she took in the over-sized menu before her, the silk tablecloth and red rose centerpiece. Their dinnerware had been laid out along with two large wine glasses.

"Well, it's pretty new. I've never eaten here myself, but I heard they had the best Italian food this side of the Mississippi," he said, looking around as he took his seat next to her.

"It's perfect, I love it."

"Good, I can take a breather now," he said with a sigh of relief opening up the large menu.

They sat quietly then perusing the menu and its large variety of appetizers, salads, entrees and rotisserie meats. Just then, a server approached them with a bottle of wine. He introduced himself and asked if they wanted to try a sample of the wine he'd brought to the table. They both obliged, then Jack declined the offered glass and ordered a bottle of a familiar Pinot Noir that he picked from the wine list.

"How did you know I was a fan of Pinot?" Nat asked.

"I didn't. I was just hoping for the best," Jack laughed.

When the server returned with the bottle, they both placed their orders and waited for their salads.

"If I forget to tell you Jack, I had a great time tonight," Natalie said, looking into his eyes.

"But, the night isn't over yet, my dear..." He smiled his charming devil of a smile.

Natalie took in Jack's appearance, looking deeper at the man she was starting to lose herself to. He'd definitely bought a new outfit for the occasion. His shirt was stylish and modern with a hint of formality to it. Only he could pull off a shirt like that with a pair of black jeans and boots. His hair was neat and lightly spiked with gel, she observed, and for once, she could see it without a cowboy hat on top of it. She'd never really noticed it before. It was a chestnut brown color with subtle highlights of golden blonde that she assumed came from working in the sun all day, they weren't dimensioned enough to be professionally done. His sexy emerald eyes seemed to sparkle in the setting sun, and his face was shaved and shiny and she reached out and touched it because she couldn't seem to resist.

Jack palmed the hand cupping his cheek with his own. His smile was one of a man genuinely pleased. He brought her hand to his lips and gently kissed each finger which the utmost tenderness. The intimacy of this act was so profound that the sexuality of it nearly undid Natalie. She gasped softly as his head lowered toward hers. She could feel his hot breath on her lips. He smelled so incredibly sexy...

Someone loudly cleared their throat and Natalie looked up to see their waiter, salads in hands, impatiently looking down at them. They split apart and Jack mumbled an apology as the waiter sat their salads down in front of them. Natalie felt her cheeks flush as she folded her napkin in her lap and began to dig into her salad with her fork. The salad looked lovely; a mix of greens, veggies, and cheeses. She noticed that she was starving as she added the dressing and began stirring her salad. She looked over at Jack who looked embarrassed as well and laughed at him.

"What?" he asked as he put a bite of salad in his mouth.

"That's never happened to me before," she said still laughing.

"Yeah well, that makes two of us!"

They ate their salads, munching on some bread that the server had brought to the table as well.

"Mom and I are going to clean out Nathan's old room and make Dallie a bedroom. I think she will like having her own room," Natalie announced.

"Yeah I think she would," Jack agreed.

"She's seems so happy at the ranch."

"Has she always loved animals?" he asked.

"Always," Natalie exclaimed. "I remember the first time I took her to the zoo, you ought to have seen her face..." Jack smiled at her recollection.

"She was so excited today when the horse responded to all of her commands," Jack said. "It made her day. She worked so hard with him, showed such determination. She's something else! I swear. I've never seen anyone with a gift like the one she has with that horse. It's the most incredible thing I've ever seen." He shook his head in wonder.

"Yes, well, this is the most interaction she's had with animals in her whole life. I blame myself for that..." she trailed off and he didn't ask why, which was just as well.

When their meals arrived, they ate not only their own food but each other's as well. Handmade cheese ravioli with a porcini mushroom cream sauce for Natalie and pappardelle pasta with veal bolognese for Jack. Natalie boxed half of hers to save room for dessert.

"Yeah, go figure! I should have known you would have a sweet tooth just like your mom does. I swear I've gained ten pounds since I started living with your parents. We have dessert after every meal," Jack grumbled. "You can tell I love a good dessert!" he said, patting his belly. That was a joke and a half. Natalie couldn't fathom where he hid it because his body showed no signs of excess fat of any kind, what she'd seen of it anyway.

"So what should we get?" she asked. "The Tiramisu or the Crème Brulee with a caramel center?"

He'd scooted his chair right next to her and put his arm around her as he looked at the selections. "Let's do the Crème Brulee."

"Sounds good, huh?" she replied.

As the server came forward, Natalie ordered the dessert and handed the menu to the waiter. When the dessert arrived and Natalie dug in, she was all too aware of Jack's eyes on her. She dared a glance in his direction, and caught him smiling at her. It wasn't just any grin; it was playful and sexual in nature. His arm was propped up on the top of his chair and he was observing her lips as she licked the spoon clean.

"What?" Natalie demanded to know why he was smiling at her as if she were the butt of a private joke.

"Oh, nothing," Jack replied, fire danced in his eyes. "The way you eat that dessert… it just has to be the sexiest thing I've ever seen you do."

"Well," Natalie said, defending herself. "It's good! Here. Have a bite." She didn't give him a second to disagree before grabbing a hefty spoonful and putting it to his lips. She gently placed it in his mouth, and then slowly, deliberately pulled it away from his closed lips. His eyes held a hint of challenge. "See, I told you."

"I think I'd rather watch you eat it," he said, giving her a wink. With that she laughed.

"Jack, this place really is great. Thank you."

"I'm sure it's not as grand as some places Chicago has, but I'm glad you're enjoying yourself, honey." He draped his arm around the shoulder of hers that was bare and began stroking it. "Natalie, have I told you how absolutely amazing you look tonight?"

She glanced over at him as she finished her dessert, putting her spoon down. His eyes held so much sincerity that she cupped his cheek in the palm of her hand. "Yes, Jack, I do believe you have."

"Well, let me say it again. Natalie, you look absolutely amazing." He pulled her closer, for a gentle kiss on the lips.

"Well, you dress up pretty good yourself, Mr. Kinsen."

"Now, I don't know about you but, I've had enough of this fancy stuff. Let's go have some fun… Jack style."

Natalie laughed a hearty laugh. "Now what exactly is Jack's style fun?" she asked, cocking her eyebrow at him.

"Oh, you'll see darlin', you'll see," he said. He smiled that charming smile of his all the while making Natalie wonder what exactly he had up his sleeve.

"*N*ATALIE!" Her ears were bombarded with familiar cat calls.

"God, you guys *really* don't get out much, do you?" she asked, putting her hands on her hips and shaking her head.

The interior décor of the Rusty Spur was just as she remembered. Loud, raucous country-western music, a platform of old billiard tables, a small bar surrounded by a large, dusty dance floor and a rusty mechanical bull; the same old honky tonk from her younger days. She greeted the handsome former jocks that had been the entertainment of her high school career. They'd surrounded both her and Jack, as he'd lead her to the billiard tables.

"Hi, Buck." She gave the tall, stocky man a big hug. "How's that leg injury doing?" She kissed his scruffy cheek and patted his big biceps.

"Oh, Nat, it's getting better. Pulled hamstring, I'm only gonna be out for a few more weeks…. I'm so glad you're home, Natalie, I've really missed you! Man, you get more beautiful every time I see you." His sincere hug proved his words.

Bobby "Buck" Jenkins was a defensive lineman in the NFL. He played for the San Antonio Stallions, and had the worst reputation for women in the league. Nicknamed Buck for his failure as a bull rider back in his freshman year, the name had always just suited him. At twenty-eight years of age, he was still as handsome as always, probably still single, with a set of baby blue eyes that could captivate a nun. His build was larger than when she'd last seen him about two years ago. He'd grown a mustache and lightened his hair, but he still had the same sweet smile and profound gentleness for his size that made women flock to him.

"You're so sweet," she smiled sheepishly. "You goin' stag tonight?" Natalie asked, winking at him. Buck just blushed to his toes. Natalie knew he was always seen surrounded by leggy blondes.

She was grabbed by the next in line, Keith Turner. Keith had married his high school sweetheart and had two beautiful daughters that Nat had seen on her last visit home.

"Natalie, it's good to see you, hon. How are you doing after all that's happened?" His look was of pure tenderness and it touched Natalie that he cared so much. Keith was also a big man, not quite as tall as Buck, and a little thick around the midsection after almost a decade; his face was softer than Buck's more rugged one. His eyes were a deep green and his blonde hair was a little grayer than she remembered.

"I'm hanging in there. How are Mary Sue and the girls?"

"They're wonderful; we got a boy on the way, due this January!"

"Well, congratulations." Natalie smiled big back into his happy face.

"Yup, ol' man just don't know when to quit, now does he?" Scottie Warden piped in.

Scottie was her second favorite of the three; he'd always kept her laughing when Troy had upset her back in high school. Buck had been her favorite because of his spontaneity and he was a good listener plus Buck was just plain fun.

Scottie looked every one of his twenty-nine years. The cigarettes he'd smoked since he was a kid had defined the crows' feet starting at his eyes. His brown goatee, mustache, and dark gray eyes were just as she'd remembered; his body and build were the same. His only noticeable change was the tattoo of a half-naked cheerleader on his arm. He'd always been a lady-killer with his quick wit and charming smile.

Natalie smiled back into those warm gray eyes. "Scottie, you haven't changed one bit."

"Same charming sonovabitch I used to be." He put his arms around Natalie a little more loving than necessary and looked over at Jack. "Now, Natalie, I got to tell ya! I'm mighty disappointed though. I thought I'd get first dips on you when you got rid of Troy, what are you doing hanging out with this rugged ol' cowpoke?"

Natalie smiled at Jack, who by then had taken a few steps

forward and had greeted Buck and Keith by tipping his cowboy hat, a typical gesture in the west, often replaced by the more common greeting of shaking hands. Natalie regretted not getting to see his hair, but he looked so sexy with the hat on. She smiled then and turned her face into Scottie's ear so only he could hear her. She whispered something profound in his ear, and although she thought no one could ever make him do it, she'd made Scottie Warden turn three shades of red.

"Well, I see," he cleared his throat, "but maybe you'd better take a look at mine before you go and make a final judgement on that." Natalie laughed and swatted him on the arm. He laughed loud and boisterously.

"Hi, Natalie," came a soothing voice she knew all too well.

She moved toward the one face she'd been avoiding, Rick Singleton's. Rick had soft, tender features that hadn't changed since high school. He had the same sky blue eyes and soft smile. Same spiky dark brown hair she remembered running her hands through. The same full lips she could remember kissing. The same lean, muscular frame she remembered lying down upon her, loving her like Troy never had. Looking at Rick now she remembered all the things she'd done with him and felt slightly disappointed in herself for allowing it to happen, even if it had felt good at the time. She hadn't seen him since the affair, would he be awkward or would he pretend like nothing had happened?

It had been a brief affair, lasting only two days. She and Troy had been married five years when it happened. It was right before she'd gotten pregnant with Dallie and she and Troy had been fighting more than normal. If it hadn't been for her being pregnant with Dallie, she would have gotten a divorce, but she'd stayed with Troy for the sake of keeping her family together. How stupid she had been to do *that*! Natalie had felt horribly guilty after the affair happened and not just simply because of her strong moral fiber, she'd used Rick and looking back now she was glad she'd ended it when she did.

"Rick, how've you been?" she asked, walking up to him. He pulled her into his arms for a tight hug. His embrace was loving and tender, maybe a little too tender, as Natalie recalled the way he'd hugged her that day on her loveseat in Chicago. She took a step back as he dropped his arms, although one hand stayed firmly on her back.

"I've been doing really well... I see you're finally free of that sonovabitch you were with." She was rather taken aback by that statement, but smiled nonetheless. Even though, he was boyishly handsome, he wasn't ruggedly sexy like Jack was, not even when she thought of him naked. Come to think of it, none of the guys, not even Buck, were as good-looking as Jack was.

"Yeah, I finally did something good for myself for a change."

"Well, it's good to see you smile again, you look incredible." His eyes darted down her chest and thighs, all the places they had been before and she felt like blushing.

"You too, Rick. You haven't changed at all," she said, smiling up into his face.

"How's your little girl doing, she okay?"

"She's never better, loves it on the ranch with Mom and Dad... and Jack."

At mention of Jack's name, Rick's head shot up, his arm dropped, and he looked over at Jack apologetically. Like a deer caught in the headlights.

"Oh, hi, Jack. How's it going, man? Been a while, huh?" His words came out quickly as he distanced himself from Natalie and walked over to Jack, shaking his hand. Natalie could see that Jack wasn't happy; he was scowling. Buck came up to her then as Rick and Jack engaged in conversation.

"He's never going to get over you, Nat," Buck whispered in her ear.

He knew almost all of her secrets. He was the one person that she'd trusted them with not too long ago. They had kept in touch throughout the years, due to her husband's close proximity with the NFL and Natalie's own desire to keep Buck a close friend as he'd always been. They would visit almost monthly and call one another frequently, until about two years ago upon returning to Chicago from Abundance when Troy had forbid it. He thought that they were having an affair. "He talks about you all the time, rarely dates, never goes home until the bar closes down... it's really kinda pathetic, if you ask me."

"You and me both, Bucko." She smiled up at him.

Scottie hauled her up against him then. "Now, Natalie, I do believe you owe me a round of pool. Last time you were here, you said that you'd play me and you never got around to it. So, let's see what ya got." He pulled her toward the billiard table, tossing a cue stick at her.

"Ok, Scottie. It's been a while, but I think I could still whip you," she said, cocking her eyebrow at him.

~

*J*ack realized that it might be a hard thing to do, keeping one's hands off a beautiful woman like Natalie seeing as it'd been a while since they'd seen her... but by God, she was his date tonight, and he was damned sick of watching her being ogled and groped by them. Well, the three single ones anyway... Damn them! She didn't seemed to notice either, but then again, maybe it was because she'd had almost two glasses of wine at dinner, a beer, a rum runner, and had just finished off two rounds of rum and cokes, doubles. She sure could hold her liquor and she was sure feeling damn good and letting everyone one else know it, including him.

He took another swig of his sixth round of Bud. She sauntered toward him then and patted his arm as her hips swayed against his. She reeked of alcohol and he felt bad about allowing her to make herself so vulnerable, but then again, he had wanted her to have a good time no matter what. If she wanted to drink he couldn't really stop her.

"Ok, Jack, show 'em what you got, baby!" She smacked him on the ass as he headed toward the pool table. They were ahead by only one ball and it was his turn. They'd decided to play teams, Natalie was his teammate and they were two-time winners. Scottie and Keith were surprisingly good competition. Rick and Buck had lost the last game; Buck had said his best ball was played on a football field and Jack believed it because the man sure as Hell sucked at billiards.

Jack was intrigued with his partner, not that that was a big shocker; she was unbelievable even in her semi-drunken stupor. He was surprised by her balance and grace, as well as precision as she made every shot she took. He was also admiring that sexy backside of hers that she kept showing him every time she leaned over the table to take a shot, if only her comrades hadn't been admiring it too… If he made this last shot, knocking in the eight ball, they would win for the third time in a row. Jack had always been competitive, and the alcohol forced him on. He'd always been good at pool too. Right now, he was slightly mad, mad because he wanted Natalie all to himself and he couldn't have that because of her rambunctious crew from high school. He watched Scottie's hand slide around her waist and down her hip for the third time tonight. He lined up his shot, and felt his blood pressure shoot up. Who in the Hell did Scottie think he was touching her like that? Dammit! She was Jack's date.

Jack called the corner right pocket through his gritted teeth, pulled the stick back, taking aim in the center of the cue ball and thrust the cue stick toward the cue ball, smacking the eight ball where it twirled onward to land right into the corner right pocket. He rose in triumph, smiling at Natalie. Walking over to her, he grabbed her around the waist and pulled her into his arms. She smiled up at him, congratulating him with her eyes. He tossed the cue stick aside and planted his hand in her massive wave of curls, bringing her head up to his. He kissed her lips fiercely, possessively moving his tongue into that soft, warm mouth of hers until she melted against him, only then did he pull back.

All four of the men looked at both of them in surprise. Jack's message was all too clear to them. Natalie was aware of his message too. He could see it in her face.

"Natalie, honey, why don't you go to the bar and get me a Bud in a bottle, will ya?" He handed her a $20 bill. Maybe this Bud should be his last. The affects of alcohol were starting to get to him too, he was getting brave and when he got brave he did stupid things.

"Sure, you guys want anything?" she asked, taking the bill from his hand, looking expectantly over at them.

They all stammered no's at her as their faces turned red. He watched her walk away hoping that he hadn't pissed her off. He then turned to the guys, who all at once found something incredibly interesting on the toes of their shoes.

~

*N*atalie walked silently to the bar. Jack was pissed, she could tell. She hadn't known they would be all over her like that. When had Rick and Scottie become so darn touchy-feely? She felt as if they were attacking her. They acted as if she were the only female they'd ever seen or touched before. Jeez! And, she'd been nice about it but man; they couldn't keep their hands to themselves. Those last two drinks had given her a buzz and she was starting to feel a little out of control. Why did it seem so far from the billiard tables to the bar and why did the bar look so fuzzy? It had been so long since she'd had an alcoholic drink; it felt so good not to have to think , or worry about Dallie...to feel so liberating...

She'd been surprised by Jack's possessiveness. It was kinda sexy, flattering, and embarrassing all at the same time. She liked having him around to protect her and take up for her especially since she obviously couldn't do it herself.

She felt a slight jerk in her heart as she turned to look at him making amends with the guys. He must really like her. It made her smile brightly as she turned to the bartender. It was Louise. She'd been there as long as Natalie could remember. She wore a tight mini-skirt and halter top that read "Got Beer?" It was a ridiculous outfit, but it fit Louise, as all her prior shirts had.

"Well, Natalie Butler, how the Hell have you been?"

"I've been doing well, Louise. And yourself?" Natalie smiled into a tanned, wrinkled face that adorned way too much make-up.

"Well, I've been just fine. Sorry to hear about you and Troy. What a surprise that was to hear that he committed those murders," Louise said, shaking her head.

Natalie wanted to change the subject, so she did.

"Can I get an Amaretto sour and a Bud, bottle please?" she asked in her nicest voice.

"You sure can, hon." She turned away to oblige Natalie's order.

"Well, I'll be damned if it ain't Ms. Natalie, after all these years," a deep voice boomed.

Natalie turned her head to see the handsome face of Luther Boyd. She was beginning to feel really disoriented and grabbed the bar to center herself. God, he'd aged and not in a bad way either. He was even more attractive than he'd been back in high school, his face more defined. His smiling brown eyes and dimpled cheeks reminded her of their kiss when they were only thirteen. She'd had a huge crush on him throughout junior high, until she'd met Troy. Looking back now, she wished that crush would have lasted longer, the kiss too.

"Luth, how are you? How are your parents?" She hugged him tightly as his arms went around her waist. He'd gained some muscle she could tell, she didn't remember him being that big. Maybe he worked out. 'Course she didn't remember him being that blurry either...

"I've been better. They sold their chicken houses and moved to Florida. You believe 'at? Big ol' house, right on the beach, it's a doozy."

"Really? Wow! So what are you doing now?"

"Aw, I bought a cattle ranch over in Dade County. About 20

minutes north of here. What in the *world* brought you back to this place?" he asked, adjusting his old black Stetson; she'd never seen him without it. She watched his eyes fall over her and linger at her breasts, making her feel unabashedly sexy.

"I'm staying with my parents for a while…to get back on my feet," she trailed off.

"Well, I sure was sorry to hear about what happened. I wasn't around when it all went down; I moved then went down to help Mom and Dad move. I heard about it from David when I got back. I was completely shocked; I would have never guessed Troy was that kind of a person. Hell! We all played football together." He shook his head. Natalie just nodded her head, which made the fuzzy feeling worse, so she stopped.

"So what's a classy woman like you doing in a bar like this one? Don't you know only hussies hang out here?" His grin was teasing.

"Well, the only hussy I see is that one over there." She pointed over to Annabella Smith, who had moved her way across the dance floor over to Dan Wilson and was rubbing on his chest with her index finger while bringing her thigh up to curve around his leg; she looked like a snake curling around him as if he were a tree branch. Annabella's desperation was pathetic. "God, she hasn't changed one bit."

"Nope, I sure as *Hell* wouldn't touch her now."

Annabella had been Luther's girlfriend at one point and time, until he caught her in bed with another man. The hurt still showed on his face. Annabella was a beautiful young woman with chestnut brown hair laced with platinum blonde, eyes the color of deep whiskey trimmed with long, thick lashes and a curvy yet slender build. Beauty wasted, Natalie thought. She had a desperation for men that had been born from her own hatred of herself. She had no self respect, no moral code, no inhibitions. Annabella'd had a rough childhood, pushed from one foster home to the next. Her innocence had been taken from her at a party at the age of 14 and she was now punishing herself by allowing men to use her at their own will. Luther had given her hope and love at one time, but she'd thrown it back in his face the night he'd found her in bed with a stranger. Sadness filled Natalie's heart as she watched her throwing herself at Dan. Did she really enjoy making a spectacle out of herself? Making herself appear to be nothing more than a sex object? Natalie secretly prayed that Dallie's own traumatic childhood wouldn't drive her to be the same way. No, it wouldn't! Natalie would make certain of that!

Louise sat Natalie's drinks down in front of her and Natalie handed her the $20 bill that Jack had given her. She took a sip of the drink she'd ordered and savored it. She hadn't intended to get inebriated, but she figured if she was on the way, she was going to do it right. She opened her hand to accept the change Louise gave her, dropping a couple bucks for a tip.

"So, you seein' anyone now, Nat?" Luther asked, his eyes twinkling.

Before she could answer, Jack was at her side.

"She's with me tonight, Luth," Jack said, throwing his arm around her waist.

"Well, Jack Kinsen. You should just be kicked out of this town. You asshole! What makes you think you can steal the heart of Abundance's most eligible bachelorette?" Luther asked, looking up at Jack, a phony challenge in his eye.

Natalie intervened then, trying to talk with her hands, "I really don't think I'm exactly labeled the most eligible—"

"Natalie, let me tell you something sweetheart," Luther interrupted, dropping his hand to rest on hers. "I've been trying to get my hands on you since grade school... you know that, as have so many other men in this town." He winked at her then.

Natalie smirked, "Well, I know Scottie and Rick have missed me..." She turned and handed Jack his beer, noticing his lack of interest in it.

"Rick's always had a boner for ya and Scottie, well he loves women... and me, shit, I can't get *away* from y'all ladies quick enough before I get in trouble."

With that they all laughed.

Buck came up at that time, smiling. "Guys, I hate to interrupt, but it sure has been a while since I got to line dance with Ms. Natalie and I really would enjoy it." He beckoned Natalie with his open hand and she took it.

"I would love to, Buck." She kissed Jack on the cheek, dropped the change in his hand, and was all too aware of the surprised look on Luther's face as she walked away with drink in hand.

~

*J*ack watched her walk away, feeling heavy hearted. He watched her disappear in the darkness of the dance floor, her body showered with the colored lights of the disco ball overhead. It took him a moment to notice Luther was trying to talk to him.

"Sorry, Luth..." he trailed off as he took a seat beside his best friend.

"Jack Kinsen, are you in love? Hell, I figured that might be it when I hadn't heard from you in over a week. I figured it was a girl... or you'd gotten whacked by someone or maybe a frickin' UFO, those things are everywhere down here." Luther laughed at his own attempted joke before taking a sip from his Coors bottle.

"Yeah, well..." Jack adjusted his hat trying to seem indifferent, but it didn't work with Luther. He knew Jack too well.

"Ah, don't worry, Buddy," Luther said, patting Jack's back with force. "Natalie loves her friends, but trust me she would never date *any* of us." Jack looked at him questioningly, "She knows us all too well."

Yeah, that wasn't the case with Rick, Jack thought. She'd had an affair with Rick. It had been about four months ago since Rick told him all about it and about thirty seconds after walking in the door that Jack had connected the two.

It'd been a dry night; he'd been craving a beer. He'd ambled into the Rusty Spur alone, sat down at the bar and noticed Rick looking like Hell sipping on a drink. His eyes were as red as his shirt, and he looked like he hadn't shaved in a month. Jack greeted him with caution and as soon as he did, Rick began rambling off like a mad man. He'd had an affair with Natalie, the woman he'd loved for so and so many years. It had been a weekend affair. He'd been on business, and knew her address and went to see her. He'd talked about how she'd ignored his calls after that and how when he finally talked to her that she'd told him she was pregnant with her husband's baby and they were trying to work it out. Rick said he wished that he'd have gotten her pregnant then he could be with her now and blah, blah, blah. He'd said he'd never told anyone and he couldn't get over her even after almost five years.... Jack had just listened to be polite. Natalie had been that woman, and it had made Jack sick to his stomach when he'd finally remembered the conversation and recognized the woman of that conversation as *his* Natalie. He wondered if she still had feelings for Rick, and silently prayed that she didn't.

"Jack?" Luther asked, punching him in the arm.

"Ow, that hurt, you—" Jack trailed off as he looked over at Luther whose patience was growing thin.

"You're acting like a love sick puppy! If you want her, go get her...Jeez."

Luther was right, Jack thought as he watched Buck and Natalie doing the Electric Slide. Despite her tender alcoholic state, she was doing an excellent job keeping the rhythm and a damn sexy job of it too. The song gradually faded into a slow song and Natalie laughed as she was pulled into Buck's embrace. Jack decided it was his turn to take his date back, so he got up from the bar, and walked, more like marched, toward the dance floor. When he got to them, he poked Buck on his bulky shoulder.

"May I?" he asked in a not so patient tone.

"Sure, Jack," Buck said, reluctantly giving her over to him. He took Natalie's empty drink from her as he walked away.

Jack took her gently into his arms, encircling her waist; her arms went over his shoulders.

"I was wondering when you were gonna start having some fun," she said, smiling up at him, her alcohol-induced words whispered in his ear. "I've been wanting to dance with you *all* night long. I mean, Buck is good-looking, don't get me wrong, but, you...I think you're *much* more sexy." This last statement was done with her tongue sliding gently over her pouty top lip. It was immediately apparent to him that the alcohol had finally kicked into full swing.

Jack smiled down into her eyes and thanked her. Her eyes closed as he pulled her tighter into his embrace and moved his chin to her neck, swaying their hips to the rhythm of the song. He loved the warmth of her body against his. Her hips pressed into his, her breasts against his chest. He was mesmerized by her smell, and all too aware of the effect she was slowly having on his mind and body and heart. It frightened him, but thrilled him at the same time.

"So, how do you know all my old buddies?" she asked.

"I met Luther through your parents. He introduced me to the rest of the guys."

"You and Luth seem pretty close." She smiled, looking over at Luther who was watching them.

"Yeah, we get along good. We go to the gym together."

"That explains a lot." She gripped his biceps and giggled. "D'you know that Luth was my first kiss?" she stated randomly.

"No, I didn't know that!" He was rather surprised by her confession.

"Yup, seventh grade! On my front porch swing... Hey, I bet y'all have a lot in common!"

"I guess so...He's my closest friend here."

"I thought I was slowly becoming your closest friend here." Her eyes twinkled and her fingers deftly unbuttoned the second button of his shirt.

"You're slowly driving my senses crazy." He laughed softly short of a groan.

"Is that a good thing or… a bad one?" she asked, getting braver by the minute as she lowered her arms and put her hands on his ass.

"When I figure that out, you'll be the first to know." He smiled down at her then lowered his lips to hers. She took them willingly, moaning as his tongue slipped inside her mouth. He tortured her with it only long enough to leave both of them wanting more, then pulled back to look at her.

Maybe he'd had one too many beers or his eyes were playing tricks on him. They were no longer showing him a clear picture; they were instruments of the Devil, showing him scenes of Natalie… dancing seductively, rocking her hips in such a provocative, promising way that no man could stop himself from thinking naughty things to do with her. She was curving her body into a sexual foreplay, touching her breasts, stroking her waist and hips, her thighs. She danced as if she were his own private performer turning her back to him and moving her bottom against his pelvis, grinding, torturing, going down to the floor and then back up, practically giving him a lap dance right there on the dance floor. He had died and gone to his own erotic heaven with her.

Then suddenly, Jack realized that these weren't visions, or wishful thinking or dreams or anything else…The music had become a hard, thumping rap song with lyrics that promised sexual intent, his date had become an exotic dancer and everyone's eyes were riveted on her. She'd turned to face him, pulling her dress up enough to get her thighs a straddle of his right leg. She then grabbed his hips; his knees had instinctively bent to accommodate her as she showed him her rhythm. She swayed her hips left and right, grinding herself against him, humping his leg as she danced. Her hands were thrown into her hair as she flung her head back then proceeded to touch her body in the way that he'd only dreamed to. Her eyes found his and she wrapped her arms around his shoulders, pulling herself up to her tiptoes, in front of him again then started from his chest working her whole body down the length of his, her hands, breasts and hips touching him all over at once, searing his skin with an invisible flame, then her hands stopped at his thighs, her head pausing at his crotch, then working back up again all the while rubbing her body into his, a finger gently tucked in her mouth.

"See what I can do to you with my body," she whispered, rubbing her breasts against him, the way a cat rubs itself against its master.

A huge lump had grown in his throat, his cock was as stiff as a two-by-four, and his heart was beating to the rhythm of the song in which Natalie was so deftly deflowering herself to. He had to stop this; he had to gain control of the situation, but his mind seemed to be in freeze mode. He looked around, his eyes finding Luther who had now joined the other four men. All of their eyes were centered on Natalie who was going to town on him. They all looked as if they were experiencing a live pornographic film from a bystander's viewpoint...eyes of amazement and lust looked on at them. Luther was not going to be of any assistance it appeared. He gazed around at everyone else whose attention had been caught by Natalie's spontaneous exploits. Even the other people who had been dancing had stopped to watch them, looks of astonishment of their faces. Then Jack's eyes fell on someone he wasn't expecting to see at the Rusty Spur tonight, Dan. Jack watched Dan's eyes follow Natalie's body as she rolled it against Jack; eyes that undressed her. Dan's gaze caught Jack's and the two men held the stare until Dan's eyes stroked at Natalie then slithered back to Jack in a challenging stare. Jack couldn't take Dan staring at her as if she were being fucked. It was simply too much. He pulled her up straight against him and took her hand, leading her to the exit door, past the guys, who were having trouble speaking as they stared at her.

Natalie was the first to break the silence with a hiccup and then a laugh. "What?" she asked impatiently. "Y'all didn't know I had moves? I was head cheerleader at Abundance High for *God's* sake!" She asked the question casually as if she'd done nothing to draw that much attention to herself.

All was silent but for a moment, then Rick spoke up, "*I knew you did.*"

Luther, Buck, Keith and Scottie stared at Rick as if he'd confessed to a murder. Rick, in turn, blushed as red as a beet. Jack felt his stomach pitch as he envisioned Natalie moving on Rick like she had on him and knew that he couldn't take anymore surprises for the night. He mumbled a good night to the guys and led Natalie out the door of the Rusty Spur.

~

*D*an was as horny as a sixteen-year old on prom night. After what he'd just witnessed, he could only imagine the body and libido that lie underneath that sexy black dress of Natalie Cameron's. He'd watched her breasts and hips rise and fall over Jack as she grinded on him, and he'd pretended that it were him. He'd wanted that woman since he'd first seen her. If only she would give herself to him as she'd given herself to Jack tonight. She was a woman who wasn't afraid to show a man how much she wanted him. She was a woman who was guaranteed to get laid tonight. That dance had tormented Jack until he couldn't take anymore and that's why he'd jetted outta there so fast.

Lucky son of a bitch! When he'd caught Jack's gaze across the floor, he'd seen the anger in his face and had loved that he'd pissed him off. He really liked pissing off Jack. He was nothing but a do-good, picture perfect, ass kisser. He'd taken Dan's job from him back at Long Winds and Dan had seduced his girlfriend for revenge. He'd loved the look on Jack's face when he'd walked in on the two of them; Dan had planned it just right.

He'd known that Jack had been wild back in his rodeo years, but so far, until tonight, he had acted like a born again virgin for as long as he'd been in Abundance. He put on a good act for Natalie, pretending to be nice, charming, work obsessed, but Dan knew better than that. He just wanted to get into Natalie's pants; that's

145

what it was all about. That's why Dan couldn't resist making Jack think that he'd been intimate with Natalie. *Yeah, in his dreams!* He wanted Natalie with a hunger that wouldn't wait. He'd fucked a lot of women in his day, but Natalie had been on the top of his lists for years maybe because he knew that she would never have him and now Jack, his biggest rival, was getting some of her tonight. It really pissed Dan off.

He looked over at Annabella, who was sauntering toward him with that sexy smile on her face. It was nothing new; he'd been with her…a lot. In fact, he was one of her favorites, she'd said. A dirty little thought planted itself innocently into his head and he smiled in triumph. It was rumored that Annabella had been with Jack, and if she had, then Dan just had to know it. She was a whore and if Jack had done her then he wasn't any better than she was. Maybe this was Jack's ticket out of Natalie's bed, and Dan's ticket in! He laughed and grabbed hold of Anna's belt loops pulling her roughly into his hard-on while sliding his hand up her shirt.

"C'mon baby, let's get outta here."

CHAPTER 7

*J*ack burst through the doors of the Rusty Spur as if he were on fire, pulling Natalie with him to the parking lot. He dropped her hand to open the truck door for her and picked her up and into the seat. He shut the door, came around to his side and quickly hopped into his seat, shutting his door. His hands were shaking as he gripped the wheel. He heard Natalie hiccup and tried to calm down.

Jack knew he shouldn't be so angry, Natalie couldn't help that she was so enticing. He dared a glance over at her and wished he hadn't. Smokey, sultry eyes stared back at him and he gulped.

"Are we going somewhere more private now?" The eagerness in her voice was unmistakable. He gulped again; if he got through this night without stripping her naked and loving every inch of her it'd be a miracle from God.

It had been *so* long for him. If he took her tonight with all her recently presented dance moves, it wouldn't last more than two seconds. But God he wanted her...

He smiled over at her because he couldn't help himself.

"Yeah, we are," he retorted, not looking at her eyes. He started the

147

truck and threw it in gear. They were going anywhere but there, he had to get away from that bar, too much excitement for one night. Then he remembered that the Rusty Spur was his idea. *So much for my idea of fun*, he thought.

They were on the road and headed through town when Jack felt something tickling his thigh. He looked down and saw Natalie's hand between his legs. His groin went rock hard just like that. It was amazing how she made his body react.

"Natalie," he warned, "what are you doing?" She was Hell bent on destroying him tonight. If only he hadn't let her drink so much...

Ignoring his question, she continued her exploration. "Oh, Jack. I'm having so much fun. I'm so glad you brought me out tonight." She rested her head on his shoulder and touched her lips to the pulse point in his neck. He quivered and at the same time grabbed her hand, moving it from his groin to his chest. He could at least tolerate her hand being there.

"Me too, hon."

Which wasn't a lie. He'd had fun tonight and he'd also learned a lot, like not to get Natalie drunk unless you wanted her naked and wild. Which wasn't far from what he wanted, but he had to be a gentleman. Her parent's would kill him if they saw her like this and that was partly his fault.

Natalie's hand began to move and before he knew what she was doing, she'd unbuttoned his shirt almost to his jeans. Her fingertips caressed his pectorals and his nipples, sending shivers up and down his spine. She moved them over each muscle, tracing his shape and then down to his navel, her fingertips flirting with the top of his jeans. Her fingers moved back down between his legs. She was slowly putting herself in the lion's mouth and didn't know it.

"Natalie, baby, you have *got* to stop that," his voice came out raspy and sounded unfamiliar to him. He refused to abandon his code of honor, no matter how amazing her fingers felt on his skin. He knew deep down that he could let this go no further, she was drunk and he wouldn't take advantage of her and that was all there was to it.

"But, Jack, didn't you like my dancing?" She looked up at him seeming so innocent, but Jack knew she was only weaving a web of pure seduction.

"Yeah, darlin', very much so." *Although now everyone in the bar thinks we're sleeping together*, he thought. This was only a bad thing because he didn't want to have the town misjudge her reputation.

Her mouth moved down to his chest and she began a rhythmic licking of his nipple that nearly sent him over the edge. Without thinking, he pulled the truck over at the first place he saw, an old abandoned gas station. He turned the truck off and forced her away from him, scooting her completely to the other side of the truck as quickly and efficiently as possible.

She took the rejection harshly and curled her legs in under her, looking over at him in the dark cab of the truck; her lips were pouty and it took everything in him not to reach over and wipe that pout right off of them with his tongue.

"Jack, don't you want me? Don't you think I'm sexy?" The pale moonlight washed over her sparkling necklace and her eyes which sparkled as equally, showing the uncertainty in them. God, didn't she realize how gorgeous she was?

The autumn night had blessed them with an unexpected cool breeze and Jack opened the door to embrace it, the sexual tension was suffocating him. When he'd gotten enough air so that he might be able to think, he slammed it shut and he turned to her, taking her hands in his. He knew he had to be gentle; he had to reject her without hurting her pride.

"Natalie, you are undoubtedly the sexiest woman I have ever seen in my life, and I want you more than anything else in this world." He watched her eyes fill with tears as he spoke, "but, aren't you the very one that said I couldn't buy my way into your pants." Her head dropped then, and Jack's heart twisted in pain. A sob escaped from her lips.

"Jack, you wouldn't have to buy me a thing, I would willingly give myself to you…You're the most wonderful person I've ever known."

"Oh, Natalie," his laugh came out as a groan. "You're tearing me apart on the inside and you have no idea."

"Jack," she said and took his hand and placed it on her left breast. "I want you here." She moved his hand to fall between her legs, up her thigh to the lacy panties beneath. "And I want you here." Jack gulped and felt the familiar stiffness, ever present when he was around her, become a painful throbbing bulge. He was in deep shit.

"Natalie, listen to me, you don't want to do this. You're drunk, you won't even remember it, and you'll regret it like Hell tomorrow." He stumbled over his words, trying to get them out quickly enough that she wouldn't try anything else…unfortunately that didn't work.

"Oh, shut up and take me…" She grabbed at his shirt which was hanging half off in the first place and threw her legs over his lap, straddling him. He parted his lips in protest as she began kissing him in wanton passion and rubbing herself against that part of him that wanted her most. Her tongue moved in calculated rhythm to seek the sensitive parts of his mouth. He resisted her at first, like any good gentleman would, and then it became too much and he gave up. He moaned aloud as she sucked his tongue and licked on his lips, her tongue tormenting him. She was a wild woman crazed by lust; a volcano of passion ready to erupt at any moment. He let her kiss him until they were both breathless, then she moved her mouth to his neck and collarbone, his chest. God, it felt so good, the feel of her silky hair on his bare skin, the dampness of her breath, the smell of her hair, her sweat, her lust for him. She began unzipping her top from the side and slipped it over her head, peeling her arm from the lacy sleeve, displaying her round, perky breasts constrained by a sexy black bra and her long, trim torso. He groaned as he remembered seeing them naked with their pink tips and felt he would die, he wanted to touch her, to see her again so badly he couldn't see straight, but knew that if he did, there would be no turning back.

He kissed her neck and shoulder and his trembling hands moved up her skirt to her panties. He fought the urge to nuzzle and kiss the full, creamy breasts that were thrust up at him, threatening to spill out of that sexy, skimpy, lacy bra, and resorted to gripping her tight little ass instead. Her head flew back and she moaned like that of a woman in pure ecstasy, Jack almost exploded.

"Oh, Jesus," he swore in torment, trying to gain what little self-control he had left. He wanted her like this. He wanted her passionate and desperate for him, but not here, not like this. He wanted to see all of her and love all of her.

"Oh, Jack, I need you so much, please...please...." her plea was frantic as she reached for his jeans, but he couldn't allow any more, couldn't take anymore. He stopped her hands and moved them around to her back, where he could finally be in control.

"No, Natalie. I can't...I can't do this to you and I won't," he stated loudly. She started her protests once again only to be rebutted by him. "Baby, please, I'm begging you. Not here, not now. I *will* make love to you, I swear, but not like this. I want you sober, and I want to be able to see you, all of you."

She stopped fighting and relented if only momentarily. "You think I'm a slut...don't you?"

"No! Of course not! I think you're just really, *really* horny, but it's okay because I am too." He smiled, trying to ease the tension.

"Oh, come off it! Don't act like you don't know what happened!" Suddenly, she was angry and Jack was confused.

"Huh?"

She crossed her arms over her half-naked chest in defense of herself as Jack released his grip on her hands. She was something else when she was drunk; horny one minute and angry the next. This might actually be amusing if he wasn't so swollen that he was absolutely miserable. He would be getting no sleep tonight for sure.

"You know about me and my past, my ex-husband... why do you *think* I'm horny?" she asked.

Jack hesitated but then decided to answer her anyway, "I think you're horny because you, like me, haven't had any in a long time and we're really attracted to each other, so why not?" Wrong answer.

"Don't play coy with me, Jack Kinsen," she said with force, poking at his rib, he yelped.

"Coy? What are you talking about?" He rubbed at his injured rib. "That hurt!"

"You, just like all of the other people in this one-horse town know about what happened in Chicago. It was all over the news, it was broadcast for millions of viewers to see it and speculate on it and judge me and my family, so don't act like you don't know what I'm talking about. My husband was a former pro wide receiver and a sportscaster for ESPN, so the whole fucking world knows my entire life story, and I'm to believe that YOU don't!" With that she jumped off of him and grabbed her top, throwing it over her head, which was disappointing to say the least.

"Natalie, I really—"

"Why the Hell else would it be so *easy* for an attractive, virile man such as yourself to be the object of my lust? With a husband like I had, a *normal* guy would have done, but you, you're like a sex god with your big muscles and good looks... Hell, I'm surprised that you would even be seen out in public with me. With my reputation, what man would want me? I'd be lucky to get into *your* pants. You'd be doing me a favor. Maybe that's why you were being so nice to me because you felt sorry for me. Yeah, that's probably it."

Seen in public? Her reputation? Doing *her* a favor? Felt sorry for her? Either she was so shit-faced she didn't know up from down, or she'd just lost her last marble. He looked at her as if she were crazy, but she wasn't looking at him, she was crying now.

"Natalie?"

"It's okay, just take me home now, please?" She wiped at the tears falling down her cheeks.

"Okay," he responded gently. Whatever she had just told him was important in a way that made Jack realize that what happened to her in Chicago had almost destroyed every faucet of her being. Not knowing how, he'd once again hurt her and could neither understand nor fix it.

~

*H*e pulled up and cut the engine behind the carport. She'd cried all the way home and Jack knew he had to do something.

As she started to open the passenger door, he stopped her. "Natalie, I want you to hear me out. Please?" She looked up at him, her eyes stained from her makeup. "I don't care if you believe me or not, but I have *no* clue what happened to you in Chicago. I took care of the ranch when you're family came out there to be with you and if you haven't noticed, I don't watch much television, news or otherwise. I don't know what pain you've suffered or how much. I just know that I want to be with you and I feel that you want to be with me and I don't care what happened in your past or the reputation you had or what kind of person you think you are. I care for the person you are now. The only reputation I have seen is one of a woman who is wanted by so many men that it's practically comical. I have seen nothing but a beautiful personality tested by an occasional flaring temper. I appreciate the fact that you want me so much; it makes me feel damn good. And I don't feel sorry for you, I just want to take you out and enjoy spending time with you. I've wanted to since I first saw you. Well actually, that was a picture of you..." he stammered and caused Natalie to laugh. "I mean, how does a person pass by a picture each night before going to bed then doesn't even recognize that person when he sees her on the side of the road? How dumb am I?"

"You didn't even know me then, I was just a picture in another city and you were just a ranch hand."

"Yeah, well I'm still just a ranch hand." That got another laugh out of her. "But the point is this: the past means nothing to me and I want you to know that. I love being with you and that's all that matters to me," he said, taking her hand.

She smiled and gave him a gentle kiss on the lips. "Thanks Jack, that means a lot to me... But is there any way that you can get me out of this truck, I think I'm gonna hurl?"

"Shit," he responded in a hurry as he jumped out and ran around the truck to get to her. He had just got her to the ground when she puked more than any drunk person he'd ever seen. He held her hair for her as she coughed and hacked. She even did it rather gracefully, he thought. Now he really felt like shit. He shouldn't have let her drink so much; this was all his fault. He'd ruined their first date.

When she'd finished, he lifted her up and into his arms. She just laid her head on his shoulder, giving into exhaustion. Her parents must have been in bed because all the lights were out, save the front porch light. The front door was unlocked and Jack silently thanked God for that piece of divine intervention. He opened it softly and eased his way inside. He then closed it with his foot and headed upstairs, taking the steps gently so as not to wake anyone. When he got to Natalie's room, the door was open so he stepped inside and sat her on the bed. He stepped back, giving her some room.

"Thanks, Jack." She sat up trying to acclimate herself to her surroundings. She put her hands on both sides of her head as if it were spinning and she were trying to stop it. "I think I'm going to need some help," she said, looking up at him.

He immediately came to her side and helped her remove her top, trying hard not to stare down at her breasts, which seemed to be pushed up higher than last time he'd seen them. They were spilling out of that damn sexy as Hell bra of hers and silently he wished he were removing it too. She lay back, slid the skirt off her hips, and handed it to Jack. He stared down at the lacy panties covering her curvy hips and muscular thighs; he'd never seen them this bare before. She had a sexy pair of legs, slim and long and muscular. He imagined how they would feel wrapped around his naked hips.... Suddenly, he thought of what Dan had said and cringed as he wondered if Dan had ever seen her like this before; he wanted to know the truth, needed to know the truth, and he knew that she would tell him. She was too drunk to lie.

"Natalie?" he asked, trying hard to lift his gaze from the little triangle of silk between her thighs. Her eyes had drifted shut, he sat on the bed next to her and said her name again, and finally she looked at him. "There's something that has been bothering me that I want to ask you about..."

"What is it Jack?" she asked, her voice growing hoarse.

If she said she had been with Dan... Would it hurt, would he be disappointed, angry? He just had to know, he didn't know why; he just knew he had to know.

"Did you sleep with Dan?" He prepared himself for the hit...

"What?" She laughed. "Why would you ever think a crazy thing like that?" She shoved him, trying to be forceful but came up short.

Relief shot through him, she hadn't!

"Well, because he kept hinting around that you two had."

"Yeah, Jack, I don't think so. I wouldn't touch that man...you should know how much I hate him."

"As much as I do! I just didn't know for sure, especially since you and Rick..." Whoops, he wasn't supposed to know that.

"Me and Rick. What about me and Rick?" He had her attention now; she sat up quickly and was looking into his eyes, searching for an answer.

"Well, you know..."

"No, I do *not* know. What are you talking about?"

He might as well go ahead and confess, since he'd chopped his own head off.

"Well, I know about the affair." That's all he had to say, she lowered her head then looked back up at him. "I just happened to be there when Rick decided to tell someone about it for the first time."

"Of course you were! Look, Jack," she sighed, hesitating only long enough to pull her ruffled hair away from her face with her hand. "That was a long time ago and it shouldn't have happened, but it did. I figure everyone knows about it anyway. It's not like you can keep a secret in this freakin' town. People find out one way or another. But, just because I slept with Rick doesn't mean that I sleep around..."

"No, of course you don't! I didn't mean it that way! You know," he frowned, "I have a right mind to beat the shit out of both of them. Dan shouldn't tell things about you that aren't true and Rick needs to keep his mouth shut. If he or Dan say anything else about you, I swear I'm gonna kick their asses."

"I appreciate that Jack." She smiled up at him then looked serious. "But why did you think I slept with Dan? What did he say?"

"Well, one of the things he said was that he *knew* you better than I did." He gauged her reaction.

"Yeah, he wishes," she said with a laugh.

"Then the other thing he said was the thing that got his nose broken the other night. He said something about fixing your attitude by screwing you and that he knew what your body felt like, so I went at him before I knew it."

She made a sound of disgust, "He's a dick."

"Well, you sleeping with him didn't make any sense at first, but then I thought about how much you hate him and that maybe that was why you did."

"So, how did you get at the fact that since I slept with Rick that I might sleep with Dan?" She was more alert than he'd originally thought she'd be with all the alcohol she'd consumed that evening, but he figured he might as well answer her questions.

"I was surprised that you slept with Rick I guess... because I thought that he was an unlikely candidate for you to sleep with so I guess somewhere in my jealous mind I assumed since Dan seemed an unlikely candidate too that maybe you slept with him too... Stupid, I know, and none of my business." Self-conscious, he pulled his hat off and brushed his hand through his hair, easily replacing the hat.

"So, why is Rick an unlikely candidate for me to sleep with?" She looked semi-amused instead of offended, which was a relief.

"Well, because he isn't good enough for you, neither is Dan."

"And just what kind of man *should* I be sleeping with?" her voice had turned sultry and she used her foot to stroke his thigh as he sat next to her on the bed. This wasn't good especially since she was already half-naked, her slender body so enticing, and he was dying to see underneath.

"Well," his voice had grown unsteady. Damn, how was it that she did that to him? "Neither one of them, for one thing. You need someone better than them."

"Someone...like... *you?*" Her eyebrow arched in question at him.

"Damn right someone like me." He jerked up off the bed before she could grab him and drag him into her trap. "Here, take my shirt," he said, unbuttoning the last two buttons of his shirt. He removed it and tossed it at her as she held her hands out to catch it. "You look...cold..."

She pulled it to her nose and smelled it, letting her eyelids flutter closed as she did so. The gesture was so utterly erotic that it took his breath; he had to get out of there before they both regretted what happened next.

"I'll see you in the morning. Sleep well, darlin'." He gulped as he watched her throw it over her shoulders, touching it gently with her fingertips as if he just given her the key to Heaven.

"Oh, I definitely will." She lay back down on the bed and looked up at him, her pouty lips doing wonderful things to his insides. She looked so incredibly astounding with her curly hair all wild around her pillow, that expensive piece of work on her neck and his big silver shirt covering her small frame, the black bra and panties peeking out beneath it. He silently groaned in torment. "Goodnight, cowboy." She slowly blew him a kiss.

"Goodnight," he stammered in sweet agony as he flipped off the light.

"Oh, Jack?" she called.

Jack stilled suddenly in pulling her door closed. "Yeah?"

"Thank you for the wonderful night."

"No, Natalie. Thank you," he said and quickly closed the door.

He would never get to sleep tonight, with visions of her dancing on him and sleeping in his shirt; there was no hope.

~

*H*e had been wrong about not being able to sleep. He had slept alright. In fact, he'd slept the best he had in, well, as long as he could remember. After he left Natalie, he'd gone to his room and taken a cold shower, then hopped into bed and fallen right to sleep, thoughts of her filling his head. And he'd dreamt…sweet, sexy dreams of her. Her smile, her kiss, her body. She'd been fun and adventurous, shy and teasing. He'd made love to her all night long… in his dreams. And he'd waken feeling great about it. Jack and Natalie felt right, it sounded right. He couldn't wait to take her out again, to kiss her again, and to feel her pressed up against him again. Maybe he *was* in love as Luther had put it, but dammit, it felt good and it made him feel alive, something he hadn't felt in a long time. She excited him and thrilled him and maybe she was exactly what he needed right now. He wanted her with a desire that he'd never had before, he longed to see her every second that he couldn't.

It was only eight in the morning and he couldn't wait to be in her presence again. He'd waken near five and headed to the barn for his daily chores, but he couldn't get those dreams out of his head. All the while, shoveling and feeding and haying, he never stopped thinking of her. He was acting ridiculous, he realized, but then he didn't care. She was everything he'd ever wanted and he was on his way to making her his. That made him smile.

~

*N*atalie awoke with a start, the clock on her beside table read 12:07 PM. She sighed and felt her head throb. Why had she gotten so drunk last night? Did she not know that she couldn't party like that anymore, she was a mom for God's sake, not a teenager? What she'd done last night was so stupid. She'd acted like such a slut in front of Jack…and the whole town. Jack must be so ashamed of her now.

"Oh, God!" she groaned as she wiped the sleep from her eyes.

How could Jack ever forgive her? She heard a throat clear; someone was in the bed with her. She cautiously turned over to find the man in question lying beside her. He was facing her with a big smile on his face.

"Good morning, sunshine!"

"Oh, God!" she stated again, covering her face.

"Oh, c'mon now, rise and shine. Time for lunch, you completely missed breakfast. Your mom was getting worried so she sent me up here to check on you." He tried pulling her hands from her face, but she rolled over.

"Does she know that I drank last night?" she asked, her voice muffled through her hands, not wanting to really know the answer.

"Uh…" He'd hesitated, that couldn't be good. "Yeah."

"You *told* her?" Natalie turned on him, appalled.

"She asked me. I couldn't lie to her." He shrugged.

"Oh, God." She covered her face again.

"Oh, c'mon, what's she gonna do, *ground* you?" He managed to get her to uncover her face. "Dallie's been asking about you, I told her you weren't feeling well. She wanted to know how the date went."

"Oh, Jack, I'm so sorry for ruining our first date. Please forgive me for the way I acted, I'm a horrible drunk."

"Oh, you were *not*. Besides, the sex was great!" He bobbed his eyebrows at her.

"What?" *Sex?* They'd had sex? Dammit! How had she managed to make love to the hottest man she'd ever seen and not remember it?

"I'm just kidding, but you sure were *damn* hard to refuse."

"Oh God, I'm so embarrassed." The memories came flooding back, all too vivid, making her blush all the way to her toes. Had she really begged him to fuck her? "Oh, how ridiculous I was."

"Natalie, honey, there's nothing for you to be embarrassed about," he said, running his hands through her hair. "You got some naughty moves on the dance floor though. You know, a lot of women would be down right jealous." He curved his hand around her hip, a naughty grin on his stubbly, handsome face.

"Jack!" She swatted at him but missed, causing a boom of laughter from his throat. "Oh God, I will never be able to show my face in that bar again..."

"Which isn't necessarily a bad thing," he added.

"Jack." She took his face in her hands. "Please, tell me that you don't think less of me, that you don't think I am some sex-crazed white trash hussy." Her eyes peered deep into his mossy green ones.

"Natalie, I really don't think that," he said reassuringly, then grinned again. "In fact, I like you a lot better now that I've seen what you can do with those hips..."

She gave him the mother of all looks then sighed. "I haven't drank that much since I was in high school and I've definitely never acted like that before. I've never been so...slutty." She said that last word in pure disgust with herself.

"It's okay, baby." He patted her thigh. "I have that affect on every woman."

"Oh, get out of here, would you?" She once again swatted his hand away, but he wouldn't be thrown so easily. He grabbed her waist and pulled her toward him, facing him.

"I'm not leaving until I get a promise that you will get out of this bed."

"I have a hangover," she pouted.

"Well, I can't help you there, that would have to be our friend ibuprofen, oh and coffee!" he said matter-of-factly then looked down at her and smiled at her with that crooked smile she loved. "Damn, don't you look hot in my shirt?"

She tossed a pillow at his head as he fled the room laughing then looked down at herself. The unbuttoned silver shirt barely covering her shoulders, her black panties and bra exposed. She felt an uncanny sense of feminine pride. She *did* look hot in his shirt. She'd always had a slim waist and athletic build, even after she had Dallie; she'd maintained her flat tummy through body pump classes at the

Y. Although she'd been underweight for the past several months, since moving home, she'd gained her weight back and filled out to what she was before.

She felt an astonishing sense of guilt as she sat up in the bed, her head spinning as she steadied it with her hands. *Oh God*, she felt so shameful and she should be ashamed of the way she'd acted with Jack last night. The way she'd grinded on him on the dance floor and practically begged him to have sex with her later in his truck. He was such an attractive man. He'd probably had hundreds of women throw themselves at him. That wasn't a new experience for him, she was sure of it, but she had begged him and thrown herself at him like some desperate two dollar hooker. When had she lost all her inhibitions with him? He'd made her feel sexy and beautiful when he complimented her on her looks and it had been a long time since she'd been given a compliment, so long since she'd been treated like a lady and taken out to a nice dinner and given such an incredible gift... And the promises he'd made to her...*I will make love to you.* He'd felt so strong and solid when he'd pushed her away from him. She'd known that he hadn't stopped her because he didn't want her; that was the farthest thing from the truth. He hadn't done it for himself; he'd done it for *her*. Because he'd known that she, in the end, wouldn't have wanted it that way. She had fought her desire for him from the very first time they kissed; he'd known that, he'd known she wasn't ready. And for that she was grateful to Jack, the forever unconditional gentleman.

But her heart sank as she suddenly realized that if Jack had truly wanted her, drunk or sober, he could have taken her. Why was it that she lost herself so in his eyes, in his touch? She was losing her self-control. Her walls were crumbling and she wasn't sure how she felt about that. Was she ready to face all the things that came along with her desire for this man? The consequences of her actions?

No. She wasn't. It was too soon. And she knew she had to stop this, she had to. Her sanity was at stake here. They couldn't continue to go around groping each other like love sick teenagers. It was ridiculous how carefree they acted with one another. And what would happen once they'd satisfied their craving for one another? Would it be over then? Would he have his fill of her? She wasn't willing to find out. She would be heartbroken and bitter all over again... She had to end this before it ever really begun.

$\sim$

"Ok, give him a little slack there, darlin'," Jack instructed Dallie as she prepared to ride Call around the arena by herself for the first time. She loosened the reins and looked cautiously back at Jack for further instruction. "Don't get nervous now. You're the boss, *you* lead *him*. Now I want you to take him one lap around the arena and bring him to a halt right here." He marked the spot with his boot. She hesitated but for a moment, worrying her bottom lip with her teeth. Then suddenly she grew taller and signaled the horse forward. He went surprisingly very willing, letting her lead him, going with her as they rode forward. She smiled, her sunny blonde locks bouncing as they took the first turn, she rode with pride and dignity, a trait succeeded to her by her mother and grandmother. She was at ease on the horse, he was at her will. All the Butlers had ridden with superiority, especially Natalie. She had won many an equestrian event in her younger days, from barrel racing in local rodeos to racing at state derbies. She'd done especially well in equestrian jumping in her teen years, succeeding many long-running champions in her field. He'd found trophies and ribbons she'd won as well as old newspaper clippings in her room while he and Corrine we're moving Natalie's things from her room into Nathan's. She'd told him all about Natalie's victories and he'd been intrigued. He hadn't really thought anything about it until Dallie had shown such an interest in horses and now he'd realized why. Natalie had once had such a knack for horseback riding and it was turning out that Dallie did too. If Natalie had been so good at it, why had she suddenly just stopped doing it?

Dallie turned Call around the last turn, headed back toward Jack. She smiled at him and his heart swelled. She looked so much like her mother, so vivacious and ambitious, so sweet and soft, yet withdrawn. He'd thought about all the things he'd overheard Dallie say to her grandmother and all the things Natalie had said to him last night. What were they so afraid of, what made them so afraid to live life? Who could even think of hurting this beautiful innocent child and her passionate, loving mother?

"Jack, I did it, I did it!" A small shrill of delight drew him from his reverie. He smiled big at her overwhelmed expression.

"Yes, you did, sweetheart. You did great! Now let's take him back to the stables and brush him down good."

"Oh, Jack! Please just one more time around?"

"We really shouldn't overdo it, Dallie. You're so little honey, you're mom would probably kill me if she knew that I let you ride him by yourself in the first place."

"Yes, I would!" An indignant voice replied. Jack mentally sighed before he turned around.

Natalie stood there, hands on her curvy hips, eyebrows raised, looking all sexy as Hell even if she were ready to tear him apart. She must have just taken a shower because her hair lay semi wet as it fell in curls down her shoulders. He gulped, not only from the lashing he would receive, but from the heat that suddenly consumed him at her appearance.

"Need I remind you, Jack, that she is only four years old?" Her voice was meant to be intimidating, but the voice he heard was sultry.

"Uh, Uh, I am almost five now, Mommy!" Dallie interceded.

Natalie ignored her and took a step closer to Jack, pointing her finger with accusation. "If I had known you were going to be so careless with my daughter I would have never agreed to this." She stepped away from him then and over to Dallie grabbing her and taking her off of the horse. Who was this angry tyrant? Where had the confident, sexy female gone that he'd taken to dinner last night?

Before he could think, she'd sat Dallie down, ordered her to the house and grabbed the horse's reins leading him to the barn. Jack stopped her.

"Hey, you know I would never do anything to endanger Dallie, I was standing here the whole time."

"Jack! You know as well as I do that that horse could crush her before you would even be able to do anything about it. Get that through your head, she is *just* a child."

"She *is* a child, but I have never seen a child do that well on a horse in all my life."

"So, that means you have to put her life on the line, to see how good she might be on a damn horse. Who are you really doing this for anyway, Jack?" By this time they weren't but a breath away from one another. She smelled so delicious that he wanted to kiss her with all his might, but he resisted because he knew she was really angry.

"Natalie, she loves it so much. She's so good with him, you should see her. I want her to follow her dreams and if that means riding Call then that's what I want her to do, I'm not pressuring her into doing anything she's afraid of. I'm just encouraging her. She begged me to ride him by herself, so I thought I could at least let her try."

"She is not to ride him again without you being right beside her and I mean it. He could kill her and you need to remember that."

"I know that, Natalie. I wouldn't let him hurt her."

"As if you could stop him, Jack! I will not let Dallie get hurt over something as stupid—"

"Is that why you stopped doing it yourself because you think it's stupid?" His tone deepened.

"Don't pretend that you know me so well, Jack! You don't know *anything* about me." That last sentence was followed with an icy glare that cut him as deep as a knife. His heart lurched and his eyes looked upon her in confusion. The eyes that stared back at him were unflinching, eyes of a woman who had been through Hell, met the Devil and dared him to take what of her soul had been left in the fiery blaze. Why was she turning on him suddenly and so ferociously? They'd had such a breakthrough; they had gotten so close, they'd began a relationship and were dating for God's sake.

But she was walking away, just like that. She'd known she'd hurt him, she had to know. And he'd hurt her too, but how? Why couldn't he make things right with her? Why was he continuing to screw this up?

"Natalie?" He wouldn't let her just turn her back on him. He grabbed her wrist and turned her toward him and into his chest where his arms embraced her. Her body was stone cold and her resistance didn't break as he'd expected it to.

"Jack, I just need some space right now, ok?" Her voice sounded strained as if she could barely speak. She wouldn't even look up at him. He wouldn't have that.

"Natalie," he said and pulled her chin up with his fingers, cupping her cheek. Her eyes had tears in them, she was troubled and he felt terrible. "I'm sorry, I never meant to hurt you; you *have* to know that. I just want Dallie to be everything she wants to be. She's so much like you, she's hard to resist when she wants something." He smiled into her blue eyes and leaned down to kiss her. Her lips weren't soft and accepting as they had been last night. She was *really* resisting him; he pulled back, a puzzled look on his face. "Natalie, what's wrong?"

She sighed, fighting back tears. "Oh, Jack. I can't do this right now. This! Us! It's too complicated, for me...for Dallie. All of this is moving too fast. I think you and I should just back off." Tears spilled from her eyes as he looked at her incredulously.

"Natalie, we've had *one* date for Christ sake! How can you decide after one date that things are *too* complicated?" He realized he was so dumbfounded by her statement that he was having a difficult time trying to speak. "You haven't even given "us" a chance yet," Jack said, moving his hand back and forth between them for emphasis.

"Jack, don't you see what happened last night? I lost control. I have never acted like that in my life. I made a complete fool of myself and of you!"

"You did not, Natalie! So you had one too many drinks. You think you are the only person to ever do that? Don't be so hard on yourself all the time, maybe you needed to let your hair down a little. Besides, nothing happened!"

"Jack, I'm a mother. I have to be more responsible for Dallie's sake, that's why I can't just make spare of the moment decisions. I need to think about this." She sighed, using her hand as he had earlier.

"I don't understand," he countered, exasperated as he swept his cowboy hat off his head with one hand, ran his other hand through his hair then dropped both hands down to his sides, tapping his hat against his thigh; he felt utterly defeated. He was a man grasping for something that had never entirely been in his reach, something he could smell and feel and taste but could never have. He hated the way that made him feel. He wasn't a quitter. "We were getting along great and you were starting to trust me. What did I do that was *so* wrong?" Confusion and disbelief were ripping his heart in two. He wanted her with a desire that was stronger than anything he'd ever felt in his life; no woman had ever made him feel the way that she did and he was so afraid that if he didn't grab and hold on to her now as tightly as ever, that he would never get another chance to do so.

"Jack, don't you see, *you* didn't do *anything* wrong. I just, I don't trust myself with you and that terrifies me." Her eyes held such sadness and regret as she spoke. Jack's head dropped. He had gotten so close and now she was pushing him away…again. He sighed and stiffened up, if she wanted space then that's what he would give her no matter that his heart had just been wrenched from his chest, but by God, he would fight to the ends of the earth to get her, no matter what.

His voice was tender as he said, "I'll wait for you for as long as you need me to. You mean so much to me, Natalie, and if you need anything you know where I'll be. Don't be afraid to ask." With that he walked away from her, he had to get away, his body and soul felt so torn that he didn't even feel whole. He didn't look back, afraid that if he did, he would *show* her that they were meant to be together.

~

he next week went by painstakingly slow. Day in and day out were much the same. Jack got up, he worked, he ate, and he went to bed, all without her. He never thought he could miss someone so badly in his life, especially someone whom he hadn't even had time to get to know. He'd only recently gotten close to her, they'd had one date, but yet he ached to be near her, to talk to her, laugh with her, touch her. And she *was* there, just not emotionally, not like she had been and they were practically avoiding each other at all costs. Oh, they were polite to one another, a little too polite to suit him. He missed when they would argue and the passion that would come out in her when they did. He missed her kiss and her laughter.

Natalie rarely initiated conversations, almost as if conversation was painful for her when she and Jack talked, and most of the time they weren't talking. Not what they should be talking about...them. Mostly, they spoke about the weather and Dallie's progress with Call. Call was definitely making headway, he was obeying commands, ground driving, and progressing with his free longeing; he was even beginning to trust Jack. Jack was grateful, but he was also distant and sometimes he felt that the horse had sympathy for him.

He was heartbroken and he didn't know what to do about it. And he was grumpy, but not with anyone in particular. He just did his work as he always had before, before she'd come into his life and turned it upside down. Everyone had noticed Natalie and Jack's distance, but no one had spoken of it. He wanted to ask her how she slept, if she dreamt of him, if she hated this detachment as much as he did.

David had made a contract deal with a film company to train some Tennessee Walkers for an upcoming movie, and the horses were brought in the first of the week, so he was busy working with them among all of the other horses in line. Natalie had even come down to help her father train them; David had asked her for help. She seemed reluctant at first, but she obliged him and if Jack didn't know any better it appeared she was enjoying it. She wouldn't work with Jack though and her avoidance hurt him. It was hard to work with her so close to him, but he did it. He just held his head high, even though he was dying inside and went through his day to day routine of commands and ground driving and riding. The crew was coming in next week to train with them and get acquainted with the horses. Three horses were to be used as one horse in the movie so they had to focus their work on coordinating the routine and personality of each of the horses. Deep down, Jack was not a fan of working with film companies. The producers and directors could be pushy and demanding. Not understanding the time and effort that was put into each animal. Plus, most of the time, they had to leave the ranch and go to the set to handle and care for the horses and filming took weeks to complete. But, thank goodness, David knowing he couldn't go it alone, had partnered up with a fellow horse rancher, William Thomason. He and his hands would be helping them this week.

That Thursday, Jack woke up like normal. He got out of bed, showered, and met everyone downstairs for breakfast. He sat in his usual spot, thanked Corrine for coffee and started eating the home-made biscuits and gravy she'd fixed for all of them. She was such a good woman, such a warm and generous hostess. She was also a beautiful woman, with her deep auburn hair and blue eyes, trim figure, gentle voice… A strong woman who could do it all; manage her household and all its responsibilities, take care of her family, enjoy some well-deserved free time and despite all her over-whelming tasks, still be able to make her husband swoon. He imag-ined that Natalie would be like her too, the kind of woman that every man secretly desired to have. Thinking of Natalie, he looked over at her; he couldn't help himself, and smiled sadly at her. She smiled obligingly back at him and lowered her head. She forked at her food, but didn't look too inclined to eat it. He wondered if she were as miserable as he was. This had to stop, he told himself. She'd had her space and what had it done for her. Nothing! The same as it had done for him.

"Jack?" Dallie intervened, and Jack turned his head to look over at her. "You didn't tell me good morning like you always do!" Her brows were drawn in a frown, her arms crossed over her little Tinkerbell shirt. She was seemingly oblivious to his despair.

"Oh, I'm sorry, kiddo. I guess I'm just kinda tired that's all," he stated, ruffling the top of her head with his hand. He was kind to Dallie as he'd always been; she seemed to brighten his day even when he felt like it couldn't get any worse and his hope had been all used up. He talked to her more than anyone else, and he spent more time with her than with anyone else.

"It's okay, I guess I can forgive you this time." She smiled, teasing him and patting his big bicep. Dallie was always so loving. Deep down Jack wondered if Natalie had once been that way before life had corrupted her spirit.

"Shoo, thank goodness, I was getting worried there." He smiled as he chucked her on the chin, his usual playful gesture.

"Do I get to help with Blaze today, like you promised?" There was such eagerness in her eyes, the same as he'd seen in her mother's eyes that night that she'd begged him to make love to her with such desperation that it had ripped down into his soul.

"Of course, sweetie, I never break a promise." He smiled over at her. It had become so hard to look at Dallie and not see Natalie in her.

"I'm going to town to look for a job tomorrow," Natalie said quietly to her mother, but Jack was eavesdropping.

"A job? Natalie, why on earth do you need a job?" Corrine asked, looking surprised. They were speaking just above a whisper and Jack kept leaning a little so as to hear them.

"Well, I want to try to get on at the paper, I miss writing and it's the only place I can think of where I could do that. Its not that I need the money. I just need something to keep me busy," Natalie suggested.

"Well, I thought you were keeping plenty busy helping your dad with those horses, but if you want to write I understand."

"I'll need you to look after Dallie for me, if you don't mind?"

Before Corrine could respond, Jack took his opportunity. "I'll look after her...." Silence followed.

Natalie spoke after what seemed like ages. "Are you sure, Jack? I know that you have much to do. What with Blaze being recently put in a halter and Call and all those new horses brought in by Mr. Sikes?"

"I wouldn't mind a change in scenery, trust me. She would be no problem at all."

"Yes, Mommy, I wanna hang out with Jack." Dallie wrapped her little arms around his big bicep, resembling ivy tangling around a massive oak tree. He grinned at her enthusiasm.

"Well, okay, if you're sure she won't drive you nuts... I should only be gone for a couple of hours."

"I would be thrilled to watch her for you." Jack couldn't help but smile as Dallie's little pearly whites shone up at him.

~

*D*avid stumbled into the kitchen after breakfast, his mind in a state of unrest. He walked over to his wife, who was working on the dishes, his beautiful, sweet, giving wife of thirty-five years. Her silky mahogany hair curled in tendrils down the back of her pale pink blouse. Corrine Anne Butler was fifty-three years old and the absolute love of his life. They had been just kids when they were married, barely out of school and so in love with the promise of life. He smiled to himself as she moved a piece of loose hair from her face. His hand inched up her back as he let her curls twirl around his fingers. He sighed; a man content in his wife's presence.

"I know that sigh…" she trailed off. She knew him too well, knew he needed to talk to her. She turned, wiping her wet hands on a dish cloth. "What's the matter, dear?" Her soft hand gripped his cheek.

He gazed deeply into her big blue eyes and couldn't help but smile at her beauty then he leaned down and kissed her plump lips, loving the feel of their warmth. He pulled her into his arms then and kissed her properly as his arms drifted to her waist. She sighed then and let herself be lost to him. She was a sucker for long kisses; that he knew for a fact. She smiled as she pulled back.

"David Alexander Butler, this isn't the reason for that sigh." She looked at him cautiously. She was right. This had nothing to do with them. It had to do with their only daughter, Natalie.

"You're right," he said. "Although, I am all too aware that I don't kiss you often enough to suit me." She just smiled, blushing to her heels. He pulled away from her embrace then and settled his back-side against the counter crossing his arms over his chest. "Have you not noticed the way Jack and Natalie have been acting toward one another?"

Corrine shrugged. "Of course, we all have."

"Well, dammit, why are they acting that way?"

"I don't know honey, but it's really none of our business, you know?" She shook her head sadly.

"It *is* our business. They are perfect for one another, why can't they see that?" he stated with conviction.

"Well," Corrine scoffed, "aren't you Mr. Matchmaker?"

"No, I just see things as they are and I don't understand what the deal is."

"Bad date?"

"Surely not! He took her to that fancy new—"

"David?" Corrine gasped his name as her hand flew to her mouth. Her eyes flew up to his, "You don't think they slept together do you?"

"Naw, Jack wouldn't have been anything but a gentleman to her! For God's sake woman, what do you think of them two anyhow?" he scolded.

"Well, it's just that Natalie was acting so funny the next day. Jack said she drank that night and neither of them have been with anyone in so long."

"Corrine!" He was surprised by her comment.

"Well, it's true! It makes a man *crazy* to go without sex for too long…" She faced him matter-of-factly.

"Well," he said and smiled like a sly fox. "You're right about that." His hand inched around her waist. Corrine blushed again.

"Really, David, do you think they did?" Her eyes were full of concern and it upset him to see her so troubled.

"No, I really don't, honey." He rubbed her back then and pulled her into him. "I think Natalie is just unsure and I think Jack is in love."

"Really? So soon? They've only known each other for a few weeks now." She looked up him so hopeful and he smiled again, kissing her lips again.

"Yes, I do…and yes so soon. I remember a man that fell head over heels for his wife on their first date."

"Oh, David." She kissed him this time and when she pulled away, he was the breathless one. "What should we do?" He just shrugged in response. "I know that we shouldn't interfere, but I want Natalie to be happy so badly, David, our baby deserves to be happy…" Her adamant pleading did him in.

"Alright, I'll talk to Jack and see what I can get out of him, okay?"

She nodded and rested her head against his shoulder. "Natalie deserves a man like her father, and Jack is so much like you."

"I know. That's what makes me think they are perfect for one another, because Natalie is so much like you." Her sparkling eyes lifted on him.

"Do you think they'll grow out of it?" She smiled.

"Not a chance!"

CHAPTER 8

hat was I thinking? Natalie thought to herself as she sat on her bed folding her laundry that same afternoon. She was a moron, an idiot at best. Why had she told him that she'd needed space; she'd lied. She needed *him*, just him. Him to soothe her at night when she'd cry herself to sleep wondering if she would ever live normally, him to kiss her tears away, him to make her feel alive again as only he had. She'd made a mistake, a big mistake, but would he be so easy to forgive her? Would her pride allow her to say that she'd been wrong?

Natalie had helped around the house so as to keep her mind from him all week and down at the barn with all those horses her father had signed on for. She settled to working with her father or Cass and wouldn't, couldn't, work with Jack. Everyone had seemed surprised at that, seeing as how her and Jack had become so close prior to that. But no one asked, not even her father, who seemed aggravated at their growing distance. Jack was so close, yet so far away from her. He worked super hard with each horse; he was completely dedicated to his labors and seemed undaunted by her presence there. But it had been too difficult for her to be working so close to him. So, she'd helped her mother around the house; doing dishes, dusting, stripping beds, folding clothes, sweeping, mopping, organizing cabinets, anything she could to keep as much distance from him as possible. She'd found things to organize that hadn't been gone through in years. They also moved all the things from Nathan's room to the attic and purchased a small bed to go in his room for Dallie. They had surprised her with it earlier that week. They'd painted the room a soft pink color with western items as accents. The comforter on the bed had a Quarter horse embroidered on it, the curtains matched and the pillows were shaped like horses. Natalie had gone all out and bought a toy chest with horseshoes for handles and a lamp with a cowboy hat for a shade. A rug of true Appaloosa hide was the finishing piece. Dallie had loved it and she almost cried in joy when they'd showed it to her. Jack had been impressed and surprised as well at their determination and hard work. He'd smiled at Natalie for the first time since their "separation" and for a moment her heart was at peace. She'd decided then that she'd been a fool to let him go. Now she was paying the price for it.

When Jack had laughed at Dallie that morning at the table, a shiver had ran all the way down her spine. She missed that laugh and his deep, sexy voice. Yes, she'd been miserable the last week, she wouldn't lie. She missed him so bad one night that she almost lost her inhibition. She was stepping into the bathroom as he was stepping out and she almost collided with him. His brown hair wet and his tan skin dewy from his shower. He'd smelled so fresh, like soap, and leather and something so originally Jack. She resisted the urge to bring her nose to his heaving chest and inhale his scent. She could feel the steam coming off his skin as he stood before her, waiting for her to speak, to do something, anything, and she wanted to beg him to hold her against him, so she could be consumed by the heat that only they shared. She longed to touch his beautiful bare chest and feel the indentation of his muscles. But she didn't, she'd just lowered her head and mumbled an apology. He stepped aside, brushing past her, leaving her to feel alone and bereft in his absence. Now, she just wanted to cry out from the pain she felt from missing him. He looked as sad as she was. He probably hated her now more than ever. Was it too late to ask him to reconsider? She pondered how she could ever right her wrong. She'd made so many stupid mistakes in her life, now this would be one more. She had to talk to him; had to explain to him… She could at least apologize, and she set her mind that she would do exactly that.

$\sim$

*A*fter breakfast, Jack walked down to the barn to check up on Call. He was looking his shoes over and brushing him, hoping that he might be able to ride him later on in the day. The horse had come a long way in the past week, and Jack was amazed at how quickly the stallion had warmed up to him. He had ridden him for the first time a couple of days ago and he was shocked that he didn't get bucked off. After Dallie had ridden him by herself, Jack just had to give it a try. He'd held his breath as he stepped up on the stirrup, but was quickly surprised at the stallion's grace and gentleness. He knew right away that he wouldn't cause him any trouble.

"That a boy," Jack said, laughing as Call nibbled greedily on the carrot Jack placed at his mouth. The horse whinnied in response.

He was brushing his mane when David yelled for him.

"Hey, Jack!" he hollered.

"Yeah!" Jack put the brush down and stepped out of the stall as David signaled him into his office.

He walked the length of the barn; the heat felt as if it was bouncing up at him. Autumn was in full swing, but they'd been cursed with a tropical system heading in from the gulf and the heat was intense on this unseasonably hot day. It felt all consuming. The long paved aisle only served to insulate the heat especially with the AC being broken.

Jack joined David in his office. The older man sat behind his desk

175

in an overstuffed red chair, his arms folded across his chest, his look stern. This meeting wasn't about business Jack realized and sighed internally. He walked over to the window AC and turned it on full blast as he wiped his forehead, letting the cool breeze drift over his face. He was prolonging the conversation that was inevitable.

"Jack, sit down, please. I apologize for the heat, the repairman will be here soon, I hope." David motioned to the chair opposite him.

Jack sat as requested and waited; waited to be lectured about Natalie.

"So," the old man began, "just how long *have* you been in love with my daughter, Jack?" His question was frank as he stared unblinking at Jack. Jack hadn't expected such a direct question; his eyes shot up to the man he respected more than anyone in the world. He dare not lie; David could see right through him, he'd always been able to.

So Jack looked him straight in the eye and told the truth; the undeniable, damning truth. "From the moment that I saw her." He'd suddenly realized that he had been in love with her all along, although he'd only known it in that instant.

"So, then what the Hell are you doing exactly?" David's glare was intense and Jack felt as if he was being squeezed like a lemon.

"Well, she doesn't exactly want me around. She told me to back off not just a week ago," he emphasized, shrugging his arms.

"That's a joke..." David smirked sarcastically.

"Oh, yeah? How do you figure?" Jack was getting angry; David was making humor of this miserable situation.

"Her mother used to look at me the way that Natalie looks at you."

Jack's anger faded immediately and a slow smiled replaced his frown, breaking a smile from David.

"So, I take it that the date didn't go so well?" His tone was now more amorous than it had been in the beginning and Jack was glad for that.

"It went...great, or so I thought, until ...but she just, she says that she needs space and I just, I can't keep on like this, David. I'm miserable not being able to be myself with her. We've had one date, how does she know she needs space?" He sighed, a man in utter confusion.

"Jack, son... Natalie has been through a lot in the past year. I don't know if you know about what happened to her, but she was hurt in a way that no one should ever be hurt and she lost a part of herself... her spirit, her confidence. Now she has a problem trusting people after what happened, especially men. This is something she has to work out on her own. And you know, Jack, right now Natalie needs a friend, someone she can lean on. She needs someone solid, someone she can put her trust in, and build a new life with. It's been a long time since she's had any stability in her life. But don't give up on her. She's like her mother, she longs to be loved. She's passionate, she's vulnerable, and she needs you right now even if she doesn't know that she does."

"So, what should I do?" Jack asked, feeling slightly confident for the first time since his unpleasant encounter with Natalie a week ago.

"Well, now, it may take some time, but you must show her what she can't see herself...that she needs you and that she can trust you. Show her that it is okay to love you. Encourage her. It will all come together after that."

~

Dan smiled to himself as he helped pull hay from the trailer. Jack and Natalie were fighting and Dan had some dirt he that couldn't wait to share with her. Life was good. Now maybe it would be his turn to get a break. Annabella had taken him to her place last week and they'd done it all night long. It'd been dirty and sexy and fun. She wasn't the woman he wanted though, she was nothing but a slut who he could bed at anytime he pleased. Natalie was the woman he wanted and had for a long time now and it was time he got his chance. When he told Natalie just what he'd learned, she would drop Jack like a hot potato. They weren't speaking now as it was, they really wouldn't be speaking when Jack's little secret came out. She would hate him and then Dan could make his move. Jack didn't deserve her anyhow just as he hadn't deserved Karen.

Dan had been extra nice to Natalie all week, offering her help with the horses and making a point to talk to her each chance he got. He was warming her up, waiting for the right time to make his move. To tell her his news, to make her aware that Jack wasn't the man that she wanted to believe he was.

He pulled his hat off and wiped the sweat from his brow. He looked over at her talking with her father in the corral, his cock growing hard. Her hair cascaded down her back, her skirt blowing in the wind, those full breasts of hers straining against that tight red top, it was too much for him. No wonder Jack was moping around like a lost kitten. Dan laughed. He couldn't wait to tell Natalie what a piece of shit he really was. It was coming!

◇

*L*ater that day, Jack was carrying Dallie on his shoulders as they led Blaze into the barn. Natalie was standing at Cheshire's stall, his big head hanging out of the opened Dutch window, petting him between his eyes. Jack smiled as he saw her, and she bowed her head as she'd done too many times in the past couple days. He silently cursed. He opened the stall for Blaze and led him in.

"You want to get the stool and brush him down?" Jack asked Dallie.

"Yeah!" she said excitedly as he sat her down onto the ground. She ran off quickly to get the stool from the closet. The gates on the barn doors were always closed now so that the incident with Call could never happen again.

Jack had garnered up the courage to finally talk to Natalie, it wouldn't be easy, he knew that, but this was going to stop, today. He worked his way over to her, stopping beside her and to his surprise; she was the first one to speak.

"He was the last horse I ever rode..." She spoke almost as if he weren't there and she were in her own silent reverie. "I won my last jumping event riding him; we could ride like the wind, he was so graceful and swift. I trusted him; he was my favorite horse, so laid back and gentle. I trained him myself, you know? My dad picked him up as a stray at a local farm. He'd been abandoned, so I trained him, I was seven years old when I got him. He's almost twenty-three years old now." She looked up at him and was quiet for a few minutes then spoke quickly, rushing the words out as if she couldn't get them out fast enough. "Jack, I'm so sorry that I yelled at you that day about Dallie and about not knowing me. I should never have said that to you! It was cruel and uncalled for...and—"

"It's okay, really. You were upset, I understand. Honestly, don't worry about it, okay?" His hand reached out to touch her arm. He knew he shouldn't have touched her, but he missed the feel of her skin so badly.

She gasped, not expecting his touch. He pulled his hand away and she looked over at him.

"So, how did it go with Blaze today?" she asked, looking to the stall with the afore mentioned colt.

"Not so good, he wouldn't let her lead him, yanked and pulled, until I had to grab him, afraid he'd take her down with him. He's just now harness-broken, just not liking ground work, it's too soon. I told her we'd work with him some more on a halter and lead later on in the week, so she's fine with it. Call's doing well though. She can mouth commands at him now, and he's letting me pet him and even let me ride him the other day."

"That's great! You two are working so hard. I'm glad to hear it's working out well."

"Yeah, we'll be selling him sooner than we originally thought."

God, she looked utterly beautiful today. Her hair was wild and wavy. Her long, flowing skirt clung to her in all the right places and her tight top revealed her shapely breasts and slender waist. He longed to pull her against him and feel her breasts and belly against his. He lowered his head, resisting the urge.

"Hey, Nat, I wanted to ask you something... There's a county fair in Denton this weekend and there's gonna be a horse show and auction tomorrow. I was wondering if I could take Dallie to it, if you don't mind."

"No, I don't mind at all. I think she would love that."

"Yeah, I thought so too. Don't tell her yet though, I want to surprise her."

Dallie came running out then with the stool and brush and headed into Blaze's stall. He watched her and then turned back to Natalie.

"So where's your interview tomorrow?"

"Oh, it isn't an interview. I'm just going to the newspaper office to see if they have any openings. I have an old friend who is the editor there; I thought she might give me a small time job."

"Well, good luck. I'd wondered if you would miss journalism when you moved out here."

"I do! I miss writing, very much."

"Yeah, well I miss *you* very much." His tone deepened and his gaze was intent on her, gauging her reaction.

At first, she looked up at him, utter surprise in her eyes. Then her head lowered and she fiddled with her hands for a bit.

"Jack, I really don't think that—"

"We *are* going to be together, Natalie. You can make it easy or you can make it hard, either way, I'm gonna prove myself to you, no matter what!"

~

*S*he'd thought about what Jack had said all that day and long into the night. It echoed in her ears at unexpected moments, sending shivers down her spine. He'd spoken so blunt and bold, so promising. She'd missed his touch and kisses even more than she wanted to admit, but she'd known she couldn't just come crawling back and say that she'd made a mistake, she would look like a fool and sometimes she felt as if her pride was all she had left.

She missed him, mostly at night right before she drifted off to sleep. She would see him in her mind, his laughter, his kindness. She'd dream about him and wonder how long their avoidance would go on. Then suddenly, out of the blue he'd unexpectedly told her that he wasn't giving up on them.

Almost a week had gone by since their falling out and they'd not mentioned what happened since. They'd only been kind to one another so as not to make things awkward. Inwardly, Natalie was glad Jack had stepped in; deep down, she wanted him to love her, but she was afraid of what would happen if she fell in love with him. She didn't know if she could love again, her fears were always lurking in the shadows, a turbulent reminder of her past and how it had affected her. For some reason, she just couldn't let go of it. Oh, but how she wanted to. She wished she could just forget it all, but that wasn't going to happen. What happened was unforgivable, unforget-table. It would always haunt her no matter what, no matter where.

That next morning, she woke up feeling refreshed for the first time all week. She was a little nervous and a little anxious. She couldn't wait to get back into the life of news; the adventure, the challenge. She hoped that there was an opening for her at the local newspaper. She yawned and peeled the covers back; her feet hadn't even touched the floor when Dallie burst in.

"Mommy, Mommy, guess what, guess what?" Her little voice squeaked.

"What?" Natalie grabbed Dallie as she rushed at her, slinging them both backward onto the bed.

"Jack's taking me to see a bunch of horses at the fair. We're gonna eat caramel apples and popcorn and ride rides…"

"Wow, you and Jack are going to have lots of fun today."

"Yup! Mommy, what happens at an auction?" she asked with eagerness in her eyes.

"Well, it is kinda like a big horse sell, you show your horse and you can sell one or buy one or…"

"Wow! I wish I could buy one." Her eyes got big at that thought.

"Maybe one day, honey." She set Dallie down onto the ground and stood up stretching. "Now, you be good and stay with Jack, don't go running off, okay?"

"I promise. I won't."

"Okay, go get dressed."

Dallie ran off downstairs instead. Natalie smiled to herself. Dallie was just like she'd been at that age; so happy go lucky, so vibrant and full of life, so in love with horses…so innocent to the world around her.

She walked into the bathroom to shower and got ready rather quickly. She adorned a sky blue sleeveless shell, a camel colored blazer and dark brown trousers, not too casual, but professional enough. She'd curled her hair into ringlets and applied cool shades to her eyes. She shoved some flats on and walked downstairs.

Jack, Dallie, David and the hands were eating breakfast, a combination of toast and meats and omelets. Jack's clothes looked dusty; he must have gone to the barn and fed the horses already. He looked up at her and she could have practically wiped the drool from his mouth. She smiled knowingly at him, and he finally came back to his senses and smiled back at her.

"You look beautiful!" he exclaimed. "I would hire you for sure."

"Thanks, Jack. I only hope that my employer will share your enthusiasm." She laughed as she approached the table.

"And if he doesn't then he doesn't deserve you."

She wouldn't correct him and tell him that her employer at the

Times, if she got the job, would be a female and wouldn't care how beautiful she looked. She decided to just leave it alone.

"How's breakfast?" she asked, looking over at her daughter.

"Really good, Mommy, I love when there's cheese *inside* the eggs." She looked so happy that Natalie felt bad about not making her more omelets in the short span of her lifetime. Life had been too rushed in Chicago; breakfast consisted of mostly cereal or granola bars, things that could be taken on the go. She caught Jack's gaze as he gave her a knowing smile.

Natalie sat herself down at an empty spot as her mother served her plate and coffee. She smiled at Dallie as she poured cream into the steaming cup and told Corrine to sit. She hated having her mother wait on her, even if she was used to it.

"You look nice today, honey, best of luck to you, huh?"

"Thanks, Mom." She took and kissed the back of her mother's hand before she helped herself to a delicious and cheesy south-western omelet.

It was another thirty minutes later of hugging Dallie and thanking everyone for the good luck before she was able to walk out the door. The wind swept her hair as she got into the car and turned the key into the ignition. It had been weeks since she had driven her car. They had used her mother's old Lincoln Towncar when they'd gone into town for groceries and items for Dallie's room.

Everyone back at the ranch wondered why Natalie wanted to work...it wasn't that she needed money. She had enough to sustain her and Dallie for years to come. It was the fact that she wanted to write again, it had been years since she had been a writer. Up until her husband's trial, she'd been the editor-in-chief at *Edge* Magazine in Chicago. *Edge* had been one of the leading women's magazines in the country, competing with top names like *Cosmopolitan* and *Women's Health*. She had loved her job, and she'd been good at it. She loved being able to put the magazine together and design the perfect cover each month. She got along with all of her co-workers and had close relationships with most of them and everyone liked her. She laughed to herself as she remembered starting out as a "How-To" girl. She'd slowly worked up to Health and Fitness, then Politics and finally five years later became the editor-in-chief of her company. Of all the people Stacey Reynolds could have chosen, it had been Natalie she'd wanted when she retired. Natalie recalled the shock and surprise that had come over her when Stacey had announced her offer.

"No, Natalie," she'd said when Natalie had shook her head in doubt. "Don't you dare for one second doubt your abilities. You, above everyone here, deserve it! You work you're tail off every day you're here, you strive for perfection and you have a knack for detail that far surpasses anyone else I know."

Natalie really had worked extremely hard to get there and it had finally paid off. Now, she just wanted something small and not too demanding of her time, to keep her busy and keep her writing, something to challenge her mind, so the first place she'd thought of was the local newspaper, *Abundance Times*.

It seemed like a never-ending drive before she finally saw the signs to the city limits. Town was quiet, but ready for business at 9:00 AM on this beautiful October day. Trees and lamplights draped in fall garland lined the sidewalks of her old hometown. Natalie spotted the florist shop and boutique. Fallen leaves crunched as people walked down the sidewalk starting their day. She passed by the ancient pink marble courthouse with its broad lawn before turning into the parking lot of the *Abundance Times*. She tried to stave off her nervousness as she took one last glimpse into her rearview mirror at the reflection of herself. She smiled, got out of her car and took the short steps into the newspaper office. She smiled at the receptionist who greeted her.

"I'm here to see Elaine Colby."

"Ok, sure, who's calling for her?" The young teen smiled.

"Natalie Cameron…Natalie Butler," she corrected, knowing that Elaine might not recognize her by her married name…*yeah right!*

"Okay, it'll be just a minute." The skinny blonde receptionist picked up the phone and mumbled into the receiver. It was only a matter of minutes before Elaine pulled her curly brown head into the lobby.

"Oh my God, Natalie? Is it really you? Someone said they saw you in town, but I thought, 'No way, that city girl will never come back to this old place!'" Elaine exclaimed, pulling her into a fierce hug. "How are you?"

When Elaine finally finished squeezing her, Natalie smiled into her old friend's freckled face. "I'm doing good, and how about you?"

"I am *great!* Come on back to my office and we'll talk. Do ya want some coffee?" She tugged on Natalie's arm even as she requested coffee from the receptionist.

"Um, no thank you. I'm fine, really."

"Oh, that's right, you probably only drink what, lattes and espressos, huh, you big city girl?"

"No, actually, I just had some coffee at breakfast..." Why did everyone assume that she had been transformed by the "big city"? She didn't finish her reverie as she was pulled into a quaint little office with a high backed chair and a metal desk with a flat screen monitor.

"Please, sit!" Elaine welcomed her guest as she motioned Natalie to a well-cushioned seat across from her desk. The door was closed behind them as Natalie did as she was instructed. "So, Nat, what brings you back to these parts?"

"Well, what better place to be than home?" That was another question she would be glad that people stopped asking her.

"Yeah, good point! Oh, by the way, I just wanted to tell you how sorry I was to hear all that about Troy, what a shocker! I thought y'all made a terrific couple...I just never would have imagined that of him..." she trailed off sensing Natalie's discomfort. "I'm sorry, Natalie, I know people have driven you crazy with questions. I just—why did you come to see me?"

So there was the real question. Natalie and Elaine hadn't been close in high school. It wasn't that they hadn't liked one another, they simply had different lives.

"Well, Elaine, I want to get back into journalism, so I was wondering if you had something, a possible opening or a column, so that I might start writing again."

Natalie could tell that Elaine was surprised by her request.

"I would be *honored* to have an editor-in-chief working for me, tickled pink in fact." Her smile was big, but then she shook her head. "But, unfortunately, Natalie, I don't have anything at all for you to do right now. I wish I did, I would love to have your expertise in this office. I just simply don't have any room for you. I really don't have any columns I could take away from anyone because of all the stories covered by the high school group."

Natalie's heart dropped slightly. Disappointment wasn't what she had expected. She wanted to start working again; she wanted to have something to do besides sit at that ranch all day drooling over Jack Kinsen.

"But you know, I am pretty sure that the bank is hiring right now, full-time in fact! Let me make a phone call and I can pretty much guarantee you the position." Elaine picked up the phone, but Natalie shook her head.

"No, that's really alright, I would only be interested in writing."

"Oh," Elaine said, once again surprised, dropping the receiver back onto its cradle. "Well, of course, how silly of me, it's not that you *need* a job. God knows you don't need the money..." She trailed off and Natalie didn't know how to respond to that comment. "Well, I tell you what, if I get an opening, you will be the *first* person I call, okay?"

Natalie smile was nonchalant at best, but she shook Elaine's hand, thanking her and stood to leave.

"Oh, Natalie, wait!" Natalie immediately sat back down in the chair as Elaine riffled through the drawers of her desk. "I have the number of the publisher at *Lone Star Living*." When Natalie didn't respond, she continued, "*You* know? That local magazine out of

Denton?" Natalie shook her head, her eyebrows raised in question. "Well, anyway, she might have something for you. It might not be anything big…"

"No, that's okay." Natalie's smile brightened. "I don't want anything big!"

"Oh, well, good! This will be right up your alley then." Elaine searched through her rolodex and grabbed the card she wanted, jotting the number down on a sticky note. "Here, give her a call. Her name is Marlene Wiseman. I think she will be pleased to know you are looking for a writing position."

≈

*P*leased had been an understatement. Marlene had been thrilled to say the least.

"Natalie Cameron! Oh my goodness! Is this really you?" Marlene had screamed into her end of the phone. She had reassured her that she was indeed herself and not some prankster. "Well, bless my soul! I can't believe it's really you." Natalie proceeded to explain to Marlene her reason for calling and was surprised to hear that she had something in the local politics section of her magazine. Natalie couldn't be more thrilled. Politics had been her specialty when she'd been writing. Marlene said she would be sending her an email with instructions on submitting an application and resume and told her she'd be contacting her next week about the magazine's deadline and schedule. She hung her cell phone up and breathed a sigh of relief. *Thank God!* Natalie was so glad she hadn't needed someone for the sex and relationships column, she would have been up a creek. Then that was the good thing about writing for a local southern magazine…there *was* no sex and relationships column. Ha!

She felt good as she rode toward the other side of town. She needed to head to the bank and open an account.

She pulled up to the remodeled brick building and parked. Tucking her cell phone in her purse, she opened the door and breathed in the cool air. Fall time was her favorite time of year and she got giddy thinking about taking Dallie on a hay ride and picking out her pumpkin and her Halloween costume. Troy had never participated in Halloween or any other holiday for that matter, "Just a waste of taxpayer's money," he'd always said. Like he didn't have it to waste… But all that was to change. Natalie would be going all out this year!

A young man in a cowboy hat opened the door for her as she stepped inside the air-conditioned lobby. She mumbled a thank-you and headed over to the receptionist.

"I need to set up an account," she replied to the attentive twenty-something girl with silver braces and black glasses. The girl motioned for her to sit at a desk over to the right side of the lobby and she obliged.

Natalie sat and waited, digging out her current check book and driver's license. She'd already gotten that changed just last week…

"Well, I'll be damned," a sassy female voice called out from the other side of the desk.

Natalie was startled at first then looked up to see a familiar face staring down at her.

"Natalie Butler! I *cannot* believe you are sitting at my desk…Come give your old girl friend a hug." Jordan Tate grabbed her over the desk as Natalie stood, pulling her into a tight embrace. Her copper red hair with its caramel highlights was as wavy as ever and her brown eyes the color of honey glowed as she smiled at Natalie. Her full breasts peeked out of the top of her silky red top and her slender thighs were barely covered by a black pencil skirt. Gold bangle bracelets adorned her wrists and gemstones of all colors shimmered on her fingers. She was still flashy but just as beautiful as she'd been in high school. "Oh my God! How have you been?" She smiled into Natalie's eyes as she sat and beckoned Natalie to do the same.

"I've been really well, how about you?" The questions were becoming rhetorical now and each time she was confronted by them she silently cringed.

"Well, I'm great. Single as ever." Jordan winked. "Although…
that's *not* what I heard about you…" *Oh great, here we go…* Natalie
thought. *I must be the latest gossip of the town.* "I heard through the
grapevine that you were dating Jack Kinsen. Please? Tell me it's a lie!"
Jordan stated, pleadingly grabbing Natalie's hand, giddy as a school
girl. Natalie felt herself turning crimson and knew Jordan saw it too.
"Oh my God," she exclaimed, quickly covering her mouth with the
hand that had been holding Natalie's. "*You* hussy, you *are* dating
him." Natalie couldn't help but laugh at that. Jordan joined in too. "I
am *so* jealous of you. Wow! Isn't he just a big ol' slice of Heaven?"
Jordan eyes closed passionately. "Those eyes, that smile, that sexy ass
of his…Oh, I'm sorry." Jordan's eyes had started to glisten. She'd
always been "boy crazy" and she herself was the very epitome of man
killer with her curvy body and flirty ways.

Unfortunately, Jordan never cared much for keeping them; she
would rather just play with them then release them, not unlike a
trophy fisherman. "Too much work," she'd informed Natalie once,
when she'd asked why Jordan wouldn't go steady. "They like to tell
us what to do, how to do it, without regard to what we want then
you hear them talking us up to their friends like we're nothing but a
stake to claim or talking about how hot another girl is… Forget it!
They're only good for fixing things, pumping gas and fuckin'. I'll take
the single life, thank you!" They'd both laughed then. If only Natalie
had been as smart about her relationships as Jordan…

"Now, I didn't go and upset you now did I, Nat?" Jordan gasped
and touched Natalie's arm in reassurance, drawing her from her
reverie.

Natalie smiled and shook her head, indicating that she wasn't
offended.

"Jack is a wonderful man." That's all she permitted herself to say.
Half the town probably already knew about that night at the Rusty
Spur, so Natalie didn't try to explain herself.

"Isn't he? He is always such a sweetheart when he comes in here."

I bet! Natalie thought; Jack was always quite a charmer. Jordan continued, "So, tell me, how's your little girl?"

"She's great. She loves being at Mom and Dad's."

"That's wonderful. She's four now, right?"

"Yes, five in December."

"Wow, it doesn't seem like that long ago."

"I know…" Natalie trailed off. Her friendship with Jordan had ended in high school. She'd seen her in town a couple times and spoken to her on her last visit. But she *had* missed her. She'd been a good friend to Natalie and come to think of it, one of the few female friends she actually had.

"You know it sure is good to see you." Jordan smiled as if reading Natalie's mind.

"You too, Jor."

"We should go to lunch one day and catch up for old time's sake."

"Sure, I would like that."

"Good! Maybe Jack has a brother you can set me up with," she said, raising her eyebrows.

With that they both laughed heartily.

~

"*J*ack, can we ride the Ferris wheel now?" Dallie begged, her little hand wrapped around Jack's middle finger, blue eyes dancing and blonde curls bouncing as she looked up at him. She'd already managed to stain the little pink dress Natalie had put her in this morning. Jack only hoped she wouldn't be upset with him about that.

"How 'bout we finish our ice creams first? We don't wanna drop them on someone's head, now do we?"

Dallie shook her head aggressively and Jack laughed deeply.

He was enjoying his outing with Dallie. It was a nice, cool fall afternoon, the sun was shining brightly above and the leaves were rustling under their feet. The mixture of children laughing and carnival music echoed in the background as they walked the midway. Dallie had been a pleasurable companion and her laughter and delight had brought Jack back to his own childhood. He'd felt like a kid again along with her. They'd snacked on popcorn and watched the horse show where Dallie had adored each horse they brought forth, especially the black female Arabian yearling. She was halter-broken and well into the stages of her ground work. Her price had been reasonable.

After a greasy lunch of hot dogs and onion rings, they headed over to the fair rides, where Dallie had wanted to ride everything in sight. And Jack being the "fun" guy he was had went along with her with no exception. Now, he was wondering if his stomach would ever be the same as they sat down on one of the park benches to finish their ice creams. Her little pink tongue licked at the big mound of strawberry ice cream as it melted down her fingers. Her mouth was covered in pink and Jack couldn't help but smile at her sweet little face. He adored her as much as he did her mother.

She smiled up at him then and he reached down into her miniature pink backpack and grabbed out a wet wipe and began attending to her mess, wiping her face first and then her fingers. He was sure glad now that Natalie had insisted they take the little pack with them.

"Jack, why are you and Mommy fightin'?" The question took him off guard and for a moment he didn't know what to say.

"Well, Dallie, sometimes we adults can complicate things." He sighed.

She looked at him inquisitively, brows drawn. "What does *that* mean?"

"Well, it means that …well, Dallie, I—I think she's afraid to get too close to me now."

Dallie shook her head vigorously. "No, she's not, she's not afraid of you… She has a *crush* on you." She sounded so sure of herself.

Jack laughed and kissed the back of her tiny hand. "Who on earth told you that?" He was dying to know.

"I heard Mommy say it to herself in the mirror... Jack, what does that mean?"

"It means that she likes me." Stars had begun sparkling in his eyes.

"Everybody likes you, you are nice and you are fun." She was so innocent; he couldn't help but smile at her. "Are you going to take her on a date, again?" Suddenly, Dallie's eyes sparkled.

"You are *really* hung up on this date thing, aren't you? Tell Grandma she needs to lay off *The Young and The Restless...*"

"You should then you can marry her and I can have a little sister." She was stretching a little, but Jack couldn't think of a better plan himself and he laughed at her sweet virtuousness.

"Sure, you want me to take her on a date again?" he asked. Dallie's head and curls bobbed a yes. "Alright! I'll take her on another date, if it will make you happy... But who's gonna be the one to tell her about your new pony?"

"Oh, no! You are on your own, mister," she replied. Jack laughed so hard he nearly wet himself. He picked her up and hugged her to him as they ran to get on the Ferris wheel.

~

hy on earth do they need to know **that***?* Natalie wondered as she filled out her online application to *Lone Star Living*. She had propped herself in one of the many rocking chairs on the front porch, her notebook atop her lap, feet propped up on the railing, cold sweet tea in hand. She was suddenly distracted as Jack pulled into the driveway in his pickup. She silently smiled to herself as Dallie waved at her through the window. Jack parked, came around and plucked Dallie from her car seat and sat her down on the ground. She raced toward the front porch her pink dress stained, hair in disarray, climbing the steps with difficulty. She finally made it to her mother and hugged her tight.

"Mommy, Mommy! We had *so* much fun!" Dallie exclaimed. Natalie hugged her back and smiled down at her daughter.

"Honey, that's great. I'm so glad." Natalie kissed her sweaty forehead and laughed.

"Yup, we rode rides and ate hot dogs and ice cream and I saw lots of horses...Jack was a really fun date."

Natalie laughed warmly. "I think so too."

"Well, good... 'cause he's gonna ask you on another date soon."

"I can't keep you quiet for *nothin'*, can I?" Jack asked, effortlessly climbing the step and grabbing Dallie up as if she were light as a feather and tickling her belly. She squealed in delight. "How 'bout you go inside and give Grandma that dress, so she can wash that big ol' stain out of it?" He kissed her plump left cheek, sat her down and she ran off inside to do as she was told.

"Yes, I see that her dress is a quite a wreck..." Natalie faked giving him a hard time.

"Yeah, I'm sorry about that...collateral damage." He gave her a fake sneer as he sat down in the rocking chair next to her. "It sure is a beautiful day, isn't it?"

"It is! I love this time of year." She joined his gaze as they looked out at the orange and red leaves falling off the oak trees in the driveway.

"Nice specs by the way." He reached over and tapped at the glasses that were perched on her nose.

"Oh." She blushed. "I only use them when I'm reading."

"Sexy..." That single word caused her body to react in a way that made her blush. She gulped. "She's right you know?"

"About what?" *Man, did the temperature just rise out here?*

"About the date," Jack stated emphatically.

"What do you mean?" Oh, it was definitely hotter than it was before *he* came onto the porch. She moved her hair off her neck to cool herself.

"Well, there's a great new Tex Mex place downtown and on

Wednesday nights they have two for one margaritas…" he trailed off, leaving her the invitation.

"Oh, well, um…tequila makes me do crazy things." She was fanning herself now.

"Exactly what kinds of things?"

Her eyes shot over to him. His eyebrows were arched and his smile was devious. He knew damn well he was making her nervous!

"Naughty things?" he asked.

"Wouldn't you like to find out?" She arched her eyebrows in challenge.

He didn't have to say anything. His eyes did all the talking. A huge lump had grown in her throat and she couldn't swallow. He looked away then and sat silent for a few minutes, possibly because he was all too aware of the sexual electricity shooting between them. He looked back over at her then; a seriousness had come over him.

"Natalie, I'm sorry."

"For what?" Her eyebrows had drawn.

"I shouldn't have said that! It was impolite of me." His look was so sincere that it touched her.

"Jack, it's okay. I'm not offended." She really hadn't been offended, she'd been turned on. "Besides," her voice was a whisper, "I like flirting with you."

His smile was big as he looked at her. "I like flirting with you too." His face became solemn again and he took her hand. "But I also need to apologize for something else…I want to apologize for the way I've acted with you these past couple weeks, being so forward with you." He was so serious that it startled her.

"What do you mean?"

"I moved too fast with you from the very beginning, and I ran you off with my sexual advances. I've behaved very badly."

"No, you haven't, Jack!" She shook her head vigorously. "I came on strong to you too, believe me, it wasn't only you."

"Yes, but you never would have if I hadn't started it…"

"I beg to differ!"

He smiled then, his face a maze of expressions. "Forgive me?"

"As if there was any doubt." He breathed a sigh of relief then.

"Friends?" he asked.

"Friends."

He shook her hand as if they were meeting for the first time and she laughed. He kissed her hand then and held it in his own as he sat in silence just rocking in his chair. She was touched by his kind gesture of sincerity and enjoyed this blissful peace that had come over her. He sat just holding her hand watching the clouds roll by for a bit then he released her hand suddenly as he looked over at her.

"Oh, I'm sorry. I'm keeping you from work."

"Oh, no, it's just an application for a job," she said, looking down at her laptop.

"Did you not get the job you were looking for?" His eyes were hopeful.

"No, I got a better one. I'm going to be doing a political column for *Lone Star Living* Magazine out of Denton."

"Oh, that's great." His eyes widened.

"Yeah, I'll actually be doing it out of Abundance, so it will be *our* local news and politics, not Denton's. They're starting to branch out and add columns for other local towns so I called her at just the right time. She was thrilled."

"That's really great, Nat. I bet you're excited."

"I am! I'll start putting my article together next week… It's only a monthly publication, so it won't require much of my time, but at least I'm writing again."

"I'm happy for you." His smile showed her that he was.

"Thanks, Jack." She looked back down at the computer then and began typing at the application again. Jack sat quietly, his presence giving her comfort as she worked. It wasn't long before Corrine poked her head out the front door and told them it was "Supper time" before heading back inside. Natalie was pleased with the inter-ruption, she'd finished the application and had moved on to her email which she hadn't checked in quite some time and wasn't too enthusiastic about checking it anytime soon. She closed the lid of her notebook and stood, tucking it under her arm. Jack stretched before standing to follow her inside. His hand touched the small of her back as she opened the door and she smiled, enjoying the way it made her feel. The crowd had already gathered at the table and Dallie was carrying around one of the growing tabby kittens in the crook of her arm like it was a baby, coddling and crooning to it as she went.

Jack smiled and shook his head. "Two peas in a pod."

"I was thinking the same thing," Natalie replied.

Corrine emerged from the kitchen then with a steaming casserole dish and Natalie's stomach growled.

"Dallie, get that darn cat away from the table," Corrine scolded as she sat the dish in the center of the table.

Natalie sat in her usual spot and Jack followed, Dallie lagged behind and finally propped herself in her spot, sulking.

"What's wrong, pumpkin?" Natalie was the first to ask.

"I just wanted Figaro to see what we were eating…"

Jack smiled over at Natalie and patted Dallie's hand. "Well, darlin', he doesn't need to see what we're eating. You know, 'cause he doesn't get to eat it…"

She crossed her arms over her chest then, lips drawn in a pout. "Well then, I don't want to eat it either!"

Great, here we go! Natalie thought. "Dallie, don't act that way, now, I mean it. That's so ugly. Grandma would be hurt at you; she worked hard on this dinner." Natalie had gotten so used to her well behaved child that when the four year old in her came out, which wasn't often, she didn't know exactly how to deal with it. Instead of straightening up, Dallie had the audacity to stick her tongue out at her mother. Natalie eyes widened, but before she could jerk her up, Jack did.

"Let's go have a talk, Dallie!" Jack's face was stern as he lifted her in his arms and took her out to the back porch. Natalie just shrugged and looked over at her mother, who looked indeed surprised.

"What on earth was that all about?" Corrine asked.

"Dallie was acting like a brat..."

Natalie knew that if anyone could appease Dallie it would have to be Jack, so she waited for her father to say the blessing before helping herself to the food surrounding her. Jack and Dallie headed back in at that time and Dallie's frown had transformed into the happy-go-lucky smile they all knew. Natalie looked at Jack perplexed. He just smiled and gave Dallie an awaiting gaze.

She looked to him then back to Natalie. "I'm sorry, Mommy," she stated with her sweetest tone and started helping herself to the biscuits in front of her. Natalie just looked at her in astonishment.

"All better now...Let's eat," Jack stated and elbowed Natalie with a grin, who in turn just shrugged.

And they did eat, in peace, thanks to whatever Jack did. Dallie wouldn't stop talking after that, telling all the hands and her grand-parents about how her and Jack rode the Ferris wheel and ate hot dogs and saw the horses. She was so excited to have an audience.

"So, Dallie, have you thought about your Halloween costume yet?" Surprisingly, Dan was the one asking the question. Come to think of it, he'd been different lately, nice...generous and helpful, it seemed a bit suspicious to her.

Dallie shook her head. "No, we don't do Halloween." Dallie's smile inverted.

"You don't *do* Halloween? Well why not? It's a lot of fun."

Natalie interrupted then, "Oh, we are *doing* Halloween this year, Dallie. We're going all out! Pumpkins, hay rides, lights, the works."

Dallie looked up at Natalie in surprise. "We are?"

"Oh, yeah!"

"I can be anything I want to be?"

"Anything you want!"

Dallie hooped and hollered then, getting a rise out of the crowd.

After dinner, Natalie made her mother go rest as she and Jack did the dishes. Dan had volunteered, but only after Jack had already started helping her. Dan's generosity, or whatever it was, was really starting to grate on her nerves. She knew there was a scheme behind it.

She was washing as Jack was drying and putting away. Dallie was in the living room watching *The Black Stallion* with her Paw-Paw, while Corrine sat knitting. All the hands were gone to the bunkhouse for the evening. It was quiet and peaceful inside the house and for once, Natalie felt at ease with herself and with Jack.

"I think I'm gonna make dinner tomorrow night and give Mom the night off…" She was thinking aloud to herself. "Maybe she and Daddy can have a date night of their own."

"That would be mighty kind of you."

"Yeah, I thought so too. You know I think we should start trading out. It really isn't fair that she cooks so often…" She stopped washing suddenly. "But what on earth will I make?"

"What do you like to cook?" Jack asked, propping his elbows on the counter and looking over at her.

"Well, anything really, but my foods are more "worldly" my Mom says, whereas Mom's foods are more southern."

"Worldly?"

"Yeah, you know, like lasagna, Mediterranean, stir fry…"

"Oh, got ya…"

"I don't really know if you guys like anything besides what Mom cooks."

"Oh, I'm sure we would enjoy whatever you decided to make."

"Don't be so sure…"

"Why not?"

"Well, no one knows this, so keep it on the D.L.," her voice became quiet and she leaned toward him a bit so that he could hear her. "I'm not quite the cook my mother is."

"That can't be true!" Jack gasped dramatically then winked at her.

"It can so to done it." He laughed at her choice of words and she joined in. "It's true. I haven't really cooked in a long time. Hey, maybe you could help me."

"Me?" His look of surprise brought a smile to her lips.

"Yeah."

"And what makes you think *I* can cook?"

"Just wishful thinking…"

He laughed heartily then and pulled a piece of her hair away from her face. "Ok, I guess I'll help you, since you're so *helpless* in the kitchen."

"Hey!" Natalie swatted at him and he made a dramatic dodge as she missed. "I never said I was helpless…" She raised her eyebrows and he just smiled. Once they finished the dishes, Jack excused himself. *Probably going to check on the horses again*, she thought.

Natalie declined the invitation to join Dallie and her father in the living room and instead headed upstairs to finish checking her emails and finish her paperwork for Marlene. She settled herself on the bed, propping her laptop up on her knees. She popped her glasses back on her face, blushing as she remembered what Jack had remarked about them. She was well over half way into the junk file of her inbox when Jack appeared at the head of the stairs. He smiled at her as he walked into the bathroom. It was just a smile, a sweet smile as if he were saying "Hi!", not a word was spoken, but it turned her thoughts straight from her emails to him. He was taking his nightly shower. He was probably shirtless right now, pulling his boots off. He would soon be naked; his chest and arms and torso exposed. She recalled seeing him up close, touching his pecs and abdomen, tracing his well-defined muscles there… Then he'd be wet… Damn him! Why did he have to make her body react this way? She was suddenly turned on and waves of yearning were sailing through her core. She tried to concentrate on the task at hand, but her mind simply wouldn't allow it. Oh, it had been so long since they had touched each other in an intimate way and try as she might she couldn't will her thoughts away from thinking about his naked body.

When she heard the shower start, she nearly came off the bed. He *was* naked now. She could see him in her mind. His broad chest and shoulders, his massive biceps, his tanned skin… She hadn't seen below his belt line, but she imagined his thighs would be as muscled as the rest of him and if she had any indication as to his manhood from having it pressed rock hard against her, she was certain it would be impressive. She wanted to touch every inch of him and run her tongue down his chest and belly and lower... She wanted to tease the furry down that scattered his chest and the straight line of hair that lead to his manhood. She wanted to feel the weight of his sex in her hands and test it. Tease him and stroke him until he couldn't take anymore. She wanted to pull him deep inside her, feel his muscular body on top of her.

Oh, was it so sinful to have these thoughts when it felt so good to imagine his hands on her? He was so solid and secure. So gentle, so affectionate. She imagined how tender he would be as a lover... She missed his touch, missed the feel on his big body against hers. This man had made her feel happiness again and she had begun to love this feeling, especially now that their relationship was actually beginning. She tried once again to focus back to her computer then jumped as Jack opened the bathroom door. *When had he cut the shower off?* She blushed to her toes, feeling her cheeks on fire, then looked down at her computer to keep her eyes off his tempting image, afraid somehow he might see what she'd been thinking, but had to squelch that idea when he knocked lightly on her door.

"Got a minute?" he asked, entering the doorway. He donned a tight grey worn in Texas A & M shirt that emphasized the broadness of his chest and baggy pajama pants with the same emblem. It was the only thing she'd seen him wear aside from Wranglers and a button down. So much for the bare chest and towel around the waist! Darn it...

"Sure, what's up?"

He made a move to sit beside her on the edge of the bed, so she scooted back to make room.

"Well, there's something I need to talk to you about..." he started. She listened patiently, wishing he would just throw her down on the bed and kiss her breathless. Unfortunately, he continued, "I probably should have asked you first before I did this, but, I bought Dallie something today…I, uh, I bought her a horse." He stopped, waiting for her response.

"A horse? A *real* horse?" Her eyes widened in shock.

"Yeah!" He laughed. "A real, living, breathing horse… well a pony, a yearling, she isn't a full grown horse yet."

"Why did you buy her a horse?" She was stunned.

"Well, because I thought she needed one and she really wanted it."

"She's four. Why on earth would she *need* a horse?" Natalie asked, semi-amused.

"Well, I mean…of course she doesn't *need* a horse. I just thought she should have one. You know, to train and raise as her own."

Natalie smirked, "She could've had Blaze…"

"Yeah, but this is the one she picked out, the one that she wanted."

"Well, I want a Porsche. Will you buy me one if I pick it out?" Her tone was playful.

Jack laughed. "You don't sound as mad as I thought you would."

"I'm *not* mad. Surprised. But not mad… But, who's supposed to help her train this horse. You are overextending yourself, Mr. Kinsen."

"Well, I thought you might could help us with that…"

"Me?"

"Yeah, you can train horses as well as anyone else here."

"Well, I don't know about that…" He gave her a retired look, "I mean, I guess I could, I don't see why I *couldn't* help…"

"Good! I think she would really enjoy that," Jack insisted.

"What kind of horse is it?"

"A female Arabian."

"An Arabian? Those aren't cheap."

"No, but she's a beauty, raven black and good news is, she's halter-broken and into round penning."

"Jack, tell me something… Why is it that you have spent so much money on me and Dallie lately? I *know* that horse was a huge chunk of money, at least ten thousand and my necklace was expensive too. Aren't you supposed to be saving for a ranch of your own?"

"I am… I just enjoy giving to my two ladies." With that he smiled and took her hand. "Besides, I have plenty. I'm not worried about money."

"Not worried? Ok, Mr. Money Bags! Still, I don't think you should be buying such pricey gifts."

"I wanted to buy them," he said, dismissing the subject.

"Will you at least let me reimburse you for the horse?"

"Wouldn't dream of it…" He pulled her hand to his mouth and kissed it, his lips were feather light on her skin, and she gasped internally wishing they were on her lips instead. His big bicep rippled as he put his other hand up to her face, cupping it and she longed for him to stay with her as he left her side and stood to leave. "Gotta go pick her up tomorrow. Mind if I bring Dallie with me?"

She shook her head, feeling bereft as he moved toward the door.

"Good night, Natalie." His smile was soft and sexy.

"Night, Jack." And with that he turned and walked out of her doorway, closing her door behind him.

CHAPTER 9

$\mathcal{N}$atalie laughed as Jack pulled the turkey out of the oven.

"Are you serious?" she asked, checking the meat thermometer as he sat the bird on the stovetop.

"Dead serious." Jack's eyebrow was cocked as he gauged her reaction.

"Well, I suppose I could..." She bent over to retrieve the two other dishes from the oven and Jack fought everything within him not to look over at her well-rounded backside. "I still have time to finish my article before it's due."

She hesitated again and he could see the wheels turning in her head. The movie cast was coming in tomorrow to start training with the horses and Jack had asked Natalie for her help because the main role in the film was a female, the only female in the movie and she had no experience with horses whatsoever. Jack thought things might go smoother if Natalie were to train her, plus he was up to his eyeballs in things to do.

"No pressure, Natalie. Just think about it...What's that?" He'd walked over to stand next to her as she sat a steaming casserole dish down on the island in front of them.

"Oh, it's a zucchini gratin. Dallie loves them and I thought it would be a good 'green dish' as Mom calls them." She smiled, delighted at her idea.

"Well, it smells great!" He bent over slightly and breathed in the scent of zucchini and cheeses. "And so do you..." He was within inches of her and he couldn't help but inhale her sweet, fruity scent.

She looked up at him then, oven mitt still on her hand, a look of surprise and desire filling her face. Her chest rose and fell, her cleavage barely covered by a thin burgundy V-neck sweater. Her long locks were pulled back away from her face in a barrette; her hair half up, half down. Her makeup was light, natural looking. If you asked her, she would consider herself dressed down, but to him she looked amazing.

Jack had been good, really good. He hadn't tempted her or touched her provocatively in any way. He'd just given her distance, given her time, and reassured her that he was there for her. He was doing as her father had said and was giving her trust and stability. He was waiting for her to make the first move, wanting her to be comfortable with him. When they moved forward it would be her decision, not his.

She inhaled sharply, not quite knowing what to say or do. He could see the want in her eyes, could see the hesitation as she stepped toward him, then back. She gulped. *So, this is what true torment must feel like.* He thought as he watched her. Almost like helplessly watching a cornered cat or a fish out of water.

Before she could respond the kitchen door swung open and who else but Dan would walk in. Natalie jumped like she'd been shot and Dan smiled as he approached them. Jack just rolled his eyes.

"Can I help with anything?" Dan asked. His Cheshire cat smile was plastered on.

Natalie reoriented herself and smiled. "Sure, umm, here, go ahead and take the turkey to the table and Jack and I will get the rest." She handed him some oven mitts as he did as he was instructed.

Something was definitely going on with Dan. He had become nice, too damned nice, to everyone, including Jack and he'd been extremely friendly to Natalie. Jack couldn't figure it out, was he trying to win her over. *Well, he'd better get that notion out of his head real quick*, Jack thought as he took the mitts Natalie handed him and picked up the casserole dish before him.

Before he could step from the kitchen, Natalie grabbed his arm. "Hey, Jack," she said. A slow, burning heat went through him. He didn't respond, just turned toward her, desire suddenly coursing through his veins. "I'll be glad to help you."

"You don't have to decide now, you can think about it."

"No, no! I don't need to. I have the time and you need me, so I'm there, okay?" Her full lips smiled up at him, bringing a smile to his own lips.

"Alright. 8 AM sharp."

She laughed, "You got it, boss." She grabbed the potatoes as he held the door for her to exit.

Everyone was seated around the table, everyone but Corrine and David who'd gone out for a dinner date as Nat had suggested. Jack sat the dish down and waited to take his seat as Natalie rearranged the dishes and moved a platter full of roasted potatoes in front of him. She sat them down next to the turkey and Jack sat down with her. Dallie said grace and afterward, Natalie took to carving the turkey.

"Wow, Miss Natalie, this is quite a feast," Billy Bob said.

"Thanks, it was really a last minute decision. I hope it's good..." Natalie blushed and it made Jack smile to see her displaying modesty.

She began passing the turkey out, and Dan piped in his two cents, "You really outdid yourself, Natalie. I'm really impressed."

Jack couldn't help but roll his eyes again, as if she needed a reason to impress *him*.

"Thank you, Dan," Natalie said.

Once everyone got a helping of the meal, Natalie held back and waited for their reactions. Jack smiled to himself; it was as if she were waiting for a bomb to go off. But it was him she was looking at. He took the hint and dug into to his turkey leg and his zucchini whatever it was. He wasn't a bit surprised to find that she was a good cook. After all, she *was* her mother's daughter.

He smiled over at her, "This is terrific." And that was all she needed to relax and breathe easily. She dug in herself as did Dallie who was telling him all about her costume ideas for Halloween.

"Well, what about a princess?" he asked.

Her frown was answer enough, "Jack, please." She propped her hands on her hips, reminding him of her mother, and Jack laughed.

"Sorry...forgive me for even mentioning it." He hugged her then and kissed the top of her sweet head. He looked over at Dan who was asking for another helping and wondered what on earth was going on with him. Jack didn't like it, whatever it was. Dan wouldn't weasel his way into the relationship he was starting to build with Natalie. This would not be a repeat performance. Jack would make certain of that...

Later that evening, Jack headed up to bed after talking on his cell phone with Luther who was whining because Jack hadn't called him. He'd said it was past time that they go out for a drink. Jack had agreed, but his heart hadn't been in it. There was only one thing he wanted and as he headed into the bathroom he found it. Natalie was attending to Dallie who was brushing her teeth with a little toothbrush adorning a pink pony. Jack smiled and propped himself in the door jamb. He remembered how excited Dallie had been to show Natalie her new pony today after they'd brought her home. She'd made her mother keep her eyes closed all the way to the barn and when Natalie had opened them, a beautiful raven black Arabian stood before her. Natalie had made a big deal over how pretty the horse was and petted her and oohed and ahhed over her. Dallie had been thrilled.

"Ok Dallie, time's up, spit and rinse," Natalie instructed as she smiled over at Jack. Dallie did as she was told and ran to Jack as she headed out the door. He picked her up and propped her against him as she hugged him.

"Will you tuck me in and read me a story?" Dallie begged. She knew he couldn't say no.

"Which one will it be tonight?" he asked.

"*Stellaluna!*"

"I was afraid you were going to say that," he feigned exasperation as he looked over at Natalie. Her beautiful blue eyes twinkling. God, he was so in love with her. When would she end this torture for him, for them both?

"Goodnight, Natalie." He wanted to be saying it next to her, not in separation.

"Goodnight, Jack." She looked disappointed; as if she had something she wanted to say but was holding back.

He laid his sweet little angel down in her bed and tucked her sheet and comforter around her. As he settled down next to her, she propped her head on his shoulder and he began to read her the book that had become their nightly ritual. She was asleep before he ever got halfway through the book and he looked down into her adorable little face and smiled. Her eyelashes were so long that they rested on her plump little cheeks. She looked so much like her mother. He moved his body away, gently placing her head on her pillow. He whispered a good night as he kissed her fleshy little cheek. He moved to stand and looked up to see Natalie positioned in the doorway, watching him. She was donning a short pink robe atop a sexy little white nightgown. Her eyes were tearful and she looked sad.

She spoke before he could ask her if she was alright. "Her father never read to her... She would beg him to, but he was always too busy or simply never there..." She trailed off, looking down.

Jack said the only thing he thought of, "He's a fool."

She nodded and turned to leave, then turned back toward him, facing him. "Thank you, Jack... For everything."

"Natalie, don't thank me." He slowly walked over to where she was standing and took her hands in his. "No thanks are necessary. I adore you and your daughter and I do things for both of you because I want to."

"I know, but it's just nice to have such kindness and generosity in our lives and I want to thank you for showing her that there are still good people left in this world."

He smiled down into her face lit only by the small lamp on Dallie's nightstand. Her eyes sparkled with unshed tears and once again he felt hate for this man that had brought such pain into their lives. She looked so frail and vulnerable in that moment that he fought everything within him not to kiss her. He dared himself to give into his earthly desires. She needed more than passion and sex. She needed a man whom she could trust; one that would be there for her, one that would love her and take care of her, one that would fulfill all of her needs and that was the man he wanted to be. Not just the man that satisfied her sexual desires.

She made no move to touch him, just stared up at him for what seemed to be long minutes. She was a woman fighting with her own feelings, a woman torn, a beautiful disaster. There was nothing to do but wait, wait for her to decide when she would stop being afraid and start living again. She gulped and whispered a good night as she turned away to go to her own room. He just sighed and turned the opposite way. They always said that time healed all wounds... It was just a matter of time.

～

She was beautiful. Of course she was beautiful! She was a celebrity. Natalie recognized her from several action movies she'd seen her in: *Paradise Unknown*, *Too Hot to Handle*, and *War Within*. Vivian Alexander was tall, lean, and had the most gorgeous natural blonde hair Natalie had ever seen, if it was indeed natural. She wore big round tortoise shell sunglasses, a straw cowboy hat and bright cherry red lipstick. Silver bangle bracelets dangled from her wrists and yellow hoop earrings adorned her ears.

Her stone washed jeans had tears, her red snakeskin boots were new and her blue shirt featured a bucking bronco and cowboy reading "Every girl loves a dirty cowboy". Her bulky brown shrug and red Coach hand bag were completely out of place, but Natalie admired her sense of style.

"Hi, are you Natalie? I'm Vivian." Her bracelets jingled as she shook Natalie's hand.

"I am. It's a pleasure to meet you, Miss Alexander."

"Oh, please call me Vivian. It's a pleasure to meet you as well. I *loved* your magazine. And thank you so much for taking the time to help me. When I was assigned this role, I was so nervous. I am scared to death of horses. I'm so glad you're here," Vivian said. Natalie's eyes lit up in astonishment. *She's scared of horses! This could be very bad!* "I'm so glad I'm not the only girl." Natalie was surprised at her subtle shyness and was eager to befriend this down-to-earth young woman who looked no older than twenty-one.

Vivian took in her surroundings as they walked the length of the barn.

"Wow, this barn is fabulous, it's huge and very modern."

"It is," Natalie confirmed. "My father had it remodeled about five years ago to accommodate his growing demand. New air conditioning, heated stables. We even have a birthing room and grooming salon." She pointed out to Vivian. "How about we introduce you to our crew before we get started, okay?" Natalie led Vivian and her assistant who looked more like a repressed vulture with his no-nonsense eyes and crooked nose into her father's office where all the hands were gathered in a meeting. "Dad, I'm sorry to interrupt, but this is Vivian Alexander." Natalie stepped back as Vivian approached her father who stood behind his desk. He pulled off his hat and took her hand.

"Miss Alexander. I'm David Butler. It's a pleasure to meet you, ma'am."

"Thank you, likewise, Mr. Butler." Vivian took his firm handshake and met it with her own.

Natalie then looked over at Jack as he stood. "Vivian, this is Jack Kinsen. He's our foreman." Jack extended his hand to her and she placed her hand in his as he gently shook it.

"Nice to meet you," he said, tipping his hat as he sat back down in his chair.

"The tall one is Dan Wilson; next to him is Billy Bob Anderson. Kyle Warren. Miguel Rodriguez and Cass Henderson." She pointed out. "Beside my father is William Thomason, he owns a ranch a few minutes from here and his crew is Jeff Andrews, Bobby McFee and Tad Walters." They all tipped their hats and greeted her. Vivian smiled back and said, "Hello!" to them. "We will leave you guys. We have a lot to work on," Natalie replied and showed Vivian out of the office.

"Wow, now I know how you feel to be the only girl working around all these hunks," Vivian blushed and Natalie laughed, bringing a laugh out of Vivian.

"It can get a bit overwhelming at times with all the testosterone flowing around here," Natalie agreed.

"Oh, I bet. Especially for someone with a figure like yours."

Natalie was again surprised by her comment but thanked her just the same. It flattered her that a movie star thought she had a nice figure.

Natalie led her confidante to the back of the barn to the shower rooms.

"Well, here's the restroom and shower room. There are also some lockers back there for you to put your belongings in if you wish. We need to get you acquainted with your horses, okay?" *And a pair of chaps and spurs as well*, Natalie thought. A real pair of cowboy boots wasn't such a bad idea either…

"Ok, great. Again, thank you so much for all this," Vivian said as she opened one of the lockers and placed her oversized bag in it.

"Oh, you're welcome. I'll meet you out in the corral when you're ready."

~

*V*ivian was a good sport and very fun to work with, Natalie saw. Once Natalie got her accustomed to all the items and equipment they would need, bits, reigns, halters, saddles, brushes, etc… The first obstacle she had to face was getting Vivian used to the horses despite her intense fear of them.

"Ok, Vivian, this is probably the most important thing that I will ever tell you," Natalie stated in all seriousness. "Never, not for one second, forget that this horse is indeed an animal, and not only an animal but a *large* animal, you must remain calm and in control. But the second you forget that, you'll be in trouble. Horses can be extremely dangerous, I'm sure you're aware of that. So even more important, you cann*ot* be afraid. I know that you are, but they can sense your fear and it makes them nervous too, which will only make this job a lot harder on all of us. So the first thing I want you to do is pretend like this horse is simply a large dog."

Vivian had been reluctant at first but had touched the horses as Natalie had instructed and talked to them as she'd explained. Each horse was, of course, unique and different in personality and it would take time for each of them to get used to their new rider, so Natalie simply encouraged Vivian to be at ease and most important in control. She had begun by letting Vivian lead each of the horses around the corral. Then she worked on commands with her and Natalie explained to her how important it was that the horses respect her and see her as their boss.

By lunch time, the backyard was a circus and Vivian had yet to ride. The video crew had arrived within the first hour to play with camera angles for each horse. The director and producer had arrived to talk to her father. Their lunch was being catered in by large vans and was being set up under tents. Vivian's body guard had shown up not too long after they had started and stood by the fence giving Natalie a grin that annoyed her each time she happened to glance his way. Vivian's assistant with his perusing eyes had stayed on the phone when he wasn't doting over Vivian or propped in his fold out chair with its purple umbrella acting for all the world like a bored three year old, checking his watch constantly, yawning and sighing. Natalie was ready for her lunch break when Jack arrived and told them to eat. She sighed in relief and joined him at the fence.

"You are my knight in shining armor," she said and smiled up at him. She looped her arm through his as they walked toward the tent covered tables stocked with trays of numerous hors d'oeuvres, meats, vegetables, pastas, and desserts.

"Glad I could rescue my princess," he laughed. "She that big a pain in the ass?"

"Not her, her body guard and assistant. The camera man too. I was ready to kill him when he shoved that camera in Bruno's face."

"I guess it's all a part of the lifestyle, but you would know," he teased. She gave him a retired look as he laughed. As they joined the others in line and began plating their food, Jack's voice became a whisper. "So, how is the progress going?"

"Well, for someone who's terrified of horses I think she's doing great," Natalie replied placing a stuffed mushroom in her mouth then scooped up a helping of sausage rigatoni with marinara onto her plate.

"Terrified of horses?" his whisper was now a bit louder as he hit the roast beef station.

"Yeah, she hasn't even got to ride yet." *Oh, garlic mashed potatoes.* Natalie thought and added that to her heaping pile of food.

"Wow, I didn't know that! Has she ever ridden a horse before?" Jack inquired and scooped up some ratatouille.

"Nope," she said and popped a piece of cauliflower in her mouth before moving to sit on the benches provided by the studio. Jack was close on her heels.

"Wow, this is gonna take longer than I thought… I only thought it would take you a couple days to train with her before we took over, but that's a joke. Does anyone else know?" He took a seat beside her and began eating his chicken carbonara.

"I don't really know. I guess it's a good thing she's got stunt doubles." Natalie laughed heartily, bringing a big grin out of Jack.

"Yeah, that's true!"

"So, what have you been doing all morning while I've been working my butt off?" she teased.

"Hey, it looks to me as if it's still there." He made a point to look around her seat. "Thank goodness," he feigned relief and Natalie laughed. "I've actually been working with the stunt doubles." They both burst into laughter at that.

"She'll get it, it will just take time. It won't happen overnight," Natalie assured.

"I know, but let's try telling that to the director. He's wanting to bump up their starting day."

"I know, I'm doing my best, I just don't want to push her."

"I understand." The look in his eyes told her that he understood all too well and she sighed knowing how he felt. He was the one waiting for *her* progression.

After lunch, most of the crowd had left. Jack had brought Dallie down from the house to meet Vivian. She'd been delighted to meet a "real movie star" and Vivian was taken with her as well. Bruno was Vivian's first horseback ride, seeing as he was the most easy going stallion in the bunch. She was afraid, but again Natalie explained to her that she was in control and must remain calm. Natalie led the horse around the corral, getting Vivian used to the feel of him. They did this for an hour before Natalie felt Vivian should go at it on her own. Her father and several of the hands had gathered at the fence to watch. Vivian felt unsure at first, but Natalie encouraged her, and she trotted him forward and around the corral slowly, then as she became more comfortable, she gained speed. She wasn't very graceful, but she was a first timer and it would take some time to get her used to riding. Overall, Natalie was as proud as Vivian was as she came to a stop in front of her. She dismounted the horse and gave Natalie an embracing hug.

"Oh, thank you so much. I couldn't have done it without you,"

Vivian exclaimed as she pulled away. The hands began clapping, along with Jack, who looked over at Natalie and smiled. "Can I try it on the other horse, what was his name, Twilight?"

"Why don't we just work on one at a time? I wouldn't overdo it today, Viv."

"Oh, but, I really want to."

Natalie looked over at her father. He shrugged and motioned for Tad to bring out the stallion. He was saddled up and reined and Vivian mounted him, grabbing the horse's mane with newfound confidence. Once again, Natalie led Vivian around the corral to get used to Twilight as she had before. After she felt comfortable, again, Natalie let her go on her own.

Dallie suddenly squirmed at the fence where she was being held in Jack's arms.

"Mommy, I want Mommy."

Natalie looked over at her to see what she needed.

"What's wrong, Dallie?" Jack asked, looking down at her.

Dallie only repeated, "I want Mommy." Natalie stepped forward to take her and pulled her to her side, holding her. "Mommy, something's wrong. He's gonna hurt her."

"Who, angel?" Natalie looked down into her daughter's pale face, her little blue eyes fixed on the horse and his rider.

"Twilight."

Just as she said his name, the horse's whinny pierced the air and he reared up, his front legs reaching for the sky. Vivian screamed in terror.

"Oh shit," Natalie cried as she set Dallie down on the ground. "Stay right there Dallie and don't move. Jack, lasso," she cried as she ran toward Vivian and the horse. Jack tossed a rope at her as he ducked through the fence and followed her with a rope of his own. Vivian's cries were infuriating the stallion who began bucking and snorting and jumping like a crazed bronco. Jack and Natalie kept their distance, but were close enough to lasso the stallion.

"Vivian, listen to me, stop crying, you have to hold on to him, grab the reins and tighten your grip with your legs," Natalie instructed as she got the noose ready and looked over at Jack, who nodded.

"On three," He replied his lasso ready as well. "One, two…three."

On three, they swung both ropes around the horse's neck and tightened them down to control the spooked animal. By then Tad, Dan and William had joined them. Dan, Will and Natalie had one side and Tad and Jack had the other. It didn't seem to be a determent at all. Twilight was still bucking and whinnying angrily, their effort was no match for his strength. Just then Natalie heard Dallie calling to her. She looked over to see Dallie running toward her.

"Dallie, No! Stop! Don't come any closer," Natalie cried.

"But I can help him, Mommy," Dallie countered.

"No, honey, you can't…" The rope burned deep into her hands as the horse pulled them back and forth. It was becoming hard to hold on to it.

Natalie's father approached then with Dallie in his arms, coming closer.

"Dad, stop! What in the Hell are you doing?" She gritted her teeth not just from anger but from the pain searing through her palms.

"She can help," her father said and moved closer, pushing Dallie out at arm's length.

"Are you out of your *fucking* mind? Get her away from that crazy horse!" she cried.

"It's okay, Mommy," Dallie exclaimed. She came at Twilight from the side, placed her little palm at the stallion's neck and began whispering to him. She stroked him as far as she could reach. Within seconds, the horse came down off his haunches and had calmed down enough to where Natalie and the hands let up on their grip, they were all breathless. The stallion breathed heavily as Dallie got closer and put both hands on his face at his cheekbones. She began singing to him and stroked him between his eyes.

"Will someone please get me off this damn horse?" Vivian begged in numbness. She was shaking as Jack pulled her off the saddle, grabbing her underneath her armpits and sat her down on solid ground.

"Tad, take Twilight back to his stall. Dan, call Dr. Green. Let's call it a day!" Jack said. He was visibly shaken as he walked Vivian back toward the fence. Dan and Tad began doing as they were told. William followed David as he hauled Dallie back out of the corral. Natalie followed perplexed, angry and suddenly in pain as she began coming down off her adrenaline high. She looked down at her burnt, bleeding, scarred palms and silently cursed. Why in Hell had she not bothered to wear her gloves? She approached Vivian, whom she assumed would be hysterical. She was sitting calmly with a tissue in hand, looking at the ground. Natalie was within arms reach of Vivian when her assistant popped up in her face, waving his finger.

"If I had any idea how reckless you people would be…You will be hearing from our attorney," he reprimanded.

"Hey," a deep voice intervened. "Let me tell you something!" Jack boomed, stepping in front of Natalie. "You'd better get your finger out of her face right now. You won't talk to her that way, not now or ever. We have a contract at this ranch, same as you do, and in that contract it states that we won't be held liable for any incident that happens here. Especially with horses that aren't even *our* horses. So before you go threatening someone, you'd better have something to back it up with." He gently took Natalie's shoulders and faced them the opposite direction, walking them toward the house. "C'mon Nat, let's go doctor your hands."

～

*L*ater that night, it was quiet at dinner as everyone sat contemplating the day. Natalie was the only one missing from the table, and it seemed empty without her. She'd gone upstairs after he brought her inside and cleaned and bandaged her hands, taken some pain killers and went to bed. Neither of them spoke as he attended her wounds, both were too awe-struck by the day's events. Jack knew she'd been upset at herself and her father. It wasn't her fault what happened, no one could've anticipated that Twilight would've gotten spooked as he had. Dr. Green had found nothing to show any reason for his behavior and had given the horse something to relax him. David was also quiet at dinner and Jack could see that he felt guilty for bringing Dallie into the middle of the commotion. Although Jack was glad he had, at the same time, David had taken great risk by putting Dallie in danger. All the hands left for the bunk house after dinner and Jack headed upstairs to check in on Natalie. He'd showered before dinner and was grateful he did because all he wanted to do was crash. Natalie's light was on in her room and he breathed a sigh of relief as he opened the door. She was sitting up on her bed, her computer in her lap and her sexy glasses perched atop her nose. Her cheeks and shoulders were sun kissed from the long day out in the Texas heat. Her hair and long pink tank top were rumpled and disheveled. She looked up at him as he approached and tears filled her eyes. She pushed the computer aside as he rushed to her and pulled her into his arms.

"Oh, baby, don't cry... Everything's fine now." Jack crooned to her.

"But I feel horrible about what happened today," Natalie said.

"I know you do. But you know what? Vivian called." He smiled, looking down into her red eyes.

"She did?" Natalie's tears began to weaken at the mention of Vivian's name. Jack swiped at them with his fingers.

"Yes, and she was calling to apologize to you for what her assistant said to you. She fired him by the way!"

"She did? Good! Good riddance to that weasel of a man."

"Vivian was upset about what happened, but she said that she was okay and that she would be here tomorrow. I told her that I didn't know if you would be though," he said, looking down at her hands, red and swollen, covered in gauze.

"They'll never look the same again." She began to sob again.

"Oh, yes they will. They'll heal in time."

"Yes, but they look like man hands now. I won't ever have pretty woman's hands again...this is what I get for not wearing my gloves. I can't even type, how am I supposed to write my article?" Her eyes filled with tears again and he bent his head down, kissing the bandages softly.

"They will always be the most beautiful hands in the world," he said, smiling into her face. She sniffled, her tears once again ceasing as she smiled back at him. His heart did a flip-flop at the look she gave him and he wanted to kiss her so badly, but again, as always, he resisted.

"How's Twilight?"

"He's fine. The vet can't find a thing wrong with him. Heck, I figured maybe he'd stepped on something, but he checked him from head to toe. Nothing!"

"How strange!" Natalie frowned.

"Too many people around, unfamiliar territory, new rider... I don't know." Jack shrugged. "It's a chance we all take with these animals." Natalie just nodded

She looked down in contemplation, then back up at him. "Jack, Dallie knew that he was about to get spooked. I don't know how, but she did. She told me that something was wrong, that he was about to hurt Vivian."

About that time, David and Dallie knocked at the door and Jack turned to see Dallie with a small vase of orchids. She was dressed in a Scooby-Doo nightgown complete with pink slippers. She smiled as she approached the bed.

"These are for you, Mommy. They're from Paw-Paw," Dallie said and handed the flowers up to Natalie, but Jack took them instead and sat them on the nightstand.

"Daddy." Natalie sighed as David stepped forward.

"I know I didn't have to, but I wanted to," David said and tucked his hands down into his pockets before continuing, a look of regret covering his face. "I shouldn't have put Dallie in the middle of it, I know that. But God help me, I had to." He paced and then sat himself at the foot of the bed. Jack stood, feeling like an outsider in the conversation although neither one of them looked inclined to tell him to leave. "I couldn't stand by and watch that horse hurt someone when I knew that Dallie could stop him," David said with conviction looking into Natalie's eyes.

Jack's gaze went from David's solemn expression to Natalie's confused one. She still didn't realize that Dallie had the gift she did. Was it denial or simply unawareness? She didn't know what to say to her father, but she didn't look as upset as she had earlier. Her expression had softened.

"I'm not angry with you, and I'm sorry, Daddy. I just want Dallie to be safe, and I was scared," Natalie said.

"I was scared too. For you and for Jack and for Vivian... I love you baby, more than anything," he said and moved to embrace her and she sat up to accept him.

"I love you too," Natalie murmured. Dallie joined them then in a group hug and Natalie kissed her forehead. "And I love you, my little angel."

"I love you too, Mommy," Dallie said and gripped the back of Natalie's hand softly and touched the bandage on her palm. "Do they hurt?"

"Badly."

"I'm sorry. I told you I could help him."

Natalie sighed then and pulled Dallie into her lap. "Baby, I know you love horses, but they can be *dangerous*...How did you know something was about to happen?" she asked, stroking her daughter's long tendrils.

"I felt it. He was shaking. He was scared," Dallie said.

He hadn't appeared that way to Jack or anyone else. It was as if Dallie had a sixth sense when it came to the horses.

"What was he scared of, Dallie?" Jack asked, taking her little hand in his as he knelt down in front of her and Natalie. She just shrugged. "So, how did you know he was scared?"

"I could feel that he was, and it made me scared."

All three of them were in awe. They had seen how quickly the horse had gotten spooked and how quickly he'd reacted to Dallie's touch.

"Well, pumpkin. Let's go tuck you in. Mommy needs to eat some dinner," David said, gathering his granddaughter into his arms and kissing her on the cheek.

"Goodnight, Mommy," Dallie said and waved as David toted her out the door.

"Goodnight, baby. Sweet dreams," Natalie returned.

"You too," She replied blowing her a kiss.

"Want me to bring up your dinner?" Jack asked, watching the two head into Dallie's room.

"Would you mind?" Nat asked.

"Would I mind? It would be my pleasure."

She smirked at his eagerness as he ran off downstairs. He returned soon after with a tray full of food and saw Natalie was eager to eat. She had removed the glasses and was sitting patiently, her injured hands atop her lap.

"Courtesy of your mother," he said, smiling.

Corrine had fixed Natalie a heaping bowl of beef stew, a buttered yeast roll, a tall glass of sweet tea and a generous helping of black-berry cobbler. Natalie grabbed the sweet tea first and gently brought it to her lips as Jack nestled the tray on either side of her and came around the bed to sit next to her.

"Bless her," she said as she grabbed up the spoon to dig into her stew. She struggled, trying to grip it, winced, and dropped the spoon in to her lap. "Dammit!"

"Here, let me help you." He plucked the spoon from her lap and placed it in the stew, scooping up a bite for her. "Open up." He brought the spoon to her pretty full lips.

"You're going to feed me?" Natalie asked, incredulously.

"Well, yeah, why not? You seem to be having trouble doing it yourself."

She shrugged and he could see it was difficult for her to admit her vulnerability. She was embarrassed and her cheeks were red as she opened her mouth to take the stew. Natalie had pride, a lot like her father. But Jack wasn't much on pride. It had never gotten him far.

"It's just embarrassing," She mumbled, swallowing her bite of stew.

"No, it isn't. You're in pain. Do you honestly expect me to let you sit here and struggle when you don't have to?" With that he shoved another bite into her mouth.

"I just don't want to inconvenience you," She replied, after chewing and swallowing the bite he'd given her.

"Do I look like I have anything better to do?" He asked earnestly. She shook her head then, smiling. He smiled back. It was nice change to see Natalie finally bend a bit. She'd been the tough, independent one for far too long and it was good to see that she couldn't do everything on her own, that she *did* need someone every now and again to help her. She needed him, and that was a good feeling for Jack.

She was able to feed herself the roll as he continued giving her spoonfuls of stew. They conversed about the day and about the ranch and it felt good to be this close to her for the first time in far too long. He was falling more in love with her as each day passed, the more he learned, the more he loved. Even though he still hadn't learned everything, she fascinated him. Everything about her fascinated him. He admired her strength and determination, her love for Dallie and her family, her courage and pride. Her father had been right. Their relationship was growing into something wonderful. He felt it. She was falling for him, she had to be. She was opening up to him; it was just a matter of time.

"Have you started working on your own ranch?" The question was completely out of the blue and Jack paused, the spoonful of cobbler stopping in midair. "Did I say something wrong?" Her eyes took on a new look, a look of apprehension.

"No, no, you didn't say anything wrong," he said. He just hadn't expected the question. "Um, well… yes and no."

"What do you mean?" She accepted the bite he placed in her mouth and again looked at him with those eyes full of worry.

"Well, I've picked out and paid for the land and picked out the layout and the house plan. But to be honest with you I hadn't thought much about it for a while."

Her brows were drawn in confusion. "Why?"

This conversation was one he'd been dreading deep down. Her father had asked him these same questions not too long ago and Jack had simply skirted around the truth, now he felt eager to tell Natalie why he had become reluctant to pursue his dream.

"Well, to be honest." He squirmed a bit. "I haven't been too enthusiastic about continuing with the ranch lately." Her eyes were riveted on him, her look captivating. "I don't know if you've noticed, but your father's," he paused, searching for the right word, "capabilities… aren't what they once were. I've been hesitant to leave your family because I feel they need me, even more than I need a ranch of my own right now." Natalie's head dropped. She knew that Jack was telling the truth. "I don't know what they will do when I leave, and to be honest, I really haven't wanted to. Your family has become a part of me. I know that your father still wants to leave the ranch to you and Nathan…" He left the sentence open because he knew as well as she that her and Nathan weren't speaking.

Natalie was quiet for long moments then spoke as if in a reverie. "Deep down, I know that my father, after all these years, is still hopeful that Nathan and I can work things out and take over the ranch when he's ready to give it to us. I just don't know if Nathan will ever forgive me." She looked up at him, pain in her eyes. He wouldn't ask what on earth she needed Nathan to forgive her for. He was simply glad for the fact that she was opening up to him about her past. Something she rarely did. He felt like he was trying to put together a puzzle; she would only give him a piece here and there and he was left to wonder about the missing portions.

She touched his hand then, gently, the bandage soft on his skin. "Jack, thank you for everything you've done for Mom and Dad.

Truly, I don't know what they would have done without you... It means a lot to me that you would consider them before yourself. But don't put your life on hold. They wouldn't want to know that you weren't living your dream because you are worried about them." She had no idea just how much her parents meant to him and he did worry about them and what would happen to the ranch when he left. He was their foreman, after all. He just nodded and plopped another bite of cobbler in her mouth, smiling at her.

"What about you, Natalie? What about your dreams?" He didn't think she would answer his question, but she surprised him.

She swallowed the bite before answering him. "Me? Well, I guess Dallie and I will stay here. I used to tell Mom that when I was a child... Dallie loves it here and I, like you, feel that Mom and Dad need me... I guess I feel obligated to stay as well since I abandoned them ten years ago." More pieces to the puzzle. Why was she telling him so much? Why was she telling him so little? He took the bait either way.

"*Abandoned* them?"

"Yeah. Abandoned them... I married Troy right out of high school. I was pregnant and I just couldn't stay behind and have my parents help raise my child while I worked endless jobs and he went off to college and lived his own life. Plus, he wanted me to go with him and I thought it was the only choice I had and I thought I was in love. God, but I was young and stupid, and I went with him. It was the worst mistake I've ever made. Well, actually, I can't say it was a mistake because if it weren't for Troy I wouldn't have Dallie..." She was staring off into space and Jack was intrigued and wanted to know more.

"So, what did you do?"

"Well, I changed colleges as fast as I could, but my journalism scholarships were void because I was supposed to go to Texas Christian. He had a football scholarship to a private school...Baldwin Mill University in Chicago, Illinois, so that's were I went. My parents couldn't come up with that kind of money, so his parents paid my way. Troy refused to go if I couldn't go with him so they caved… We were married at their house, you know. I always felt that they thought I wasn't good enough for their son…ha, imagine that! You know where Cameron manor is?" He nodded his head indicating that he did. "Yeah, *great* in-laws might I add…" She was quiet after that, but Jack was hanging by a thread. He needed more, had to have more.

"Why do you say that you "abandoned" your family? I mean, yeah, so you left to be with the man you thought you loved to start your own family, but is that really "abandonment"?" He was prying he knew, but he had to know why she felt that way.

"Because we were all so close, me and Mom and Dad and Nathan. And there was an unspoken understanding between me and my brother, that we would live here all of our lives and take over the ranch when Mom and Dad wanted to retire. Daddy always said he wanted to travel the world one day. Nathan has never forgiven me. He was so hurt and betrayed. He will never let me forget it…" She looked down then.

"Yeah, well, he needs to grow up and get the Hell over it," Jack stated, annoyed. She looked up, surprised at his words but said nothing. *That was a pretty selfish idea in the first place*, Jack thought. "People grow up, change their minds and sometimes go their separate ways in life. That's just how it is. Just like me and my brothers, we all three live in different places, but that doesn't make us any less of a family because we do…"

He continued questioning her. As long as she was willing to answer his questions, he was going to ask them. "What happened to the baby?" Dallie was too young to have been born that long ago…

"I lost it. First quarter of college at Baldwin Mill," she smirked. "It was just as well, I guess. He had never really wanted it in the first place and deep down I was scared to death…I know I would have loved it no matter what but I truly wasn't ready to be a mom then."

"And Dallie?"

"She was quite a surprise." Natalie smiled at the recollection. "But at least we were more prepared for her. I had been working at *Edge* for about two years and then Rick came up to visit...I felt really guilty after that, really disappointed in myself and was determined to work on my marriage. I had been raised that marriage was a sacred bond and that you should try to work things out, besides Troy and I were in a good place in life as far as everything else was concerned. We both loved our jobs, we were financially stable, and we had a beautiful home. I tried to treat him with the love I had felt when we first got together in high school and for a while he recipro-cated that. A few months later, I was pregnant, but then Troy got hurt right in the middle of my pregnancy and had to leave the NFL. He was never really the same after that..."

To his surprise, she continued.

"Dallie was the most beautiful thing in the whole world when she was born. I had never felt such love in all of my life when I held her in my arms for the first time. I know everyone says that but it's completely true! For a while Troy seemed to be happy again. But then..." She stopped then and he could see her mentally shut down. Her confession was over and he was left with more questions than answers. Again, just bits and pieces to the whole story. He was dying to know more about her life. What had led up to her coming here? But he couldn't press her and he knew it. She was making headway and that was a start.

They sat quietly as he continued to feed her the last of the cobbler. Questions filled his head and heart as he pulled the tray away from her and set it on the ground. She touched his hand again and smiled up at him.

"Thank you, Jack."

"No problem. You would do the same for me, I'm sure." At that, she nodded.

"I know, but I really want you to know how grateful I am for all you've done for me...and for my family. I couldn't have survived this past month without you." Jack didn't fully understand that comment and was rather surprised by it, but didn't reply as she slowly moved her hand up to his face, cupping it with her bandaged palm. He felt the stirrings of desire swarm his body as she moved her torso toward him. He moved toward her instinctively and his arm went around to her back. Their eyes met. Her head was within inches of his as she brought her lips to meet his. They were warm and supple and smelled of that sweet blackberry cobbler she'd just eaten. Her full lips were soft against his and he kissed them back, gently, wanting to deepen the kiss but not wanting to encroach on her passionate embrace. She was in control and she would stay that way until she said otherwise. She didn't make the kiss sexual, just pressed her lips to his ever so gently. It was a tender kiss of appreciation, and although Jack wanted more, he didn't allow himself to take anything she wasn't giving him. She pulled away and just as quickly as it had begun, it ended. She didn't move her hand just looked at him deeply in the eyes.

"Well, darlin', I think you have mastered the art of a proper thank you. I think I've taught you well." He winked at her. "And anytime you want to thank me again, I'll be right here ready to accept your gratitude." With that, she laughed loudly.

～

The next couple days were difficult to complete with rope burned hands, Natalie found out. It was hard to shower, it was hard to eat, and it was hard to work. But she didn't complain any more after that first night, even when Jack offered to feed her again in the privacy of her room. She had declined respectfully even though she really would have loved to let him. Not just because of the pain, but because it had been rather sexy letting him feed her, if somewhat humbling. Natalie wasn't able to work with the horses either, but she had tried. And she had a newfound respect for Vivian Alexander. Vivian had indeed shown up the next day to work with them, which had really surprised Natalie. Vivian had, at first, seemed like the type of woman who would easily give up, but she had shown determination when she got back on that horse again the day after it had almost bucked her off. Jack was working with them again today and Natalie felt somewhat jealous of the way he and Vivian laughed and flirted together. She had gotten through that first day by instructing as Jack went through the motions, but she felt useless, she might as well have her hands tied behind her back. Today, Vivian would be riding by herself and it would be all up to Jack. She just stood on the sidelines feeling like a benched quarterback. She had looked forward to riding with Vivian until she'd gotten her hands scarred up. She still had so much she wanted to teach her.

Vivian was a kind girl and very down to earth, but Natalie didn't like the way she flitted her hair when Jack was talking to her. *It must be a celebrity thing,* Natalie thought. All those girls let the fame go to their prissy little heads. *How pathetic!* As if they didn't have enough men to choose from out in Hollywood, they had to go and infringe on ordinary people as well. Well, if he wanted her, he could have her, Natalie decided watching as Jack laughed at something Vivian said. Natalie cursed her bandaged hands as she watched Jack boost Vivian onto her saddle. *Isn't that what a stirrup and saddle horn are for?* She turned, embarrassed by her jealousy. Since when had she started to care so much?

Her father had asked her to help with his bookkeeping and it seemed as if Jack didn't need her in the corral, so she headed back to the barn to keep busy, almost running headlong into Dan in the process.

"Jesus," she swore as she looked up at him, his sweaty blonde hair concealed by a dusty tan Stetson. His dark brown eyes were intense as he looked at her.

"Sorry, Natalie."

"Could you watch where you're going?" She would've hated her condescending tone had she been talking to anyone else.

"I'm really sorry. I didn't mean to startle you." He removed his hat and swiped at the sweat on his forehead, giving her a weak smile. "Look, uh, there's somethin' I really want to talk to you about."

"Well, I'm sorry Dan, but I'm busy now. Can it wait?" Instead of being curious as to what he wanted to talk to her about, she preferred to postpone the conversation. *What could he possibly have to say that would be important anyway?* She asked herself.

"Uh, yeah, sure. I'll catch up with you later."

"Ok." She waved nonchalantly as she walked back to her father's office. What was his deal lately? He no longer appeared to be the arrogant, male sexist he'd once been. It irritated her and puzzled her. He seemed like a boy scout lately, doing no wrong. He was sucking up to her. That was it! But, why? What did he want? Maybe she should have talked to him after all.

Natalie kept herself busy updating her father's checkbook, entering invoices into the computer and filing a stack of papers the size of her beloved state. For a moment she went back in time, she was home again; doing all the "dirty work" her father always hated and put off until the last minute. She felt like she'd done this practice a million times before and it lightened her mood, if only momentarily. She was just finishing up when Jack walked in, looking sweaty and sexy as all get out.

"Hey… damn, its hot out there." He was out of breath as he moved in front of the AC and pulled his hat off, letting the cool breeze fan his face. His big bicep flexed as he did so and she watched the sweat drip from him. She tried hard to swallow the huge lump that had grown in her throat in the process. Her body's demands were becoming hard to resist with this man. Everything about him oozed sex and masculinity, from his hard muscles to his big smile. "Whatcha doing?" he asked.

It took her a moment to answer him, afraid her voice would catch.

"Uh, just organizing Daddy's desk."

"Oh, yeah, I see that." He hitched his finger toward the front door. "Ya kinda went MIA there for a while."

"Yeah, well, you looked like you were doing just fine without me, so I wanted to do something productive." She tried to sound casual as she answered him, keeping her voice steady, trying to sound less irritated than she really was. He looked intently at her for a moment before he shrugged and sat down in the chair in front of her, placing his hat on his bent knee.

"Well, if its not too much trouble would you mind showing Vivian the proper way to ride, I mean, once your hands have healed up? She needs to look more...well, lady-like and more comfortable in the saddle."

"More lady-like?" Natalie asked, giving him an exasperated look.

"Yeah, you know she's— well, she's slouching in the saddle. She needs to improve her posture and I thought you'd do a better job instructing her with that than I could."

"Have you ever seen me ride?" The question was somewhat rhetorical and she knew it, but she asked anyway.

"Well, yeah, I mean when you rode with Dallie...why?" His gaze was intent as he searched her eyes.

"What makes you think I can *teach* something like that? It's a *natural* ability." Her tone was smart and he picked up on it. His eyebrow cocked at her comment.

"Well, perhaps you could give her a few pointers, *if* you would." He propped his elbows on his thighs and rested his chin on his intertwined fingers giving her a retired look.

Like how to keep her hands to herself? "I think I could watch her and see what I could do."

He smiled then, pulling his hat back over his head. "Thank you!" He watched her for a minute then stood. "It's lunch time. Come eat with me." He was too irresistible to say no to, so she nodded and stood, taking the arm that was extended to her. Maybe he had realized that he had hurt her feelings, or maybe he was just being his usual self, she couldn't tell. He looked down at her and smiled as they walked. "It appears that I am overdue for that date I've been meaning to ask you about."

She tried to hide her smile but failed. "Oh?"

"Yeah, see, there's this adorable little girl who is in dire need of a costume for Halloween and it's only about two weeks away. So, I thought we could go grab a bite to eat and head to Denton to find her one. What do you think?"

"Well, I guess we really should make sure that she gets a costume," she retorted.

He laughed as they headed toward the catering tent.

Later that afternoon, Natalie was back in the corral with Jack and Vivian telling her how to position her hands, her chest and her legs as she rode to appear more "lady-like" as Jack had put it. She was definitely droopy before Natalie had improved her posture. However, Vivian was becoming more comfortable in the saddle and that was a great start. As they ended the day, Natalie walked with Vivian back to the barn to the shower room.

"How do you do it?" Vivian asked randomly.

"Do what?"

"Work with all these men? I mean... Wow, Jack is one of the best looking men I think I've ever seen..." Natalie rolled her eyes. *Oh God, rub it in why don't you!* She thought. "He's got a great body and he's so sweet, but he only has eyes for *you*." Natalie stopped dead in her tracks, eyebrows drawn in surprise as she looked up at Vivian.

"What?"

"I'm really sorry, Natalie, I didn't know that you two were an item. I mean, I realize I was probably flirting with him. I mean, I *know* I was... but it's my personality... I'm sorry. Please don't be upset with me!" She had taken Natalie's bandaged hands gently in her own. Natalie just stared up at her, not knowing what to say, only knowing that her heart was fluttering. "Besides," Vivian replied slyly. "That Tad is one fine hunk of man himself." Vivian winked and left her then to stare into space as she went to retrieve her things from the shower room.

Did Jack really only have eyes for her?

~

*J*ack was ready for a night out with his two girls. He finished up at the barn before heading to the house for a quick shower. Natalie had appeared jealous today if his assessment was correct and he'd loved it. That meant she cared for him. He smiled as he soaped up and rinsed off. She was really starting to get to him. The way she looked, those eyes, that body, those looks she gave him... But it wasn't time yet. He knew that. And although he was madly in love with her, he wouldn't push her into something she wasn't ready for, even if he was dying inside. He turned the water off and grabbed his towel. He realized he was starving as he dried off and wrapped the towel around his waist. Within twenty minutes he was dressed and out of the bathroom. Dallie ran out of her room then and greeted him by wrapping her little arms around his legs. He scooped her up and planted a kiss on her little cheek.

"I really get to go this time?" Dallie asked. Joy danced in her eyes.

"Yes, darlin', you really do. This date is all about *you!*"

"Where are we going to eat?" she asked as he walked them down the stairs.

"Well, where do you want to go?" he asked. She shrugged with all the innocence of a four year old. He just smiled. "Let's ask Mommy then, shall we?" She nodded at that. Jack picked his keys up off the vanity at the end of the stairwell as he followed Natalie's voice into the kitchen.

"Well, of course... We'll be fine while you're gone. I can go get some groceries and take care of the house. It's not a big deal." Natalie was talking to her mother and Jack paused not wanting her to feel rushed.

"I know, but I don't want to inconvenience you, dear," Corrine replied.

"Mother, please, I live here too now, I need to carry my weight just like everyone else. I would be glad to look after things while you're gone."

"Alright, if you're sure that you're okay with it…"

"Yes, I am. I promise. You and Dad go and have fun in Houston. You deserve to have a few nights off from this place. I can handle the boys!" Natalie said and looked up at Jack and Dallie then and smiled. "It's these two I'm worried about."

"Oh, those two are the least of your worries," Corrine said as she walked over to Jack and Dallie. "Have fun tonight, my sugar plum," she replied, kissing Dallie's cheek and patting Jack's hand. Corrine stepped out into the dining room as Natalie joined Jack and Dallie.

She had showered and was donning a silky turquoise tank top with a turtleneck collar that wrapped around her slim neck. Her dark hair lay in curls down her shoulders and matching turquoise earrings dangled in her ears. She'd paired the outfit with a tight pair of jeans accompanied by tan snakeskin boots and a long, oversized cream covered cardigan. She looked down right edible.

As they walked down the front steps to Jack's truck, Dallie asked her mother what she wanted for dinner.

"Oh, I don't know, what do you want?"

"Tacos!" Dallie squealed.

Jack smiled. "Tacos it is!"

As they strapped Dallie in and headed down the road, Jack's curiosity got the best of him.

"What were you and your mother talking about?" Jack asked.

She ran her hand through her wavy long hair as she answered him and he felt that familiar stiffness grow between his legs. Damn, she looked hot tonight! "Oh, she and Daddy will be leaving in a couple weeks to go to Houston. They are beginning filming. Bill and Deb are going too. I know you've been the one that's worked with the horses the most though, so I kinda feel that it should be you going instead of Daddy…"

"Nah, I'm the foreman, besides this is your father's deal. Not mine."

"Yes, but Jack you deserve to get to go…"

He shook his head. "No, your father's been beside me the whole time, besides I would rather he go anyway. I hate doing films."

"But Jack, don't let him take the credit for what you've done."

She was taking up for him and it made him feel good, but he saw it a bit different and told her so. "I don't see it that way. It's my job to train and break the horses just as it is your father's. So what if your dad stood back this time? He still does his part and he wants to go, so I don't see any problem with it." She lowered her head then, looking defeated. "But it means a lot to me that you see how hard I work."

"You *do* work hard and you are so dedicated to your work. You've done a wonderful job with those horses," she said.

He smiled as he chanced a look over at Dallie. Her head was leaned over against the car seat. She was out cold, dead to the world asleep. Then he looked over at Natalie. She was looking at him in admiration and his heart rate quickened. She'd looked at him this way before, but this time it hit him hard. He wanted to see her look at him this way forever. God, he was so in love with her. He stretched his hand across Dallie's car seat and took her hand in his. She gladly accepted it and they rode that way to the restaurant.

When he parked, Jack unbuckled Dallie and perched her on his shoulder, her little head resting against him. He joined Natalie at the curb and once again took her soft, albeit injured hand in his. Her soft, small hand fit snuggly in his. It felt right, it felt good. Being with these two females tonight, both with whom he'd fallen in love with, felt as natural to him as breathing did. As they sat down at the table, Dallie stirred and awoke, perky as ever and was begging for cheese dip and a taco. Her eagerness and obliviousness made Jack laugh. Before long, they were eating tortilla chips and cheese dip and both he and Natalie were sipping frozen margaritas. They were laughing at Dallie and each other and once again Jack felt at home in their presence.

"I thought you said tequila made you do crazy things?" Jack stated, giving Natalie a sinister smile.

"It does…" she retorted.

"Really, what exactly does it do to you?"

"There are some things that simply should not be repeated Jack Kinsen, and this will be one of them." Damn! But she was such a classy woman, classy and fun.

Since she wasn't going to entertain him with her story, he moved onto Dallie.

"So, any ideas yet about a costume?" he asked.

Dallie shook her head as she bit into her taco. Cheese and meat came out the other end and fell to her plate.

Jack thought about the perfect costume for Dallie as they left the restaurant and heading toward Denton. He and Natalie spoke about the new pony and Call and how they would be selling him soon. They arrived at the Halloween store around seven and Dallie squealed in glee as they entered the door. Costumes, masks, decorations, props, lights and animated creatures of all kinds filled the large warehouse-like store. Cobwebs hung in the corners and spooky music filled the air. Everything needed for Halloween was in this store from fangs to wigs to fake blood to candy corn.

"Mommy, is that real?" Dallie asked, looking anxiously up at a Jason Voorhees replica complete with a machete.

"Of course not, Dallie. He just looks real," Jack answered instead. He slowly walked closer to the animatronic villain with Dallie in his arms. Her hold on him became tighter as he reached out and touched it. "See, he's just plastic." Dallie screamed as noise emerged from Jason, but timidly reached her hand out to verify Jack's claim. She laughed when she realized he was telling the truth.

"This place is amazing…" Natalie stated as she picked up a set of talking skeleton heads. "Halloween has really changed since I was a kid."

"Yeah, tell me about it," Jack said as he walked over to the costumes. "Well, baby, you got your pick…from Tinker Bell to vampires." He set Dallie down to peruse the exhibit as he moved over a foot to the women's section. He picked up a sexy red she-devil costume and held it up for Natalie to see it.

"Feeling a little naughty, Nat?" he asked, smiling. She simply cocked her eyebrow at him and walked over to where he stood.

Dallie scanned each costume carefully, her brows drawn in concentration. She found a horse costume and squealed with delight as she brought it over to Natalie.

"This is what I want to be!"

"Of course, how could I *not* have guessed," Natalie said and pulled the costume up so that Jack could see it. Jack smiled and shook his head in amusement. Walking over to the men's selection, he found a costume of his own. With his eyebrow cocked, he looked back over at Natalie, showing her his selection and she immediately burst into laughter.

CHAPTER 10

"The Lone Ranger and Silver, I should have known." Natalie was pleased if not a bit surprised that Jack had volunteered to not only accompany her and Dallie trick-or-treating but dress up as well.

"Well, you know, not every man could pull it off."

"No, no they couldn't." Natalie rolled her eyes as Jack laughed. Then a seriousness came over her. "I hope you're doing this for Dallie and not to win me over."

She couldn't see his expression in the dark as they rode home in his truck, but she could sense he was offended by her statement.

"Of course it's for Dallie," he said with sincerity. He sat silent for a few moments, and then his tone softened. "You're *not* the only female in my life, Natalie." His hand gently embraced hers as they laughed together. "She makes it *easy* to love her," he said, his tone once again changing.

She knew that she hadn't made it easy for Jack. Her wounds were still raw, but they were slowly healing. She was becoming more comfortable with him each day, but he couldn't expect her to just abandon her inhibitions. She was trying to trust him and let her fear go. He had to be patient. Or maybe she was just making excuses....

"I'm trying, Jack." Was all she said.

"I know." With that they sat in silence all the way home. Her mind reeled with thoughts. Would he give up on her? Was she taking too long? Why couldn't she just let go and give herself to him uncon-ditionally as he had her? She was way overdue for love to come into her life. Why was she fighting it so? Was she afraid of him or herself? These questions bombarded her mind to the point that she felt drained. She hadn't realized they had pulled up to the house until he brushed her cheek with his hand.

"You okay, darlin'?" he asked so gently that she thought she would cry. He was everything she'd ever wanted, but even now her uncertainties prevented her from telling him so.

"Yeah," she stated, turning from him, unstrapping herself and turning to Dallie in her car seat. Her little head was once again flopped against the seat, sleep had taken her.

"I got 'er," he stated, opening his door and flooding the cab with light. He scooped her up as if her long, limp body weighed nothing more than a feather which Natalie knew that it did. Dallie was dead weight when she was asleep.

As they stepped up onto the porch, Jack stopped dead in his tracks. His gaze was fixed on the porch swing and Natalie followed it, but didn't understand what caught his attention until she saw the smoke ring circle the stranger's head as he bent forward.

"Well, Hello lil' sis."

~

"*N*athan?" Natalie's question was one of shock and surprise. It had been almost ten years since she'd seen her big brother.

"Natalie, I see you've finally made your way back home." The voice that greeted her was unfamiliar. Grave, solemn, lacking compassion. "I told you so just doesn't seem to do itself justice, does it?" His voice leaked of sarcasm. He stood then and she gulped at the face that looked strange to her now.

His raven black hair, almost the same color as hers, matched his beard and mustache and was long, halfway to his shoulders, under his tan cowboy hat. His sapphire blue eyes were full of pain and looked tired and worn. His skin was heavily tanned; his complexion was russet-colored, showing their Cherokee heritage. His build was larger than she remembered. He seemed taller, more muscular, although not near as broad as Jack. His face was scruffy and needed a good shave. He looked older than he should at thirty-two with the beginnings of crow's feet scratching at the corners of his eyes. Too much sun and too much smoking, she thought.

Jack spoke up then and Natalie could see that he was weary of Nathan approaching her. "Natalie…" he said, his voice dreadful.

"It's okay, Jack, just take Dallie up to bed, will you?"

"But…"

"Jack, how are ya?" Nathan approached Jack then, his cigarette smoke leaving a trail behind him. "Is this my niece, Nat?" He touched her little arm and Natalie could see Jack's jaw clinch. Nathan turned to her then. "Dallas! Isn't that original?" He laughed. "I bet Troy came up with that one, didn't he?"

"Natalie?" Jack was becoming impatient with Nathan. But Nathan ignored him.

"How old is she now?"

"She'll be five in December." Her answer was robotic. She still felt stunned by his presence.

"Nice. It's about time I finally get to see my niece, especially since she's almost five and I've never laid eyes on her." His voice was getting louder and more cynical by the minute.

"Well, the blame can't lie solely on me…you might have gotten to see her if you hadn't been off in some damn rodeo circuit aimed to get yourself killed." Natalie's voice got louder too and she could feel her heart beating faster, ready for this fight. Ready, after ten years, to lay the cards on the table.

"Don't even go there, lil' sis! You made your choice…"

"Yeah, and I made a bad one didn't I, Nathan? Why don't you just go ahead and tell me how badly I fucked that one up, huh? Go ahead; throw it in my face if it makes you feel better!" She had moved closer to him, her body within inches of his, her finger thrust in his face. She was tough, just as damn tough as he was and she wouldn't let him run over her. She'd be damned if anyone *ever* ran over her again. "Come on, Nate, I'm waiting! Lash at me!" When he didn't, she continued. "I made a mistake, a huge one, the biggest mistake I've ever made in my life. You don't think I have to live with that *every* day of my life and look at my child and know that I might have been able to put a stop to her misery had I but known what type of man I married?" She paused. Her voice was loud and unwavering. She took in a deep breath. "There! You happy now, Nathan! You were right and I was wrong!" He was speechless, taken aback by her statements. He hadn't been expecting her to fight back. She'd been the sweet one, the quiet one, the one that just went along with whatever everyone else wanted. Well not anymore! She was a fighter now and she would let him see how much of a fighter she was. "What's the matter, big brother? Cat got your tongue?" She went on when he didn't respond.

"Why don't you tell Jack?" She looked over at Jack then, his face a maze of confusion and surprise. "Tell him… Tell him how you begged me not to go! How you threatened me if I left! It didn't matter that I was as scared and upset as you were. It was all about *you* and what you wanted! To Hell with me and the fact that I was pregnant and didn't choose to take your way out! Tell him how you told me I had forgotten where I came from and who I was. That if I left, you wouldn't be here if I ever came back. That you would be *done* with me! 'I never knew you: depart from me', that's what you said."

There were tears streaming down her face now. "Dammit, I'm

239

just as human as you are. I'm your fucking sister, your very own flesh and blood! You were supposed to be my big brother, there for me through it all and where were you when I fell from grace, huh? Where the Hell were *you?*" She collapsed then, falling to her knees onto the porch that her father built with his own two hands. Her body shook as she cried for time lost, time she could never get back. Strong arms embraced her then and she took comfort in them, immediately realizing that they were not Jack's, but her brother's. "Oh, Nathan! I was sorry the moment I left this place, you *have* to know that! I never meant to leave all of you. I can't tell you how much I missed you. I love you so much. I never wanted to hurt you!" He said nothing, but she could feel his hot cheeks as his tears fell onto her own face. She had missed her brother, although she hadn't realized just how much until that moment. Neither of them said a word as he stood her up and pulled her into his arms.

"I'm sorry that I wasn't there for you," he said after a long silence.

～

That next morning, Natalie felt well rested. She was finally starting to feel better about her life. Last night's confrontation hadn't been easy and it hadn't been pleasant, but it had been necessary. She was relieved to know that she and Nathan had finally spoken after almost a decade and eased the bitterness between them. Her demons were slowly diminishing, one by one. Jack had been a trooper last night. He'd been once again put in the middle of Natalie's drama but had handled it like a gentleman as always. Poor Jack. He'd taken Dallie up to bed then came to see to her after she'd bid Nathan a good night downstairs. It would take them time to forgive one another, but as long as they were speaking there was hope for them. Jack had come to her then and made sure she was okay. He was her rock and her solace, but she had felt peace, not sorrow, and she hadn't needed his comfort. She'd needed his love, but pride and fear had deterred her from asking him to lay with her and make love to her.

She was on a mission this morning as she woke early, showered, and roused Dallie. She was nervous as she descended the stairs with her daughter. All the hands were laughing as well as her parents as she entered the room. Then silence followed as their eyes fell on Natalie and Dallie. Jack especially tensed as he looked at her. Nathan sat at the head of table. Apparently, no one had heard the squabble between them last night and tension seemed to swallow the room as Natalie approached Nathan; everyone's eyes bouncing from Natalie to Nathan and back again. A big smile came over his face as his eyes drifted to Dallie. Her hair in disarray around her head, sleepy eyes she continued to shove her little fists into, her My Little Pony nightgown and bare feet. Natalie sat down beside Nathan and perched Dallie on her lap. Dallie looked up intently on the stranger she'd never seen before.

"Dallie, I want you to meet your Uncle Nathan," Nat said.

"Hi!" Dallie replied sweetly. "You're really my uncle?"

Nathan smiled at her and said, "I really am. I'm your Mommy's brother."

"I've seen pictures of you... Are you a cowboy?"

"Yes ma'am, I ride bulls."

Dallie's eyes widened. "Real ones?" Natalie's eyes were welling up as she watched Dallie interact with Nathan.

"Yeah, real ones." Nathan laughed, flashing his pearly whites. "Ever been to a rodeo?" Dallie shook her head.

"What's a rodeo?" Her question was aimed to Jack who stepped over closer to her then.

"It's a competition for cowboys and cowgirls. They ride bulls and horses and rope calves. They even have clowns," Jack replied.

"Like the circus?" Dallie asked.

"Kinda like the circus... only without the elephants and tigers."

"Oh, I want to go to a rodeo!" She squealed. "Can I?"

"In due time, baby," Jack said as he sat down next to Natalie.

"Can I watch you rodeo?" she asked Nathan.

"Sure you can."

"Oh boy!"

Corrine had tears in her eyes. Natalie knew it touched her to have both her children under her roof together again. Natalie doubted it would last long, but felt comfort just the same. It was pleasant eating together and catching up on old times. Nathan was laughing and telling Dallie stories of his life in the rodeo circuit. After breakfast, the hands left and Jack took Dallie upstairs to get her dressed as Natalie talked with her brother.

"She looks like you, you know?" Nathan remarked to his sister, tilting his head in Dallie's direction as his gaze followed her upstairs.

"Everyone says that," Natalie said.

"It's true. Spitting image. I swear it."

"She looks like *you*, Nathan," their mother stated, smiling. "You had those same curls when you were a child." Nathan smiled as well.

"She's full of spunk too, just like you. It's amazing!" Nate added.

"Everyone says that too…. She loves horses, you know?" Natalie said.

"Well, that doesn't surprise me. She came from horse people." His hands gestured to her, her father and mother.

"She has a gift," her father said.

"Oh, Dad, please? Don't start with all that nonsense…" Natalie harrumphed, brushing off her father's comment.

"No, really, Natalie, she does. Tell your brother the truth."

"What's he talking about?" Nathan's brows were drawn as he looked at her face. She felt herself flush as she answered him.

"Daddy thinks she can 'talk' to horses." Natalie raised her eyebrows and shrugged her shoulders.

"She's a whisperer." David revealed.

"Sure she is, Daddy," Natalie stated, rolling her eyes.

"Your sister is in denial, we've all seen it with our very own eyes. Jack believes it as much as I do."

"Yeah, well, it's all circumstantial," Natalie argued.

"Circumstantial, my ass!" David scoffed and turned his chair toward her brother, "Nathan, it's incredible. You have to watch her with them. I've never seen anything like it."

"Well, I think someone has seen one too many movies..." Natalie laughed.

"You don't believe it?" Nathan asked her.

"No, I don't. I think she's just more sensitive to them than we are. Do I think she can hear them and talk to them? No. She's not Dr. Dolittle."

"But what if they do exist?" Nate asked.

"What? People like Dr. Dolittle?"

"No, horse whisperers... What if I told you that I've met one?"

"See, Natalie, I told you that I wasn't a fool," her father intervened.

"You've met one?" She asked incredulously.

"Yes, and I've seen what he can do. It is real, Natalie."

"I've heard of them and worked with all kinds of trainers just as you have and I believe certain people are better with horses than others, but I don't believe that my four-year old is a horse whisperer. She never even saw a horse until two years ago."

"She has a gift!" her father concluded.

~

*J*ack and Dallie were working with her pony today, the pony that had yet to be named. Vivian had the day off and Jack was grateful for that. She was wearing him out. Sweet girl, but it was nice to work with someone who knew what they were doing for a change, even if she *was* only four.

Jack was looking forward to the evening anyway, he had a surprise in store for Natalie. He was cooking her a chuckwagon dinner that he'd begun earlier this morning. He planted the hot coals deep in the ground and had some barbeque beans cooking in a large Dutch oven with big pieces of onion and bacon. It was his turn to impress her with his cooking skills even if they were scarce.

The sight he'd seen last night was quiet humbling to him; humbling and heart-breaking. Natalie had opened her heart and her soul to both him and Nathan in that moment and it had made him love her even more. There had been no pride in her voice, only shame. She'd confessed that she'd been wrong and Jack knew that it'd been hard for her. Once again, he only had bits and pieces of the whole story, but he was getting a better idea of who Natalie had married...this Troy Cameron, whoever he'd been, had almost tore this family apart.

"Jack, do you like the name Ameera?" Dallie asked as Jack helped her lead the pony in the back pasture. They were working on bending and stelling.

"That's a beautiful name, Dallie."

"Mommy said it means princess in Arabic."

"I like it; she has all the grace of a princess."

"What's Arabic?" Dallie asked innocently.

"It's a language, a culture of the Middle East, across the world... where this pony's line is from. You know Dallie, Arabians are known for their endurance and speed!" Come to think of it, this Arabian horse would be the first on their ranch. She was really something, she was smart and fast and muscular. She would make Dallie a fine horse. Natalie came up then with Nathan in tow.

"Mommy, Jack liked Ameera."

"Well, so I guess Nadia is out of the question then," Natalie piped in.

"What does it mean?" Jack asked.

"The beginning, the first."

"See that's rather fitting too... but ultimately Dallie, honey, it's up to you. She's *your* horse," he said looking down at Dallie.

She looked from her mother to Jack, back and forth, thinking it over.

"Umm, I think I like Ameera better."

"Hey, then Ameera it is," Jack said smiling. The horse whinnied then. "See, even she likes it." With that they all laughed.

"So, Dallie, your Mommy tells me you have a gift with horses…" Nathan began. Dallie just nodded. "Can you talk to them?"

"Sometimes."

"Can they talk to you?"

"Umm, they don't talk to me, but sometimes I feel what they feel. Like the horse that hurt Mommy's hands. He was scared, but he didn't tell me. I felt it."

"And how do you calm them so easily?"

"I just touch them and whisper to them." Nathan gave Natalie a knowing look. "How many times has she done this?"

"A couple. The first time was with a wild stallion. A mustang some guy had just brought in from Wyoming the day before," Natalie answered.

"You shittin' me?"

"No, I'm not *shitting* you! He was running right at her and the next thing we knew, she was petting him like he was a kitten."

"Well, I'll be damned!"

"You keep talking like that in front of your niece and you *will* be," she said, poking him in the rib.

"Sorry," he said as he yelped.

"Hey, Nathan would you take over for a second. I need to talk to Natalie," Jack requested.

"Sure." Nathan opened the gate and walked over to them. Jack passed him the lead.

"She knows what to do," Jack said as he patted Nathans' back.

He headed out the gate and took Natalie's arm as they walked out of earshot.

"You got any plans for tonight?" he asked.

"No, should I?"

"Well, you do now. I have a surprise for you. Just bring your hat and your riding gear. We'll go about six."

"Is this a date?" she asked, gazing up at him, amused.

245

"You're darn right it is." He kissed her hand then and turned to head back to the corral. She pondered his surprise. Another date, huh? He was trying to break her down and he was doing a good job of it. He looked good today, not unlike every other day...he'd shaved and his clothes had smelled so fresh and clean despite already being dusty and sweaty.

As she and Nathan headed back to the house, she noticed it looked like it would rain, the sky was growing dark and clouds were building high in the troposphere. She waited for Nathan to ask the question she knew was coming because he kept eyeing her suspiciously.

"Ok! What, Nathan?" She couldn't take it anymore. She stopped before they got to the back porch, her hands on her hips.

"You doin' him?" he asked. She gasped her protest and shoved him. He laughed. "Sorry I asked. Jeez!"

"That was such a rude question," she said, shoving him again.

"Seriously, sis," he said, turning to look at her. "What's up with you two?"

"Well, we're talking. Actually, we're dating...we're friends."

"Yeah, I look at my *friends* that way all the time..."

"What are you talking about?"

"The look..." He rolled his eyes. "Don't act like you don't see that look he's giving you, or the one you give him for that matter. It's down right dirty."

"Oh, will you stop it," she exclaimed and waved her hand.

"Yeah, ok, you know the truth! You two have a *thing*," he stated. She rolled her eyes but laughed in the process. "You're happy. I don't remember the last time I saw your eyes light up like that. It's becoming."

"Thanks, bro!" She smiled. She took his arm as he led her up the steps. "Jack is quite a guy." She sighed.

"Yeah, I've known him for a while now.... A more honest worker there never was. Quite the lady's man while he was in the circuit though, I must say. But, he's different now...in a good way." He corrected as her eyes bore holes into him. He gave her an "I'm in trouble look" and she laughed.

After lunch, Natalie headed back to the barn to work at her father's disheveled desk. She felt as if there was no end to the paper-work on it. *Does he ever file anything?* She asked herself then typed her password into the computer, jumping as a knock came at the door. She looked up to see Dan standing in the doorway.

"Hey Nat. Sorry to interrupt, but I've been needin' to speak with you," he said and came in, closing the door behind him. Her mood was lighter than when it'd been the last time he'd mentioned speaking with her so she signaled for him to take a seat.

"What's on your mind, Dan?" She stopped her work and focused on him.

"Well, there's something that's been bothering me and I wanted to talk to you about it…See, I don't really think Jack is the man he's portrayed himself to be."

"Oh, okay? And why is that?" she asked, curiously. So this was about her and Jack, she should have known.

"Well, I know some things about him that would say otherwise."

"What kind of things?"

"Well, for starters, he's been with Annabella Smith."

"Really?" she asked, doubtingly. His statement caught her by surprise, but she wasn't taking the bait just yet. "And how do you know that?"

"She told me along with some other people who witnessed him taking her home one night."

"Well you of all people should know she's a bold faced liar," Natalie stated with conviction.

"She may be, but what about the witnesses… You can't discredit them."

"Maybe I can and maybe I can't."

Annabella wasn't the kind of woman Jack would be with; Natalie felt with all her heart that it just wasn't so.

"Dammit, Natalie!" His voice got louder. "If he's been with her then he's no better than she is. Why must you defend him?"

"Because I don't believe he would sleep with her." She *knew* he wouldn't!

"Why? What makes him so much different than anyone else?"

"He just is! He wouldn't *want* someone like her. He had his fill of trashy women when he was done with the rodeo circuit."

"Yeah, says *him*."

"Look, Dan, we can sit here all day and fight about this. But I'm sorry I have work to do." She stood, signaling to him that the conversation was over as far as she was concerned.

He didn't budge and gave her an exhausting look. "What makes him so much different than me?"

"Honestly? You're two very different people. He wants different things than you do. He is kind to me."

"I'm kind to you."

"Yeah, *now* you are. That can't be said for our past conversations."

"I want to be kind to you always."

She rolled her eyes and drove her point home. "Jack has morals."

"Yeah, says *you*."

"What is this really about anyway, Dan? Annabella or no Annabella. What difference would it make?"

"I want you. I've always wanted you."

"You've got a very strange way of showing it."

"But I've changed, Natalie. I just want to make you happy!"

She put her hands up, silencing him. Dan wasn't an unattractive man by any means. He was tall and muscular with blonde hair and brown eyes. He just completely turned Natalie off and always had with his attitude towards women. "Ok, let me just say this so there's no confusion, Dan," she said. "I'm not trying to hurt your feelings, but honestly, I'm not attracted to you. You aren't my type." His face went from disappointment, to hurt, to anger and he lashed out at her as he stood.

"Well, I'm not Troy Cameron that's for *damn* sure."

Her face drained of color and before she could scramble over the desk to claw his eyeballs out, the door opened. It was Jack but her eyes were fixed on Dan and his eyes were on her. Anger met anger.

"Oh, I'm sorry, I didn't mean to interrupt," he stated, but their eyes didn't move from each other.

"Well, *look*, Natalie, there he is now, your knight in *shining* armor." Dan's voice dripped with sarcasm as he looked over at Jack who just stood there trying to figure out what was going on between the two of them. "Why don't you ask him yourself and we can get the truth right here on the table, here and now?"

Her eyes were riveted on him. "I don't need to ask him. I told you that I already knew the answer."

"Ask me what?" Jack voice held a trace of frustration and perplexity.

"He *claims* that you slept with Annabella." Natalie wasn't looking at Jack. Her eyes had a signed death warrant out for Dan and they would burn him down before this conversation was over.

"Annabella? As in Annabella *Smith*? Are you serious?" Jack asked and looked over at Dan, disgust in his voice. "That's the best you can come up with?" He sneered.

"You're a fuckin' liar. I've got three witnesses that saw you drive her drunk ass home last September," Dan said and ran over to confront Jack. Jack pushed him back from him with one hand, as if swatting a fly away. If this turned into another brawl, Natalie was putting her money on Jack.

"I *did* drive her home," Jack said and looked over at Natalie. "She *was* drunk." He agreed, looking at Dan, then back to Natalie. "We were both at the Rusty Spur that night and had she not been my best friend's recent ex-girlfriend I would have left her ass sitting right where it was. But I didn't, I felt sorry for her. I didn't even really know who she was at the time. So I took her home, unlocked her door and set her down on the couch. She threw herself at me, but I refused, so after that she decided to spread her little rumor." His gaze moved to Dan. "You heard about that rumor a year ago.

But yet you're just now investigating it? Isn't that convenient?" He looked back over at Natalie. "I swear to you, I *never* touched her. I dumped her on the couch and left." His gaze then flew back to Dan. "I haven't ever been *that* hard up." His voice tinged with revulsion. Jack crossed his arms over his chest then looked back over at Natalie.

She'd known all along that Jack would never touch Annabella Smith. He wasn't Dan.

Her eyebrow was raised as she waited for Dan to say something, do something. His gaze just matched hers. He then walked back over to her and was the first to break the silence.

"You know what? Fine! Believe him if you want, but you know something else—" He had moved directly across the desk from her, his finger in her face and that's when she went for him. She reached for his throat in a quick second and grabbed his collar, pulling him toward her. Her eyes were unmerciful and vengeful as she looked into his dirt streaked face.

"I *will* believe what I want! And let me tell you this Dan Wilson. Don't you ever, *ever* again compare what I want to Troy Cameron. You don't know anything about me *or* what I want. You are nothing to me and never will be. Now get out of my father's office."

He sneered at her as she released her grip. "Make me!" He wanted a fight from her.

"Dan," Jack said and stepped closer, wanting to extinguish this conversation as soon as possible. "Come on, just do as she asks."

"No. This isn't her office yet and she can't make me leave it." Challenge showed in Dan's eyes as he stared Natalie down, he even had the audacity to smile.

"No, she can't," Jack said. "But *I* can…it may not be her office yet, but as your foreman, I'm telling you to get the Hell out of David Butler's office. Now."

Dan's eyes met Jack's, then Natalie's. Hate was all she saw and all she felt in that moment and he finally turned and exited. Making sure he brushed aggressively past Jack on the way out. She breathed a sigh of relief and literally fell into her father's chair. Jack walked over to her then.

"Are you okay?" The look of concern on his face vanquished her residual anger.

"I'm okay. He's such a jerk. I just want him gone once and for all."

"I know, me too."

∿

ater that day, Natalie was working on her laptop on the front porch as Jack and Dallie raced up the stairs, Jack making a big scene of her "beating him". Dallie went inside to see her Grandma and Jack sat down beside Natalie.

"Mom and Dad are going out tonight to meet some of the crew members so I don't have anyone to watch Dallie." She frowned and looked at him disappointed.

"She can come with us. I don't mind, if you don't."

"I can watch her," Nathan said and approached them then, coming up the front porch stairs. "I could use the company."

"You're sure you don't mind? We won't be gone long."

"Of course I don't mind. I wouldn't have volunteered if I'd minded. Besides, it's high time I get to know my niece."

She smiled and thanked him, heading inside to prepare herself to ride.

She hadn't been riding with Jack before and the thought thrilled her. She dressed in a tight pair of Gloria Vanderbilt jeans, a sexy one shouldered fringed top and her old brown Stetson to match. Maybe it was over the top but she was on a date after all.

Her parents had already left when she came downstairs. She was grateful in a way; her mother would never approve of her riding in the outfit she had on.

She kissed Dallie and told her to be good for her Uncle Nathan. Nathan gave her a cat call on her way out the back door and she shot him her best "go-to-Hell" look. Well, she may not have seen her brother in over ten years, but he still seemed to have his easy going, fun loving disposition and Natalie smiled. It was nice to have her playful brother back and he seemed to enjoy being back in her life. Things were looking up for her.

Jack stood at the railing with the demeanor of an All-American cowboy. His blue linen button down shirt, the first two buttons hanging loose giving her a shot of his chest, was tucked into his tight Wrangler jeans. His ever present hat was black tonight and he'd changed his usual boots to a pair of black snakeskin ones; he was every woman's secret fantasy. His eyes looked her over from head to toe.

"Wow! I'll bet there ain't a cowboy alive that didn't wish he could go riding with a looker like you." He tipped his hat at her before escorting her down the back stairs to the barn.

"Well, thank you cowboy. You're quite a looker yourself."

"Much obliged, ma'am," he said. She laughed at his poke at old diction.

He led her to the stables where Midnight and Cheshire waited, their saddles ready.

"Your chariot awaits, m'lady," he declared. She smiled again as he helped boost her onto her thoroughbred gelding. His hands were gentle on her backside and she flushed at the feel of them on her skin.

"If I didn't know any better, I'd think you were trying to cop a cheap feel, Mr. Kinsen."

"As I recall, Ms. Cameron, you did say that you didn't kiss on the *first* date and if my calculations are correct, this would be our third date. You never said anything about our third date...." His grin was wicked as he looked over at her.

"Behave yourself!" She scolded playfully as she turned her gelding around toward the barn door. Jack joined her on his stallion and they trotted forward toward the back pasture. "Where are we headed?"

"East." He signaled to the woods. "On the other side of that thicket of trees."

"Toward the creek?"

"Yes, ma'am."

It had been some time since she'd ridden into the east side of their property. She'd brought a light jacket and tucked it into her saddlebag just in case this October weather decided to give them a chilly night once the sun set. He was a pleasant riding companion as they rode into the dense blanket of oak trees. The trees wouldn't last for long, she knew, as she looked up into the shadows. Birds called in the early evening and crickets chirped. She smiled loving the sudden activity that the small thicket held. Before long they were in a clearing headed toward the creek, she could see the smoke of a fire rising up into the air.

"Race ya!" She challenged and looked over at Jack.

"You're on!" With that she shoved her heel into Cheshire's flanks and with a "Heeyah", they were off. Jack was close behind, but she wouldn't let him catch her. This was what these two were born to do, ride and ride swiftly. The wind threw her wavy hair wildly around her head and she loved the feeling she felt at that moment. She was a young girl again, free to ride, free to dream, and free to love. But Cheshire was old and he tuckered out before Midnight did. Natalie cursed her fate and congratulated Jack on his win.

As they closed in on the camp Jack had set up, Natalie saw her father's old chuckwagon sitting next to a campfire with a log seat. A big fleece blanket was laid out with a small vase full of wild daisies and a bucket of ice that held a bottle of champagne. She felt her heart flip-flop. He was such a romantic.

"Jack, this is...this is beautiful," she said as he dismounted and tied Midnight to a hitching post he'd fashioned from an old tree trunk. He came to her side and pulled her from her horse. "Thank you, you're always so thoughtful. I don't deserve this." She slid down his hard body as his hands went around her waist.

"Natalie, you deserve the best that I have to offer. Besides I wanted to make you dinner."

"Oh, my! I am surely impressed, cowboy," she stated and he laughed and shook his head at her southern belle accent.

They walked hand-in-hand toward the chuck wagon where Jack pulled out a bag of steaks from a cooler. There were two ribeye steaks that looked as if they'd been marinating for a while. He'd done a lot of work for this date, she saw. A Dutch oven sat in a pit of coals, while a hot skillet sat on top of a makeshift grill over the campfire. She wondered what was in the skillet. The steaks were large and well marbled she noted as Jack put them into a large cast iron skillet and set it on the grill. Her mouth watered as she heard the familiar sizzling, she couldn't remember how long it had been since she'd eaten a steak.

"How do like yours?" he asked. "*Steak* that is." His raised his brow.

"Medium."

"Aww, darn, I thought you were gonna say hot and juicy." He pouted. She threw her head back and laughed.

"Well, I do like them hot and juicy as well."

"Oh, baby, talk dirty to me."

He smiled as he pulled her toward the large red blanket with him as they lay back, feet extended, elbows propped up on the blanket. The brook babbled beside them, water swirling over pebbles. The sounds of the coming night were calming as birds, frogs and bugs sang. Natalie felt serene in this open lot of land with this man she was starting to love being around.

She signaled her head over to the chuck wagon. "Did you restore it?"

"Yeah, somewhat. It's got new wheels and a cover but it still needs some work."

"Thank you for this, Jack."

"You're welcome. I needed a break from all the excitement and I know you did too. How're your hands doing?"

She looked down at her no longer bandaged palms. "Better,

they're starting to scab over. I'll just be glad when they look like mine again."

He took her right hand in his and examined it closely as he traced the long, red wound that ran down the length of her palm. The tender touch of his fingertip to her palm sent a tingle through her most sensitive areas. She gulped, hoping he couldn't see how aroused he was making her with what should have been a platonic touch. But he felt it, as she looked up into his eyes, knowing she shouldn't have but did anyway, she saw the look he was giving her. The look Nathan and Vivian had spoken of, the look of desire, of agony. He was a man of patience and she was holding out on him. Afraid to love him, afraid to give in to her feelings. Her heart was racing and she was frozen. Frozen in time with this stunning man and his incredible personality. This man who had done nothing but proven himself to her, time and time again. He was frozen too, unmoving as he watched her fight with herself. His eyes were green torrents of emotion and she found herself lost to them, to him. He was deathly still; it was to be her that made this move if it were to be made. She swallowed hard as her body leaned toward him. Her chest heaved as she looked at his sexy mouth, at those full lips that haunted her dreams. Her hand went to his face, touching his clean shaven jaw and her head tilted. His mouth parted as her eyes closed and her lips connected with his. His lips were soft and yielding to hers and he moaned as she deepened the kiss. His tongue was gentle yet eager as it delved into her mouth. At her moan, his hand enveloped the small of her back and he leaned into her, his chest touching hers. He kissed her fiercely and breathlessly. And she matched his fervor with her own. His kiss moved to her cheek, her ear, her neck, his hands moved up her leg which had somehow gotten wrapped around the back of his thigh. His hand gently moved along her buttocks, her spine, making electricity spike through her body. She was melting beneath his touch, her center wet and throbbing for him. She moaned as his hand grazed her breast and his lips met her collarbone.

"Oh, baby, you feel so good." He groaned. Her hands went to his buttocks then and she squeezed his tight ass, loving how he growled a response. His hands worked up her shirt and he leaned her back a bit so he could remove it, kissing her neck and chest in the process.

"Jack, I want you." She began unbuttoning his shirt as well and grabbed at his jeans as she knocked her hat off her head. This was it, they were going to make love right here on this soft blanket. She and this rugged, sexy cowboy with his big muscular body and his sea green eyes were going to finally have what they'd both been wanting for so long now. She licked her lips as her hands and eyes admired his solid bare chest and flat stomach and that tempting fan of hair that trailed to his unbuttoned jeans and boxers. His skin was so tan, a stark contrast to those white boxers, captivating her. She was mesmerized by his sheer sexiness with his shirt completely unbuttoned and his cowboy hat still perched on his head. Her eyes took in his pectoral muscles and his rock hard abdominals, every muscle rippling with each breath he took, and she drooled as she traced the indentation of his muscles with her fingertips. His breathing was becoming labored. Her gaze flew to that most fascinating part of him and she worried her lip as she took in the big bulge in his jeans straining for release. God, how she wanted to see that part of him. She chanced a look at his eyes. They were dark with desire and she brought herself up on her knees and spread her legs over him, straddling his lap in a seated position. She fiddled with the down of his happy trail, feeling his hard erection pressed rigidly against her inner thigh as her fingers clumsily groped at the fasten on his jeans. His hands came to her breasts then and she moaned aloud as he reshaped her and kneaded her and fingered her hungry nipples through her bra. With each swipe of his thumbs her body grew more and more urgent for him, her nipples becoming rigid peaks beneath the silk of her bra. Each moan, each touch, brought waves of pleasure and desire with it, her sex throbbing almost painfully for release. Their eyes locked but for a moment before he gently took her face in his hands and pulled her down to the ground with him, kissing her lips longingly, his tongue plunging inside her mouth. His hands lowered to her bottom, rocking her back and forth against his restrained erection. She rocked with him, her eyes closing in ecstasy as her body responded to the stimulation of his movements. They were both breathless within seconds. She wanted him inside her. Needed him there. Her hands reached down again between then fighting to unzip his jeans, she heard the fly open. *Success.* He cupped her breasts again, his mouth going to her neck, his hands moving to reach behind her to remove her bra, and as her head came back up, something caught her eye as the horses began to move restlessly. She pulled back and so did he.

"What's wrong?" he asked, looking into her face, but she wasn't looking at him. Her gaze was fixed in the distance. She said nothing but moved his face in the direction where she was looking.

"Shit!" He jumped up quickly, rolling Natalie to the side and ran toward the covered wagon.

It appeared to be a coyote, running at them with torpedo speed. She looked over at Jack and watched him load a rifle and cock it. He bent to his knees and aimed the rifle toward the canine. The horses were whinnying now and rearing up.

"Jack!" She ran to move behind him, waiting for him to pull the trigger. She covered her ears, anticipating the loud reverberation of gun fire. He waited, patiently, silently as he focused on the wild animal. He waited until it was almost on them before pulling the trigger. The animal was thrown backwards several feet, the kickback from the round echoing in the open pasture. The animal gave a sharp whimper before keeling over about 20 yards in front of them. Natalie was silent as she took in what just happened. Jack gave a sigh of relief and stood up, allowing the rifle to fall to his side. He turned to her then and looked her over.

"You okay?" he asked. She just nodded. He took her hand and they walked together over toward the dead animal. Natalie grimaced as it lay there, covered in blood, smoke rising from the gun shot wound. "He looks to be rabid." Jack observed, pointing at his mouth.

"That's the only reason a coyote would come within a hundred yards of a human." He turned toward her then looking at her. She saw the shame hit his eyes and she came to him then, "Natalie, I'm sorry…"

She put her finger to his lips and shook her head. "Don't, Jack, don't apologize." She smiled up at him and kissed his nose. "Let's enjoy the rest of our night."

He nodded and replaced the rifle in the wagon. He used a tarp to cover the coyote so they could eat without having to look at it. Natalie didn't put her shirt back on. She just threw her jacket on and zipped it up. Jack, on the other hand, didn't even bother with his shirt and Natalie was glad for the view.

She was pleased with the chuckwagon fare of steak, skillet potatoes, cowboy beans and champagne. He'd even surprised her with sour dough biscuits drizzled with honey and strawberries. They ate on the blanket that had almost been their sinful downfall and laughed together as they enjoyed Jack's meal.

"That was delicious, Jack. You really outdid yourself once again." She smiled as they sat hand in hand watching the sunset.

"Thanks, it was nothing."

"Oh, it was something all right. You're always one-upping yourself with me. You're quite the romantic. "

"I try," he said smiling over at her.

"Who taught you how to cook chuckwagon style?"

"Your dad did, actually. We went camping one weekend, and he showed me all the different things you can cook in a Dutch oven, it was very enlightening."

"I, myself, know a few things about Dutch oven cooking…" she stated proudly.

"Well, maybe we should share recipes." They both laughed heartily at his statement. "Oh man, as much as I hate for this evening to end, I guess we should head back before we're completely in the dark."

"Oh, do we have to?"

"Well, do you really wanna camp out here all night with the

coyotes?" When she shook her head, he added, "Didn't think so….Damn, I guess I better bury him or we'll have big problems on our hands." He rose to attend to the carcass.

"I'll help."

"Really?"

"Yeah! It doesn't bother me."

"No, I can't let you do that. Just, uh, I tell you what, just hold the lamp up for me and I'll do it, okay?"

They went back to the chuck wagon and Natalie grabbed an old oil lamp and matches to light it as Jack grabbed a shovel, put on some gloves, and wrapped the coyote in the tarp. He picked it up and took it farther into the clearing. She followed him with the lamp and held it up for him to see. He dug quickly and powerfully and before they knew it, Jack was pushing the carcass into the hole. He covered him with dirt and stepped back wiping the sweat off his brow with his forearm.

"Ok, well, that's that."

$\sim$

Nathan laughed as Dallie looked up at him, a funny look of her face. "You haven't ever eaten a corn dog?" Her brows were drawn as she shook her head. "Well, you are in for a treat."

He'd fried them up some corn dogs and tater tots, probably to his sister's dismay, but Dallie was a kid and hanging out with her tonight had made him crave some kid food. He sat the plate down in front of her and took a seat beside her at the table. She was such a beautiful little girl and she reminded him so much of his sister when she was younger. Natalie had never had those curls or golden blonde hair but she had those same curious, big blue eyes and Nate smiled into Dallie's sweet face as she watched him pick up the stick of his corn dog. She followed suit and watched as he bit into the top of it and again did the same.

"Mm, Uncle Nate." She chewed loudly in pleasure. "This is SO good."

Nate laughed again. "Right? I told you that you would like it."

"It's like a hot dog." She dipped the top of her bitten corn dog into some ketchup he had put on her plate and took another big bite, smearing ketchup onto her plump little cheek.

"Yup!" He took a napkin and wiped it off. "I'm gonna have to fuss at my sister for not feeding you a corn dog, you know?" She just nodded as she continued to devour the greasy food.

He thought about how stupid he'd been these last ten years and how much he'd missed of Dallie's life, her birth, everything. How had he sat idly back when Natalie had come to visit two years ago and not at least come to meet his niece? How had he ignored what they'd been through and not been there for his sister in her time of need? Because he'd been angry and jealous and…very selfish. He was a scum bag and an idiot. Looking into her sweet face now, he felt his heart tear with regret and remorse. He hadn't been there…not for Natalie…not for Dallie…not for anything. He'd missed so very much.

But that could change, right here and now! And it was going to. No matter the fact that he still wasn't happy about what his sister had done and how she'd just up and left, he was making a vow at this very moment to be there for his family. Dallie would know him and love him and he would do the same with her. He smiled at this new found realization and they finished eating.

Afterward they'd gone down to the pasture to bring the horses in for the night and feed them and she'd made her rounds giving each one of them a little love on their muzzles, calling them by name and telling them goodnight at Nate's amusement. He'd got her ready for bed then they'd piled up on the couch and watched *Hidalgo* and Dallie's eyes never left the screen. He'd made her some hot cocoa and later she'd fallen asleep on his shoulder. He'd kissed her sweet smelling forehead and swore to make good on his newfound promise of being there for his family. He scooped her up and carried her to her bed, tucking her in and kissing her plump, warm little cheek and smiled. Things were going to be better now that Nat was home, he just knew it.

~

*A*fter the coyote was buried, Jack and Natalie headed back to the camp fire, extinguishing it and gathered the blanket and cookware, packed up and watered the horses before placing collars and harnesses on them, removing their saddles and hitching them up to the wagon. They jumped in the wagon seat and headed back to the barn into the clearing, avoiding the deep thicket of trees this time. Natalie burst into song as Jack whistled "Deep in the Heart of Texas", clapping when prompted and laughing after they'd finished the song.

"I love what that champagne does to you," Jack stated.

"Hey, what if it's not the champagne?" It wasn't the champagne. She felt good, for the first time in a long time she felt really good. Jack had put her on cloud nine and she felt free to laugh, to enjoy life again.

Jack brought the horses to a stop in front of the barn and unhooked the chuck wagon, leaving it out front. Natalie began helping Jack remove the attachments from the horses. He smiled at her as he walked into the barn and she gulped. She didn't want this evening to end. She was starting to fall for this man; she could feel it as her heart slammed into her ribs. He was breaking her walls down, and it was both liberating and exciting. They worked in companionable silence, Jack taking the harnesses and reins and bringing her a brush as he brought the horses some water. Neither knew what to say, afraid if they spoke, they would end up on the floor of the barn naked before either of them knew what had happened.

It was well past dark when they headed in after finishing up with the horses. They walked into the dimly lit house together, hand in hand. Nathan was asleep on the couch, the TV drowning his face in shades of blue and yellow. Dallie was more than likely asleep upstairs, Nat knew. Jack went to lock the door and Natalie turned off the TV, covering her brother with a blanket from the back of the couch and headed upstairs. She went immediately to Dallie's room and checked her sleeping daughter. She repositioned the cover and kissed her sweaty cheek, smiling down at her lovable little girl.

Her precious innocent angel who'd never asked for anyone to harm her. But her father had. What truly amazed Natalie was that Jack was everything Dallie's father had never been. Dallie's friend, Dallie's hero, Dallie's Superman. In the time that they had moved back home, Jack had been more of a father to Dallie than Troy had ever been. This recognition was like a kick to the stomach. Her head lowered and tears filled her eyes as she turned to leave before she woke Dallie. She gasped as she saw Jack's silhouette in the doorway.

"I'm sorry," he whispered. "I just wanted to check on her." His gaze swept her face and he stepped closer. "Are you okay?"

She nodded her head. "Yeah, I just...I get emotional sometimes when I look at her." She didn't want to admit the real reason for her tears.

Jack smiled. "She has that effect sometimes. She's really the best child anyone could ever ask to have," Jack stated. Natalie nodded again.

She wanted to get out of there before she burst into tears, but the look on Jack's face held her captive. His eyes were so tender as he spoke of her child and it made Natalie turn mushy inside. She crossed her arms as she moved forward to exit the door. Jack closed it behind them, leaving only a crack between the door and the door frame.

"Well, I guess I will see you in the morning. Good night, Natalie. I had a wonderful time with you." His voice was a touch louder as he faced her. Her arms still crossed over her chest, she smiled up at him. The house seemed colder than it had been outside and she craved to be nestled in his warm, solid arms.

"I did too, Jack. Thank you again for such a great time," she answered.

He leaned down to kiss her cheek then pulled back. They stood there just staring into one another's eyes, inches apart, fighting their desire for one another. Neither moved, neither spoke. But Natalie recognized the look in his eyes; it was an invitation, an unspoken beckoning that she heard as clear as if he'd asked. He waited endless moments then shifted, removing his hat. He tipped his head to her then and turned around, leaving her. She silently screamed at him not to leave, that she wasn't quite ready yet, to be patient with her. But it was no use! He went into her old room, flipped the light on and closed the door. She turned then as well and felt a great emptiness inside her as she entered her room. She began stripping her clothes off, tossing them into the wastebasket at the foot of the bed. She wanted to open that door, throw herself at him and never look back. Why, why did she fight it so? She was a flesh and blood woman with needs and wants and he was the here and now. She sat looking at the closed door wishing it would disappear and she would be in his arms. She knew deep down she was scared to death of what sex would bring into their relationship, but God, she was tired of living with these concrete walls she'd created so high that they were isolating her from living.

She tossed and turned that night seeing his naked body on top of her, making endless love to her. She saw him as he'd been in the pasture. Hot and hard and ready to love her. She saw his eyes as they'd been; dark, deep emeralds full of passion and desire. For the night, he was her dream lover. Her merciful fantasy. Her deliverance. Her freedom. He was tearing her walls down, until there was nothing left but just the two of them. No fear. No pain. No past... Only the present.

CHAPTER 11

*J*ack felt like a chicken running around with its head cut off that next week. He and Natalie and David had worked themselves into oblivion. That week had been Hell week at Starlight Valley Stables. The director had bumped up the filming schedule, and they were starting in a week instead of two. They worked every day from dawn until far past dusk. Natalie had been a God send. She'd taught Vivian everything she knew and for once, Vivian looked like a true equestrian. Natalie had accepted nothing but perfection from her. David had started to work with them as well to get used to the horses. Even they were begging for rest at the end of the day. By dinner time, Natalie, David and Jack were so exhausted that they ate dinner quickly and headed straight to bed. Corrine and Dallie were in the house much of the week. Natalie and Dallie worked in the afternoons with Ameera. Blaze was on hold and Call was ridden in the evenings when and if Jack got a chance to ride him. They'd all worked so hard and Jack finally got to see the passion and spirit that Natalie had been lacking when she'd first arrived. She was at home on her father's horse ranch. This was what she did and what she'd excelled at. She was so completely natural and intriguing on horseback. Intriguing and beautiful. As she'd been that night in the pasture. She'd wanted him that night and she'd meant to have him. If it hadn't been for that damn coyote...But Jack had been grateful in a way. She didn't seem ready. There was desire in her eyes, there was no doubting that, but there had also been fear and doubt in them too. He'd seen it that same night before they'd gone to their separate rooms. All she'd had to say was the word and he'd have taken her, but she'd hesitated. And he'd known then that it still wasn't time.

Jack felt like he'd run a marathon by Friday. His arms and back ached. His head throbbed, and he longed for a cold beer and a dip in a hot tub to soothe his sore muscles. He stood at the fence watching Natalie dismount Shasta, one of the Tennessee Walkers. He watched her pull her hat off her head and run her hands in her wavy dark hair and his mouth went dry. In his mind, he added her to the hot tub and cold beer...in a tight red bikini. *Oh Yeah!* She approached him, hips swaying, breasts bouncing and it was all he could do not to pull her to him and kiss her breathless. He hadn't been unable to kiss her with all the people around this week. He was overdue, *way* overdue. She came through the gate and walked over to stand beside him.

"Hey, would you mind if I cut out and go grab some lunch with a friend?" Nat asked. *As long as the friend isn't a guy,* was his first thought.

"Well, no, I don't mind. You've worked your ass off this week, you deserve it." He turned her around then, giving her the once over. "Actually, it's still there. Thank God!"

"Ha, funny," she said, swatting at his hand.

"But I do have one request," his voice lowered because they were surrounded by people. "When you get back, you have to kiss the *Hell* out of me... I mean a long, deep, blow my shoes off kinda kiss." Her grin was slow and her eyebrow was cocked.

"I thought you'd never ask." She gave him the once over as she headed toward the house and he swore he'd never loved anything more in his life.

~

"*I*'m so glad you came," Jordan said as she hugged Natalie to her.

"Well, forgive me. I'm all dusty and dirty, but I'm here," Natalie said, smiling as she sat down into her chair.

"Oh, you look great. Besides, you've been busy all week, you said."

"Yes! Oh my God! It's been never ending." They both laughed.

Jordan had invited Natalie to go to lunch with her and she'd had to put her off all week until she'd finally decided she simply had to have a break from the ranch. So, she'd called and met Jordan at a quaint little bistro down town. The menu was limited so Natalie settled for a chicken salad sandwich and a cup of homemade vegetable soup.

"And a large sweet tea, biggest one you got," she said to the young waitress as she left their table.

"So, you've really been working like a cowgirl again, I see." Jordan gestured to Natalie's plaid cotton button down and jeans.

"Yes, Jack and Dad and I have been training the actress and her doubles for a movie their filming in Houston. They decided at the last minute that they want to start shooting next week instead of two weeks from now. So, we've been crazy busy."

"Well, that sucks, but it's good to see you're in your element again."

It was true. It was nice to be back in her "element" as Jordan had put it. Natalie loved working with horses and realized recently just how much she'd missed it. She had even thought that she'd take it up again and start working with her father and Jack when she wasn't working on her column.

"So, you just have to tell me because I'm simply dying to know, how is he in bed?" The question was completely off the subject and Natalie felt herself blush all the way to her toes.

"Jordan!"

"What? I've just got to know… Dammit, he has to be good. I

know he is! Just tell me how good he is... A 10, oh I bet he's an 11...
What?" Natalie couldn't help but laugh at the desperation in her
friend's voice. "You tell me right this instant, Natalie Butler, you are
the most envied woman in town right now and I think I deserve to
know if he's really as good as he looks...How big is he? Is he big? I
bet he's big!" Natalie just looked at Jordan with a sly smile and a
bright red face. "Oh my God! You haven't slept with him yet, have
you?" Jordan eyes looked like they would bulge out of her head.
"Wow! What on *earth* is stopping you, are you out of your mind?"
Natalie's eyes fell. She didn't know herself what was stopping her
from sleeping with Jack. She hadn't had a good night's sleep since
the night of their last date not quite a week ago. Jordan took Natalie's hand then.

"I'm sorry, Nat. Forgive me for being so rude! I'm just jealous is
all... I mean, the man is drop dead gorgeous, has the body of a Greek
god and he's rich. You couldn't *stop* me from having sex with him...
and lots of it too." Natalie hadn't heard her last sentence; she was still
hearing the word rich coming from Jordan's mouth. Had she heard
her correctly? Rich? Jack was *rich*? Rich with what exactly?

"What?" Natalie asked in disbelief.

"Well, I'm just saying if it were me, you know, I'd have probably
slept with him on the first date, but you, of course, have always had
more self-control than I have..." Jordan laughed.

"No, you said rich. What do you mean rich?"

"Rich. Wealthy. Has lots of money..."

"Jack? My Jack? Jack *Kinsen?*"

"Yeah," Jordan's eyebrows went up in affirmation.

"Jack Kinsen is rich?"

"Yes!" Jordan declared. Natalie's heart had started to pound in her
ears, she was thoroughly confused.

"But how? He's a foreman at my father's ranch for God's sake.
How in the Hell is he *rich*?" Jordan watched Natalie in her reverie
and then a pained look came over her face.

"Oh, Natalie! I'm sorry. I thought you knew." Jordan took her hands again. "I shouldn't have said anything. I only know because I work at the bank."

"But you don't know *how* he's rich?" Nat asked. Jordan shook her head. "Why hasn't he told me?" Her voice lowered and her heart broke. He'd kept it a secret from her all this time. She'd trusted him and she was falling in love with him and all this time, he'd not even trusted her enough to tell her that he was wealthy. Natalie's head shot up then and anger filled her eyes.

"Jordan, what else do I need to know?" She was no longer hurt, now she was furious.

"Uh, I don't know of anything else. Just that he has money. But like I said the only reason I know that is because I work for the bank and I've seen his accounts. I really don't think very many people know that Jack has money, Natalie." She was trying to make her feel better but it wasn't going to work. Natalie felt hurt, angry and betrayed by this man who had been so wonderful to her.

"You don't know of anything else that I should know about Jack?" If he'd lied to her about one thing, there could be more.

"Not that I know of," Jordan said then her face changed. "Well, there is one more thing...there was speculation that Jack was the one that paid your father's bank note off when they were going to foreclose on the ranch." Natalie felt her stomach pitch.

"Foreclosure? When?" She was in shock.

"Oh, this was back about a year ago, I guess. Your parents were about to file bankruptcy. They hadn't been doing so well at the ranch and the bank was going to take it, but not long after Jack showed up, the note had been paid in full, anonymously."

Natalie was dumbfounded, when had they been struggling so badly that they nearly lost the ranch? They'd never told her any of this. Why? Shame? Pride? Now she knew why her parents loved Jack so much, he'd saved them from losing everything they'd ever had. But she was their daughter and it should have been her responsibility to take care of them. She felt so empty inside that she nearly cried out from it.

"Jordan, I'm sorry, but I must go." She stood to leave.

"Oh, Natalie. I'm sorry. Please don't be upset with me." Jordan stood as well.

"It's not you I'm upset with. Please understand, I need to go sort this out, okay?"

"Okay, but if you need me, you'd better call."

"I will. Thank you." She hugged her friend as she left.

She took her time getting back to the ranch. She ran errands and tried to calm herself down before she faced him. More than anything, she'd been crushed by the news, simply because he'd kept it from her. He could've told her, many times before now. About the money, about paying off the note. They had almost become lovers and he was keeping things from her. It hurt to know that he couldn't tell her these things. It also hurt that her parents hadn't came to her when they were about to lose the ranch. Even though, deep down, she knew they never would have.

She returned home around 3:30 PM and went into the house. She couldn't face Jack just yet. She would crumble and she didn't want him seeing her that way, even if he had seen her that way before. She heard her mother and Dallie in the kitchen so she joined them and shed all emotion from her face.

"Hey, what're y'all doing?"

"Mommy!" Dallie squealed and ran to her. Natalie picked her up and hugged her to her chest. She loved how soft and complacent her little body was in her arms. She wouldn't be little forever, Natalie knew, and she would cherish this time while it lasted.

"Hi, honey, we're making muffins for the trip," her mother said.

"Oh, they smell wonderful, just like my little Dallie." Dallie giggled as Natalie kissed her cheek and neck. Natalie hugged her tighter and tucked her head beneath her chin.

"Your favorite, pumpkin and apple streusel." Corrine walked over to Natalie then and placed a kiss on her cheek. "Don't worry. I'm leaving a batch here for you for in the morning." She winked at her.

"Thanks, Mom."

"You're welcome." Corrine walked back over to the oven and pulled a pan of them out. Natalie inhaled the smells of cinnamon, brown sugar, and pumpkin that wafted through the air. Her stomach growled.

"Mommy, can I go with Grandma and Paw-Paw?" Dallie asked, looking up into Natalie's face.

"I don't know if that's such a good idea, Dallie. Grandma and Paw-Paw need a break and that means from you too."

"Ooh," Dallie griped. "I wanna go. Grandma said I could." Natalie's gaze crept over to her mother, who shrugged.

"Mom, you really want her to go with you?"

"You know I don't mind. I thought she would have fun."

"She's not too much to handle?"

"Of course not, she's my granddaughter."

Natalie debated with the idea. "Well, it's just so far away...."

"It's only about four hours from here. They are starting in Conroe."

"That's still a long way, what if she needed me?"

"Oh, Natalie, you worry too much!"

Worried too much? Wasn't that part of being a mother? "I just don't know."

"Please, Mommy..." Dallie's little blue eyes sparkled.

"Come on, Natalie, she can stay with us for a few days and then you can come get her before Halloween."

Once again, Natalie played with the idea. "Oh, all right, but I'm coming to get you on Wednesday, no if, ands, or buts."

She sat Dallie down who squealed in delight and ran to her grandmother's legs. They had really bonded since Natalie had returned home and it warmed her heart to know that Dallie loved her mother so much. Natalie remembered how fond she'd been of her own grandmother. She was such a pioneer woman. They'd go on cattle drives for days when she was a young girl and her and her Gigi would fish and hunt and cook over a roaring campfire. She would tell her ghost stories under the stars and fashion her moccasins out of real cow hide. Her grandmother had been half Cherokee, half cowgirl and full of life, just like Natalie's mother.

Corrine turned then and looked over at Natalie. "Well, you'd better go get her packed. We're leaving in an hour. I gotta finish these muffins. Dallie go gather up Pinkie Pie and some toys for our trip and don't forget your cowboy hat." Dallie squealed again and ran off.

"An hour! Jeez, Mom."

"Well, if you'd 'a high tailed it back here before four o'clock, I'd of had time to get things done." She was giving her the guilt trip.

"I'm sorry. I had things I had to get done in town. I lost track of time."

It was a bold faced lie and Natalie hated lies, but she couldn't talk to her mother about such a personal subject. Her mother would be ashamed to admit that she and Natalie's father needed financial help from her or anyone. They'd always worked for what they had. They'd built Starlight Valley from the ground up. No, this would be something that Natalie would just have to discuss with Jack and Jack alone.

"Well, go put the towels in the dryer so that you and Jack will have clean ones while we're gone. Oh and there's ground deer in the fridge, if you wanna make a meatloaf tonight," she said to Natalie's retreating back.

She ran to do as her mother had asked then ran upstairs to get Dallie packed for the trip. She was rushing, placing shoes, clothes and toiletries into Dallie's overnight bag, all the while, she ultimately dreaded the coming conversation she would be having with Jack. She was just coming downstairs when her father opened the front door.

"Y'all ready?" he boomed.

"Yeah, here's Dallie's bag," she said handing it to him.

"I'm glad you're letting her go with us. She'll have such a good time. And if you or Jack need anything, you just holler okay." He pulled her into a hug. "Oh and Nathan's going too."

"Gosh, is *anyone* staying here?"

"Yup, you and Jack... and all the hands." Natalie looked suspiciously into her father's eyes. Had she not known any better she'd think that he and her mother had planned this on purpose. His blue eyes just twinkled back at her as he gathered the luggage her mother had parked at the door.

"Wait for me, Paw-Paw," Dallie said, running up to them. "Bye, Mommy." She waved.

"Hey, do I get a hug or what?" Natalie asked and Dallie sighed impatiently as Natalie scooped her up, kissing her soft little cheek.

"Be good for them okay? I love you."

"I love you too." Dallie jumped from her arms and ran out the door. About that time, Jack grabbed her up on her way down the stairs. Natalie felt her stomach take at the sight of him.

"And just where do you think you're going without hugging me?" he asked.

Dallie laughed in delight as he planted kisses all over her face, hugging her to him.

"Stop it," Dallie said between giggles as he tickled her belly. Natalie felt her heart beat faster, she would be alone with him in the house for the next six days and she was furious with him. Damn her luck!

~

"You think this will work?" Corrine asked her husband as they headed down the road. Dallie had fallen asleep in her car seat between them and Corrine ran her fingers through her bright blonde locks. David looked handsome in his old black Stetson and Corrine's heart beat quickened.

"If it doesn't, I don't know what will," he added, looking over at her. "I mean they've had all the time in the world. Now with no one around maybe they won't have any excuses."

They were once again playing match maker. They just wanted

their daughter to fall in love and be happy. When Nathan had volunteered to accompany them, they knew that they had to get Dallie to come along too, so that maybe Jack and Natalie could have the house to themselves and were forced to spend as much time together as possible. They'd worked hard this week and needed the break from everyone else. They were going to fall in love. It was going to happen. It was just a matter of time. Everyone saw how Natalie and Jack looked at one another. But Corrine still saw the hesitation in her daughter's eyes, the fear. David had been the one to suggest leaving them the house for the week. Corrine had been unsure at first, but finally agreed with him. They needed time alone, to bond, to get to know one another. Corrine prayed that it would work as she took David's outstretched hand.

~

*S*he would pay for lying to him, that bitch! He was going to hurt her in every way possible. This would be the last time she ever lied to anyone. She was nothing but a low life two-bit whore that deserved everything he was gonna do to her. Dan headed away from the ranch and toward the Rusty Spur to get drunk. Maybe he could get some followers while he was there. That would be good enough for her. Annabella didn't know what was coming, but either way, she would be punished for her deceitful tongue. When he finished with her, she would beg him for forgiveness. There would be no mercy. He was going to attack her full force with his vengeance. She had it coming.

~

*J*ack couldn't find Natalie. Just where the Hell was she? They had the night to themselves *and* the house and Jack was going to make sure they took full advantage of this situation while it lasted. He searched the house. No sign of her. Her car was there... Wait! Maybe she was in the barn, in her father's office working. Of course! What a workaholic she was. Well, work was over. It was playtime.

All work and no play.... He laughed to himself as he headed out the back door and toward the barn. The sky split then. The dark clouds that had been threatening all week were finally following through. Large droplets of rain spilled from the sky, but Jack welcomed it as it washed over him. It was cleansing, refreshing, cool on his body. He picked up speed as he got to the office door, and sure enough, there she was, going through her father's checkbook.

"Hey, there you are! I've been searching everywhere for you," he stated catching his breath. She didn't look at him as he came through the door, but was intent on the checkbook as he pulled his hat off and shook the water from it. "Hey, come on, take a break! You can work on that later. The night is young. You owe me about a thousand kisses and I'm thinking we should go out and celebrate our victory. What'd 'a ya say?"

She looked up at him then, tears in her eyes. "It's true..." she said, her voice barely a whisper.

"Well, yeah, it's true! Hell week is over! Let's get out of here!" He approached the desk.

Her head lowered and he realized then that she was upset about something. "You were the one that paid the note off... weren't you?"

He paused, not knowing what to say. This wasn't how she was supposed to find out. He swallowed simultaneously with the roll of thunder that rumbled overhead. He sighed and sat in the chair opposite her.

"It *was* you, wasn't it?" she asked again. He just looked her straight in the eyes and nodded. "How? How could you afford to give them $300,000? Are you rich?" Again, he just nodded. "How rich are you? How much money are we talking here?" Her voice was deathly calm. He hated that she'd found out this way, but it was time to tell her the complete truth.

"Well not quite as much as you have I'm sure, but... I've got over a million right now."

"Jesus," she swore and closed the book. "You're a millionaire and you never told me?" The look she gave him was incredulous. "How did you become a millionaire?"

"My parents apparently went without for years so that my brothers and I would never have to... They had insurance policies, their land, their own inheritance, several patents on some equestrian equipment..."

"Why would you keep this from me?" She was hurt more by his secrecy than anything else.

"Natalie, baby, I never meant for this to hurt you. I don't know how you found out, but you have to know that I was going to tell you..."

"When? You've had plenty of opportunities to tell me."

"Really? When was I supposed to tell you? When you weren't speaking to me? When we were working from sun up to sundown?"

"Oh, don't give me that! You could have told me the night you bought Dallie that horse, for starters..."

"Ok, ok, you're right. I should have told you then. But I didn't, and I'm sorry that I didn't." He stood, but her brows drew.

"Why didn't anyone ever tell me about Mom and Dad?"

"Oh, Natalie... you have to understand how ashamed they were of their situation. I only found out because I overheard them talking about it. I had been here right at six months when it happened. Apparently, they were several months behind on their mortgage and the bank was calling them, mailing them, harassing them. I went that very next day and paid it off so that it was done. They wouldn't have known that it was me, but your father point blank asked me. He was pretty upset at first, but I told him that I had no use for money and that he needed it so I'd put it to good use. He begged me to let him pay me back and of course, I refused. I said the only way he could pay me back was if he let me buy some of his land. He gave me 100 acres and he refused to let me pay him for it. That was that!" He felt sorry for her, for the look she was giving him. "Natalie, baby, I'm sorry that you had to find out this way."

She shook her head. "They should have told me. I would have helped them."

"According to them, you had enough problems of your own to worry about."

"It hurts that you wouldn't tell me. You *kept* it from me." The way she looked at him tore his heart out.

"Natalie, I didn't keep it from you, I swear. The right time just never came up to tell you, that's all."

"No, that's not all… You *purposefully* hid it from me." She stood then. Her fears echoed in her eyes.

"No, that's not true!" He came closer toward the desk, but she held her hand up, stopping him.

"Yes, it is!" She pointed her finger into his chest.

"Natalie, you're just assuming…"

"Why else wouldn't you tell me?"

"It wasn't like that. Besides, you never told me *you* had money, now did you?" For a moment, he had her and her face paled. Then the anger returned.

"I didn't *have* to tell you, Jack. You already knew!" She was yelling now and his heart was pounding in his chest.

"I only knew that you were a journalist. I never knew that your husband was in the NFL, I never knew he was a broadcaster. You're parents left him out of the picture. And while we're on the subject, aren't there a lot of things your keeping from *me?*" There he'd gotten it off his chest, but he wasn't finished. "There are so many things about you that I don't know, Natalie. I have only bits and pieces, but not the whole picture. You've never told me the whole story and I've never asked you to because I've waited for you to tell me."

"This is different…"

"How is this different? Keeping secrets is keeping secrets. Let's call a spade a spade! You seem to find it so upsetting that I didn't tell you about the fact that I have money. Well, who cares? Money means nothing to me. Nothing! It never has... The only thing that matters to me now is you. And I know that I've upset you and I will do anything to make this better." She wasn't looking at him now as she crossed her arms over her chest.

"It just goes to show..."

"Show what?"

"You really *are* too good to be true!" With that, she turned the other way and ran out of the office. Oh, she wasn't getting off that easily!

He followed her down the long, paved breezeway and had to run to catch up to her, when he twisted her around to him, she fought him.

"Stop it, don't you touch me." She clawed at him with her hands, but he grabbed her wrists.

"*You* stop it. Calm down." He backed her into the barn door with his body. The strong wind whipped stinging rain at them as he held her hands down against her sides. "Now, you tell me what's going on... Where is this coming from? Why did you say that?"

"Because it's *true*! I knew that you were just too damn good to be for real. I knew you weren't as perfect as you seemed. There had to be a catch." Her eyes were flames of blue as she stared into the windows of his soul.

"Natalie, of course I'm not perfect. No one is. What are you talking about?"

"You didn't tell me the truth. You know I have trust issues, you know I wanted to trust you more than anything. Now you see why I can't trust anyone! If you can lie to me then anyone can." He felt her chest heave against his. The rain lashed at them, soaking their clothes and their hair. The angry storm outside matched the one within.

"I'm sorry, Natalie. I'm sorry that I didn't *tell* you and I should have... But there is *no* catch. Baby, this is me! You know me! This is who I am!" He said, pointing his fingers at his chest. "I've never lead you to believe any different! I've *never* lied to you! The fact that I have money changes nothing. I work hard, I live a simple life. That's it! There's no ulterior motive. I just want to be with you more than anything in this world."

"I don't believe you!" She struggled to break free from him. They were yelling now, not only from their pent up anger, but in order to hear one another in the raging storm.

"Yes, you do. I know you want to believe me. Why are you acting this way?"

"Because I'm scared!" She broke into a sob then, her body quivered against his and he held her tightly to him, willing her fears away.

"I know, baby, I know you are. I am too. I'm scared to death." He took her face in his hands, his eyes bore into hers.

"Why?" She drew her brows in confusion.

"I'm scared that I'm not good enough for you, that I don't deserve you. I'm scared that I'll disappoint you."

"You are?" she asked, surprise in her voice.

"Yes!"

"But you're everything I've ever wanted."

"Then Natalie, you *have* to believe that it's real! The way I feel about you, it's different, different than anything I've ever felt before. When we touch, when we kiss, when I hold you, I feel something I've never felt with anyone else. There's a *reason* for that, Natalie! We are meant for each other! And I know you feel it too. I know you do or you wouldn't look at me the way you're looking at me right now. Everything I've ever told you is 100% from my heart. You *know* that what we have is real, just believe in it!"

"I don't….I don't know if I can!" She cried out as her eyes tore into his soul.

"Natalie, baby, please just look inside yourself. Stop allowing your mind to come between what you feel. What does your heart tell you? You know that I would never hurt you. You know I would never lie to you. You know that you can trust me. You *have* to believe that."

"I don't know what to believe anymore!"

He looked deeply at her, willing her to listen to him and trust in him, in what they had together. But her eyes were a black hole of anguish, full of doubt, full of pain, full of fear. He sighed and looked down. All that he'd done to prove himself to her had been in vain. She wasn't going to stop being afraid to be with him. He couldn't make her trust him; he couldn't make her love him...

He sighed again, his hands leaving her sides, all the fight within him gone. Replaced now only with sadness and disappointment. He stepped back then and turned from her, facing toward the interior of the barn. He forced the heels of his hands into his eye sockets, then through his hair, finally shoving them into the pockets of his jeans, a man whose soul was being tortured.

When he turned back toward her, his voice was deathly calm. "Natalie, I can't... I can't do this anymore. I can't keep getting so close to you only to keep getting pushed away. It's tearing me apart. I want you more than I've ever wanted anything in my whole life." He gently touched her face then, tears filling his eyes as he spoke, "I'm in love with you and I need you, but I can't make you fall in love with me. I've tried. I've tried to prove myself to you, but to no avail. The only thing I can say is that when you're as tired of being alone as I am and you know you can't go to bed at night without wishing that I was there with you then you'll know the time is right. When you believe that what we have is worth the risk, you'll know. I can't tell you when you're ready for this relationship. I can only wait for you to decide when it's right. But when you're ready, when you're *really* ready, I'll be right here waiting for you when that day comes."

With that he walked away from her, his clothes and hat and spirit ravaged by the rain and wind...and her indifference. His heart was breaking in two, but even when she called his name and the pain of it ripped through him like a knife, he kept walking. He couldn't turn back. It was up to her now.

∼

*S*he lay in torment, sweating, and tossing and turning. She couldn't sleep. Especially not knowing where he was or when he'd return. She'd stood her ground, forcing herself not to run after him even as she called his name into the raging storm. When he hadn't so much as looked back, she collapsed to the ground and sobbed. In that moment she felt as if she'd lost him forever. Damn her pride! This was the man of her dreams and she'd just let him walk away...

She'd gone to the house after clearing her tears and saw that his truck was gone and then cursed herself for being so hard on him, cursed herself for allowing him to believe that she didn't feel something for him. She'd robotically made dinner for the hands and herself and afterward sat and waited for him to return, but he never did. He'd been right. And she wanted to tell him that. Right about everything. Oh, why had she acted so selfishly over the fact that he had money? So what if he had money or even no money at all? So what if he hadn't yet told her? She'd not told him anything of her past and he didn't stop loving her because of it. And he did love her; he was *in love* with her, he'd said. Oh, she wanted him to come back so badly. Wanted to apologize to him. Wanted to tell him she was ready and that she meant it. She cried again, cried herself to sleep and awoke when she heard his bedroom door slam shut.

He was home! Her pulse quickened and butterflies filled her stomach. She could be scared of being hurt again for the rest of her life or she could take a chance on this man whom she'd realized on this very night she was madly in love with. It was now or never!

~

*J*ack pulled the towel from his waist and used it to dry his damp hair again. He turned down his bed and flipped his light off. The covers were cool as they touched each inch of his naked body. It would have felt great had he not been in such a sour mood. The hot shower had helped some, but he was still beating himself up for being so hard on Natalie. She was scared, dammit. Like a child. And he'd just turned and walked away because he'd been too frustrated to do anything else, frustrated and dejected. He'd also been wrong.

He'd left the ranch... and gone into town. He ended up at the Rusty Spur with Luther. He couldn't even finish his beer, he hadn't had the heart. He just listened to Luth talk, pretending that nothing was wrong. Then he'd ridden around town, aimlessly, not quite ready to face her. Then he'd come home after eleven, exhausted from the day, ate the plate Natalie had fixed and left for him in the microwave and then he'd showered. If her door hadn't been closed and the light off, he'd have talked to her, but she probably wasn't in the mood to hear what he had to say. He listened to the rain against the rooftop as he closed his eyes. In the morning he would apologize for his behavior. He would make everything right.

Suddenly, as if on cue the foot of the bed sank in as if someone had sat on it and he gasped as he smelled Natalie's perfume sweet in his nostrils. She had come to him! He was both thrilled and surprised at her presence and longed to turn and embrace her, but waited. Mostly out of curiosity. His back was to her and he wished he could see her eyes as she sighed. Silence followed for long moments before she spoke with a soft shaky voice.

"Troy and I never had what you would call a good marriage... I guess part of the reason I say that is because we were so young when we got married, we didn't know how to communicate with each other and we began to have problems...Problems that never seemed to work themselves out. I started to hate living with someone I couldn't talk to, couldn't be myself with. I hadn't realized how bad it really was until after Rick showed up at my door and we had the affair. I hadn't realized how desperate I was for attention...it was so pathetic...Afterwards, I felt determined to make things right and I got pregnant with Dallie. Troy was playing for the Bears when he was tackled and his knee literally shattered. He couldn't play after that and he changed. He wasn't the same as he'd been before the accident. He became violent and aggressive. He never hurt me, not while I was pregnant but I started to wonder and fear he would. He was very jealous, especially of my relationship with Buck. He accused us of having an affair and forbid me from talking to him or seeing him about two years ago. He never had a clue about Rick...

"After Dallie was born, things got better for a little while. He started to act like the man I originally married, but it wasn't too long before I started to realize just how much I had begun despising him. See...Troy had a very...authoritative attitude. It was his way or no way. He was an only child and he was raised to have what he wanted. And when Dallie came along all the attention was on her, he didn't get his way and he didn't like that. He became jealous of his own daughter. So he didn't make a big deal about holidays. Probably so he could take her fun away for his own selfish reasons. He hated animals too and refused to let Dallie associate with them. And he was completely obsessed with looking good for television and wanted us to look happy whether we were or not. He didn't spend a lot of time with Dallie and when he did he was always so belligerent to her. He was always out at a social gathering somewhere and he was always wanting me to tag along. He said I made a good 'arm ornament' and that I was good for his publicity. For the most part, I put up with him. I loved my work and my daughter and that's what I focused my life on."

Jack said nothing just listened intently to her. Then suddenly her voice changed, it was no longer reminiscent, it was sorrowful.

"Troy started to come around the older Dallie got. He wanted to spend more time with her and I thought he was finally stepping up and becoming a father to her." She breathed in and out then trying to stay calm. Jack turned and sat up then, facing her. The light of the full moon splashed over Natalie's face and he saw the silent tears come as she spoke, "I had started leaving her with him at night when I worked later than normal. I never thought anything about it... I thought he was being good to her. I never knew...God, how could I not have known?" She crumbled then and Jack took the hand she wasn't wiping her face with. He saw how difficult it was for her to tell him about her past. "I came home one evening and the house was dark... I thought he'd put Dallie to bed and went on himself, so as always I went in to check on her." She paused again, violent spasms racked her body as she tried to speak, tears streamed her face. "He was...he was on top of her, Jack. She was naked and...he— he was touching her. She was cry—crying for me...Oh, God!" She covered her face with her hands.

Jack inhaled sharply. Jack's stomach pitched as the unwelcome picture filled his head. His mind reeled and he felt as if some unseen force had come in suddenly and ripped the heart right out of his chest. Oh, God, this man *had* been a monster after all...What kind of barbarian could do something like that? And to their own child? Poor Dallie. Poor Natalie. How helpless they must have felt. No wonder this woman was so afraid for her daughter and herself.

"My poor, innocent baby girl! She was only three years old! He'd been doing it all along..."

"Jesus, Natalie. I'm so sorry. I had no idea. God...I'm—I'm sorry!" Jack gripped her shoulders, pulling her to him as she collapsed into his arms. He held her and stroked her hair and her back as he'd done in the past. He now knew the reasoning behind her hesitations, her fears. The torment she fought that existed inside her mind and her soul. This amazing woman had truly been through Hell and back. His heart went out to her as she looked up at him and swiped at her face.

"There's more..." She looked down, then back up again, tears glistening in her eyes. "While he awaited trial... I found out that he's—he's...a— a murderer."

"Jesus!" *When did it end?*

"He raped and strangled a woman one night while she was out running on our campus. We were in college at the time; it was during our junior year. Then before Dallie was born, he kidnapped a six year old girl in our neighborhood. He did horrible things to her,

Jack, gruesome things..." She looked down again, the sobs picking up where they'd left off. "There isn't a day that goes by that I don't wonder what he would have eventually done to my daughter had I not found him that night."

"Baby, I'm so sorry." He repeated. What else could he say? Nothing would make this better. How could anyone every forgive something like this? How could anyone forget something this horrific? She would be haunted forever, he knew.

He sat silently stroking her soft flesh as he held her. Her sobs gradually turned to whimpers. He said nothing, just sat there holding her and absorbed her frame of mind. Feeling the things she must have felt. Anger. Shock. Sorrow. Disgust. Fear. Torment of the entire body, mind and soul. He now knew the pain she'd suffered and why she'd responded to him as she had this whole time. Inside he felt torn and shamed and then hate took over him, hate for this man who'd hurt the two most important people in his life.

They sat there for such a long time, her cries eventually fading, he just softly stroked her and the only sound was their breathing which was slow and even. They were both quiet for a long time. Then Natalie pulled back suddenly and looked at him, a new emotion showed in her twinkling, tear-streaked eyes and for a moment he didn't know what it was. Then he recognized it as need. Her breathing had calmed, but her chest was heaving as if she were tried to control herself. He gulped as he looked down at her. The moonlight was bathing her peachy skin in shades of blue and silver and as his gaze fell down her body, he saw that she wore only a silk teddy. Her breasts threatened to spill out of the lacy top of it, her thighs were bare, peeking up at him. His member went rock hard in seconds flat and he was all too aware of the heat rising from their bodies. His eyes flew back up to hers and once again those eyes bore straight into his, like heat seeking missiles. They tore his insides out. She gulped then too. Her eyes fell down over him until she got to the sheet and could see no more. His heart rate quickened and anticipation seized him. She looked so gorgeous sitting there. Her wavy dark hair streaked with mahogany curled around her shoulders and fell down to her breasts, a mass of ringlets teasing him. He reached for it, wanting to test the softness of the curl. His finger brushed her cheek and he leaned in closer.

"Jack..." Her voice was sultry now... needy, erotic and it thrilled him.

"Yeah?" He was having trouble answering as she moved her body closer to his.

"Make love to me," she whispered, almost breathlessly. Her lips were but a breath away and he closed his eyes as she brought her face to his. She wouldn't have to ask him twice.

His lips found hers as he slowly pulled her down tilting their bodies to where he was on top. His mouth was eager and soft as he caressed her lips. Then he deepened the kiss, using his tongue gently, yet powerfully. One of his hands went to her leg, stroking up to her slender thigh and her hip. The other was behind her head, kneading her scalp as his fingers tangled in her thick mass of hair. His mouth continued it's exploration as his hand snaked up from her hip to her thin gown, moving across her lean tummy to find her breast. She rose for a breath and moaned as she began caressing his shoulders with her fingernails, the soft tickling sensation only added to his desire for her. His thumb grazed her pebbled nipple and he teased it with his fingertip. Another sexy sound escaped her throat as he squeezed her big, full breast, reshaping it in his hand. He cursed then, this was all part of his fantasy but, dammit, he couldn't see her. He flipped away from her then and flooded the room with light from the bedside lamp then rolled over, back to her side. She was breathless as she looked at him.

"I want to see you," he said, looking down at her. She gave him an enticing smile.

"I want to see you too." Her hands went to the bottom of the short, sexy, tiny negligee as she crawled to her knees and peeled it over her head. He sighed longingly as his eyes fell over her.

"God, you're the most beautiful woman I've ever seen, Natalie."
She smiled sweetly at that.

She really was the most beautiful woman he'd ever seen with her
long, lean torso, her perky, full breasts with their pink tips and her
flat tummy. Her skin was so flawless and creamy and he longed to
stroke and kiss and taste every inch of it. His eyes fell to her curvy
hips and lean thighs to a skimpy pair of black thongs and he
gestured to them.

"Hey, you're cheating….I want to see ALL of you."

She raised her eyebrow at him. "You want 'em off, you take 'em
off." He smiled then and grabbed her, pulling her back down beneath
him. He started at one leg using only his fingertips; he followed it up
to her thigh, then to her groin and grabbed the string of the under-
wear, tucking his finger underneath it. His other hand came to her
other leg and he watched her intake of breath as his other finger
followed suit.

"These just simply have to go…" His eyes sought hers.

"No fair," she said. "I haven't seen you yet." She pouted.

"Oh, trust me, baby, you'll be able to look your fill before too
long." His head lowered and his tongue traced the line of her panties
not far from her belly button. She sighed and threw her head back,
his lips followed and he began kissing and licking his way around
the thin silk. As he got to the strings, his tongue traced the line of
her groin and she nearly leapt off the bed. He smiled to himself,
loving that he could make her do things like that. He then began
kissing the fabric itself, working his way down to the delta between
her thighs. His tongue darted at her, reaching her through the thin
layer of silk.

"Oh, Jack, oh, please I want to see you!" she begged. Again he
loved her breathless reaction. In a flash he had pulled the thongs
from her body and threw them on the ground. His eyes fell upon her
and again he smiled.

"Whatever the lady wants, the lady gets," he said, peeling the
covers off of himself slowly as he rose to his knees. She was able to

look her fill then and if her eyes were any indication, she liked what she saw.

"Jordan was right..."

"What?" he smirked, taken aback.

"You *do* have the body of a Greek god."

"And just how the Hell would *she* know?" He laughed heartily then stopped as her hands went at him, stroking the hot, hard length of him. He groaned, sucking in his breath as her fingertips touched each part of him. When he couldn't take anymore, he ended the torture, stretching his body out atop of hers, too close for her to touch him. His chest aligned with hers, his belly touched hers, his hardness pressed against her thigh. Her hands went to his face as he kissed her breathlessly once again. Their kiss was hot, passionate, needy. His mouth moved to her neck bringing the most wonderful sounds from her throat as he lightly nibbled there. His hands went to her breasts again, squeezing her firm, plump flesh, his thumbs bringing her nipples to hard points.

"Jack, oh please," she groaned with need.

His head lowered and she anticipated feeling his hot mouth on her. He kissed her creamy skin randomly from one breast to the other, her cleavage, continuing his torment with his thumbs, slow, long kisses using his tongue to torture her. Then slowly his breath fell on her. She moaned hungrily as he flicked her nipple with his tongue, his lips closing over the throbbing peak and gently pulling on it, drawing her deepest desires with it; his hand torturing her other breast with rhythmic circles. She moaned loudly, her body writhing, his mouth bringing her so close to oblivion. Then he let the other one have a turn. When he was finished loving them, his mouth fell lower to her belly, her belly button, to the little triangle of hair between her legs. Her body ached, her womanhood pulsing with newfound desire that longed to be quenched.

He had to touch her, taste her, every inch of her. His head fell and he parted her, using his fingertips on her to elicit sexy noises from her throat. His finger entered her silky warmth and she writhed against him as his finger plunged then withdrew, plunged again.

"Jack..." she cried breathlessly, feeling her body slowly unravel into waves of pleasure.

"Yes, baby." His tongue found her and he licked a trail all his own, gently sucking at her sensitive skin as his finger continued to explore her. She cried out, her breathing became labored.

"Jack, please," she begged, "not without you." He smiled then and came to his knees giving her a moment to breath, but her look was just as sultry as before. "Don't I get a turn?" she asked with challenge in her eyes as her gaze fell between his legs.

"A turn?" He was preparing to slide his sex into her.

"I want you in *my* mouth." He gulped; he wouldn't argue with her.

She made him turn and lay on his back as she lay atop him and kissed him. Her lips darted over his cheeks, his nose, his chin and she worked her way down to his big muscled chest. Her mouth was hot as she stroked at his skin with her tongue, planting messy kisses on his flesh. She flicked his nipples as his breath hissed through his teeth. She smiled as she moved down his chiseled stomach then to his groin. Her fingers traced him and he thought he would die with anticipation. Then she took him in her hand and began stroking the length of him, teasing the velvety tip of him with her fingertips. His heart hammered in his chest and his breathing became ragged. Then her head lowered to him and he almost jumped off the bed as she took him into her hot mouth, inch by tormenting inch.

"Dear God." He swore as pleasure overcame him.

Her dark hair fell over his thighs, her sultry eyes looking up at him as she tortured his rock-hard flesh. She licked the head of his sex, up and down, round and round then encircled the base of it with her fist, pulling gently on him as her mouth enclosed the tip gently sucking. Then her mouth fully encompassed him and she moved her fist up the length of him as her mouth came back to the tip; Up and down, milking his sex with her mouth and her fist simultaneously. It was exquisite. She was exquisite. He gave an animalistic groan, fighting the urge to spill himself into her mouth. She continued to lick and stroke and suck with that stunning mouth of hers until he absolutely couldn't take anymore. He took her hands.

"Natalie...please, baby....I can't..." Her teasing grin said she was happy with herself. Then she surprised him once more by straddling his hips and bringing herself down over his erection. He nearly came undone as the tip of him entered her sweet softness. They both gasped in torment as inch by nerve-racking inch she impaled herself upon him until his sex filled her completely. Suddenly, he was engulfed in her silky heat, his sex and his mind, and he grabbed her hips, stilling them for a moment, afraid he would lose himself to the warmth that was hers alone.

"Just a minute, darlin'." A hot sweat broke out on his forehead as he restrained himself from the natural instincts of his body.

"What's wrong, Jack?" she asked, her hands splaying across his abdomen.

"You're just so sexy baby, so sweet, you feel *so* good...So very good." He willed himself not to lose control and slowed his breathing as he tilted his head back and gritted his teeth in glorious agony. Then slowly he eased his grip and she began to rise and fall on him, loving him with her body and her eyes. His hands stroked her breasts, her back, her muscular little rear-end as he watched her bounce upon him, slow at first and then faster, more needy.

"Oh God, Natalie!" He was again close to climax, but he wasn't ready to give in just yet. He suddenly flipped them both over to where she was on her back, his body covering hers. Then he began gently thrusting deep inside her as he kissed her mouth.

He wanted her to go first. He wanted to see her fall apart to his touch, his body, his eyes. His hand lowered to where their bodies met and he began caressing her. She moaned loudly and called his name, spurring him on. He drove into her slowly, softly. Making love to her, stroking her with his sex.

"Natalie, baby. I'm so in love with you," he said. His eyes met hers as he loved her, his touch ever so light on her. Her eyes mirrored his. They were pools of raw emotion as she matched his rhythm. Her breathing became shorter, sharper and little moans escaped her lips. She was getting close, he knew…then her head flew back suddenly and she succumbed to him. Her release came quickly, her flesh quickening around his and her body was racked with fierce tremors, her cries echoing rapture. A tear fell down her cheek and he kissed it away. He rode the wave of her orgasm, letting her return slowly. Then suddenly, her legs gripped his hips and her eyes returned to his. She was back for more, he realized and smiled. His thrusts became more urgent and their breathing became ragged and broken as they moaned their ecstasy with each plunge of his hips.

"Jack, oh, Jack." She cried out in orgasm once again and his resistance faltered as her body contracted around him once more. He finally gave in to sexual bliss and spilled himself deep inside her, growling a pleasure cry of his own. After he slowly came back to earth, he stayed there, still inside her body, watching her as their breathing gradually slowed. He looked down at their entangled bodies, intertwined in such a way that no one could tell where one began and the other ended.

He smiled then and kissed her; a soft, slow kiss and she smiled up at him as he pulled back. He slowly drew himself from her and fell to her side, propping his head up on his arm watching her. She turned to face him then and he brushed a lock of her hair away from her eyes.

"Wow, Jack…" she began.

"Incredible," he murmured.

"Yeah." She smiled, her cheeks turned crimson. He stroked her face with his hand then pulled her toward him, kissing her lips. "Can we try reverse cowgirl?"

"Reverse cowgirl? What the heck is that?" Although he knew, he feigned ignorance for her benefit.

"I'll show you," she said, her hands falling on him as he moaned.

~

*L*uther Boyd sat wide awake, beer in hand, watching an old
Saturday Night Live rerun on TV. He was getting used to
nights like these. Alone, bored, envious of his best friend…
Jack hadn't looked too happy tonight, no matter how much he
pretended he was. Jack had everything in the world to be happy
about, though. He was dating… and dating Natalie Cameron at that.
Any man would be envious. Best friend or not.

Ah, who was he kiddin'? He was just jealous because he hadn't
slept with anyone in a long time. He sighed, he missed having
someone to cuddle up to at night, he missed the touch of a woman,
the smell of a woman. He burped loudly and got up out of the
recliner for another beer. He glanced over at the clock. Two in the
morning. Great!

As he headed into the kitchen, the doorbell rang.

"Now, who in the Hell could that be at this time 'a night?" he
asked, ambling toward the door. "Jack, that better not be you! I
swear I'll kick your ass for that one, bud. You better not tell me that
you have her all to yourself tonight in an empty house and you're
heading your sorry ass over here."

He flipped the porch light on and quickly swung the door open.
"If you—"

He stopped. The person on his front porch wasn't Jack.

"Luther…" came a raspy, weak female voice.

Annabella Smith looked at him through one good eye, the other
was purple and swollen the size of a softball. Her face was scratched,
her lip busted and bloody, and her hair matted with twigs and leaves.
He swallowed as he dared to look beyond her face. Her clothes were
torn, he could see the swell of one breast and her entire stomach
which too was scratched, bruises covered it and her arms and blood
pooled between her legs, streaming down to her ankles.

"Jesus Christ, Bella. What the Hell happened to you?"

"Please, help me!" With that, she collapsed and he moved quickly

291

to gather her into his arms, she was limp, out cold. He moved swiftly, not knowing how badly she'd been injured just knowing he had to get her to the hospital as fast as possible. Adrenaline took over. He scrambled, looking for his keys, and found them on the coffee table. Grabbing them, he ran for the door, throwing on his bedroom shoes as he passed the foyer then he slammed the door and hauled ass to his pickup. He sat Annabella down gently in the passenger seat, not even bothering with a buckle. He came around the other side of the truck, started the ignition and threw the truck in reverse, heading out toward town. His heart slammed into his ribs as he flew down his gravel driveway. He pressed his fingers into her carotid artery to check her pulse. It was low. Way too low. His foot slammed the petal to the floorboard. He had to hurry or she was gonna die right there on his seat.

CHAPTER 12

*N*atalie awoke to the sunlight streaming through her bedroom window. She felt Jack's arm slung over her waist and his warm breath tickling her ear. She smiled to herself. Wow! Last night had been more wonderful than she'd ever dreamt it could be. He'd been a sexy and strong lover. Fun and exciting and passionate. They'd made love throughout the night, falling to sleep only to wake up caressing one another. It was like an erotic dream come true. She stretched her arms up to the bedpost in a stretch and remembered how much she'd loved her old bed. His hand crawled up to gently squeeze her breast then and she squealed in surprise.

"Jack, you bad boy!"

"Oh, sorry, that was a total accident."

"Sure, it was." She rolled over into his strong, solid chest then and kissed his lips slowly, lovingly. She remembered how tender he'd been last night, surprising since his body was so big and muscular. She looked down at his chest admiring his masculine strength. She delicately fingered the lines of his muscles. He tucked his hands behind his head as he stretched and smiled at her lying naked across him.

"So, do we want to stay in bed all day?" It was a Saturday after all. The horses had to be fed, but other than that they had nothing too pressing to do.

"It's awfully tempting…" she said, raising her brows at him.

"Awfully!" he agreed. "Hey, I have an idea!" he said suddenly. "Let's go get some stuff to decorate the house for Halloween." She smiled at him. He was always thinking about Dallie. He adored her child so much.

"Ok, lets!"

They took a shower together and ended up making love under the spray of the water. It was exhilarating to Natalie because she'd never done it in a shower before. Afterward, they dressed. Jack went to go feed the horses while Natalie baked up the batch of muffins her mother had left in the fridge. She was pulling them out of the oven when he came in the door.

"My, those smell almost as good as you do." He grabbed her waist from behind and pulled her against his chest, kissing her neck. She reveled in it, loving the way he made her feel.

After breakfast, they headed into town for Halloween decorations. Jack had this master plan to light the porch up and turn the front yard into a graveyard scene. She laughed at his enthusiasm. They stopped by the farmer's market first and picked out some pumpkins, gourds and wreaths made of fake maple leaves, glitter and ribbons as well as vegetables and fruits for her to cook for the week. Then they headed to Denton to the Halloween store they'd went to a little over a week ago and got lights, props and tombstones. Natalie picked out a few things for inside the house too. They stopped for lunch at a Mediterranean grill and added gyros and hummus to their lists of favorite foods. As they headed home, Natalie decided to call and see about Dallie. She got her father's voicemail.

"Hey Dad, it's me…I just wanted to call and talk to Dallie and see how she was doing. I hope she's being good for you! Anyway, tell her I miss and I love her…"

"I miss her and love her too!" Jack yelled.

"...and Jack misses and loves her too. So, anyway, call me later. I love you guys, bye." She hung up the phone, slightly disappointed.

Jack looked over at her and took her hand. "Hey, you alright?"

"Yeah, I'm just starting to miss her. I don't think I've ever been this long without her. Without talking to her even. You know?" He just smiled over at her.

When they got home, she put away the fresh produce and headed outside to help Jack decorate. They hung orange and black lights and electric candelabras. They took the makeshift tombstones and placed them in the front yard, covering them in moss and setting lights in front of them to illuminate them for the evening. They filled large cauldrons with mini pumpkins and set them on either side of the door. They stuffed some of her father's old clothes with hay and perched the dummy in one of the rocking chairs. He was complete with a pumpkin head, which Natalie drew a silly face on, and a straw hat. Then they started on the inside, using the wreaths on the doors and the gourds and pumpkins on the mantle and for a table center piece. They admired their work then started a supper of roasted lamb and butternut squash, creamed spinach and orzo salad. Before nightfall, they sat in companionable silence watching the sunset. He smiled over at her in the orange and crimson glow of the sun, a mischievous look in his eyes.

"You ever done it in the hayloft before?"

She laughed. "Are you serious?"

"Do I look serious?" he stated, smiling and arching an eyebrow at her. After a few moments he said, "Well, come on, now's as good 'a time as any..." He pulled her from her seat and down the back stairs.

She was completely in love with him and his thirst for life. And when they were both naked and breathless on a saddle blanket perched in the hayloft, she told him.

"I love you, Jack."

He smiled that big, sexy smile of his. "I love you too, my darling."

With that he kissed her breathless, his hands gently caressing her body as he made her his.

⁓

She was alive. Thank God for that! Luther paced the waiting room as he had much of the entire day. Annabella had been in the ICU for almost twenty-four hours now. She'd been raped, multiple times, beaten, cut and left for dead. She had been cut vaginally from the inside out. That explained the vast amount of blood that was falling down her legs when he'd first seen her. Whoever had done this to her had intended to punish her, ruin her for life, and ultimately kill her. Whoever had done this to her would pay severely. There had been several of them and that was before they'd tried to fillet her with a hunting knife. Luther was beyond irate. He didn't love Anna as he once had, he didn't even like her right now. But no woman, no matter how promiscuous she was, deserved what this creep and his cronies had done to her. The minute she woke up, he was gonna find out who it was and when he did, they'd better pray that he didn't find them.

⁓

On Sunday, Jack took Natalie fishing. They rode to Lake Dallas and fished at Lewisville Lake, catching catfish by the pounds. When they came home, Jack gutted and skinned the fish and Natalie fried the pieces to crunchy perfection along with hushpuppies. She paired the fried vitals with fresh coleslaw and dill potato salad. They froze what they didn't cook and it appeared they would have enough catfish to last until next year. They enjoyed their dinner as they sat together at her parent's dining room table.

"Man, I'm glad I got a woman that knows how to cook," Jack said with a bite of slaw in his mouth. Natalie laughed at him.

"Well, you said I was my mother's daughter after all."

"And thank the sweet Lord above for that," he said, plopping another hushpuppy into his mouth. "Hey," he said swallowing his bite. "Wanna watch a scary movie tonight? I'll make us some popcorn..." She nodded in agreement.

He made her feel like a teenager again; Entertaining her as he did then sneaking her off to make love to her in random places. Like this afternoon when he'd suggested they make love on the staircase. She of course had obliged. She couldn't say no to him. It was impossible. For the first time in her life, she felt good enough for someone. She felt she finally deserved to be happy. She deserved Jack Kinsen.

Natalie phoned her father to talk to Dallie as she went into the living room after supper. He'd finally called right before they headed off for bed last night and she was relieved to hear her daughter's voice in the background.

"Hi Mommy," Dallie answered the phone.

"Hey baby, what are you doing?"

"Just eating supper with Grandma and Paw-Paw and Vivian. They cooked us chicken over a campfire. And you would be so proud, Mommy. I ate it all gone."

"You did? I'm so proud of you," Natalie murmured into the phone. Jack joined her on the couch, handing her a cup of hot chocolate as he smiled at her.

"Did you know that that's how cowboys ate back then?"

"I sure did, do you feel like a real cowgirl?"

"Yes, and guess what, I got to ride with Uncle Nathan today!"

"Well, that's great, sweetie. I'm so glad that you're having a good time. I miss you!"

"I miss you too...Where's Jack?" She hadn't left him out of either of their last two conversations.

"He's right here. Do you want to talk to him?" Jack signaled for Natalie to hand him the phone and she did before hearing Dallie's response which she knew would be a yes.

"Hello, my little darlin'... I am...Ameera is fine...yup and Blaze too," He winked at Natalie and smiled as he continued. "Mommy and

I are just hanging out about to watch a movie. You did? How neat! Well, I have a surprise for you when you get home…Well, you'll just have to wait and see. I miss you too. I love you… Here's Mommy." Tears came to her eyes then as she got the phone back and told Dallie goodnight and that she loved her. That should have been a conversation that Troy had with Dallie but he'd never been as kind or as caring of her as Jack was. She put the phone on the coffee table and leaned back into the couch. Jack looked down at her then and she looked up at him with tears in her eyes.

"You really miss her, don't you?" he asked. She just nodded afraid to tell him that he would have made Dallie the greatest father in the world.

~

On Monday, Jack came into her father's office as she worked once again on invoices and balancing. She decided that her father should hire her part time so that the paper work got done when it was supposed to. She looked up at him and he looked at her with that all too familiar twinkle in his eyes.

"What?" she asked playfully, not sure she wanted to know.

"Here! On the desk?" He cocked his eyebrow.

"Jackson Edward Kinsen!"

"What? It'll be fun." He raised his hands in an innocent gesture. "Maybe you can put those sexy specs of yours on…"

"I will have you know that this is my father's desk!"

"It can be cleaned off." He raised his eyebrow in challenge and she smiled, knowing that despite her teasing protests that she would give in to him.

"You are bad," she muttered as he leaned down over the desk to her.

"You've made me that way," he said, bringing his lips to hers. She returned the long kiss and as she pulled back they heard a ruckus in the breezeway.

"Where is that son of a bitch?" Came a familiar voice. Jack hurried to go find out what was going on and Natalie followed. They both stared in shock as they saw Luther Boyd approaching with a Louisville Slugger. His clothes were in disarray, like he'd worn them for days. He had a major five o'clock shadow and his eyes were bloodshot.

"Who, Luth?" Jack demanded.

"Dan... he's a dead man! Where the fuck is he?" His voice was grave and he spoke softly, slowly.

"For the love of God, *what* is going on?" Jack asked. "You look like Hell!"

"He tried to kill Annabella."

"When?"

"He raped her Friday night, him and a bunch of his friends. They beat her and used a hunting knife to cut her inside and left her to die on the side of the road."

"Oh my God!" Natalie exclaimed, covering her mouth with both hands.

"Now, where...is...he?" Luther's eyes looked crazy as he once again repeated himself, raising the bat.

"Luther, I don't know, buddy. Now, why don't you just put the bat down?" Jack asked calmly, approaching Luther gently, his hand up.

"No, I'm going to take pleasure in bashing his damn brains in." Luther tapped the bat against his shoe.

"Look, as much as I dislike him myself, he really isn't worth going to prison for. If he did what you say that he did then he will be tried for it. There's just no sense in you—"

"Jack, you're not stupid enough to believe that anyone would go to trial for raping a slut like her, do you? There will be no evidence because no one cares; No one but me. God damn him." Luther fell to his knees then, the bat falling to the ground. He sobbed.

Jack approached his friend, stopping in front of him. Natalie followed and crouched on her knees, looking into his eyes.

"You ought to have seen what they did to her. I've never seen anything like it in my life. I thought she would die before I got her to the hospital. There was so much blood…So much! The doctor says it's a miracle she's even alive." Natalie took his hands trying to calm him. "I've been at the hospital for two days now. I finally saw her this morning. She looks like death, but they say that she's going to live. She'll never be able to have children though. Not that she'd ever wanted any but, all the same." Jack stooped down then and grabbed his friend's shoulder.

"I'm sorry, Luther. I truly am."

"Yeah, I know. I'm a damn idiot. You can say it! Dammit! I'm still in love with her. God help me! I didn't even realize it until this morning when she looked up at me and thanked me for saving her life. I still don't know how she walked that far…She's black and blue all over and cut from one end to the other."

Natalie took his face in her hands. "How long has it been since you've eaten?" The look he gave her was dumbfounded.

"I don't know."

"Well, come on. You and I are going back to the house. I have a pot of beef stew cooking and you're going to eat some of it if I have to force it down your throat."

Jack would take care of Dan. For now, she was taking care of Luther.

When they got to the house, Luther sat at the table while she scooped him up a bowl of stew and cut him a piece of hot cornbread, placing a dollop of butter atop it. He sat with his face in his hands, shivering. She knew exactly what he was feeling. She'd felt it before. Hopelessness, suffering, fear, loathing. She sat the bowl down in front of him and he took it eagerly.

"Thank you, Natalie," he said as he began scooping big spoonfuls into his mouth. He ate as if he was starving. She sat the tea she'd fixed in front of him and he drank it greedily as well. When he finished his stew, he again thanked her as she fixed him a second helping. He took her hand before he dug in and began speaking.

"I've never hated someone so bad in my life for what he did to her." He looked down, his eyes looking pained and guilty at the same time.

"I know Luth, I know. I despise him too, but trust me the cops will handle him. It's a law that any rape must be investigated thoroughly. Justice will be served. Just get a good lawyer, preferably one from out of town and everything will work out."

"Natalie:...do you think I'm a fool? I mean she's bedded half this town and the next one over and yet I still want her...What the hell is the matter with me?"

"No, Luth. I don't think you're a fool." She cupped his scruffy face in her hand. "The heart wants what the heart wants and there's nothing you can do to change who you love."

That night, Luther slept in the guest room after calling to check on Annabella. Natalie and Jack went to see her and even though Natalie had never liked her, she'd felt deep sorrow for the horrible things that had been done to this young girl. Annabella's face and lips were swollen and bruised; four distinct scratch marks ran from the corner of one eye all the way down her cheek to her chin, as if someone dug his nasty fingernails into her there. Her right eye was swollen shut and black and blue. Deep cuts ran down her arms and legs which were also dotted with purple bruises of various sizes. Her spirit looked as broken down as her body. Her voice was extremely weak and she begged their forgiveness for her trouble. This experience had been humbling for her. She acted nothing like the same person they'd both come to know. When they left, Jack had told her that Dan would be turned over to the police if he showed up at the ranch. They had an APB out on him. He'd never come in for work the day before and no one knew where he was. None of the guys had seen him since Friday night. It was oddly suspicious, especially if he was innocent. Although after tonight, Natalie knew he had done it; out of anger toward Anna for lying to him about Jack. That was exactly why he'd done it. The thought made her nauseous.

"I always thought Dan was scum, but I never imagined he would do something like this," Natalie said on their way home, feeling as if she were in a daze. "You know what's so odd, is that just the other day...in Dad's office, he told me that he wasn't Troy Cameron... Now, he's just put himself on the same level with Troy..."

"Yeah, well, it just goes to show you, I guess. I never thought he was capable of doing it either, but I guess we didn't know him as well as we thought we did," Jack responded, taking her hand and giving her a sorrowful glance.

Natalie was angry. How could anyone hurt someone that way? Then again, how could Troy have hurt the people he'd hurt, even his own daughter? There were no answers for the cruelties people could inflict on others. Natalie silently cried all the way home.

When they finally went to bed, Natalie slept unsoundly. She had nightmares. She saw images of Troy killing the little girl on their street; her name had been Sarah, Sarah Richards. She was six and had loved dolls and swings and singing. Natalie saw her sweet little face in her dream, she was carefree and happy, and Troy took her life without a second thought, then she saw Dan raping and beating Annabella without mercy. She awoke screaming, clawing, fighting them, hating them. Jack awoke too and flooded the room in light, taking her in his arms and stroking her as she dried her tears. It had been too real, too much for her, and she asked that he leave the light on. He obliged and held her in his arms as she fell to sleep once again.

By Wednesday, Natalie was ready to come get her baby girl. She'd spent many wonderful days and nights with Jack, but she missed her daughter and wanted her with her. Jack seemed just as excited as she was. Natalie knew that he missed her too, maybe not quite as much as she did, but he missed her all the same.

They were meeting her parents outside of Conroe that evening. Natalie had once camped on Lake Conroe and absolutely loved it. She and Jordan and the boys had taken Buck's father's boat out and camped off one of the islands. It had been a fun time, even if she'd been with Troy then.

They met her parents at a Western Sizzlin' because her father had been craving "some red meat" he'd said. When they parked and got out of the truck, Natalie watched as Dallie ran to her and tears filled her eyes. God, she'd missed her little angel. She bent to take her into her arms and swept her around in circles as she hugged her tightly to her chest.

"Oh, my darling, I missed you so."

"I missed you too, Mommy," Dallie said, squeezing her neck. "Jack!" She squealed as Natalie set her down. She ran to him too and he effortlessly lifted her into his arms as he hugged her to him. She kissed his scruffy cheek and Natalie's heart melted. If she didn't know any better she'd think her daughter was as in love with Jack as she was... Nah!

"Let's go grab a bite to eat and then I have a surprise for you," Jack said and Dallie squealed in delight.

"Can't I have it *already*?"

"Not yet. Let's eat and then you can, okay?"

"Ohhh, alright," she sighed.

As they ate, Natalie kept watching her parents. They were eyeing Jack and Natalie suspiciously as if they were waiting for them to tell them something. Natalie blew it off. She knew how eager they were to have Jack for their son-in-law; perhaps that was it. They talked about the ranch and how filming was going and Natalie told them about what happened to Annabella, spelling some words so that Dallie didn't get what she was saying. They were both shocked and horrified at the news. Natalie told them that Dan had yet to be apprehended.

"Dan was always a jerk. I just never knew he was a—a...like that. And to think he almost mu—M-U-R-D-E-R-E-D her," her father said, sadly shaking his head. Dan would eventually need to be replaced, but that was neither here nor there.

They bid their farewells as they left the restaurant and headed toward home. Jack stopped off at the home of a client. He was in and out quickly but came back carrying a crate, he motioned for them to get out of the car, pulling something from the crate. When he turned, Natalie saw it was a black and white border collie pup, only about 11 weeks old, a small, sweet little thing. Dallie screamed with joy.

"A puppy! A real puppy! Is it mine?" She approached Jack and extended her hand to pet the little dog.

"He's all yours, Dallie," Jack said. The collie licked at her little fingers and Dallie giggled.

"Oh, Mommy look! Isn't he sooo cute?" Dallie cooed. Jack handed her the puppy and she cradled it as she walked toward Natalie.

"He is! Did you thank Jack?" Natalie asked.

"Thank you, oh thank you," she cried as she turned toward Jack.

"You're welcome, my little darlin'."

As they headed down the road and Natalie watched Dallie laughing and playing with her new puppy, she confronted Jack.

"A new pony *and* a new puppy... and it's not yet Christmas," she said, her eyebrow cocked.

"She deserved it. Of all the kids in the world, she deserved both of them." He was right. Dallie'd had to do without the animals that she'd loved until now and Jack was making up for it. That meant a lot to Natalie.

"Just don't spoil her, Jack."

"What makes you think I would do such a thing like that?" he asked as he grabbed her hand and kissed it. She gave him a knowing glance.

When they got home, it was still too early to turn the lights on but Dallie saw the yard and was overjoyed by what they'd done.

"Oh, Mommy, it looks like *Hocus Pocus*," she said, referring to her favorite Halloween movie.

Before nightfall they'd carved three jack-o-lanterns and made popcorn balls with candy corn eyes. When the sun set, Jack placed the pumpkins on the front steps, lit their candles and turned the lights on. Dallie was mesmerized by the scene before her.

Afterward, Natalie was busy making supper as Jack and Dallie played with the new puppy.

"You think Dash likes me?" Dallie asked. She was referring to the puppy she'd swiftly named for his quick, playful movements.

"Of course he likes you," Jack replied. "You're his favorite person in the whole world." She smiled at that.

After supper, they ate their popcorn balls and watched some old Halloween cartoons on television. Jack took Dallie up to bed, while Natalie typed on her laptop. When he came back down, he smiled at her.

"What?" she asked.

"She wouldn't go to sleep without Dash." He came to sit beside her.

"That doesn't surprise me."

"Well, I guess it could be worse, at least he's had his shots." She smiled at his comment and focused back to her computer screen as he grabbed her feet, massaging them. "She's so much like you sometimes."

"Scary, isn't it?" He just smiled at her assessment.

"So, how come your in-laws never come around?" Her hands paused on the keyboard and she turned her head to face him. His question was random and she hadn't expected it. She took in a deep breath. He sensed her discomfort and waited.

"Well, when we lived in Chicago, they were around all the time, especially for holidays. They probably came to visit at least once a month. But then after…that night… that Troy was…" She cleared her throat. "After that night, they've not seen Dallie since."

"That doesn't make any sense, I mean, she's still their grand-daughter."

"Yeah, well, I'm sure that Troy told them otherwise…Who knows what he told them really, either way, I'm sure they're convinced that I was the one to corrupt him…" She shrugged. "Oh well, at least Dallie has one set of grandparents that love her and want to see her. The less contact with them, the better, I guess."

"You couldn't corrupt a fly…" He smiled. Then she looked over at him and asked him a random question.

"How about your family, do you ever see them?"

"I haven't seen them but twice in the last year. I flew out to Cheyenne for Christmas, then again this May, but I haven't been out there since."

"You said you have two brothers?"

"That's right, Carson is my older brother. He's thirty-five. He's got a wife, Olivia, and two boys, Alex and Ethan. My younger brother, Gavin, he's the one that lives in Corpus Christi. He's twenty-seven, single, business-like, completely opposite of me and my older brother."

"Why?"

"Well, because Gavin's more concerned about what he wears and how he looks. He's a bit cocky. Doesn't like to get his hands dirty."

"And you and Carson do?"

"Oh, yeah, we're both ranchers. Carson owns a Hereford farm up in Cheyenne. He used to work with horses too, but says cows are easier because you don't have to do as much with them. We both used to say that we had no idea where Gavin came from…"

Natalie laughed. "So, you guys get together for holidays? Like a big get together."

"Yeah, mostly. I was there for a week both times I flew out. I stayed with Carson and Olivia. We had a good time." His eyes met her as he spoke. "I've gotten closer to my brothers since I've come here. We call each other every now and again to catch up."

"Do you miss them?"

"Yeah, sometimes I miss them greatly. But we all have our own lives now…"

"You gonna go out there for Christmas this year?"

"I dunno." He shrugged. "I'd kinda like to spend Christmas here this year." He smiled at her, his eyes looking deeply into hers as he leaned forward to kiss her. "I seem to have found a reason to stick around here for a while."

"Oh, really," she teased, her lips but a whisper from his. "And what's that?"

"Jack! Mommy! Jack!" Dallie cried at that moment. It wasn't cries of happiness, Natalie noticed, it was cries of fear. They both jumped up off the couch, the laptop thrown into the cushions, and ran for her bedroom. Jack took the stairs two at a time, reaching her first. "Mommy! Jack!" she cried again as Jack grabbed her up and into his arms. He sat on the bed and cradled her head to his shoulder, all the while the playful puppy licking at their cheeks.

"Shh, it's okay. We're right here!"

"Mommy!" Her face was red as she turned to look at Natalie, who'd come to sit beside Jack.

"What is it, baby, did you have a bad dream?" Natalie asked as Jack passed Dallie over to her. She just nodded her small head. Natalie breathed a sigh of relief and gave Jack a knowing look as he rubbed her back.

"It was Daddy again, scaring me. He was in a black robe and he had red eyes and he was yelling."

"I think we've been watching too many episodes of *Scooby-Doo*," Jack replied, his big hand covering Dallie's back as he rubbed. Natalie did recall the last villain as a cloaked figure with red eyes, maybe Jack was right.

"Ok, no more Scooby for a while," Natalie agreed.

"No, Mommy, please..." she begged. "It wasn't Scooby, it was Daddy... I don't like him anymore." That wasn't such a bad thing, Natalie thought.

"Well, you don't have to like him, if you don't want to, ok, Dallie? But realize, honey, that it wasn't real, it was just a dream."

～

On Halloween, Jack dressed in his cowboy garb and black mask as the Lone Ranger and waiting on the back porch for his two girls, made up his mind. He was going to ask Natalie to marry him. It wouldn't be right away, another month would probably be long enough to wait, but he was already thinking of how he would propose to her. She would need a solitaire, a big beautiful diamond solitaire for her sexy, slim finger. Princess cut with a gold band and diamonds on either side... She deserved a beautiful ring and a beautiful proposal. Something special. As he became absorbed in his thoughts, out the door walked his companionable steed and Natalie, dressed herself, as a sexy cowgirl. She was complete in a bandana like halter top, mini denim skirt and cowboy boots. Her red hat and lipstick matched and he had to wipe the drool from his face.

"Where on earth have you been hiding *that* outfit?" His eyes locked with hers as he watched her saunter towards him.

"I'm full of surprises," she said and planted a kiss on his lips.

"Don't I know it!" He took her hands in his.

"Well, I thought you might need a damsel in distress," she stated proudly, giving him a knowing smile.

"More than you know." His own grin widened as his eyes stroked down her body. "You're going to be a hit with the fathers of this town."

"Should I change?" Concern hit her face as she asked. He wasn't going to tell her that had it not been Halloween, her outfit would have been somewhat less than modest. Ha! His last thought was an understatement... She was a walking wet dream and she was clueless about it.

"How do *I* look?" Dallie interrupted and Jack focused his attention to her in her white pony costume. Natalie had painted her face, which the costume didn't cover, white to match the outfit.

"You look great, honey."

"You ready?" Natalie asked.

"Yup!" she said, swinging her pumpkin candy basket.

"Come Silver!" Jack yelled and shot his toy pistols in the air, getting a laugh out of the girls. Jack hummed the theme song to "The Lone Ranger" as they headed to the truck. "We should've had Nathan dress up as Tonto." Natalie laughed at his statement. "He would have made a good one…"

"Yeah, right!" She laughed again. "I could see that one flying over really easily."

Jack had always loved holidays as a kid, especially Halloween. His father had taken them on hayrides and told them ghost stories around a campfire when the leaves started changing. Most of their costumes were made by his mother because she'd been too conservative to buy them. Jack had fond memories of him and his brothers bobbing for apples and his mother judging them in pumpkin carving contests. She'd always made each holiday special with her creative touches.

When they got into town, the streets were covered with parents and children dressed as ghosts, witches, pumpkins, even princesses and pirates, characters of all kinds. Dallie thoroughly enjoyed herself and Natalie told Jack that this was the first time she'd ever trick-or-treated before. She blamed herself he could see that, but although one couldn't change the past, Jack felt you could always make up for it and he intended to do just that for Dallie. They stopped at every house on Main Street admiring the lengths that many residents had gone to in decorating for the occasion. They even stopped in to the Halloween carnival at the elementary school where they did the cake walk and played bingo. They feasted on corndogs and pumpkin rolls. Dallie was thrilled and Jack's heart warmed knowing how happy they had made her. As they left the school, they hopped a carriage ride driven by a "skeleton" where he told them the history of their town.

As darkness fell, they returned home to admire their own decorations and before long Dallie's head slumped over in sleep. Jack carried her up to bed, while Natalie wiped the paint off her face with a washcloth. Natalie stripped Dallie's pony costume off and threw a nightgown over her head and all the while Dallie was out like a light. Jack brought Dash up to lie next to her and he curled in a ball right beside her. They both smiled at the sweet scene.

As Natalie prepared herself for bed in the bathroom, Jack stripped himself down. He was buck naked save for the black mask over his eyes. Natalie stepped out of the bathroom and into his bedroom where he lay sprawled across the comforter. She laughed as she saw him.

"Well, Happy Halloween to you too, Mr. Ranger!"

"I'm glad you left that on." He gestured to the outfit she wore.

"I see that," she said, gesturing to his erection, which was now full throttle. Her eyes changed as she looked at him, showing humor then arousal. He smiled as she ambled toward him, swinging her hips as she shed the boots, then the shirt, her bare breasts reached his eyes and he licked his lips. She watched him, all the while, slowly removing her panties. Leaving only her skirt, she walked over to one of the four posts of the bed. She began moving her body over it erotically and his mouth went dry. She crawled over the footboard and onto the bed, her eyes never leaving his. She crept atop him and kissed his lips slowly, torturing him. His hands went to her back and down to her bottom, naked beneath the short denim skirt. He squeezed her buttocks, pulling her hips into his solid hard-on. She moaned.

"Mmm, Jack, I want you inside me." She squirmed, reaching for his sex, but he wiggled around not letting her touch him. Anticipation was the game he was playing and he was going to torture her as she had tortured him with that sassy little costume of hers all night. He flipped her then and was on top of her, his hungry lips bore down on hers and he passionately kissed her yielding lips. His hands were on her then and he caressed and stroked and squeezed. Then his mouth moved over her slender body, licking, sucking, and loving the skin that quivered beneath him. She gasped and moaned and finally begged for him to take her. And he did, loving her with all his might, with a rhythm as old as time itself. They climbed together, sweating, moaning, reaching Heaven. When she cried out mindlessly in climax, he came with her, loving the sounds that escaped her throat as she gave herself to him completely. She was his lover, his passion, his desire, everything he'd ever wanted or needed in a companion. She was his friend, his torment, his reward. She was his, completely, and as he lay there holding her that night as she slept in his arms, he knew that he could never be happier with anyone else. He kissed her warm cheek as his pelvis touched her bottom and his chest rested against her back. He closed his eyes and dreamt of what their lives would be like together.

~

*A*nnabella was discharged one week from the night of the incident. Luther drove his truck back to his house as they rode in companionable silence toward the setting sun. She had only spoken when necessary and her withdrawal was heart-wrenching to him. Luther realized that this was probably how she'd reacted when, at the young age of fourteen, some random teenage boy at a rave had taken her innocence. Both events had been just as devastating. Pain, violation, numbness; these were not new emotions to Anna.

He didn't force her to speak. He only sat quietly as they pulled into his gravel driveway. He parked then and came around to her side of the car to escort her into the house. He'd gone to her house earlier that week to retrieve some of her things and had bought her some clothes that she could go home in seeing that nothing she owned was suitable or comfortable enough for her homecoming. He opened her car door and helped her to her feet. She was weak and had a hard time walking, having to lean on him. She had a line of stitches from one end to the other and in about three weeks they would have to be removed and yet another surgery performed. When they finally got to the couch, he sat her down gently and she sighed breathlessly as if the short distance had taken everything out of her. She stared blankly at the coffee table and went catatonic, like she'd been the past week. He grabbed a pillow and blanket from the bedroom and returned to her to lay her down.

"Here, baby! Lay back and rest now." She only looked up at him as he tilted her back and onto the pillow, covering her with the soft, micro fleece blanket. She didn't say it but her eyes echoed gratitude.

He went into the kitchen then and began making them dinner. He started a pot of boiling water for corn and a skillet of grease for chicken. He thought about how long it had most likely been since she had eaten a decent meal. She was a woman who never stayed in the same place very long. A rambler. A follower. Whoever housed her was who she stayed with. She followed the rodeos and the concerts. She'd never settled anywhere. She'd only moved back to her biological father's house a year and a half ago after he died because it was somewhere to stay.

It had been over a year ago when Luther had found her in bed with another man. A stranger. A nobody. He'd been devastated. He had loved her with all his heart and believed that she had changed and that she loved him. He'd been wrong! Some things just never changed. Some people just never moved on from their past. It was heart-breaking that someone as beautiful as Annabella could destroy her life as she had. Her own irresponsibility had made her the black hole she'd become.

He picked up the phone to call Jack. Jack had asked that he call him when they got back to the house.

"Hey, man, how's it goin'?" Luth asked into the receiver.

"Hey Luth, I'm doing good, buddy. How's Annabella?"

"She's here…just lifeless and withdrawn."

"I'm sorry, Luth." He could tell Jack meant it. Annabella wasn't exactly the town hero, but she was still a human being. "Hey, uh, Natalie wants to talk to you."

"Ok." He waited as he heard Jack hand the phone to Natalie.

"Hi, sweetie! How are you holding up?" Her tender voice asked.

"I've been better," he answered truthfully.

"Well, Jack and I are going to come over and bring y'all dinner tomorrow night… I want you to know that we're both here for you if you need us."

"Thank you, Natalie, truly. You two are the best friends a guy could ask for."

"Well, we love you," she said and handed the phone back to Jack.

"Luth, if you need anything, just holler alright. I'll be here all day tomorrow. If you need anything from town or anything...."

"Alright, thanks Jack! I really appreciate it! I'll talk to you later." He hung up the phone and sighed as he returned to the chicken.

A little while later, he woke Annabella as he sat a tray of food in front of her and watched her gulp as she eyed it. She gave him a feeble "thank you" as she dug in. She ate slowly and purposefully. He would eat later. For now, he wanted to make sure she was taken care of. When she finished, although she hadn't eaten much, again, she thanked him and drifted back into her motionless state. He took her hand then, wanting to beg her to not to withdraw from him.

"Bella, honey, do you need anything?" She slowly, almost robotically shook her head. After long moments of silence, she spoke, still not looking directly at him.

"I shouldn't have lied..." Her voice was soft and cracked a bit.

"What?" he asked in confusion.

"To Dan. I shouldn't have lied to him."

"Is that why he did what he did?" She nodded. "What did you lie to him about?"

"Jack. He asked me if I had slept with Jack and I bold face lied to him... I told him that I had."

"Why?" She lifted her shoulders in a light shrug. "Why would he want to know if you slept with Jack?" Again another shrug.

"Anna, look at me." She slowly turned her head towards his, her eyes reluctant to meet his. He gently took her face and forced her to look at him. "It doesn't matter what you said or what you did, Dan should never have laid a hand on you." Her whiskey colored eyes drifted back out into space, lifeless, empty.

"It's because I'm nothing. I deserve to be treated that way... I never made it a point to be treated like a lady so no one has ever treated me like one..." Her eyes moved back to his, dead, hopeless eyes. "Except you, Luth." Her face crinkled, pain crossed her eyebrows, regret, anger. "And look what I did to you...You were *so* good to me...but I just couldn't accept it..."

"Why?" He'd never asked her why she'd cheated on him. He'd never spoken to her after he left her. He'd just turned away and never looked back. They'd never gotten that final talk...He'd just assumed she didn't love him.

"Because you were too good for me!" she stated matter-of-factly. "I never deserved you..."A smirk crossed her face, a cynical smile.

"That's not true, Annabella. You do deserve me, as much as I deserve you."

"Ha!" It was more an expulsion of breath than a laugh. "You deserve someone much better than me...someone like...like Natalie Butler."

"Natalie is a wonderful person..." He nodded. "But it's not her that I'm in love with." Confusion crossed her face as she jerked her head in his direction. Her lips parted in surprise.

"Luther Boyd, you honestly expect me to believe that you're still in love with me..." he nodded. "After all this time, after all the pain I put you through, after all the men I've thrown myself at? You're still in love with me?" She was shocked. "Are you a fool?"

"I must be!" He laughed and gently squeezed her hand. "I really couldn't believe it myself until I held you in my arms thinking you were gonna die on me."

He'd never been able to explain it himself. He'd been attracted to her since the moment he saw her on the dance floor that night at the Rusty Spur. He'd known she was young, twenty-one years old at the time. He'd heard about her reputation in his town, but it hadn't stopped him from dancing with her, from sleeping with her, from falling in love with her. He believed that there was someone out there for everyone. He'd also believed that it was his job to save her, from herself, from life, from damnation. And once again, he was doing just that.

"God, Luth, you really *are* a fool!" For the first time in a week, he saw warmth in her eyes and he smiled. She frowned then, dropping her head. "I can't promise you anything, Luth. I don't know if I can stay good to you…"

"Do you love me, Bella?" he asked. If she did, she'd never told him. For a moment, he was afraid she would say no. Then tears filled her eyes as she looked at his face and sighed.

"More than anything!" *Oh, Thank God!* He hugged her then, being as gentle as possible. Her arms came slowly around him, pulling herself into him as tightly as she could, as if she were absorbing him, his strength, his love. "I always did…I always did, Luth… I'm so sorry I hurt you."

"I'm sorry too, darlin'! I never should have left you… I should have stayed and worked it out. Got us some help. Talked to someone." She nodded into his shoulder, her tears flowing down the collar of his shirt. "It's not too late, darlin'. I want to be with you. If you'll have me…" His last sentence was more like a question. She just nodded again as he held her and let her cry herself into oblivion.

CHAPTER 13

"*N*o, Nathan. Please, don't leave!" Natalie begged her brother as he headed down the front steps carrying a duffle bag with her close on his heels. "You've only been home for what...three weeks now and you're leaving."

"I have to go." He shoved the bag into the back of his pickup and threw his cigarette on the ground.

"No, you don't!" She stopped him from opening his door, grabbing his arm. "Dallie will be crushed when she comes home to find that you aren't here."

"I have work to do."

"No, you don't!"

"I do, Natalie. I have people that depend on me and I won't let them down."

"The season is over," she said, fishing for excuses.

"No, no it isn't. The finals are coming up and I have to train."

"I have a bad feeling, Nathan, please?"

"Natalie..." He gave her a retired look.

"Is it ever going to be enough for you? Do you have to kill yourself to finally realize it isn't worth it? That your family needs you here?" Her eyes filled with tears. They'd gotten so close in the last week and now suddenly he was leaving the safety of his family to go back to bull-riding.

"I'll be back. Don't worry. You'll see me for Thanksgiving." She wasn't so sure as he kissed her cheek and pulled her into his arms. "I promise! I'll be back."

She held fast not wanting him to see how upset she was, but not wanting him to leave either. "I love you."

"I love you, too. I'll call you, okay?"

She nodded. That bit of information gave her a sense of comfort as he opened the door and started the ignition.

She sighed as she watched his 57' Chevy pull out of the driveway. They'd worked together on the ranch for the last week and it had seemed like old times again...They'd talked for hours at a time about nothing and everything, about her leaving. He was the first to withdrawal then and she knew that it was hard for him to open up to her, but they had started to bond in the last week. And although she knew there was still much to discuss and that they still needed time to heal the wounds of their past, she felt they were headed in the right direction. She waved at him and held back a sob. The screen door opened then and Jack came up behind her, snaking his arm around her waist.

"Baby." He fingered the tear on her cheek. "He said he'd be back."

"I know but I just hate the distance. We've come so far..."

"He'll be back, Natalie. I know he will."

She hated it for Dallie too. Dallie had started to warm up to Nathan and he was one of her favorite playmates now second only to Jack and Dash, David coming in a close third. She prayed for this part of his rambling life to be over and his safe return home. For now, she had a story to write for her column. She'd spent the week interviewing the mayor and commissioner about the roads and a new construction project on the west side of town. She'd also enrolled Dallie in pre-school since she wouldn't be starting elementary school until next September due to her age and birthday. Her first day would be in January and Natalie felt eager and anxious about it at the same time.

She and Jack headed back in to finish up their dishes from supper. Luther and Bella had come to eat with them and they seemed so happy together. Luther had asked them to call her Bella now; there was no Annabella to speak of. That woman didn't exist anymore, Luther had said. It was Annabella's request. It made all the sense in the world to Natalie but Jack thought it was the most ridiculous thing he'd ever heard of.

Dan had been arrested earlier that week. He'd been spotted at a gas station some ten miles out of San Antonio. The cops suspected he was on his way across the border. They'd found a fake passport and I.D. in the glove compartment of his stolen Buick. Natalie was still in shock over the whole situation, but she thanked God that he'd finally been found.

Her parents and Dallie were coming in for the weekend and Natalie was looking forward to their homecoming. She missed them and would be glad when filming would finally be over.

Jack dried the dishes and was putting them away as she wiped the counters down. She and Jack had continued to bask in their love for one another and Natalie was finally starting to see what being in love truly was. Jack was affectionate and giving and respectful to her and demanded that other's respect her as well. He had become her best friend, her rock, her strength. They laughed together, talked together and made love like there was no tomorrow.

In the bedroom, Jack was a tiger...he was bold and cunning and always eager... and he was always a gentleman. Out in pubic, they were affectionate but not enough to bring attention to themselves and although they had not openly admitted their relationship she suspected her parents knew something was different. Nathan had... and she assumed that most of the town folk still circulated the story of their night at the Rusty Spur.

Natalie was completely content, however, because she could finally open up her heart to Jack and know there would be no pain.

She could finally be herself and not have to worry about what society thought about it. She could finally move on with her life.

"Luth said that he and Ann—I mean—Bella were in couples' therapy," Jack stated out of the blue as he stacked the plates together and watched Dallie's puppy chasing her cat. He smiled at them.

"Oh," Natalie responded, turning to him. "Well, that's great! I think it will be good for them both, especially Bella."

"Yeah, I guess... it was her doctor that suggested the whole 'Bella' thing," Jack said, rolling his eyes, she smiled at him. He thought the idea was a complete crock.

"I think it's a good idea. It will give her a new identity. She'll be able to start over as someone new without the pain of her past haunting her."

"Hey!" He eyed her suspiciously. "That's what the doc said...You ever thought about becoming a psychologist?"

She laughed at his pun. "Yeah right, you couldn't pay me to go to medical school."

Jack continued putting away the dishes and spoke after a few minutes of silence. "Luth got a good lawyer, he said."

"Good, but I really don't think he'll need one now that Dan decided to run." She stopped swiping the stove and turned to him, propping her hips against the island counter. "You know, that man has some nerve! I mean, he couldn't even face the music, he just decides to up and run and believes that he won't be caught." She frowned incredulously, shaking her head.

"Some people just can't face the consequences of their actions, I guess."

"Like Nathan!" She continued as if she didn't hear him. "I mean what does he hope to gain from bull riding? Fame? Fortune? Death? What? I don't understand it! I feel like I'm partially to blame. He didn't even like damn rodeos until I left Texas..."

"Hey, don't blame yourself for your brother's irresponsibility." He came up to her then and tilted her chin up to him. "What ever reason he's doing it for isn't because of you."

"How do you know?"

"Because he's no longer angry with you. I can see it in his eyes. He just doesn't know what to do with himself."

"But isn't it obvious?" she asked. Jack cocked his head, waiting for her to answer her own question. "He needs to be here, at home, with his family. Helping Dad. That's what he's always wanted. Why is he running from me?"

Jack shook his head. "You're not what he's running from.... I think he's ashamed to ask your father for a job. He has as much pride as you do. Besides, he's not the same man he was when you left..." His sentence faded out. Because in all honesty, Jack hadn't known Nathan before Natalie had left for Chicago. But his statement was true. Nathan had been a different person. Fun. Kind. Warm. Loving. And eager to be their father's right hand man. He had loved working alongside their father and it was his dream to take over the ranch. She wondered if he was jealous of Jack...Jack who'd come to their family's aid when no one else had. Jack, the man who'd been their parent's savior.

She had seen pieces of the old Nathan these past couple weeks, the Nathan that she'd known up until he was twenty-one years of age, but she had also seen how drastic he had changed in ten years. He appeared bitter, cold and unfeeling at times. He was hard, harder than he'd ever been in their past. His life had been affected just as hers had been and not just by Troy Cameron but by the pressures Nathan had put upon himself.

Despite their talks over the weeks, Nathan had never come out and told her that he'd forgiven her and that bothered Natalie. After all this time, he might be sorry for not being there for her, but he still didn't forgive her for betraying their friendship. She pondered these thoughts as her eyelids fluttered closed that night. She lay on her belly, her arm thrown across Jack's broad chest, their legs tangled together. The only sound she heard were the sounds coming through the open window; sounds of katydids and crickets and frogs. Jack's chest rose and fell, his breathing shallow as she watched him. She sighed, loving the comfort she took from this man and his love and wondered if her brother would ever be able to forgive her and truly move on with his life.

~

*M*aybe Natalie was right. It was time to give up this wild and dangerous hobby. It had been fun at first and exciting as Hell. The crowds, the money, the women, the freedom, the distinction. He had craved it and loved it. But now Nate Butler just wanted out. His legs and arms ached all over and his head throbbed as he threw down a painkiller with a sip of beer. He lay back on the hard bed of an old Streamline trailer, stacked his hands behind his head and sighed.

He'd never realized how much he'd missed his baby sister until she'd collapsed in tears on him that night three weeks ago, begging him for understanding. And he'd felt bad, but he'd never understood and probably never would understand why she'd left their family for that dirty S.O.B. Troy Cameron. Nathan had pegged him from day one and he should have put a stop to the relationship then, but hadn't wanted to interfere. Looking back now, he wished he would have then maybe the last ten years of their lives wouldn't have been wasted.

He was glad she hadn't asked him for forgiveness yet, he wasn't sure if he was ready to give that to her. They had been close before she left, as close as two siblings could be. Anyone who messed with Nathan Butler's little sister, messed with him. Of course, they fought as kids, even as teenagers, and sometimes as bad as cats and dogs, but they had always loved one another unconditionally. Her opinion had meant more to him than anyone else's. And when she had chosen Troy Cameron over their family, he had been crushed; crushed that the one person he cared for most in the world would abandon her home and her legacy to be with someone who had been so obviously wrong for her.

He knew that he had been damn selfish and that Natalie's life was her own to live as she saw fit, but the way he'd seen it was if she could leave then, by God, he could too. A stupid idea at the time, he now knew. And who had suffered the cost for it, not just him but his parents too. Just because Natalie had chosen to live her life separately from them, didn't mean that Nathan had to do the same. But he had and where was he now?

"Living like a fucking carny...in a nasty Streamline with no A/C, no money and no damn life to speak of," he loudly told himself.

Not that he specifically wanted to settle down with a family, like Jack wanted. Hell no! That was too permanent. But to reestablish the bond with his mother and father...and of course his sister would be a good start. To regain his father's trust as his son and heir to Starlight Valley Stables would no doubt be appreciated. But would his father welcome him back to the family business with open arms?

"Well, I guess there's only one way to find out..."

～

"Natalie, my dear, just the girl I was looking for," David said as Jack and Natalie entered his office door hand in hand. They'd been laughing and were coming in for a quick coffee break when her father's voice boomed in.

"Me? What for?" She smiled as she sat across from him, Jack taking the seat next to hers.

"Well, both of you, since you're here."

"What's up, Daddy?"

Her father was smiling and Natalie knew the news must be good. He was unusually happy today and it caught her by surprise.

"Well, first off, I want to thank you both for the hard work you put into the horses and the cast for the upcoming movie. Without you two it never would have gone so smoothly. Filming is nearing the end, well in this part of the country anyway and the horses were perfect. I couldn't ask for a better team."

"Well, you should have known. We're good... what can I say?" Natalie laughed and glanced over at Jack with a knowing look. He smiled and shook his head.

"Well either way, I truly appreciate all you've done," David replied.

"No problem, David. Only my best for you... I'm glad things are going so well," Jack replied, tipping his hat at his boss.

"And Natalie, I must say, I'm proud of you. My daughter who was the reigning barrel racing queen..."

"Oh, Dad, come on, that was a decade ago..." Natalie blushed.

"Well, you were!" David smiled. "But I want you to know that you're getting a cut on commission for your work with Vivian."

"Oh, No! No, you're not paying me for that!"

"Oh, yes I am! You worked as hard as Jack or any other hand I've got did and you deserve to be paid for your time."

"No, Dad, I didn't come back home so that you could add me to payroll, I won't have it."

"You will. You're a part of this family and this team and as a future heir to this ranch you will be paid for your efforts." When she began to protest again, he held his hand up in outranked authority, Natalie fell silent. "And another thing, you've done a fine job getting these invoices in order. I'm paying you for that too and don't think about arguing about it." Natalie sighed and looked over at Jack, who shrugged.

"Daddy, you know I don't need the money!" she said, facing her father.

"Then give it to someone who does." Was all he said as he dared her to argue.

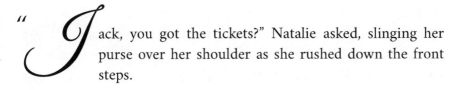

"Jack, you got the tickets?" Natalie asked, slinging her purse over her shoulder as she rushed down the front steps.

"Right here, baby!" He patted his back jean pocket as he lifted Dallie up and into her car seat.

"Ok, good. I got the camera. Dallie you all set?" Natalie asked as she pulled the truck door behind her and sat down in the passenger seat.

"Yup!" Dallie said as Natalie smiled at her daughter's growing accent. If she hadn't known any better she'd think Dallie actually grew up in south instead of the north. She buckled Dallie in as Jack came around to the driver's side and started the truck. He threw it in gear and headed to Dallas.

Dallie had been excited about this night since Nathan had called a week ago and asked if they wanted to come see him rodeo. She was also thrilled to see the city for which she'd been named and had asked to be dressed in a "real cowgirl" outfit, so Natalie had bought her a pink western shirt, white frill vest and boots and a pink cowboy hat that very day. So much for telling Jack not to spoil her…

The last two weeks had been steady. Natalie finished her latest column for the magazine and her boss, Marlene, had been impressed with Natalie's work over the past several weeks. She'd already begun interviewing the town council about the upcoming Christmas celebration and its role in the town's economy for her next column. She also continued working in her father's office helping him with invoices and bookkeeping and found herself out in the corral with Dallie and Ameera most afternoons. Jack had been busy with Blaze and Call who was sold just the day before to a man from Bremond. Dallie had cried and cried, but Jack, her Superman, had "saved the day" and took the three of them out for ice cream. They had received two thoroughbreds last Tuesday for boarding and two young quarter horses for show that Friday and Jack had started working with them as well.

The minute her parent's came home, Natalie, against her own wishes, had gone back to the guestroom. Jack made her virtue a priority and told her that it was not only disrespectful to her parents for the two of them to be sleeping together under her parent's own

ABUNDANCE

roof, but it would also be uncomfortable for him. She'd rolled her eyes and obliged, even though he'd been the very one to haul her off to the barn in the middle of the night after two days without her. She hadn't minded, in fact, she'd been thoroughly thrilled. They'd had to make adjustments like that for the last week. The barn, the truck, the pasture. She loved the spontaneity and adventure of doing it somewhere out of the ordinary.

When Corrine had stepped across the threshold she'd begun decorating for her annual Thanksgiving Day feast. The house looked as if they'd stepped right into a harvest wonderland, but Natalie was pleased that her mother had something to look forward to. Her father was still going back and forth to Houston but told them he would be home for Thanksgiving week. With all that had gone on in the last two weeks, Natalie was thoroughly exhausted, even more so than usual and if it weren't for Dallie's excitement over watching her uncle Nathan ride bulls, she would have rather stayed in bed, but a loving mother always put her children first.

When they arrived at the arena, Natalie wasn't surprised to see that it was completely packed. They parked, found their seats which as it turned out were very good seats close to the action, then Jack went to go grab some refreshments as they waited for the show to begin. Dallie had requested a corndog and some cotton candy.

"And for you my darlin'?" Jack asked, kissing Natalie's cheek as he took mental notes.

"Oh, nothing too greasy, just a coke and some popcorn." She had to yell over the crowd as he nodded and retreated. Something they'd eaten last night must not have sat well in her stomach because she'd awoken that morning with a bout of nausea. She hoped there was nothing going around, the last thing she needed was to get sick right before Thanksgiving...

When Jack returned with the food, he took Dallie from her who was squealing in delight as she watched the rodeo clowns squirting water at one another. Natalie couldn't help but smile at her daughter's happiness, although as it was, she was already ready for this

325

charade to be over... The enclosed arena was terribly hot causing beads of sweat to gather at the base of her neck and her popcorn was as stale as week old bread. She watched as the lights turned into swirling strobes of color and the announcer began to speak.

"Ladies and gentlemen, boys and girls, we have come together to watch the best of the best face off against one another...Tonight, we have riders from all over the state here to prove to *you* that they have what it takes to be number one."

Natalie couldn't help but fear for her brother as she watched the first rider mount the angry Brahma bull and raise his arm in preparation. The announcer told the name of the rider and his adversary before the horn sounded and the bull tore out of the gate in a whirlwind. Her heart pounded as the giant animal bucked and snorted and thrashed sending clouds of dust swirling around him. Her skin crawled as she watched the rider get literally thrown off the 1600 lb. bull within the first three seconds, his body shooting high into the air, and wondered why on earth she'd come. She'd always enjoyed the sport of rodeo. She herself had barrel raced for years but all that had changed when she found out her brother was a bull rider. It was pure torture having to sit and wait and watch and ponder if he would be one of the many injured when his turn came. She wondered how many rodeos he'd participated in the last ten years, how many times he'd been injured. She set her popcorn aside, her appetite disappearing.

She looked over at Dallie then, she was mesmerized by the thrill of this sport, her little eyes sparkling with admiration and curiosity. Jack was telling her how it all worked. Natalie looked at his handsome face, at the angle of his chin, the crook of his smile and thought about his days as a bull rider. The thought sickened her; what if he had been injured or even killed while participating. What if he'd been crushed under the bull's hooves or broken his neck when he'd been tossed to the ground? If she'd never met him, her life would still be chaotic and empty and painful. Because of him she'd grown to love as she never had before, because of him she'd grown to accept herself and her life, because of him she was alive in every sense of the word. When he looked over at her, she smiled, the smile of a woman in love. He smiled back equally as radiant and she knew in that moment that she could not live without him. He was her future. What he did, would be what she did. Her and Dallie.

"Jack, it's Uncle Nate, look?" Natalie's heart rate quickened as she looked to where Dallie was pointing and confirmed that it was indeed Nathan getting ready to battle with a two ton bull named Gus.

"Oh, God," she groaned and felt Jack's hand take hers as they watched the gate open and the bull and rider emerge. Natalie prayed with each second that went by mentally counting down the time. She watched her brother gracefully stay with the bull matching his movements stroke for stroke; his arm thrown high, his thighs gripped the bull's back. When eight seconds had passed, he jumped from the bull and raised his arms in victory as Natalie expelled her breath in relief. But Big Gus wasn't quite done yet, he charged at her brother as quick as lightning. Natalie and Jack stood, Dallie clinging nervously to Jack as she watched on. Natalie yelled to her brother and a gasp came from the crowd as Gus's head and one of his sharp horns thrust into Nathan's chest, pushing him violently to the ground.

"Oh my God!" She looked on as the rodeo clowns drew the bull's attention away and Gus rounded on one of them, Nathan's face was contorted in pain as he held the right side of his chest. Medics grabbed his arms and pulled him up and out of the arena. Natalie's heart felt as if it would explode as she watched them carry him away. She looked over at Jack, whose worry showed in his eyes. "Jack, did he get him?"

"I—I don't know. I couldn't tell." She was referring to whether the bull's horn made contact with Nathan's skin. She hadn't been able to verify it either.

"I should go check on him."

"Let me go! They know me," Jack insisted. She nodded and took

Dallie as he headed down the stairs and toward the area where the bulls were pinned. The announcer's voice boomed in then that they would announce Nathan's condition when it had been assessed and moved on to the next rider. Natalie sat patiently waiting for Jack to return, her nervousness increased with each minute that ticked by.

"Mommy," Dallie said after several moments had passed. "Will Uncle Nate be okay?"

"I don't know, Dallie. I'm sure he's fine." Even though deep down, she knew he wasn't.

It was another ten minutes of excruciating anticipation when Jack finally came back to them.

"Let's go. Get your stuff. We're going to follow the ambulance." Natalie looked up in horror as he took her hand.

"Am—Ambulance?" she croaked.

~

*D*allie slept in Jack's arms as he and Natalie sat in the small waiting room of the ICU. This had been an exciting and fearful night for all three of them. Although Nathan wasn't his family by blood, Jack had come to see him as a brother. He was Natalie's brother, the woman who would soon be his wife; therefore he was family to Jack.

The official had recognized Jack immediately and taken him back to see Nathan. He'd been groaning, barley moving and Jack had feared the worst. Blood covered his shirt which had been torn open by the medics; a large bandage had been placed over a portion of Nathan's ribcage, leading Jack to believe that the horn had indeed punctured his skin. One of the medics was placing electrodes on Nathan's chest to monitor his heart rate; a pulse oximeter was clamped on his finger. The other medic was attaching an oxygen mask to Nathan's face. His lips were blue and his chest heaved rapidly as he fought to breath; rasping, harsh sounds came from him as he tried to cough. Jack sighed, asking if he would live.

"Well, we've got to get him stabilized. His pulse is weak, his O2 sats are down and he's losing consciousness. Damn horn punctured his lung." The medics began rolling Nathan's gurney into the cab of the ambulance. Jack asked what hospital they were heading to and waited only long enough for the answer before heading back to Natalie.

He'd never forget the look she gave him when he told her that they were going to follow the ambulance. All the blood had drained from her face and her eyes had searched his for an explanation. His heart felt as if it'd been torn out when she got to the truck and began to cry as he related what he'd seen in as little detail as possible. He sat quietly then and held Dallie's quivering hand as he followed the roaring siren and blue and red lights of the ambulance.

They'd been waiting in a tiny, cold waiting room for two hours and Natalie had paced, then she'd sat quietly, then she'd come to Jack for comfort. Her head was on his shoulder, she was resting when the doctor finally appeared. The young female doctor looked as if she'd come straight out of *Vogue* magazine with her curly blonde hair and red lips. She approached them and they stood to greet her.

"I'm Dr. Marishca Schander. Your brother's stabilized now. He has a hemopneumothorax." They both looked at her as if she had spoken in an alien language. "A collapsed lung with an accumulation of blood," she continued, "as a result of the...uh...the tussle, but he's going to be alright. I've placed a chest tube in his pleural space to drain the blood and excess air and put him on a ventilator. His wound has been cleaned and sewn and I've put him on IV antibiotics to prevent infection."

"So... he's okay?" Tears had filled Natalie's beautiful eyes as she squeezed a tissue in her hand.

"Yes, we'll have to do some more chest x-rays over the next couple days to see if the hemopneumothorax has cleared up, but I feel his prognosis is good. He should be free to go in a few days." Natalie thanked the doctor then and asked to see Nathan, but she refused saying he needed his rest. Jack saw the exasperation hit her then and her balance shifted, her hand shook violently as she brought it to her head, which itself began to reel and before Jack could reach her with Dallie in his arms, the doctor took her shoulders to steady her, sitting her down in the chair next to Jack, she called a nurse to her.

"Natalie?" Jack asked, concerned as he looked into her ghostly pale face. "Are you okay?"

"Miss Butler..." The doctor tapped at her cheek.

"Cameron." Jack corrected.

"Miss Cameron, when have you eaten last?" They watched Natalie close her eyes, her head spinning on its own axis, she was about to faint. "Shari, grab a cold compression and glass of juice for this young lady," Dr. Schander demanded when the nurse arrived. "Quickly!" she added. "Miss Cameron, stay with me, are you a diabetic?"

"No, she's not," Jack answered for her.

"Has she eaten today?"

"Not a lot," Jack remembered seeing her eat a piece of toast and a boiled egg for breakfast and some popcorn at the arena earlier that evening. "Is she going to be alright?"

"I'm sure she's experiencing an episode of hypoglycemia." Jack just looked at her in confusion, brows raised. "Low blood sugar," she translated.

The nurse came then with the compress and a glass of juice. The doctor planted the ice pack on Natalie's forehead and shoved the glass at her. "Drink this, now, Miss Cameron. I don't need you passing out on me..." The doctor attempted a smile as Natalie weakly took the straw in her mouth and sucked at the contents of the glass. The doctor then moved the compress to the back of her neck and Natalie's color started to return. "There now, I'll have Shari refill that glass and escort you to your vehicle, but I want you to eat something and head straight to bed. This night has been trying for all of you. Mr. Butler will be fine. You can see him tomorrow, okay?" Natalie weakly nodded and Jack thanked the doctor. Then he headed out the door to get the truck as the nurse sat with Natalie. He placed a sleeping Dallie in her car seat, pulled up to the ER doors and went back in for Natalie, helping her to the truck and gently sitting her down into the passenger seat. He drove to the nearest fast food restaurant, got some burgers then headed toward the interstate as he handed Natalie the food. She weakly opened her sandwich and began eating it. It looked as though they would be spending the night in Dallas and it looked as if he would be the one having to wake up David and Corrine to tell them the news. Damn Nathan Butler!

~

"*Mother*, I said I'm fine." Natalie jumped as she heard Nathan's voice coming upstairs, but her eyes were still fixed on the piece of plastic.

"No, it just can't be true! It's wrong. It's broken..." She tried convincing herself even though she'd taken three tests now. She threw her head backed and sighed.

This wasn't how she wanted to start her relationship with Jack. What would he say? What would he think? Would he be angry?

"Dammit," she whispered.

When had she missed a cycle... then again when in the last year had her cycle been regular. She couldn't even remember the last time she'd had a period...

"Oh little sis, hurry it up in there would you? I gotta take a piss!" She rolled her eyes at Nate's language.

"Just a minute!" she yelled back.

She was glad Nathan was finally home. He'd spent three days in that hospital in Dallas, giving the nurses and the doctor who saved him pure Hell, but he'd been discharged after they found no traces of blood in his lungs and removed the chest tube they'd placed. Natalie and Jack had stayed one night in Dallas, visited him the next morning and left to return to the ranch only after Nathan's doctor had assured them that he was going to be okay. His mother and father had driven to Dallas that very same day and returned with Nathan two days later. He had come home in a relatively good mood but their mother of course had told him to go easy until after Thanksgiving. He had protested and that had been the story thus far for the last several days.

Nathan had a huge scar where the bull's horn had punctured his chest and Dallie had squealed when he finally removed the bandage to show it to her. "That doesn't look so bad..." she'd said and he'd laughed and tickled her until she was breathless.

"Natalie, for the love of God, you've been in there for an hour. What is taking you so long?" With the irritation in his tone, she gathered all three of her tests, shoved them into the pharmacy bag and looked at herself in the mirror. Her eyes were red from tears and once again she was battling the nausea that had been persistent for a week now. She swiped at her hair and opened the door, making sure she gave her brother a devious look.

"Hey... hey," he said, grabbing her arm as she crossed in front of him. She stopped and looked up at him. "You okay?"

"Fine," she lied.

"You're not still upset with me over this, are ya?" he asked, pointing to the scar on his bare chest. She looked away. "Natalie, I meant what I said. I'm done, I swear." He had told her the same thing the night her parents brought him home from the hospital and she'd cried and told him how afraid she'd been that he would die. She shook her head and he relaxed a bit. He didn't press her for an answer as she walked away and went downstairs. She went into the kitchen with her mother wondering how on earth she was going to tell Jack that she was pregnant.

~

*J*ack was more anxious than he'd ever been in his life. He had thought he could wait until Thanksgiving Day, take Natalie off and propose to her then but he couldn't wait that long. He'd had the ring in his nightstand for two weeks now where it was eating at him each time he went to bed and he just couldn't take it any longer. Today was the day! He shoved his hand in his pocket and fingered at the velvety black box as he walked into the kitchen. Natalie stood there with her mother helping her prepare a dinner of cornbread, coleslaw, fried chicken, green beans, and corn. Sweat broke out on his forehead as she looked over at him. He gulped and his pulse quickened.

"Uh, Mrs. Butler?" Jack cleared his throat. "If it's not too much trouble, could I, uh, could I borrow Natalie for a bit?"

Corrine cocked a suspicious eyebrow at Jack then looked over at Natalie whose face suddenly turned as red as the tomato she was cutting. He saw her gulp as well as she put down the knife and turned expectantly toward her mother.

"Well, I reckon you can... y'all just be back for supper, alright?"

Jack tried his best to smile, but came up short, "Yes, ma'am."

He took Natalie's hand as they walked toward the truck. She seemed as nervous as he was but then again she couldn't be, she wasn't welled up inside with emotion that was ready to be expelled at any second. He shut the passenger door when Natalie was tucked in the seat and came around the truck, hopping in and starting the engine with his shaky hands. She said nothing as they headed down the old dirt road and onto the blacktop, where he turned right and cruised at a speed of 35 miles per hour. After about three miles, he turned onto the small road that had yet to be graveled and drove for about a half of a mile before the house came in sight. He noticed that Natalie had stopped fiddling with her hands to look up at the almost finished three story Cape Cod style house. She gasped as she took it in. It had a basement, two car garage, six bedrooms, four bathrooms, a wrap-around porch and two chimneys. The third floor could serve as an entertainment room, attic, or very large suite, they would decide that later. Jack glanced over at her as he pulled right up to the porch. She was mesmerized and he smiled as he stepped out of the truck and came around to meet her. She'd already exited the truck and was looking up at the recently framed and dry-walled house in admiration.

"This...this is yours?" she asked as he took her hand.

He nodded, not mentioning that it would be hers too. He helped her up the steps and through the front door as she took in the huge great room with its cathedral ceiling.

"See, uh, after we had our little talk that night. I, uh, I thought about what you said and I decided to go ahead and start building the house instead of waiting."

She looked over at him then and smiled. "That's wonderful, Jack. This house is...well, it's...."

"Amazing."

"Yeah, that's a good word and big, really big," she trailed off as she headed into the soon-to-be kitchen that was separated from the great room by a huge bar.

"So, you like it?" he asked.

"Like it? Are you crazy? This house will be incredible when you finish it."

She took in the open bay window overlooking the miles of pasture ahead and the grove of pecan trees next to a creek.

"That's the breakfast nook...the island will go here...the stove here," he said, showing her the lay out of their dream house. She continued to peruse the grand structure as he took her hand and led her upstairs to the master bedroom with its double trey ceiling and large walk-in closets.

"Oh, wow!" she stated as they walked through the doorway to the master bathroom. The oversized jetted tub had already been put in as well as the large step in stone shower with a shower head on either side. "Jack, this is...this is going to be the most gorgeous house." She laughed.

"I know," he said and started the speech that he'd practiced a hundred times in the last two days. "That's why I want you to share it with me." Her brows drew and she turned her body to face him. "Yeah, see, I built this house with not one person in mind, but three. Me... you... and Dallie." Tears came to her eyes then and he stepped closer to her, taking her hands in his. "I have loved you, Natalie Anne Butler Cameron, since the moment I saw you on the road that night almost two months ago. You were sexy and feisty and brave as Hell and I knew that I had to make you mine. I never imagined that I could ever be as in love with someone as I am with you... and your daughter." By this point, tears were falling down both their cheeks. "I can't live without you, baby. I want to wake up to you each morning and go to bed with you each night. You are my heart, my soul, my everything, Natalie..." he professed, falling to one knee and withdrawing the small box opening it to expose the gorgeous one carat princess cut diamond to her and watched as she clasped her mouth in shock, her eyes seeking his.

"Oh, Jack!" She fell to her knees before him and covered her face in her hands before he could finish his proposal. She then calmly uncovered her face and sighed, looking deeply into his confused face. "Oh, Jack, before you ask me to marry you—you have to know something. I have to tell you something..." He waited then, patiently waited, for her to explain herself. "Oh, God, this wasn't how I wanted to tell you..."

"What is it, Natalie?" He was dying from anticipation, he took her hands.

"Oh, Jack, I'm....I'm pregnant."

CHAPTER 14

She waited for the anger to hit his face, but watched as his eyebrows lifted and drew downward as if he didn't truly understand what she'd told him.

"You're pregnant?" She just nodded and bit into her bottom lip as she was known to do when she was nervous. "That means...that... we're going to have a baby?" *Yeah, usually, that's what it meant!* Again, she only nodded. "We're going to have a baby! Oh my God! Natalie, we're going to have a baby!" He laughed then and pulled her against him, kissing her cheeks and lips and forehead. She was surprised by his reaction, but couldn't display the same happiness. "Oh, wow!" he stated and looked down at her abdomen which just recently showed any sign of pregnancy, he gently pressed his palm against her and smiled lovingly into her eyes. "How long have you known?"

"I just found out today...I haven't been to the doctor, but I took three different tests to be sure."

"Wow," he stated again. "I'm going to be a dad..." His eyes glistened then and he pulled her back into his arms and into a soft, sexy kiss. His tongue slide between her lips, one hand snaked up through her hair, the other staying where his baby was lodged. He deepened the kiss and just before they were breathless, pulled away. "Thank you, Natalie." *Thank you?* That was an odd statement.

"For what?" she asked incredulously.

"For making me a father..." She wouldn't correct him and tell him that *he'd* been the one to fertilize *her* egg, not the other way around. For at least one of them was happy about it. She remembered when she'd told Troy the first time she was pregnant.

"Dammit, Natalie," he'd said. "What the fuck am I paying for birth control for anyway?" She bowed her head, trying to block out the painful memory of it.

Jack, sensing her discomfort, moved his hand to her chin, bringing her face up to meet his eyes. "What's wrong, Natalie?" he waited then added, "You're not happy about this baby are you?" She shook her head, tears filling her eyes once again. "Oh darlin'! Why? We made a baby together!" He was still bewildered by their capability to create a child. She expelled her breath on a sob.

"I know, but this...this isn't the way I wanted it to be! I want to marry you with no strings attached. Now everyone will think you married me because of the baby." She crumbled against him; her head perching on that spot on his shoulder that had been made specifically for her. "It'll be just like when I married Troy." She covered her face and began weeping on him.

"Hey! Hey, hush now." He pulled them to their feet and once again he brought her face up to his. "This won't be anything like when you married Troy. I can promise you that! I'm in love with you and I can't wait to marry you and...and, well, now, I have more to look forward to than just the honeymoon." He winked at her then and she laughed at his goofy expression. "Now, are you going to let me propose to you or not?"

She nodded and smiled, he laughed as he bent down on his knee again.

"Natalie, do us both a favor and end this torture for me." He laughed humorlessly. "Will you make me the happiest man in the world, will you marry me?"

"Jack Kinsen, I would love to marry you!" With that he sprang up and pulled her back into his arms, kissing her breathless, loving her mouth with his own. He took the ring from the box and placed it gently onto her left ring finger and admired it there then he began unbuttoning her shirt and tore it from her shoulders as if he couldn't get to her fast enough. She followed his lead and in minutes flat they were both naked and ready for one another. He pulled her down to a blanket that he fetched from one of the closets. "For emergencies…" He shrugged as she'd eyed him suspiciously. *Sure!* She thought, knowing that he'd planned to make love to her today in this house he was building for them.

Slowly, he brought himself down over her, propping himself on his knees and elbows. His body lightly touched her, all his parts but a breath away from hers. Then he looked down into her eyes and smiled.

"I don't know what I'd have done if you hadn't come into my life," he stated, whispering into her ear as his tongue licked lightly at her lobe then her neck.

"Oh, whatever." She stroked his back as she rubbed herself against his erection. "You're *my* knight in shining armor, not the other way around!"

He leaned back on his haunches then and she moaned as she grabbed him in her hands and brought the velvety tip of his manhood to rest against her softness, rubbing him against her, rocking his smooth steel member between the valley of her thighs. He moaned deeply as he watched her use his sex to pleasure herself, the act wholly erotic in nature, his sex pulsing with each swipe against her. Finally when he'd had enough of her kinky torture, he moved, his body coming down upon her. His hands sought her tender breasts and reshaped them in his big, strong hands, rewarding them with his mouth, striking her nipples with a skillful tongue.

"God, you're so beautiful, Natalie," he groaned as his hands again captured her breasts. Her head flew back as he tortured her close to climax, then finally he settled himself between her legs and pushed his hot hardness inside her. His mouth found hers as he pulled her arms over her head and intertwined their fingers then his mouth fell, hot on her collarbone. His thick sex pushing deep inside her, stretching her until she fully encompassed him. He sighed and then pulled back only to thrust again, and then suddenly he stopped. "Will I hurt the baby?" he asked, concern showing in his eyes as he looked down at her.

"No, you can't hurt the baby, he's safe." She kissed his nose. Jack sighed, a combination of relief and desire, as he picked up where he left off. His body became a stiff missile with one set target as sweat beaded on his chest and hair line, he removed his hands from hers and grabbed her hips angling them up toward him as he moved back to his haunches. He rocked their bodies closer to oblivion and Natalie began to feel the stirrings of sexual bliss rocket through her center. Wave upon wave took her and when his hand moved up her thigh, she cried out as mindless pleasure seized her body. Her softness milked at his sex like a silken fist and she felt his body go rigid as he moaned his release and settled back down over her, bracing himself on his elbows. He stayed inside her as their breathing returned to normal then he cupped her cheek and gave her a soft kiss there.

"I want to get married right away, don't you?" Jack asked as giddy as a child with a new toy. She smiled and nodded. "Ok, where do we want to get married? I know the house won't be finished until January probably."

"Let's get married at Mom and Dads."

"Alright. That works for me!" His hand moved back down to her lower abdomen and a seriousness came over him as he lowered his head. "Natalie, there's something else I wanted to talk to you about. It's about Dallie. I—I want to adopt her. If that's okay?" He looked up at her then and once again her emotions got the best of her.

"Oh, Jack..." Tears streamed down her cheeks.

"I want her to be as much mine as she is yours. We'll wait until after we're married then we'll go to court and make her a Kinsen."

"Dallas Noel Kinsen...I love it!"

~

A few days later, they were sitting down to Thanksgiving dinner. Corrine and Natalie had prepared a beautiful feast with a fat, golden turkey as a center piece and all the fixings, traditional sides and pies by the pounds. It was enough to feed an army. Natalie, Jack, Dallie, Corrine, David, and Nathan bowed their heads as the blessing was said, then suddenly Nathan stood, took his fork and clanged it against his glass.

"I have an announcement that I'd like to make..." Everyone looked intently upon his smiling face. Jack himself was quite surprised when he added, "I've left the rodeo circuit for good, as you all know, and I would like to return to my roots and settle down here at Starlight Valley. That is, Dad, if you'll have me back." David stood then and hugged his son, bringing tears to Corrine's eyes. Natalie smiled over at Jack who in turn looked over at Dallie. She crossed her arms, eyebrows drawn, ungrateful for the interruption. Natalie stifled a laugh.

"Nathan, I couldn't be more proud to hear that you've finally come home for good, of course I'll have you back," David said as he playfully slugged at Nathan's arm. "The only issue is where you're gonna sleep. I hate that you're on the couch, son, but I've got no extra beds, the bunkhouse is full and so is the upstairs."

Natalie looked to Jack then to make the announcement he had planned to make today before Nathan beat him to the punch. He looked around, cleared his throat and stood.

"Well, uh, see that won't be a problem here before too long..."

"What do you mean, Jack?" Corrine asked, eyeing him suspiciously.

"Well, um, Mrs. Butler, see, I've uh...I've started building my house...and..."

"Jack! You're leaving?" David asked incredulously.

Natalie stood then and looped her arm through Jack's, her face turning red as she spoke. "Well, Daddy, see...what Jack's trying to say is that...he—he asked me to marry him..." Dallie and Corrine squealed simultaneously in delight. "And I said yes!"

Corrine stood then and grabbed Jack's cheek, kissing it fervently. "I always said I wanted you for my son-in-law." She then moved to Natalie, embracing her.

Dallie flew into Jack's arms then and hugged him to her. "Does this mean you're going to be my Daddy?" she whispered to him with stars in her eyes.

"Do you want me to be?" Jack asked. She nodded with exuberance and he hugged her tightly.

Before Jack could respond, he saw the look in David's eye and cringed with shame. He'd neither warned David of his leaving nor asked for his daughter's hand in marriage. He felt like a heel.

Jack sat Dallie down in her chair and walked over to David as he stood to confront him.

"Sir, I want to apologize for not asking your permission..."

David interrupted him then, "Jack, you had my permission a long time ago. You've brought my daughter back to life... I'm happy for you son!" He surprisingly grabbed Jack and pulled him into a big hug. "But you could've asked me..." He laughed and playfully punched at Jack's middle. Jack just nodded as his eyes fell to Natalie.

Pregnancy became her and only he knew about it. She had a glow to her skin that made her even more beautiful with each passing day. Nathan hugged her then and congratulated her. He shook Jack's hand as well and laughed as he told Jack that he was a brave man.

As they finally sat down to eat, Corrine and Natalie discussed wedding plans and before Jack knew what had happened, they'd set a date. He and Natalie were to be wed in three weeks on a Friday afternoon, 10 days before Christmas Eve. Reverend Rich Baldwin would be marrying them. Corrine had volunteered herself to decorate and make Natalie and Dallie's dresses. Nathan told him that he would make them an altar. Natalie thanked them for their generosity and kindness, then her emotions got the best of her and she began to cry. She had done that a lot lately, Jack recalled and handed her his napkin to attend to herself. He just smiled lovingly at her when she regained her composure. They ate until their bellies could hold no more then retired to the living room to play dominoes and watch the football game. After giving their food time to settle, Natalie introduced her family to her famous pumpkin pie and passed it around along with hazelnut coffee which she declined herself due to the baby. Jack couldn't remember a happier time and toasted to Natalie and their upcoming life together.

Later that evening, after kissing his girls goodnight and undressing, a knock came on Jack's bedroom door. Only adorning a pair of boxers, he opened it anyway, assuming it to be Natalie.

"Jack, my brother would like to ask you something…" He'd assumed right. Natalie stood silhouetted in his doorway in her sexy white gown and fuzzy slippers. She rolled her eyes and pointed her thumb back to Nathan who stood behind her.

"What's up, Nate?" Jack asked, crossing his arms over his chest.

"Look, man, lets call it a truce here, okay? I've been sleeping on the couch with a sore chest for a week now and you have a beautiful bride-to-be who has a bed I crave, so let's cut the shit and do what's right!" Nate remarked. Jack crooked his eyebrow at Nathan then looked at Natalie who shrugged. "Look, Mom and Dad weren't born yesterday, alright? Besides, you guys are engaged now and no one has to know besides you, me and her!" he said, pointing at Natalie. "Come on, Jack, please?"

He mulled Nathan's words over then smiled at Natalie, "Alright, come on in, future Mrs. Kinsen." He draped an arm around her as she walked into the room. "Good night, Nathan."

"Thanks, Jack. I won't forget this buddy. That altar will be the most beautiful thing you've ever seen in your life."

Jack laughed as he shut the door. Natalie sighed and left his embrace to go toward her queen bed. She kicked off her slippers and slide down into the covers, sighing as she settled her head against the pillow.

"Just what do you think you're doing?" Jack cocked his eyebrow at her, crossing his arms over his broad chest again.

"Well, I'm going to bed, what does it *look* like I'm doing?"

"Huh, uh! Not like that you're not."

"Excuse me?" Her eyes were incredulous as he approached her.

"The people in this room must sleep naked." His voice was sultry as he rounded on her.

"Jackson Edward Kinsen!" she exclaimed, even as he was peeling her gown over her head. "You are naughty." Her panties were thrown to the ground with little disregard as he climbed atop of her.

"You, darlin', have no idea…just wait until you marry me." Her hand snaked into his boxers and squeezed the hard bulging sex that resided there. His mouth took hers and loved it as his hand did some squeezing of its own.

"Oh, is that a threat?" she asked then sighed as his mouth fell to her breast.

"No, it's a promise," he muttered, smiling as they fell under one another's spell.

*I*t was a done deal. It had been meticulously planned and there was no going back. Troy Cameron would either get out or die trying. It would happen at daybreak on Christmas Day during shift change. When the officers were least likely to expect an escape. The day when there would be fewer officers on duty. They would take one guard hostage during a planned prisoner fight and riot then disarm as many as they needed to for escape, taking them one by one and killing them only if they had to. They would use the guard's security badge to open the doors to their freedom. There were ten of them involved.

343

Troy had stewed and simmered and wasted away to nothingness in this Hellhole of a pen. He'd been beaten, harassed, raped... despite his good behavior, despite his friendship with Bull, despite his keeping to himself. He was a sex offender and a child molester and that's how he'd been treated here. The only thing he could do to keep himself from going insane was to think about revenge...sweet revenge and freedom. The sun on his face, the wind in his hair, the feel of blood on his hands. His lawyer was first. He had a plan for him. Then Natalie would come next. He would kill her with bitter-sweet torture, cutting her, biting her, tasting her blood, before finally slitting that beautiful throat of hers. He would of course have his way with her, after all, she was his wife, but he wouldn't be doing it for pleasure only for pain. Her pain. The pain she'd put him through. Then there was Dallie, whom he finally decided he'd let live. She was his child, his flesh and blood. No need to kill her. Just the ones who'd dishonored him. He laughed as he sat in solitude and pondered these thoughts... Revenge. Sweet Revenge.

*J*ack's brothers had flown in the day before the wedding and would be staying through Christmas. Natalie had been delighted to meet them when they'd arrived. First came Jack's older brother Carson, along with his wife Olivia and their two sons, Alex and Ethan. Carson was older than Jack by five years, his voice was deeper, his hair darker and his eyes softer. He was taller by only a few inches, but once again when comparing other men to her beloved Jack, Natalie couldn't help noticing that Jack was much more handsome...and bigger. Perhaps his father had been the same way.

Olivia was darling. She was a petite blonde with a soft voice and delicate eyes. Natalie liked her immediately. The boys were playful but well-mannered and Natalie admired how strict their parents were. Alex was tall, dark and fun-loving just like his Uncle Jack. Ethan was more fair-skinned, blonde, and quiet like his mother. Alex

344

was six and Ethan was four. Dallie was stuck right in the middle of them. She'd turned five just two days before the boys arrived and they'd taken her to Dallas for her birthday. They'd shopped and toured and dined. They'd also taken her to see Santa Claus and she'd been utterly thrilled. Jack and Natalie had surprised her with a doll-house that was an exact replica of the house Jack was building for them. Her parent's gift had been a Barbie dressed in western attire which her mother had designed and made herself. Dallie had been so happy and hugged all of them before running off to play with her new toys.

The boys had embraced Jack upon their arrival and Natalie had seen just how much they adored him, as much as Dallie did. Jack just had a way with children; Children loved to play with him and clung to him. Dallie had been as eager to meet the boys as they were to meet her. Olivia had said that the boys always loved a new playmate. Jack had introduced her to them as their soon-to-be new cousin and it had almost made Natalie cry.

Gavin had shown up later, a briefcase in his hand and an earbud in his ear. Instead of giving Jack a big bear hug as Carson had, Gavin impersonally shook his hand and congratulated him on his upcoming wedding. He was long and lean, shorter than both his brothers but equally as attractive and charming. Gavin was however much more reserved than either Jack or Carson and Natalie could see why Jack thought he'd come from a different crop. He greeted Natalie with warmth as he took her hand, welcoming her to their family. Once again, Natalie almost cried.

She had been that way for weeks now. She'd never been so emotional in her all her life, even when she was pregnant with Dallie, but if someone said something kind or she saw a Hallmark commercial she'd nearly lose it. Just the other night, they'd watched *Miracle on 34th Street* and she'd burst into tears at the end. Jack had held her and Nathan had laughed at her.

Jack and Natalie had decided to keep their baby a secret, for Natalie's sake...at least until after the first trimester. She'd gone to the doctor the week before and he'd confirmed that she was about seven weeks along. No one suspected, not even her mother who'd been running around like a madwoman trying to get everything ready for the wedding. She and Natalie had rushed out the very day after Jack had announced their engagement and bought layers of fabrics, decorations, and bows. Corrine had sewn and cut and hemmed and fixed until her fingers had blisters. She'd also called the bakery, the photographer, the florist and the priest. Her mother had been a God send and even Nathan had upheld his part of the bargain by finishing the altar she and Jack would wed beneath.

Tomorrow afternoon at two PM, they would be married in holy matrimony. Natalie thought back to when she married Troy, how apprehensive she'd been about the whole situation. She'd been eighteen and pregnant with nothing but fear in her heart, fear of a new life, a new town. She had felt anger and regret for not being able to start her life and her college career without the worries of becoming a wife and mother. It had been too soon. She'd been too young. Too naïve. But even now, knowing that she and Jack had a child on the way and wishing he'd have only waited a little while longer to be brought into the world, she was thrilled to marry Jack. Jack. Her knight in shining armor, her daughter's Superman....There was no hesitation, no fear. She was older, wiser, and completely in love. She was marrying the man of her dreams and she couldn't wait to begin her life with him. She was even starting to love the idea of having a baby with him. Jack would be a father for the first time in his life, Dallie would have a sibling, her parents would have a new grandchild...Natalie wondered what the baby would look like. She only hoped he would be healthy and strong just like his father.

When they sat down to dinner that night, Natalie took in the serenity she felt being among their combined families gathered together for the first time ever. Jack's brothers were polite and thankful for her mother's hospitality. They were such a well-mannered family and they fit in with her family so easily. The conversation was light and entertaining as they laughed with one another, sharing their lives and their pasts and their futures.

Before they were half way through with their meal, Carson lifted his glass. "To the woman who has made my brother happier than he's ever been." He smiled over at Jack, who looked to Natalie. Jack lifted her hand in his and brought it to his lips, tears in his eyes. She almost lost it at that point, but squeezed her lips together and gave him a loving look, willing herself not to break into tears. Everyone raised their glasses and Jack and Natalie followed.

After dinner, Dallie and the boys played on the floor with Dash and the growing kittens as the adults sipped homemade wassail. Jack's hand rested on Natalie's thigh as they all talked about the wedding and where Natalie and Jack were honeymooning. They had chosen to head down to Galveston for a few days before coming home for Christmas; Neither one of them had ever been and Natalie was looking forward to going to the beach, even if it was going to be chilly this time of year.

The sleeping arrangements that evening were pretty tight. Dallie was to take the trundle bed in her grandparent's room; Natalie had Dallie's bed. Gavin took the guest room, Carson and Olivia took Natalie's bed and the boys had an air mattress on the floor. Nathan and Jack were confined to the living room sofas. Before he headed downstairs, Jack tucked Natalie into Dallie's twin bed and kissed her softly on the lips.

"Your family is wonderful," she said as he sat down next to her.

"Yeah, they are pretty great, huh?" he asked. She nodded. "Well, your family is great too." She shook her head, teasingly. "Yes, they are!" he argued. "I mean, you can't help it if Nathan's a black sheep." She laughed then.

"Hey, I heard that!" Nathan called from the hallway as he stepped into the room. He came up to Jack then as Jack turned to face him. Nathan extended his hand to him and Jack took it, shaking his in return. "Jack," Nathan sighed. "I truly appreciate you and all you've done for my family, especially what you've done for Natalie and

Dallie. I haven't been there for them as I should've been and I regret that, but now you've come into their lives and turned it around for the better. I know you'll take care of both of them as they should be cared for."

"You can bet on that," Jack said as he nodded that he would. Nathan just smiled at Jack and blew Natalie a kiss as he exited the room as suddenly as he'd entered it. Jack focused his attention back to his bride. "I can't wait to have you for my wife," he said as his hand fell to her cheek.

"I can't wait to have you for my husband," she responded as she brought his hand to her lips. "Are you nervous about tomorrow?"

"No, not really. You?" She shook her head. "How's our baby doing?" His voice became more tender as his palm cupped her lower abdomen where his baby grew.

"He's perfect." She smiled and caressed the hand that touched her. She was convinced that their child was a boy.

"Just like his Mommy," Jack said as he once again brought his lips to hers.

Corrine stepped in as Jack was pulling away.

"Ok, you two! Save it for the honeymoon." She smiled as she patted Jack on the back. He took Natalie's hand and kissed it again, a big smile across his face.

"Good night, my darling. I love you," he said as he stood.

"Good night. I love you too," she said before he turned and exited the room.

"Now, you get some rest and don't be nervous about tomorrow, everything is going to be perfect," Corrine said as she took Natalie's hand.

"I'm not nervous. Just ready to be Mrs. Kinsen..." Natalie said dreamily as she looked up at her mother.

"I know, me too!" Corrine grinned.

"Mom, can I ask you something?" Natalie pulled herself to a sitting position.

"What is it, dear?" her mother asked as she sat on the bed where Jack had just been.

"Is it wrong for me to be remarrying, especially so soon?" That question had plagued her for days now. She'd only known Jack for a little over two months and although she was deeply in love with him, she worried about remarriage and how people would feel about it.

"Do you feel that it is wrong?"

Natalie thought about that for a minute then responded, "No."

"Well, honey, sometimes you have to do what's best for yourself and we all know how good falling in love with Jack has been for you and Dallie and how happy you are now. Sometimes you just have to please yourself and to Hell with everyone else." With that Natalie smiled, then looked back up at her mother.

"Is Daddy upset with Jack and me?"

"Oh, of course he's not upset with you. He couldn't be happier for the both of you."

"Well, I just hate that he's going to be losing Jack and I don't want that to change things between them or hurt his business."

"Natalie, don't you worry about any of that. You just worry too much lately about everything… Your father will always love Jack and appreciate all he's done for us and I think the business will be just fine, especially now that your brother has decided to step in."

With that Natalie smiled and as her mother was leaving, shut her eyes and dreamt of her soon to be husband, the most handsome cowboy in Abundance, Texas.

*J*ack had lied. Well, not intentionally. But he had. He'd told Natalie last night that he wasn't nervous about today, but he really hadn't been nervous until the day began. He'd awoken to the smell of bacon frying and his belly growled in hunger. He joined his family and the Butlers at the breakfast table save for Natalie, his bride, whom he wasn't allowed to see before the wedding. Corrine and Dallie ate quickly and left with

Natalie to go to the salon. Jack did his usual chores at the barn under David's protest before heading back to the house to shower. David and Nathan were out clearing the yard of leaves and setting up the altar and chairs for the ceremony. Jack's brothers were helping and sweet Olivia was busy calling the caterer and rental service.

Later, Jack left with Gavin to go into town to get his tuxedo and the wedding band he'd picked out for Natalie. They grabbed a quick lunch before returning to a variable circus of people at the ranch.

The reverend had arrived, along with the caterer, the photographer and the florist. The rental service had been to set up tents, tables and candelabras that were garnished with bows. A white runner had been placed down the length of the walkway to the house and David and Nathan had placed the altar a few feet from the front steps which were covered with baskets of red and white flowers with gold ribbons. The altar also adorned the same flowers. The chairs were arranged around the walkway facing the altar. The tents had been placed under the pecan trees where empty silver trays were being laid on tables covered in white and red linens. It was a beautiful sight and Jack's heart rate quickened knowing that he would soon be wed here. He hurried inside as Corrine directed him to her and David's room to dress. Natalie, she said, would be getting her picture taken so Jack was confined to the room until he was called upon. He had changed into his suit and was sitting in an old antique chair staring at the wall when the reverend entered the room. He and Natalie had decided not to have a rehearsal dinner last night due to the simplicity of the wedding, but they had met with the reverend several days ago, who, at the time, told them the motions they would take on the day of the wedding.

The reverend greeted Jack with a nod.

"Who's got the band?" he asked.

"Carson does," Jack answered.

"Are you nervous, Jack?"

Jack looked up into the reverend's rugged face, "Actually, now I am, sir." He felt eagerness and excitement as well but he was definitely nervous about marrying the woman of his dreams.

"Well," the old man laughed. "I remember my wedding day some fifty two years ago. I was just a young man, about eighteen when I married my sweet sixteen year old wife. Boy, I tell you, I was more nervous about consummating the marriage than the actual ceremony…"

The consummation was the least of his worries, but he wouldn't tell the priest that. He just let him ramble on about his wedding day and then about the importance of marriage and faithfulness as Jack checked his watch, anticipation growing in his tummy until finally Gavin opened the door and signaled the time. Jack's stomach filled with butterflies as he walked out the door and toward the porch, the reverend behind him.

He saw Luther and Bella, Natalie's friend, Jordan. He saw all the hands, excluding Dan of course, Buck, Keith and his family, Scottie, Louise and even Rick had shown up, a withering look on his face. Jack couldn't help but feel sorry for the poor fool and his unrequited love for Natalie. At one time, he'd known exactly how he felt. Natalie had almost hated Jack in the beginning, just two and a half months ago, and now they were about to be married. Love was ironic at times.

Corrine sat next to Nathan who was positioned next to Jack's family in the front row of seats. Carson stood next to Jack as he took his place and the priest stepped beneath the altar. As Pachelbel's Canon in D minor began to play, Dallie stepped forward and began to drop paper flower petals onto the walkway. She looked adorable with her blonde hair pinned up high on her head, her little curls flowing down her back. Her white long-sleeved dress had a lacy top and a red ribbon around the waistband. Jack's smile brightened as he caught her gaze. Soon, she would be his daughter, not by birth but by law, by love. She would be his and Natalie's daughter. The thought thrilled and excited him. She stopped on the side of the altar opposite him and smiled. She appeared as eager as he was, but he knew there was no way that was true.

Just then everyone began to stand and Jack's eyes flew to his stunning bride and her father. The sight of her took his breath away. His nervousness faded immediately and he was overcome with love for this perfect woman who carried his heart and his baby. She looked amazing in the strapless white gown that her mother had made her. It was tight and long and straight and lacy with a red ribbon that flowed from the middle of her chest around her waist to her back. Her curves filled out every inch of the dress and he swore that he'd never seen her in anything more becoming. Her wavy dark hair was half up, half down with a veil that covered her face. The diamond necklace he'd bought her was wrapped around her neck, glistening in the sunlight. His heart began to hammer in his chest. She bit her plump bottom lip as she looked at him, trying her best not to cry, he knew. Her beautiful sky blue eyes were watery with unshed tears. Jack sucked in his breath as she came closer, a tear falling down his cheek. He swiped at it and smiled down at her as David lifted her veil, kissed her cheek, and placed her hands into Jacks'. The reverend began to speak once David took his seat next to Corrine who'd already begun to cry.

"You're the most beautiful bride in the whole world," Jack whispered as he looked his fill of her.

"Shh, don't make me cry," she mouthed at him and he smiled.

He held her hands in his as he continued to look at her and take in the words the preacher was saying. He spoke of love and trust, of honesty and respect, of loyalty and fidelity. He told them about the importance of communication in a marriage as well as prayer. He then asked Jack to repeat after him, to repeat his vows to Natalie. Natalie began to tear up as Jack promised to love, honor and cherish her. Then it was his turn to well up at her vows to him as he knew she meant every word she said. They exchanged their wedding bands and soon after, he was able to lay a soft, sexy kiss on her sweet lips. It was a long, tender, meaningful kiss as he took her head in one hand and her waist in the other, her hands coming to his chest. Their audience applauded greatly and as they pulled away from the embrace, they smiled at them then at one another.

"May I present to you, Mr. and Mrs. Jack Kinsen," the reverend stated and congratulated the new couple. At that time, they faced their guests and practically skipped down the walkway and into the grove of pecan trees where Jack pulled her into him and kissed her fervently as he twirled her around.

"You're finally mine," he said and she smiled up at him as Dallie joined them.

"I've been yours for quite some time now..."

After more picture taking, they were finally able to greet their guests and grab a bite to eat. The tables were scattered with trays of vegetables, fruits, sandwiches, shrimp cocktail, hors d'oeuvres, and petit fours. Their wedding cake was a three layer white cake with red and gold trim. His groom's cake was in the shape of a thoroughbred which Dallie had picked out. It was chocolate.

After they ate, they stood around their cake and toasted glasses of champagne. Then they cut their cake together, feeding one another and laughing at the mess they'd made.

Later, Jack gathered her into his arms as they danced their first dance as a married couple. Jack had picked out the song, a Shania Twain classic, "From this Moment."

As they rode away in horse and carriage, Jack once again pulled her against him for a kiss. "You doin' alright, sweetheart...or should I say, my wife?" Natalie laughed as his cocked his brows at her, giving her a big grin.

"I'm great. Never better," she said as she looked up at him.

It had been a whirlwind of a day and they'd enjoyed their union with their friends and families, but now both of them were spent. He knew Natalie had to be. Her pregnancy had taken a lot out of her. The last few weeks had been tiresome and she'd spent the last three days with morning sickness. She laid her head on his shoulder as they rode toward the hotel they would be staying in for the evening before heading off to Galveston. Their luggage had already been delivered, their room rented, courtesy of Jack's younger brother, Gavin. Jack had the key in his pocket.

"Are you up for a little marital activity?" he asked, stroking her waistline.

"As if there was any question!" she stated and kissed his cheek.

~

"Oh, Jack!" she exclaimed as he opened the door to the honeymoon suite of the small but opulent historic downtown hotel. She took in the lit candles, the rose petals covering the bed, the strawberries and chocolates. "It's so romantic." She turned to him and brushed his lips with her own.

"All for you, my love," he said as he picked her up and over the threshold of the door.

He set her down slowly on the bed as he brought himself down over her. His lips took hers, and she reached for his shoulders as his arms wrapped around her waist. He moved his body where he was beside her and pulled away to look at her, propping his elbow on the bed and resting his chin on his fist.

"Why'd you marry me, Natalie Kinsen?" She laughed at his calling her new name for the first time and his question.

"Well, because I think you're just too damn sexy to resist." She teased as she reached to unbutton his shirt. "Plus, I'm absolutely head over heels in love with you. Why'd you marry me, Mr. Kinsen?"

"So I can make love to you whenever I want to."

"As if you couldn't anyway!" She flirted, her lips finding his neck, using her tongue on his hot flesh.

"Yeah, but now your mine forever," he groaned as her mouth moved to his ear.

"Yes, I am," she whispered and groaned herself as his fingers traced the part of her cleavage that the dress didn't cover. His hands reached for her zipper then.

"As much as I love this dress on you, it really must go."

"Oh, but baby, you said I was beautiful in it." The zipper gave and he pulled it down as far as it would go.

"Oh, God," he sighed as her hand went to his groin. "You are baby, you are, but you're even more beautiful when you're naked." She stood and his hands worked the dress, inch by tormenting inch, down her body to reveal a lacy white corset with a girdle attaching two leggings to her sexy legs. He sighed as he looked at her. "My, you are just *full* of surprises, aren't you?"

She giggled, a sensual, throaty sound as he peeled the dress off her feet and folded it over a nearby chair, only to return as she stretched out across the bed. He noticed then that she wore a lacy pair of thong panties and he gulped as her hand descended incredibly slowly down her body toward them. She cocked her eyebrow seductively at him and he moaned at the sexuality that radiated from her. She looked like every man's bridal fantasy come true and he couldn't wait to make their union official. He licked his lips as he watched her touch herself in such an erotic way.

Once he started loving her, he couldn't stop. He removed the corset first with an eager mouth and hands, then her girdle, then the panties, finally the leggings. By the time he was there, she was begging him for release. He smiled all the while loving how her sexual appetite for him was insatiable. As insatiable as his was for her. Her hand moved unconsciously to her lower abdomen where their baby slept. The small baby bump, as she'd called it, was only noticeable to her. Her figure looked the same to him, her belly as flat as it had always been. He gently planted a kiss there then moved back to her lips as she removed his shirt and pants and slipped her hand inside his boxers. He moaned as her hand gripped his rock hard flesh.

"Oh, baby," he sighed as he removed his boxers and settled down over her nakedness. "God, I love you so much," he said as his mouth found that spot on her neck that made her writhe beneath him.

"Oh, Jack, I love you too...oh, how I love you..." she moaned breathlessly as her legs wrapped around his hips, his sex dipping into her sweet depth, the place that had been made just for him. He began a rhythm, soft and slow and sensual, feeling each inch of her stretch and take him into her tightness. Then his need became more pressing and his drive faster, deeper. He watched her eyes as she resisted the urge to close them in passion then he smiled as her head tilted back, a cry ravaged her lips and she gave into him, her body squeezing him, racking her in spasms as he slowed his rhythm to feel her around him. He shivered as each spasm milked him, bringing him closer to oblivion himself but he wanted her to fall apart again to him, for them to come together. He began pumping inside her again, plunging deeper, unable to quench his thirst for her. He grabbed her hips, angling her up for his taking, gripping her bottom, the pleasure accelerating. He felt her slip away again in orgasm as he too left reality, spilling his seed deep within her as he felt the very essence of what separated them as man and woman but what brought them together in love. He kissed her forehead then and held himself high over her, their bodies sweaty from their loving.

Later, they were in the large Jacuzzi tub bathing one another when her eyes took on a sexy glow and she pulled his hard member inside her as she sat on his lap. It was erotic and mind-blowing the way she adored his body with her own. They didn't stop there. They couldn't stop. Stopping would be pointless because they would only want more of one another.

Several hours later, they dined on tilapia with mango salsa, jasmine rice, and salad courtesy of room service. They also indulged themselves on chocolate silk pie which began a new phase of eroticism all its own.

Their love was new and sacred. It was alive and uncontrollable. It was both thrilling and humbling. They lived to satisfy one another, they lived to love and be loved.

That evening as they once again lay in bed, Natalie lay across his chest as he stroked her bare back looking into her deep eyes.

"Will it always be like this?" she asked him meekly, almost child-like. His answer was important to her and he knew it. Her past had been something she'd just recently let go of and it was imperative that he say the right thing to reassure her.

"Darlin', as long as there's a breath left in my body, I will strive everyday to make it be like this."

She smiled, satisfied with his answer as she kissed his cheek and tucked her head in the crook of his shoulder. They fell into deep slumber then as exhaustion took them. Tomorrow they would be in Galveston on their honeymoon, Jack Kinsen and his wife, Natalie.

～

*B*efore they knew it, their honeymoon was over and Christmas was upon them. Natalie had thoroughly enjoyed the five days they'd spent in Galveston. They'd spent days in town, on the beach, in their room. They'd eaten new foods, shopped exotic stores, and toured the historic streets then at night they tore the sheets up as if they couldn't get to one another fast enough. They'd walked the beach several nights and on one night in particular, Jack had begged Natalie to lay their blanket down and make love. She'd fought hard to resist the temptation, telling him that she'd hate to miss Christmas if they were arrested for public indecency. He'd laughed but took her then and there and made some waves of his own. They definitely acted like a newlywed couple, touching, flirting, and kissing as they did.

Everyone had been glad to see them when they returned home; especially Dallie who'd told Natalie that her new cousins were fun playmates. Natalie was thrilled that she was enjoying their company.

That Christmas Eve, they ate a grand dinner of honey-baked ham, dressing and vegetables and everyone asked about Jack and Natalie's trip for which Jack laughingly said was none of their business. This got a rile out of Nathan, who in turn got the entire table cracked up. Natalie was embarrassed to her toes and back and it didn't help when Dallie innocently asked what they meant.

Later, as they were seated in the living room eating pecan pie and sipping coffee, Natalie looked up the fireplace to the five stockings that hung there. Three were for the kids and the other two were for Blaze and Ameera. Dallie had asked that Santa bring them some salt licks and apples. At the time, Natalie had rolled her eyes, but Jack had scooped Dallie up and told her what a great idea that had been.

The sleeping arrangements were much the same, only Gavin had given Jack and Natalie the guest room and took Dallie's room, which Natalie thought was a kind gesture. Natalie and Jack had kissed Dallie before she'd headed off to her grandparent's room and Natalie was excited about seeing her expression tomorrow morning.

Although Troy had not been a fan of most holidays, Natalie had never let him take Christmas and the joy of Santa Claus away from Dallie. That was one holiday that she would not budge on. He hadn't liked it, but he'd had to deal with it. Jack, who'd been Troy's opposite on the idea of holidays, was thrilled while they were in Galveston when he'd found some toys he thought Dallie'd like. As if the child needed anything else to junk up their new house with, but Natalie had smiled at his enthusiasm.

As he kissed her goodnight and scooped her up in his arms, Natalie drifted off to sleep only to awaken sometime later as Jack called to her. Light flooded her eyes as she looked up into her husband's face.

"Natalie, baby, you're okay. Stop screaming." He held her tightly to his chest as he stroked her hair.

Had she been screaming? The nightmare had seemed so real, so true. She was wringing with sweat, her face felt as hot as a firecracker. Had she been crying?

There was a knock on the door then it was opened and Natalie looked to see that it was Gavin.

"You guys, okay?" he asked.

"Yeah, she had a bad dream, that's all," Jack said.

Gavin's brow drew downward, "Well, I'm sorry. Is there anything I can get you, Natalie?" he asked, truly concerned.

She knew she must look a sight with her red tear-streaked face, but told him no and thanked him, then looked up to Jack as Gavin closed the door behind him.

"Baby, what did you dream about?" Jack asked, still stroking her hair.

"Oh, it was horrifying, Jack. He was trying to kill me…"

"Who?"

"Troy!" Jack looked thoughtful then as Natalie continued, "He was trying to kill me and he was here, in this house…and all I could think about was Dallie and that I would never see her again…or you…or the baby…"

"Oh, sweetie, it wasn't real. It's just a dream. Don't let it bother you. He's in prison. He's not coming here. Ever," he said as he kissed her forehead. She tried to take comfort from his words but an uneasiness settled over her, an uneasiness that she couldn't shake so she asked Jack to make love to her. And he did. Taking her to a plane where nothing existed but the two of them and the comfort they took from one another. Her restlessness faded if only momentarily and she drifted back to sleep in his solid arms, listening to his breathing, feeling his big chest solid against hers. He wouldn't let anything happen to her, that she knew for a fact and she let that truth sink in as she slept.

The next morning, Dallie woke them as she squealed, "Santa came, Mommy. He came." Natalie sleepily opened her eyes to see Dallie lugging a big blanket in her arms. Natalie smiled down at her daughter, whose grin was priceless.

Jack sat up and smiled at Dallie as he made sure his nakedness was covered. "Well, he sure did, didn't he? Look at that, a new saddle blanket for Ameera…" He turned to Natalie and kissed her cheek.

Carson came in at that time and picked Dallie up. "Come on, kiddo, don't you know you got to knock on the doors of newly-weds…don't want any surprises now do we?" He winked at them as he shut their door, Dallie giving him a confused look which caused Natalie and Jack to laugh. They dressed quickly and headed downstairs to the smell of sausage cooking. Her mother, the ever gracious hostess, was at it again. Natalie kissed Jack and left him to help her mother.

Natalie's uneasy feeling returned during breakfast and stayed with her as the kids opened their gifts. She hated the feeling of impending danger. Jack gave her confused looks, knowing something was amiss, but she smiled at him, trying not to let her feelings get to her on Christmas Day. Dallie had already opened a new saddle from her grandparents, a pair of riding boots from Gavin, a new cowboy hat and western pocket book from Carson and Olivia and a case full of farm animals from the boys. When she opened one of the gifts from Jack and Natalie, she looked confused at the envelope. Natalie smiled and helped her open it. She pulled out three long tickets.

"Dallie, they're tickets to Disney World," Natalie said.

Dallie's mouth flew open. "Disney World?" she asked and examined the tickets to see if they were authentic.

"Yes."

She squealed and hugged Natalie's neck in joy. "We're going to Disney World?"

"We sure are, darlin'!" Jack said and grabbed her little body for a hug.

The adoption papers had been filed and it was official, Dallie was now a Kinsen. It had been another Christmas gift straight from Jack to Dallie. When he'd told her after their return from Galveston, she smiled big and asked him if she could call him Daddy. Both Natalie and Jack had teared up then. Jack had nodded, told her that he'd like that, and held her to him as he'd fought everything in him not to let anyone see him crying. Natalie had to turn away from them as her emotions got the best of her. Corrine had also cried.

As she watched the two of them now, she knew that it was meant for them to be father and daughter.

Dallie continued to stare down at the tickets as if they weren't real. "When are we going?" she asked.

"In three weeks," Jack answered. "Right after we are moved into the new house." She smiled back at him and handed the tickets to Natalie for safe keeping.

Everyone else opened their gifts. Natalie received new items for the house courtesy of Gavin, Carson and Olivia, her parents and Nathan. She thanked everyone graciously. Jack had told her his gift for her was for later and she'd smiled up at him wondering what he had in store for her.

They enjoyed each others company that day as they watched the kids play together with Dash and the kittens. They watched movies and sang Christmas carols while Corrine played the piano. It was a happy day and Natalie cherished the time she was getting to spend with her new family, even as the uneasiness returned. Later, Jack and the guys took Dallie and the boys down to the barn to tend to the horses as the women started dinner.

That evening with the house filled with toys and the stockings emptied of their candy, everyone retired to bed in their given locations. When she'd returned to the guest room to retire after changing into her nightgown and brushing her teeth, she found Jack waiting patiently on the bed with a box and an envelope. Natalie smiled at him as she shut the door and eagerly came to sit next to him. She'd also waited until tonight to give him her gift.

He handed her the envelope first. "This gift," he explained, "is really more for the baby..." She opened it and pulled out a business card with the name Harrison Banks on it. She looked up at him questioningly. "He's a decorator. Out of Dallas. He specializes in nurseries." Her eyes lit up then and she smiled. "It's not much really, but..."

"Oh, Jack..." She reached for him then and kissed his lips soundly.

"He, uh, actually comes to your house and sits down with you to layout the perfect nursery. He's really good. His work is top notch."

"This is a wonderful gift. You're so thoughtful." She looked at him deeply then he handed her a little black velvety box. She opened it with eagerness as well to find a pair of diamond studs. Her mouth flew open.

"To match your necklace…" he added, blushing.

"Jack, you really shouldn't have."

"Well, I thought you'd be getting so much stuff for the house that you might need something for yourself."

She looked up at him then grabbed his face and kissed him again. "You really are the most wonderful husband, you know that?" He just blushed and smiled at her. Then she remembered her gift. "Oh, I got you something too…" She, in turn, went to her vanity, opened a drawer, pulled out an envelope and handed it to him then sat back down beside him, rubbing his back. He slowly opened the white envelope and pulled out a picture of an oversized solid oak desk. It was one he'd seen while they were shopping in Galveston that he'd gotten excited about. She'd called after they'd left and ordered it for his office for the barn.

"Natalie, is this what I think it is?" He looked up at her.

"Yup!"

"Honey, this desk was outrageously expensive."

"I know, but you wanted it. So, I got it for you. It will be delivered as soon as you say the word."

"Natalie! Wow. I don't know what to say…"

"Well, I believe a thank you would be in order!" She smiled seductively at him, cocking her eyebrow at him as she leaned into him.

"Oh, do you need to be *properly* thanked?" He smiled devilishly.

"Oh, I believe I do!" She laughed even as he brought her down on the bed and kissed her breathlessly.

~

*N*athan sat at the Rusty Spur drinking a beer two days after Christmas. His mood was lighter these days as he felt he was working toward something and not fighting for it for a change. His sister had recently been married and was as happy as she'd ever been. That she'd had the opportunity to change her life around had been heart warming to him. She and Dallie had been through pure Hell and back and both of them deserved a better life than the one they'd had in Chicago. Now, Jack Kinsen had stepped in and given them that.

Nathan wondered how long it'd been since he himself had been truly happy and couldn't remember a time in the last ten years except before Natalie had left. He wondered what he would do with his life. He knew it wouldn't be much longer before his father retired and left him Starlight Valley, but what then? What did he have to look forward to besides raising and training horses?

There had never been a stable woman in his life. The only women he'd been with had been rodeo junkies. He'd never really even dated a woman before. Back in high school, he'd had a few girl-friends but did it count as a date if you were just a teenager? Women had been on his mind a lot lately. Hell, it was probably because Jack and Natalie were so happy together that it put thoughts in his head of a future. Not that he was in any hurry to settle down and have kids. He just wanted a date. A woman whose company he could enjoy.

He looked up at the television screen as something caught his eye.

"Hey, Louise. Turn that up, will ya?" he asked as his eyes narrowed.

He watched as a female broadcaster took the screen then turned her gaze to a maximum security prison, somewhere, she stated, in Illinois.

"On Christmas Day, nine prisoners escaped this Illinois state penitentiary. They took a guard hostage as they started a riot. They used her security badge to open the doors to their escape as a getaway car with these tags escorted them out of state. One prisoner and three guards were killed and six more were injured in the midst of the chaos. Among those escapees was former NFL star and sports caster Troy Cameron who as most remember was convicted just four months ago under charges of child molestation, rape and two counts of first degree murder...." Nathan's blood had frozen as he watched the screen, his heart gripped in terror. "Another twist in this horrific tale, sources tell us that Cameron's attorney, Lloyd Williams, was found brutally murdered yesterday. His body was unidentifiable as police..."

Nathan didn't wait for the rest. He was up and out the door as fast as he could react. He knew Troy would be coming for Natalie, he knew beyond the shadow of a doubt that he would kill her as he knew beyond the shadow of a doubt that Troy'd been the one who'd killed his own lawyer. Nathan's parents were gone with Dallie for the day; that Nathan thanked God for. But Natalie would be unsuspecting of Troy, unknowing of the escape. She was alone at their parent's house. Jack was working at his house.

"God, please don't let me be too late," he prayed as he grabbed his rifle, racing his truck down the road as if the very gates of Hell were upon him.

CHAPTER 15

*N*atalie sat on her bed with her computer atop her lap checking her emails when the phone rang. She grabbed it and put it to her ear, giving a sweet Hello to the caller.

"Natalie!" It was Nathan's voice. It was shaky and alarmed as static sizzled in the background.

"Nathan, are you okay?"

"No, Natalie, listen to me! You have to get out of the house! Get *out* of the house! Get to your new house as fast as you can! Now!"

"What? Why? What's wrong?" Fear caught in her throat as she tried to swallow, moving her computer aside and sitting up on the bed, gripping the receiver in her hand tightly.

"Just listen to me, dammit! You have to get..." Just then the reception cut out and her ears were filled with a busy signal. She gulped again as the phone fell to the bed. She jumped up quickly and ran out the door and into the hallway only to stop dead in her tracks.

The person she saw made her blood curdle. He just stood there in the hallway propped against the wall, staring at her. She gasped. Her whole body froze, her heartbeat pounding in her eyes, tears coming to her eyes as she watched a sly smile cross his lips. His wicked eyes, his dark stubble, that evil smile. It was an exact replica of the nightmare she'd had on Christmas Eve. She gulped. He wasn't real. He couldn't be real. Her lips quivered and she wished with everything inside her that he couldn't see her fear.

"Tr—Troy?" she said his name, willing this to be a dream.

"Natalie..." he responded. It was anything but a dream. "I told you I would come back for you." Her first instinct was to run but she knew he would catch her. He was and had always been much faster than she was. She felt as if she were about to faint, all the blood left her face. He laughed then, the horrific sound made her want to vomit. "You look as if you've seen a ghost," he replied. She felt as if she had. He wasn't supposed to be here. How had he escaped? How was he really here? "Where's my daughter, Natalie?" His tone had turned sinister, demanding. She felt hot tears stream down her numb face. She dare not answer him for her voice had been taken away. She couldn't speak. He stepped toward her and she moved backward a step.

Her voice finally took hold, "No...no...please." He was but a breath from her as her back hit the doorframe. She wanted to scream. He had her cornered now and he knew it. Again, his terrifying grin took hold of her soul. He grabbed her throat then and tilted her head back, making her face him. He was going to kill her, of that she was certain, and there was nothing she could do about it. He was too big, too strong for her to fight. He moved her sideways then and out the doorway, his eyes never leaving hers. It seemed forever before he stopped, his grip lightening on her constricted throat. Then his evil smile returned. She felt her heels touch nothing and knew he had backed her toward the stairs. *Oh, God,* she begged silently, *please don't let Dallie find me this way.*

"Such a tragedy..." he said as he let go of her neck and with the heel of his hand shoved against her chest.

She screamed as she fell backwards. She tumbled, end over end. Her head, face, back, bottom, hands, and legs hitting the stairs at different times. The pain came immediately as she fell forever, her momentum gaining. Then suddenly her abdomen slammed against something hard, stopping her...the curio cabinet at the base of the stairwell. Pain shot through her middle and she fell to the floor, drawing her knees in as dizziness enveloped her. Nausea took hold then and she gagged as the pain intensified, feeling heat flood her whole body. She thought she heard Jack calling to her, but then she heard the menacing laughter as footfalls echoed on the stairs. She remembered her dream as the unconsciousness enveloped her, knowing she would never again see Jack, Dallie, her family. She surrendered to the darkness knowing now that it hadn't been a dream, it'd been a premonition.

$\sim$

*J*ack was walking up the porch steps as he heard Natalie's blood curdling scream. He ran forward and into the house only to watch as she slammed into the antique cabinet at the base of the stairs.

"Natalie!" he cried as she slumped over, drew her knees in and passed out. A sinister laugh echoed from upstairs and Jack felt his heart fill with anger. Someone had pushed her down the stairs and was now going to die...

His first reaction was to see to Natalie. She was out cold; her pulse was low and her skin clammy. She would be going into shock soon, he assumed, he didn't know what all she had broken with a fall like that. As he examined her face, he saw a large bloody gash. He ripped the bottom portion of his shirt and placed it there, applying pressure. He then looked up into the face of something purely evil. He knew in an instant that he was looking at Troy Cameron. The man who'd taken Dallie's innocence, the man who'd tormented Jack's beloved wife, who now lay unconscious before him at the hands of this monster. Troy descended the stairs slowly, deliberately and walked over toward him. Jack waited for a breath before he lunged at this intruder, tackling him to the ground, practically howling in anger. Jack's fists assaulted the man's face as his hatred for him spurred him on. Blood flew and Troy groaned as hit by hit Jack fulfilled the rage that was seizing him. He ignored the pain in his own knuckles; he was going to beat his last breath out of him. Jack received little resistance before the man finally lost consciousness. Jack stopped flailing him as reality took hold and he looked over to Natalie, his whole body shaking in rage. Blood had begun to saturate her dress, lots of it, between her legs, under her back. *Where the Hell was she bleeding that much from?* Then he realized. *Oh, my God, the baby.* Jack jumped off of Troy then kicked him in the gut before he removed his shirt and wrapped it between his wife's legs. It did little to staunch the flow of blood, but he lifted her gently into his arms and was walking toward the door when Nathan faced him with a rifle in his grasp.

"Move, Jack," Nathan stated calmly.

Jack did as he was instructed, turning in the process to see Troy headed toward him, a large butcher knife in his hand. That's when the gun went off, a loud explosion of sound overtook Jack's ears and he watched as a hole appeared in Troy's middle, red blood soaking his shirt as the blast halted him. Troy looked down at the fatal wound in his belly and back up to them, his eyes an empty blackness, before falling to the floor, dead. Jack gave Nathan a knowing look. Nathan looked down at his sister then, a frightened look on his face as he took in her limp body in Jack's arms.

"Let's go," Jack said. "We've got to get her to the hospital...now!"

~

*N*atalie woke to the sound of a faint beeping noise echoing in her ears. She opened her eyes slowly, groggily and looked over to see Jack sitting across from her in a chair that was too small for him, his head buried in his big hands which were covered in sterile gauze. She couldn't tell if he were awake or asleep. She could tell she was in a hospital bed, she saw the IV pole. Flowers and cards covered everything.

Something had happened. She didn't feel the same. She felt different, as if she were in a bad dream. She tried to think of the last thing she remembered as she closed her eyes. Then she gasped, her eyes opening so quickly that it hurt.

"Dallie!" she cried.

Jack awoke with a start then, and came toward her. His face was covered in stubble; his beautiful green eyes were red and blood-shot, dark circles framing them. He looked as if he hadn't slept in days.

"Where's Dallie?" Natalie asked weakly, her voice cracking.

"Shh, she's safe. She's perfectly safe…" He smiled big then looked deeply at her. "Oh my love…Thank God, you're finally awake." Tears filled his eyes as he took her hand in his and brought it to his lips. "Oh baby, I was so scared."

"Jack, what happened?" She remembered nothing beyond the fall and told him so.

"You've been here for two days now."

"Two days? Was I in a coma?"

"No, just sleeping. You've had quite an ordeal. You had a concussion."

She remembered hitting her head several times as she fell down the stairs and she reached up to touch her forehead, feeling a bandage there. She felt a scratch over her nose and wondered at the damage on her face. "Jack, is my face okay?"

"Your face is more than okay," he half laughed, a tear falling down his cheek, as if she were being ridiculous. "It's perfect. Those scratches will heal in no time."

She sighed laying her head back. She looked down at her arms; one arm was covered in scratches and bruises, the other in a cast.

"My arm!" she protested.

"Yeah, it's fractured. You'll have to wear that for several months and your ankle is sprained. You've got a huge bruise on your knee…

they had to pop it back into place..." He stopped, his voice tearing, he shook his head, a tear falling from his eye.

Her stomach had taken a big hit too and...

"Oh, Jack! The baby... is he?" The look he gave her echoed sadness and he lowered his head then. She suddenly realized that she didn't feel pregnant anymore. She felt emptiness. "I lost the baby?" she asked, her voice once again cracking. He just nodded. "Oh, God," she sighed and tilted her head back, tears filling her eyes. Another mark for Troy Cameron; something else he had taken from her. "How?" She suddenly wanted to know.

Jack stepped away and drew his chair closer to her bed. He sat down in it and cupped his face in his hands, looking as he had when she'd first woken up. He sat silent for a long time before he spoke, his voice uneven.

"You lost a lot of blood, Natalie. When you hit the cabinet..." He shook his head. "There was immediate hemorrhaging. There was nothing they could do. It was such a violent blow that it crushed..." He stopped there and she sighed, feeling a deep sense of loss, what a terrible way to lose the child growing in your womb. Jack had wanted that baby so much that he'd ached for it. Now, there would be no baby. "Dammit," Jack cursed as he looked up at her, tears streaming his face. "Natalie, I should have been there for you. He could have killed you! I'm your husband, I'm supposed to protect you and I wasn't there...I wasn't there."

She grabbed for his hand and he took it, placing it against his hot tear-streaked face. "Jack, you *were* there. You kept him from killing me..."

"Yes, but I didn't stop him from hurting you or from killing our baby."

"Oh, Jack. You did all you could. You didn't know he would be there."

"Nathan did," he stated.

"He did? How?"

"He saw it on the news. He came just in time..."

"Is Troy dead?" Natalie needed to know. Jack just nodded. "Who killed him?"

"He was going to attack us. Nathan didn't have any other choice, he shot him."

Natalie didn't need gory details. They sat quietly then as Jack stroked her hand and she watched him. Watched him as he looked at her. Watched his eyes, watched his beautiful tear-stricken face. Then he smiled, a hopeful gesture in such a grim hour.

"I *do* have good news," he said, eagerness in his tone.

"What is that?"

"The doctor said we will be able to have more children!"

Natalie smiled up at her handsome husband then and laughed as tears filled her eyes.

EPILOGUE

*I*t had been six months since they'd moved into their beautiful new home on one hundred acres of her father's land. She remembered how ecstatic she'd been when Jack brought her in to see the finished product for the first time. It looked like a dream home, one that would be seen on television with its vaulted ceilings and hardwood floors, the chandelier in the dining room, the arched doorways and crown molding. She and Jack had picked out all of the colors and furniture save for Dallie's bedroom. The colors in the living room were earthy and neutral with colorful paintings of rugged landscapes. The furniture was also neutral colors which Natalie paired with bright throw pillows and rugs. Dallie's bedroom had a horse theme, similar to the one at her grandparent's home and Jack and Natalie's master bedroom was a deep red color with autumn accents. The kitchen and breakfast nook had an old west theme with cowboys, horses and cactus. That had been Jack's idea. One of the upstairs bedrooms served as a guest room while another served as Natalie's office with a large desk, shelves and a filing cabinet. The other two bedrooms were in wait, Jack said. Natalie had smiled at that.

He was so eager to father children and Natalie couldn't wait to announce to him that she was pregnant. It had taken her about six weeks to recover after she'd returned home, but once she got a clean bill of health her doctor had told her she could start trying again. She hadn't told Jack, but she'd been trying to conceive the last couple months. She had wanted so much to give him back what Troy had taken from them and now she was one hundred percent positive of her pregnancy as she returned home from her doctor's visit.

She opened the big cherry wood door, a few bags of groceries in her hands, and called to her family. Jack barreled out of the living room then with Dallie on his back squealing.

"Honey, let me get those for you." He sat Dallie on the ground and grabbed the bags from her, pulling her to him for a quick kiss. She smiled as she pulled back and looked at him. He took her hand as they walked to the kitchen.

"I've invited Mom and Dad and Nathan over for dinner, if that's okay," she said as Jack helped her put the groceries away.

"Yeah, that's ok."

"I thought it would do him good to be around all of us while Mom and Dad are in town." Jack just nodded and gave her a weak smile.

Her father had announced his retirement just last month, a few weeks after Natalie was out of her cast and had gotten a clean bill of health. He and her mother were traveling down in Florida and were home for a few days before heading in the opposite direction to take an RV trip from Texas to California. They couldn't wait! They seemed so happy with their decision to retire.

Nathan, on the other hand, appeared to be a lost soul these last six months. He had started acting like the old Nathan again before Troy Cameron had shown up two days after Christmas with the intention of killing her. Now, however, he seemed completely miserable, disgusted with himself and life in general. He was doing well with the ranch though and was kind to Natalie and Jack and especially Dallie when he came around, but he'd become so withdrawn and anti-social lately; a stark contrast to his former self. Natalie couldn't help but partially blame herself for his personality change. She remembered how different he'd been even the first day he'd seen her after her recovery.

"Oh, Nathan." She had pulled him to her and sobbed into his shoulder.

"I thought I'd lost you. God, I thought I'd really lost you this time," he'd said as he held her tightly to him for a long time. She tried to get him to talk to her about what happened, but he wouldn't answer her questions. He'd just looked at her, deep into her eyes, his own eyes mirrors of emptiness. Dark and damaged. The sight had made her weep and she'd pulled him back to her and held him for a long time before he'd finally pulled away.

"Me and Dallie are headed down to the barn to ride Ameera, wanna come?" Jack asked. She shook her head.

Business had been good thus far for them. Jack was a reputable trainer and apparently very popular in the horse world. They'd gotten calls for many projects in the past few months from as far out as Montana. Jack had hired on three men to help him and, of course, Dallie was tagging along. Natalie was back in her saddle again as well, working alongside her husband and daughter when she wasn't writing her column for *Lone Star Living*. She'd actually gotten a promotion and was now writing a column on her town as a whole and not merely just politics. She'd given it the name, "In Abundance", and thus far it was a popular piece.

They'd had to postpone their Disney trip to April due to Natalie's condition, but it had been the perfect first family vacation and Natalie thought that she and Jack had more fun than Dallie did riding all the rides and seeing their favorite childhood characters.

Dallie had also started preschool in January and had absolutely loved it. She'd learned so much and made many friends. In September, she would begin kindergarten. That fact almost made Natalie want to burst into tears.

"Is everything okay?" Jack asked, his hand going to the small of her back as he looked down at her. He was always able to sense her discomfort which was most of the time a good thing, but it also made her so readable. She nodded and smiled up at him. God, how she loved him.

"Yeah, I want to tell you something...where'd Dallie go?"

"Dallie, honey, Mommy wants you," he boomed.

"Yes, Daddy!" Dallie hollered, coming up to them. Jack smiled and picked her up and into his arms as he planted a kiss on her sweet little face. He still got excited when she called him that. It warmed Natalie's heart.

God, when had Dallie gotten so tall? She'd grown nearly a foot in six months, it just didn't seem right. She and Jack looked at Natalie expectantly.

Nat cleared her throat before saying, "Um, let's go into the living room." They followed as she sat on the big oversized sofa. Jack sat down beside her, Dallie on his lap. "Well, I have some good news..." she began and smiled because she just couldn't contain it. "I'm going to have a baby." She waited for their reactions. Dallie squealed and Jack looked at her incredulously.

"Really? You really are?" he asked beaming from ear to ear and she nodded, smiling as tears came to her eyes. He'd reacted how she'd hoped he would. "Oh, darlin', I can't believe it. I'm so happy!" He reached out for her and pulled her to him, Dallie's arm grabbing her as well in a group hug. Jack planted a kiss on her lips and lingered for a moment. "When is the baby due?" he asked, his nose touching hers, his hands gently stroking her belly.

"February."

"Wow, we have so much to do! We can turn the room next to ours into a nursery..." He said, thoughtfully.

"Mommy," Dallie interrupted and Natalie pulled back to look down at her.

"What is it, baby?" she asked, taking Dallie's small hand into her own.

"Is it a boy or a girl?"

Natalie gave Jack a knowing smile. "Well, I don't know yet. I won't find out until August… or we can let it be a surprise."

"Ooh, I like surprises!" Dallie exclaimed.

Natalie smiled and looked up at Jack. "Well, let's ask Daddy what he wants."

Jack smiled down at his two girls and nodded. "Yeah, let's be surprised." He looked into Natalie's teary eyes and his hand captured her head as he pulled her to him for another gentle kiss. He deepened it then, touching his tongue to hers, and they heard Dallie grunt in protest.

When he pulled back, his eyes twinkled like the stars over Texas and Natalie knew in that moment that she would always be in love with this man, Jack, her knight in shining armor, Dallie's Superman.

ABOUT THE AUTHOR

Shanna Swenson is the author of *Abundance* and *Return to Abundance*, endearing romance novels that showcase true love's ability to conquer any tragedy.

Shanna is a Georgia native who spent many of her childhood summers traveling across the south to her father's home state of Texas, which only served to fuel her love of travel and family. She started writing her first works, including the ground work for her first three novels, at the age of fourteen and now writes predominately romance, including paranormal and fantasy.

She married her own "knight in shining armor" in 2015 and when she's not on her laptop typing away her next novel, she enjoys traveling, hiking, yoga, watching football, movies of the action and horror genres, photography, music, reading all kinds of books and being on the water.

Visit her website at www.shannaswenson.com

51838379R00231

Made in the USA
Columbia, SC
26 February 2019